Praise for *Hurry Up* ...

'With strong characters, a cleverly constructed story and
masses of period detail, this vivid evocation of life in 1985
is a fine second book from a writer who first won
the *Mail on Sunday* Novel Competition.'
Daily Mail

'Ashdown's depiction of a vulnerable teenager
and the magnetic pull of a toxic friendship
will have you wincing with recognition.'
Glamour

'Haunting fiction.'
Stylist

'Ashdown's debut novel *Glasshopper* was named
as one of the best books of 2009, and this well-crafted
follow-up doesn't disappoint.'
Heat

'Funny, insightful and often tragic. A fascinating
book whose apparent simplicity masks complexity
as it reveals once again the strength of Ashdown's
talent as a perceptive and engaging writer.'
NewBooks Magazine

'A darkly compelling read. A school reunion opens
the floodgates to uncomfortable memories from
25 years ago in this powerfully compelling
examination of the volatile and often toxic nature
of adolescent relationships.'
Easy Living

'A very enjoyable and engaging read.
Those who lived the eighties to the full
will find lots to entertain them.'
Between the Lines

Summer of '76

ISABEL ASHDOWN

Myriad Editions

Published in 2013 by

Myriad Editions
59 Lansdowne Place
Brighton BN3 1FL

www.myriadeditions.com

3 5 7 9 10 8 6 4 2

A CIP catalogue record for this book is available from the
British Library.

ISBN: 978-1-908434-33-3

Printed on FSC-accredited paper by
CPI Group (UK) Ltd, Croydon, CR0 4YY

For my father Jules (1940–1990)

'Little islands are all large prisons:
one cannot look at the sea
without wishing for the wings of a swallow.'

Sir Richard Francis Burton

JOANNA

Bembridge, Isle of Wight
New Year, 1971

PROLOGUE

Met Office report for the Isle of Wight, 31 December 1970:
Minimum temperature 26°F/−3.3°C

As 1970 gives way to '71, a hard frost settles across the ground, its icy fingers reaching out over town and farmland, cloaking houses and gardens from one end of the island to the other. Out on the gravelled driveway of the McKees' seafront home, white mist settles on the bare branches of the cherry tree, freezing the water of the ornamental bird bath, sending a frosty chill through the mirrored hallway as homeward-bound guests collect their coats and make their merry way.

Joanna understands how this night will play out; Marie explained it to her carefully at the start of the evening. When midnight has rolled by − when only the most steadfast revellers remain − it's the women who will pick the keys from the bowl. It couldn't be simpler. Up here, in John and Marie's candlelit living room, the last dozen guests gather on the sofas, champagne and anticipation shining in their eyes. Beyond the glass of the balcony doors, the moon reflects brightly over the clawing drag of high tide, the view clear and crisp from this warm bubble of New Year cheer, high above the icy shingle and shoreline below.

Thrilled, and yet anxious, Joanna draws up her stockinged feet, tucking them beneath her as she settles against the velvet cushions, leaning into Richard, linking her fingers with his.

He squeezes her hand, pushing away tendrils of tawny hair as he kisses her ear. Simon and Laura sit on the sofa opposite, a fist-sized gap between them. Laura is engaged in discussion with the older woman to her left, who extends a sinewy brown leg, turning it this way and that to illustrate some yoga position or other. Laura attempts to mimic the move, laughing freely at her own failings, as Simon runs forefinger and thumb across his upper lip in a self-soothing motion. Someone changes the record over, and the sounds of the room are softened by Bob Dylan's 'Lay Lady Lay'. Richard glances back at Joanna and smiles, a shared intimacy, before returning to chat with the guests to his other side. Joanna wants to make conversation too, to break down the tension that's rising behind her ribcage as the reality of the moment grows ever nearer. She wants this evening to happen more than anything, and yet her every instinct tells her she should be at home now, tucked up in her marital bed with Richard by her side, her son asleep in the room next door. Across the coffee table Simon is silent too, and, as she observes this, their eyes meet and linger and she recognises his shame. With a jolt she looks away, unable to return the steady gaze of one of her oldest friends, and, fleetingly, she considers her escape.

In that moment, their hosts breeze in, bringing with them the scent of pine needles and Paco Rabanne. White-haired John holds another bottle aloft, looking suddenly youthful and alert in the twinkling light of the Christmas tree; Marie bends to stoke the fire, mischievously running her hands over the seat of her trouser suit as she turns and smiles at the gathered friends.

'Are we ready?' she asks, her neat little palms coming together like a prayer.

When Marie conjures up the glass bowl, there's applause. She places it on the coffee table with a flourish, and firelight dances in the crystal-cut surface, casting shards of light-reflection over the balcony doors and out into the darkness of the night.

'I think our new guests should go first, don't you, John?' Marie slips out of her sandals and pads across the room to lean on the sofa-back between Simon and Laura.

John eases the cork from the new bottle and circles the room to top up glasses. 'Of course! Let the youngsters kick it off. So who's to be first – Laura or Joanna?'

Joanna suppresses a gasp as Laura springs forward, unhesitant, to plunge her hand into the bowl of keys on the table before her. With her free hand she pushes back a lock of shiny black hair, boldly eyeing every male in the room before pulling out her chosen key with a challenging jangle.

A younger man at the end of the sofa raises his hand like a schoolboy, and amidst claps and murmurs of amusement Laura leads him from the room, directed along the corridor by Marie, who smiles after them like a proud parent.

'So, Joanna?' she says, gesturing at the bowl of keys as if it were nothing more than a plate of canapés.

Joanna feels the soft tread of the carpet beneath her feet as she lowers her legs from the sofa, and she turns to look at Richard. He nods, gently urging her forward, his fingertips tender in the small of her back. She can't raise her eyes, can't brazen it out like Laura. So instead she slips her hand into the tangle of keys and searches it out. Time slows as her fingers fumble around the contents of the bowl, trying to locate a particular key fob, panic flooding her veins when nothing feels familiar. At last she finds it, recognises the spongy texture of the little orb, and she wraps her fingers around it, pulls it from the bowl and raises it like a question mark.

LUKE

Sandown, Isle of Wight, 1976

1

Met Office report for the Isle of Wight, early May 1976:
Maximum temperature 75°F/24°C

There's a taste of things to come in early May, when soaring temperatures create a mini-heatwave across the country. Standing in the sunlight of his front drive, Luke Wolff wipes his oily hands on the back of his patched-up jeans and stands back to admire his new scooter. It's a 1969 orange Vespa – a little rusty around the bodywork, but it's his, bought with his own money despite his mother's anxious complaints. In the quiet heat of afternoon, white sunlight spreads over the driveway and out across the small lawn at the front of the bungalow, reflecting brightly in the polished chrome of the scooter's headlamp. There's a breathless quality in the air, a comforting sense of being here alone on his front drive, while the rest of the neighbourhood is absent, working or at school.

Luke gives the vinyl seat a final polish with his new chamois and pulls his T-shirt over his head, flinging it on the doorstep and absently wiping a smudge of oil across his sweaty brow. As he starts to clear up his gear, the familiar pop-pop-sputter of Martin's scooter bounces along the avenue, growing louder as he draws up on the path beyond the open metal gate. Luke watches as his friend turns into the drive and heel-steps towards the house, looking as if he's riding a kiddie bike, with his pale bony knees bent up too

9

high. He's six foot five and thin as a rake. He really shouldn't be wearing shorts with those legs. It's not a cool look.

Martin unclips his helmet and untangles himself from the seat like a grasshopper. Tucking the helmet under his arm, he steps around Luke's new scooter, rubbing his chin with his large hand, his shoulder-length hair hanging sweaty and dull where the helmet has pressed it against his head.

'Like it?' Luke asks, automatically stepping back on to the doorstep to bring himself closer to Martin's level. 'I've been working on it all morning. You know, checking the oil, polishing the chrome and all that. Took her along the seafront earlier on. She goes like a dream.'

A slow smile passes over Martin's face and he runs his fingers around the globe of the front lamp. 'Very nice.' His hand rests there for a moment, while his pale green eyes travel over the bodywork for a second look. He nods appreciatively and turns back to his own bike to unstrap a stack of LPs held together in a plastic carrier bag.

Luke picks up his T-shirt and pushes open the front door. In contrast to the bright glare of outdoors, the cool, narrow hallway renders him momentarily blind as he makes his way through to his bedroom, where he pours them both a glass of lukewarm lemonade. Luke eases himself up on to the window ledge, resting his feet on his desk as he studies the sleeve of one of Martin's LPs, running his finger along the curling white smoke trail of David Bowie's cigarette. Sunshine pours in through the open window, heating his back and filling the room with the honeysuckle scent of the front garden.

'Man, I *love* this album. This is officially my favourite record of the year. I'll get it myself when I've got a bit of spare cash again. I put just about everything I'd saved into getting that scooter.'

Martin is lying on Luke's single bed, air-drumming, his feet hooked through the bars of the headboard and his head hanging over the edge of the divan. His hair dangles like dull tassels.

Luke turns the album cover over to scrutinise the playlist on the back.

'"Young Americans" is the best track. No contest.'

'Agreed.' Martin hits a final air-cymbal and swings his long legs up and off the bed, rucking up the yellow candlewick bedspread as he brings his feet to the floor. He picks up a dusty book from the bedside cabinet and starts to thumb through the pages, not really looking at the words. 'Any good?' he asks, holding it up.

'Dunno. I can't seem to concentrate on reading at the moment. I was meant to be revising today, but it's too hot.' Luke rests his chin on the album cover. 'So, whaddya know?'

'Not much,' says Martin. 'It's all work, work, work at our place. The only time I get a break is when I'm revising. But we've got swallows nesting in the eaves of the workshop. I'm surprised they're there at all, with all the noise we make, but still, they're there. I think they like the long grasses in the garden; plenty of insects for them, I suppose.'

'Have they laid eggs?'

'Think so. I'm keeping a close eye.' Martin gazes past Luke, out through the open window. 'You know, the Egyptians thought swallows were the souls of the dead.'

Luke drops off the desk and starts thumbing through his album collection. 'Maybe that's my grandad you've got in your eaves.'

'Or my mum,' Martin replies, his eyes vacant. 'Imagine that. If your soul really was separate from your body? So even when your body stops working, your soul could fly.'

'Deep, man.' Luke smirks, pulling out another record and stretching across to pass it to Martin. Martin looks up and takes the album from him, flipping it over without interest.

'It would be good, though, wouldn't it? To fly?'

Luke looks at his strange friend, trying to see him as others do. He's been around him so long now that he just sees *Martin*, not the giant they all see, broken-nosed and lantern-jawed. Even his hands are giant, like long, elegant shovels. 'Tell you what would be good, mate. A girlfriend. It's been bloody ages since I went out with anyone. Surely we'll get to meet some nice girls this summer.' He picks up a pencil and lobs it at Martin's lap.

Martin's eyes zone back in and he gives a slow nod. 'But you'll meet loads of new people at college, won't you? Don't know what chance I've got, stuck in this place.'

A static image of Martin at the workbench seeps into Luke's mind, like an ageless photograph, trapped in time. 'You'll be fine, mate,' he says.

Martin links his fingers, cracking his knuckles loudly. 'I'm starving. D'you think your mum'll let us have something to eat?'

'Yeah. Come on, then.' Gesturing for Martin to get off the bed, Luke straightens up his covers before lifting the needle off the record and lowering the perspex lid.

As they reach the kitchen, Dad calls out from the living room, 'Is that you, Luke? Get me a beer from the fridge, will you?'

'What did your last slave die of?' Luke shouts back.

'Nothing! She's in the kitchen!'

Luke groans as Dad's laughter trails away, and the lads enter the light-filled kitchen, where they find Mum and Kitty making dough babies on the floury table, poking in eyes and bellybuttons with the end of a paintbrush.

'Mart-eeee!' Kitty screams, waving her floury hands above her head.

'Hello, Martin,' Mum says, handing the brush to Kitty, who frowns hard at Luke.

Martin tucks a strand of hair behind one ear, a pink tinge rising in his high cheeks. 'Hello, Mrs Wolff.' Kitty bashes the brush on the table, still trying to get his attention. 'Hey, Kitty,' he replies, raising a hand.

Mum looks up. 'You get taller every time we see you, doesn't he, Kitty?'

'*Mum*?' Luke rolls his eyes and opens the fridge, tutting as the door of the tiny freezer compartment falls open with a crack, scattering ice dust.

Kitty presses her thumb down on a dough baby's head, squashing its face into the table. 'I'm *four*,' she says, assertively waving four fingers in the air.

'Nearly old enough for school,' says Martin, accepting an ice pop from Luke.

Kitty smiles proudly and returns her attention to the dough babies.

'Phewee! What about this weather, then, boys?' Mum pinches her loose smocked shirt and wafts it at the neckline. 'Just look at Luke – he's already so brown you'd think he'd been to the South of France! Who'd imagine May could possibly be as hot as this?'

Martin holds his arm up against Luke's, comparing his pale skin to his friend's chestnut tan, as Mum stretches over the sink, filling the kettle and setting it down on the side. She looks at Luke and sighs.

'You ought to do something about your hair, Luke. It's getting a bit long. Although I'd kill for dark shiny hair like yours. Look at it – straight as a poker.' She rakes fingers through her own wavy hair, drawing it over one shoulder. 'Your dad's was just the same as yours when I first met him.'

Luke ignores her.

'Your hair's lovely, Mrs Wolff,' says Martin, staring at his ice pop. 'Sort of honey-coloured.'

'Pack it in, Mart.' Luke grimaces and loads up two plates with roughly made sandwiches and crisps. Martin looks away, rubbing a thumb down his long crooked nose.

'Aw, Martin! *You* can come again,' Mum says, twirling her hair into a bunch. 'Although this weather is playing havoc with it. There's *so* much static.' She reaches into the cupboard for a mug.

'How many cups of tea do you drink a day, Mum?' Luke asks irritably.

She flicks the switch at the wall. 'I don't know. Six? Maybe eight?'

'Urgh.'

'What d'you mean, "urgh"? What's wrong with tea all of a sudden?'

Luke hands a plate to Martin, and looks back at Mum, pushing his fringe from his face. 'I think you've got too much time on your hands.'

Martin, clearly uncomfortable, takes a special interest in Kitty's dough babies, scanning the table with a fixed expression of concentration.

'Goodness me, Luke, it's not like I'm drinking gin all day long, or smoking pot. You are a strange boy sometimes.' She turns away to get on with her tea-making. 'So, how's your dad, Martin? Is business good? I haven't seen him in the town for months.'

Martin clears his throat.

'He just got another big order in, so we're really busy. I'm going to be working for him full-time when exams are over. Some of the new frames he's making are really big – the biggest is six or seven foot tall, so you need two men on that kind of job.'

Mum reaches into the low fridge to fetch a beer for Dad, handing it to Luke, along with the bottle opener. 'I hope you'll have a bit of a break, Martin, before you get stuck into all that work. You've been studying hard too – harder than old slack-chops here.'

Martin grins as Luke pushes him. 'Yeah, well, I need to – he'll get good marks whatever he does. I've got a weekend off soon, so we're gonna go round the island on our scooters, aren't we, Luke?'

Luke rolls Dad's beer bottle from one hand to the other. 'Uh-huh. We'll take the tent, make a weekend of it. Martin wants to do a bit of bird-spotting.' He smirks. 'He'll be busy looking up in the sky with his binoculars, while I'll be trying to spot birds of the mammalian kind.'

Mum purses her lips. '*Luke*. I hate it when you say that.'

'What – *mammalian*?' He laughs, putting a saucy accent on the word.

'Yes.'

'But women *are* mammals, aren't they? So, strictly speaking, they're mammalian.'

She scowls harder. 'And "birds". It's sexist.'

When Luke notices Martin's awkwardness, he laughs even louder. Mum flicks him with the teatowel and turns away to clear the washing-up. Martin's eyes linger a moment on her small waist. Luke frowns at him to let him know he's noticed and gives him a little shove towards the door, making a point of pulling a face at Kitty as he goes. She squawks, throwing her paintbrush to the floor.

'Oh, that reminds me,' Mum calls after them before they disappear into the hallway. 'Any chance you could babysit on Saturday night, Luke? You're more than welcome to come over too, Martin.'

Luke shrugs. 'Alright, but only if we can have a couple of drinks.'

'Deal.' Mum flashes a bright smile at the boys. 'There you go, Kitty. You've got your favourite friend Marty coming to babysit.'

Kitty reaches above her head and claps her floury hands, sending white dust clouds billowing, and Martin laughs, giving her the thumbs-up as they leave the room.

In the living room, Dad's sitting in his armchair with his feet on the footstool. He's got the newspaper on his lap and he's carefully folding it back along the crease to make it easier to handle. Luke's seen him do it a thousand times before. 'Ah!' he says, slapping the paper down on the side table so he can stand, taking the beer from Luke with his left hand, simultaneously offering Martin a handshake with his right. 'Just the ticket.' He raises his bottle. 'Cheers! It's a hot one today, eh? *May*? Feels more like August. Look, I've already got the old legs out.'

Luke cringes at his father's faded denim shorts and Jesus sandals. He's not even wearing a shirt.

'Not bad for forty-something. Look at that!' He pats himself on the stomach, indicating for Martin to do the same. 'Go on, feel it. My abdominals are as tight today as they were twenty years ago.'

Martin stretches out his arm and gently prods Mr Wolff's stomach. 'Wow,' he says, sincerely. He looks at Luke. 'That really is firm.'

'So, I suppose you two have come out of your pit to watch *Top of the Pops*?' Dad says, dropping back into his seat and reaching for his newspaper and ballpoint pen. He points his biro towards the television. 'Flick it on, son. We don't want to miss the dancing girls, do we?'

Martin sits on the sofa as Luke switches programmes, giving the old television set a smack on the side to make the picture settle. 'He means Pan's People,' he says, waggling his eyebrows. 'You know they're not on any more, Dad.'

'Of course they are. It's *Top of the Pops*.'

'Really, Pan's People aren't on any more. I saw their last show a few weeks back.'

'Typical!' Dad says, throwing down his pen. It's just about the only thing worth paying the licence fee for these days! This'll be down to that harridan Mary Whitehouse and her bloody decency laws.'

Luke and Martin eat their sandwiches, chatting over various songs until Noel Edmonds introduces a new act, a mixed dance troupe, who come on to 'Can't Help Falling in Love' by the Stylistics.

'Who's this?' Martin asks.

'I can tell you one thing – it's not bloody well Pan's People!' Dad shakes his head, shifting to the edge of his seat where he stares intently at the screen. 'Good God! They've even got men at it!'

Luke laughs, almost spitting out his sandwich. 'Urgh, it's putting me off my food.'

'Well I hope Mary Whitehouse is watching *this*. Talk about indecent. Look at those outfits. You can clearly see their meat and two veg.' Dad gets up to lean on the mantelpiece for a better view, moving in so close that he's obscuring it entirely. 'You know what? That one used to be a model – the brunette. You know how I know?'

'Go on then,' Luke replies with a sigh. 'I can see you're dying to tell us.'

Martin has zoned out altogether as he chews his way through his chicken paste sandwich.

'Because I went out with her. Back in my London days.'

'Really?' asks Martin, refocusing as he gulps down his last mouthful.

'*Really*.' Dad raises one eyebrow and drops his voice. 'A lovely girl, if you know what I mean.'

'*Dirty* old man,' Luke says.

'But, you know how it is. I had to break it off with her. She was getting too clingy, wanted more from the relationship than I did, blah blah blah...' Dad flops back into his seat, waving his hand in the air, gazing into the middle distance as if imagining the long-ago affair.

'So, what was her name, then?' Luke raises his eyebrows suspiciously.

'Name? God knows!' Dad laughs uproariously, taking a swig of his beer. 'Bunty? Sindy? Heaven only knows!'

'How can you not remember something like that?' Luke stands and takes Martin's empty plate, stacking it on top of his own.

'Ah, so many women. So long ago...'

Luke rests his arm on the mantelpiece, flipping a box of matches with the tip of his free hand. 'You see, Martin, the thing you need to remember about my dad is that he's full of – '

'Luke!' Mum shouts from the hallway. 'Is this your motorbike mess on the drive? Someone'll end up breaking their neck if you leave it there! *Clear it up!*'

Dad pulls a smug face at Luke and turns back towards the television. 'Nice to see you, boys.'

It's past ten o'clock when Luke rises on Sunday morning. He clears the draining board and eats boiled eggs with Kitty before leaving the house, pausing to knock once at his parents' door on his way out.

'Mum? I'm off. Kitty's on her own now.'

They were out late last night, at one of their parties, and judging by the silence from the other side of the door they won't be up for a while. Luke's bedside clock told him it was gone two in the morning when he heard them return, and he could tell they'd had a good time; they were giggling and whispering, Mum joking with Dad to keep the noise down as he dropped his key fob on the front doorstep with a clatter. At least they're not arguing, Luke thought vaguely, before rolling over and going back to sleep.

He wheels his scooter down the front drive, turning to wave at Kitty as she bangs on the front window with her Tiny Tears doll, wobbling her head from side to side to make him laugh.

When he arrives at Sandown seafront Martin is already waiting for him by the pier, and they set off up the island together, to travel the eight or nine miles towards Nanna's house in Wootton Creek. By the time they arrive, the heat of the day is already taking hold, and they're glad of the shade of the wooded back roads that fork off beyond Kite Hill.

Nanna's home is a simple, low-ceilinged bungalow set on a large plot of lawn that slopes down to the creek beyond a screen of trees and bracken at the bottom. The front garden is almost always in shadow, facing dense trees and wooded pathways which snake off in several directions towards the various stretches of coastline at the top of the island. Beyond the low wall to her front garden there's a cluster of old pine trees where Nan has set up a wooden bird table, on to which she scrapes bacon rinds and crusts

18

each morning after breakfast. Several peanut feeders and home-made fat-balls dangle from the branches of the trees, and they now swing wildly as a burst of garden birds takes flight, alarmed by the sound of the bike engines turning on to the gravel path.

'Squirrel,' says Martin, smiling lazily and pointing at the small chestnut rodent as it scoots up the trunk and into the foliage above.

They leave their scooters in a sunny patch of light at the side of the outhouse, hooking their helmets over the handlebars. Luke runs his hands up through his sweaty hair and opens the front door without knocking. 'Hi, Nanna! It's me – Luke!'

There's a pause, before Nan's voice trails back faintly. 'I'm in the back, love. Just adjusting my ankle strap.'

'Where?'

'In the back!'

The lads walk through the narrow hallway, until they reach the living room and the bright, warm conservatory at the back of the house.

'Bleedin' hell, it's hot!' Nanna's sitting in one of the sun-bleached wicker chairs, with her foot up on the tiled coffee table. There's a support bandage hanging limply from the end of her toes. 'Here, give us a hand with this, love. Bloody thing. Pain in the arse, it is.'

'*Language*, Nanna.' Luke laughs, sitting on the seat beside her. 'Look, I've brought Martin with me.' He gives her a nudge and she looks up at Martin wickedly.

'Oh, don't mind me, Marty, love. Put it down to my age if you like.'

Luke eases the tube bandage along her foot, noticing the silvery slip of her skin as it resists the tight elastic. After a bit of tugging and adjusting, he fits it neatly over her heel. 'So, how's the ankle doing at the moment, Nanna?'

'Oh, it's alright, love,' she replies, using his shoulder for support as she gets to her feet, wriggling them into her pink velour slippers. 'Just a bit crumbly. Like me.' She picks up her wooden walking stick and beckons for them to follow her into the kitchen, where a freshly baked lemon cake is sitting on the side. 'Fancy a slice?'

Luke kisses her cheek and fills the kettle at the sink. 'Grab a seat, Mart. And you, Nan. I'll make us a nice cup of tea.'

Nan sighs heavily as she sits at the small square table, rearranging her thin little legs to get comfortable. 'What are you boys up to today? Off down the beach or something nice like that?'

'We're on our way over to Sunshine Bay,' Luke replies, placing a fresh bottle of milk on the table. The silver foil lid has a wide hole torn in it, where the blue tits have pecked their way through to get at the cream. As he reaches back to fetch the teapot he notices the row of rinsed bottles lined up along the windowsill, and makes a mental note to put them down on the doorstep for Nan on his way out. 'I start my new job at the holiday camp soon, so they want me to come and collect my uniform.'

'Entertaining the grockles?' Nanna asks.

'Nothing so glamorous,' he replies with a snort. 'I'll be cleaning out chalets and minding the pool. Just part-time until after my exams, then I'll do more shifts. The money's not too bad – and if you work there you get a free pass for the pool. And cheap food.'

'*And* you'll get lots of nice girls down there if you're lucky.' Nan gives Martin a wink. 'What about you, Martin, love? You looking for a job too?'

He rubs his nose self-consciously, and looks down at his hands. 'Oh, no. I'm working for my dad, you know, making picture frames. It's the family business.'

'That's nice,' she says, pinching at her blouse collar and blowing up over her face to cool off. 'Though I don't s'pose you meet many girls in that line of work, do you?'

Martin shakes his head and gives an embarrassed little smile.

'Of course, she's right, mate,' Luke says, sitting at the table and pouring the tea. 'Once I start work down at Sunshine Bay, I'm gonna be fighting 'em off. I won't know which way to turn for girls throwing themselves at my feet.' He raises his eyebrows at Nan, who chuckles.

Martin covers his cake-filled mouth.

'Just think of all those girls in bikinis, Mart,' Luke grins. 'Like Honey Ryder in *Doctor No*.'

'Or Raquel Welch in *One Million Years BC*,' Martin replies, chewing slowly on his cake.

Nan points at the sugar bowl on the side, and Luke passes it over. 'If it's naked girls you're after, you'd have liked it round here back in the day.'

'How's that?' asks Luke.

'Well, we had our own nudist colony up at Woodside, when it was still just the big house. Run by Reverend something-or-other. Bare bottoms everywhere. And not all of 'em that nice to look at, I'll bet.'

'A vicar? Are you pulling our legs, Nan?'

She looks affronted. 'No, I'm bloody not! It only closed down ten or so years ago, before they turned all that land into the holiday camp, as if we needed another one. You ask anyone. They were supposed to stay in the paddock if they were in the altogether, but no end of 'em used to get down on the beach, frolicking about under the tamarisks!' She giggles to herself. 'I remember it clearly, because it all started up the year your dad was born, not long after we'd moved on to the island. Lots of the locals were up in arms about it – couldn't believe a vicar would encourage such shenanigans! Some of the youngsters used to cycle up to the bay and stand on their saddles trying to peek over the hedges. I even heard that the lads from Ryde rowing club used to take a regular trip across the creek just to get a sneaky look on their way down to the Sloop. Well, we didn't have all the dirty magazines in them days. Probably the first time some of 'em had seen a naked body!'

She gives Martin a little shove across the table and the boys fall about laughing. 'Bloody hell, Nan,' says Luke. 'I've never heard of that before. What about you and Grandad? Didn't you ever fancy getting yourself a nice all-over tan?'

'You cheeky bugger!' she hoots, slicing them all a second piece of cake. 'No, we did not! Mind you, I once had to give him a right bollocking, when I heard him and his daft mate Eric Stubbs had cycled down there for a look one Saturday night. Eric's wife, well, she heard him bragging at the front gate and dragged him round here to get it out of them.'

'No! What did Grandad say to you?'

'Not much. He said he was so drunk at the time that all he remembered was falling into the hedge and tearing his shirt collar. He said Eric was a bleedin' idiot for thinking they'd all still be out in the gardens at that time of night. It must've been midnight by the time they got up there – all the nudies were tucked up nice and cosy in their beds by then!'

'I bet you were mad at him, weren't you?' Luke licks his finger and cleans up the crumbs from his plate.

'Me? Nah. He's just a man, after all. Anyway, talking of daft men, how's that dad of yours? Hasn't been over to see me in weeks – since he bought me that bloody thing over there.' She flicks her hand towards the small fridge in the corner of the kitchen. 'Waste of space. What do I need a fridge for?'

Luke stacks the plates and puts them on the side. 'You'll be glad of it if this weather keeps up, Nan. But yeah, Dad's fine. Looking forward to the end of term, I think. He's always threatening to jack his job in, but you know he never will. He never stops moaning about teaching, but I think he's glad of it when the long school holidays come round.'

'He always was a lazy git.'

'*Nan.*'

'Well, he was.'

Martin hides his face behind his teacup, draining every drop with his last mouthful. The sun shines through the window into his eyes and he blinks like a mole.

'Actually it was him who came up with the idea of me getting a job at the holiday camp. He said he was a Bluecoat at Pontins for a while when he was my age.'

Nan splutters. 'A Bluecoat?' She wipes her lashes with a crumpled lavender hanky. 'The closest he ever got to it was a singing competition he went in for when he was nine!'

Luke's jaw drops. 'He wasn't a Bluecoat?'

She raises her eyes theatrically. '*And* he came last, poor little bugger. Tone deaf.' She eases herself out of her seat and hobbles over to the sink, where she pauses to watch the rise and fall of the birds beyond the windowpane. 'Poor old Richard,' she says with a gentle sigh. 'He always was full of shit.'

2

Met Office report for the Isle of Wight, mid-May 1976:
Maximum temperature 64°F/17.5°C

The middle of May is beautiful, with a steady warmth taking
hold across the island. Any rainfall is rare and short-lived,
and a strange kind of hush descends as the breeze drops
from the air. After their first exams, Luke and Martin take
their scooters around the island for the weekend, planning
the route with precision, a two-man tent strapped to the
back of Martin's bike. They avoid the resorts, skirting along
the coastal roads where they can, stopping off at viewing
points for lunch and a stretch. At St Boniface Down they
leave the bikes and climb up the steep south side, where the
fabled wishing well is said to be found if the climber ascends
towards the apex without looking back down. Halfway up,
a pair of tawny-coloured goats is grazing on the path above
them; the gull-eyed creatures stop chewing and stand rigid,
staring down the path at the lads, each goat a mirror image
of the other.

Martin clears his throat nervously.

'They're alright,' Luke says striding on towards them.
The goats turn and canter away, up over the summit and out
of view.

At the top the boys take off their rucksacks and lie back
on the dry grass, feeling the sun bleaching down on their

arms and legs. Luke closes his eyes as his heart rate decreases steadily and his limbs sink into the hillside. There's no sound from Martin, who is stretched out just inches away; Luke stays perfectly still as he listens to the light chatter of skylarks dancing in and out of their meadow nests in the surrounding grasses. He exhales, forcing all the air from his lungs, opening his eyelids narrowly against the glare of the wide sky. Swallows glide and dip overhead, briefly cutting out the sun as they dive into the meadows.

'So, we didn't find it, then,' he says, 'the wishing well.'

'Knew we wouldn't,' Martin replies. 'My dad told me it was a load of rubbish when I said we were going to look for it.'

Luke props himself up on his elbows and gazes out across the water. 'I don't know why you bother telling him stuff, mate. I mean, all he ever does is put you down.'

'He wasn't putting me down, was he?' Martin says, screwing his face up against the light. 'He was saying the wishing well was rubbish, not that I'm rubbish.'

There's a long bramble scratch running down the length of Martin's shin, and a small trickle of dried blood merges with the ingrained dirt and dust that clings to his pale skin. Luke stares at him. 'Yeah, but essentially, mate, it's the same thing. If he says the wishing well is rubbish, what he's really saying is that you're rubbish for thinking you might find it.'

'Can you hear the birds?' Martin asks, sitting up and tipping his head to one side. 'Wish I had a camera. You could get some brilliant photos of those swallows if you hung around long enough.'

'How can you tell they're swallows and not swifts?'

He looks deep in thought. 'Just can. Longer tail streamers, I think.'

Luke reaches for his bag and starts to unpack their picnic. 'Sorry, Mart. About your old man – I shouldn't have said that. He's your dad. You don't want to hear me running him down.'

'He also said I was a useless, overgrown waste of space,' Martin says, pulling himself up into a gangly cross-legged position. 'So I s'pose you might have a point.' Reaching for a sandwich, he takes a large bite, his expression losing focus as he starts to chew. 'He's been getting worse lately. I never know what kind of mood he's going to wake up in. Yesterday I knocked a cup off the side when I was washing up, and he went mad. He grabbed the rest of the cups off the draining board and chucked them at the wall. Said we might as well make a mess worth sweeping up. We've only got two left now, and a few glasses.'

Luke shakes his head, breaking his sandwich into two pieces. 'Man, you've gotta get out of there. Hey, maybe we could get a place together? You could come with me to the mainland?' He prods Martin with his toe. 'Mart? It would be a laugh! You and me, living together? You could do that photography course you keep going on about.'

Martin continues chewing until his sandwich is finished, and reaches for another. 'I couldn't do that, mate. I haven't saved enough for the camera yet – and I don't want one of those cheap ones. It's got to be a good one if I'm going to do a proper course. Anyway, you'll be busy getting to know all your new mates at poly.'

'Don't be an idiot. Once an islander, always an islander. Seriously, you could get a job over there, no problem.'

Martin turns the sandwich over in his hands. 'But I've got my job with Dad. He's getting more orders than ever these days, and I know he wants me to carry on the business.'

'But what about what *you* want to do? You always said you wanted to work with animals, like David Attenborough.'

'Or Johnny Morris.'

'Don't you want to do that any more?'

Martin doesn't answer for a moment. 'Dad says there's no money in it, and you can't live on fresh air. He's just had an order in from this big new gallery in London – forty frames – and they want them done really quick. He couldn't do it all with just the one pair of hands. He couldn't manage without me.'

'But you must have ambitions, Mart. I look at my folks and think, I don't want to end up like them, stuck in the same old place, doing the same old things. I'd rather top myself.' He turns his face skyward as a cluster of noisy gulls passes over. 'I mean, you must have some things you want to achieve before you die?'

'I'd like to go on Concorde,' Martin replies, after a minute's thought. 'Or hang-gliding. Like those fellas we saw over at Compton Down.'

Luke brushes the crumbs from his lap. 'Sorry, Mart. It's just – it won't be the same when I'm over there.'

Martin drinks deeply from his water flask, wiping his mouth on the back of his hand. 'That's OK. You'll be back some weekends anyway, won't you? You said it yourself – Brighton's not that far away.'

Luke shields his eyes as he looks out over the endless horizon. 'You're right,' he says, watching the sunlight as it ripples and shimmers across the water.

'I know I am,' says Martin, stretching out his long hairy legs and brushing the crumbs into the grass. 'You'll be back. Just like nothing's ever changed.'

Later that day, they set up their tent on the south side of the island, at a large cliffside campsite along the Military Road with views across the channel. It's not overly crowded, but the owner has asked campers to stick to the near end of the site while they're busy getting the place ready for the tourist season. The whirr of lawnmowers buzzes in the breeze as gardeners clear the overgrown borders, cutting down the meadow grasses at the edges, lopping off the fresh daisy heads before they've had a chance to unfurl. Before long, Luke knows, the campsites across the island will fill up with holidaymakers, crowding in from the mainland with their caravans and tents and hordes of noisy children. But for now it's relatively peaceful, with just twenty or so pitches taken across the gently sloping hillside.

Martin and Luke find a spot towards the top of the field where the grass is bathed in sunshine, away from the boisterous young families who congregate closest to the washing-up stations and showers. The sun is bright, but up here the wind whips and howls around the tents and guy ropes, tugging and swirling at Luke's hair as if it's caught in a vortex. He swipes his fringe aside, while Martin lunges clumsily, grasping for a corner of the tent which has slipped its peg as they struggle to get it anchored.

There's a small group a few tents away, perhaps in their late teens. They've got that polished city look; they're definitely not from round here and they don't look like seasoned campers. One of the girls is wearing a beige trouser suit, with flared bottoms and a short-sleeved jacket. She wears the jacket open, and beneath it Luke can glimpse a bright white bikini top. Nothing else. She catches Luke's eye every time he glances in her direction, and after this has happened a few times he smiles uncertainly and gives her a little nod. She's got long straight hair, dark blonde at the roots, graduating in colour all the way down her back to where the ends are pale and sun-bleached. The girl returns his smile and looks away, pulling a floppy sunhat down over her head.

He drops to his knees to peer inside their own small tent. 'How are we doing with the groundsheet, Mart?'

Martin is scrambling around inside, trying to hook the plastic cover under the canvas walls and on to the pegs on the outside. He sprawls across the sheet with one side of his face pressed against the plastic surface in concentration, a tiny pink tip of tongue protruding from the corner of his mouth.

'Near-ly... there!' He pushes himself into a sitting position and brushes the dust from his hands. 'That should do the trick.'

Luke crawls inside and sits beside him, cross-legged, looking up and around their sleeping space. 'Bloody hell,

Mart, it's not that big in here is it? You'll have to sleep with your feet sticking out of the tent.'

Martin lies down and stretches himself out to try it for size. He's too long to lie flat. 'I'll have to sleep on my side, then,' he says, rubbing a grubby finger along the bridge of his nose. 'Don't know how they can call it a two-man tent. It's not even long enough for one man.'

Luke hops on to his feet and looms over him with a menacing snarl. 'Not for a super-freak like you, maybe!' He jabs Martin in the ribs, making him shriek. It's a high-pitched 'Yeeearghhh!' sound and Martin lashes out in reflex, knocking Luke over so that he tumbles out of the tent flap, in full view of their neighbours. When he gets to his feet, the blonde girl's looking over again. She's whispering with the others in her group, who are now all craning to get a good look.

'What's the matter?' one of them calls over, a snooty-looking girl with a big flicky fringe. 'Did oo see a ickle bumble bee?'

The group howls with laughter, including two lads in ironed shorts and shirts who are returning from the standpipe with plastic tanks of water. Everything in their party looks brand new, even the guy ropes.

'Daft girls,' Luke mutters, offering up a small embarrassed shrug and wandering round to the other side of the tent. He self-consciously brushes dust patches from the seat of his cut-off jeans, suddenly aware of his scruffy appearance. He's only brought one spare T-shirt with him, and he's already started to whiff a bit.

Martin crawls out and gets to his feet, stretching his arms high above his head, so that his long, thin shadow cuts across the faded orange canvas.

'Who's daft?' he asks, lazily scratching at his armpit and yawning.

Luke cocks a discreet thumb in their direction, allowing himself another quick peek at the girl with the long hair. She's very pretty.

Martin puts his hands on his hips and looks over, squinting into the afternoon light for a better look. His tiny shorts look ridiculous. 'What, them?' he says, too loudly, and he points right at them.

'Oh, my God, Mart! Do you have to be so uncool?' Luke drops to the ground so that he's obscured by the tent. He rubs his hands across his face and groans. 'Fucking hell!'

Martin shrugs and sits down beside him. 'Sorry, mate. So what are we gonna do for food tonight?'

Luke gets up and starts to unstrap the rucksack from the back of his scooter, unrolling his sleeping bag and laying his belongings out on his side of the tent, before crawling out backwards and flicking the earth and grass from his knees. 'Fish and chips? We could stop off for a pint somewhere at the same time. I'll need something to knock me out if I've got to spend the night cramped up in a tiny tent with you and your stinky feet.'

Martin snorts a little laugh and unpacks his few items, throwing them into the tent in a small heap. Making a pillow of his jacket, Luke lies back against the grass. The wind has dropped a little now, and the sun feels warm against his skin. Martin stands beside him, looking out across the campsite, casting a shadow across Luke's face, shielding him from the sun. Luke frowns up at him. 'Cheers, mate. I was hoping to get a nice Martin-shaped tan mark across my forehead.' He props himself up on his elbows and nods towards the ground. 'Chill out, man. We're meant to be taking a proper break from revising, clear our minds.'

Martin pulls his T-shirt over his head and lies on the grass alongside Luke, stretching his arms above his head like a man about to do military sit-ups. 'God, I'm white,' he says, taking a good look at his broad, bony chest.

Luke snorts, and reaches for his sunglasses. 'I'm definitely gonna need these now.'

For a while they lie there, side by side, just watching the other campers come and go, soaking up the warmth of the afternoon in companionable silence. The blonde girl passes by and takes a good look at them before returning to her group. 'See that one?' Luke says, when she's gone. 'She reminds me of Samantha Dyas.'

'From the year below us?' Martin says. 'She's a bit like her. You know she's going out with Len now?'

'Who, Samantha?'

Martin nods.

'Bloody hell, what's wrong with the world? *Len Dickens*? She must be mad. He's a thug.'

'He wasn't always,' Martin says, pressing his fingertips against the skin of his chest to test the heat.

'I don't know why you'd defend him, Mart. He's never given you anything but grief.'

'I'm just saying, he wasn't always that way. He was a good mate back in primary school.'

'Yeah, well, that was a long time ago. Before he turned into a mental case.' Luke gets to his feet and yawns. 'Right! I need a piss.' He chances a glance at the nearby group, who are now distracted as they try to decipher the instructions on a new tin of camping gas. 'I'll fill up the water bottle while I'm down there.'

He takes the path to the toilet block, going the long way round, to avoid the blonde girl and her mainland friends. He wonders if they're staring at him, taking the mickey out of his scruffy clothes and unkempt hair, laughing at his pale giant of a friend.

As he nears the block, his attention is diverted by a huge black dog, a Rottweiler, galloping down the slope from the other side of the campsite, and in a split second Luke realises that it has him in his sights. In one fluid movement the dog jumps at him, knocking him to the ground with ease. He lands on his side, balled up beneath the huge beast as it barks great bellowing woofs across the campsite for everyone to hear. The rear end of the dog looms over Luke's face, its grotesque testicles swinging between thick, muscular hind legs.

'Dillon!' In the distance, Luke can hear the dog's owner jogging down the hill to retrieve him. 'Dill!'

The dog steps over Luke and sits beside him, accepting treats from the woman's wrinkly brown hand. Luke scrabbles to his feet, brushing himself off and glancing up the hill to see all the residents of the campsite looking in his direction. He tugs at his earlobe.

'Oh, you are a naughty little dog, aren't you?' says the small woman, massaging the beast's jowls vigorously. She nuzzles his head with her face, and when she looks up Luke recognises her as a local from his part of town. He's embarrassed to see that, apart from the camera looped around her neck, she's covered by just a faded navy blue bikini which hangs limply on her bony frame. She looks as if she's spent her whole life lying in the sun, slowly frazzling away like a raisin.

'I wouldn't exactly describe him as "little",' he says, picking up the water flask knocked from his grasp during the assault.

The woman studies Luke closely, narrowing her eyes. 'Aren't you Richard Wolff's lad?'

Luke blinks, surprised.

'Hmm, thought so.'

He juggles the flask from one hand to the other. 'Sorry – I don't think I know – '

'No, you wouldn't. I've seen you with your dad in the town a couple of times, but I didn't like to come over. You look like him.'

There's an awkward pause. 'So, how do you know my dad?' Luke asks, more to fill the gap than out of interest.

'I met him at one of the McKees' parties.'

'Oh, right.' He glances past her to see if the others are all still watching.

'That was a few years back now.' She stares at him as if she's asked him a question and is waiting for some answer.

'Oh.' Luke gives her a polite smile. 'I've heard Mum and Dad talking about the McKees' parties.'

'Of course you have. *Everyone*'s heard of the McKees' parties. I used to be Marie's yoga teacher,' she says archly, stretching out her turtley neck and rolling her shoulders, as if to illustrate the point. The slobbering dog pushes his muzzle into the palm of her hand and she looks up at Luke sternly. 'Not any more.'

Something in her unblinking pale eyes sets his teeth on edge. 'Well, I suppose I'd better get going,' he says, holding up the flask.

'Tell your dad you bumped into Sara Newbury. Though of course he might not remember me.' She tilts her head.

Luke smiles flatly and starts to walk away.

'How's your mum?' she calls after him.

He doesn't like her tone; he turns briefly to scowl back at her as he continues to walk. She raises her thin eyebrows. 'Still going to those parties, are they?'

Luke stops, puzzled, and watches as she pulls her chin in primly, hunching down to feed another treat into the dog's slobbering mouth. Luke can see each gnarly vertebra that runs down her darkly tanned back.

'You should keep that dog under control,' he calls over, struggling to restrain his rising irritation. 'He's too big to be running about off the lead.'

The woman visibly bristles, her little hands balling into fists at her side. With a flick of her grizzled head she walks away, back up the slope towards her caravan, with the beast trotting obediently at her side.

Fleetingly, Luke's mind separates from his body. The sky is wide and unending overhead, the light too vivid, this patch of island too small. As the woman finally disappears into her caravan at the top of the field, Luke exhales, at once conscious of his surroundings, and heads for the toilet block, stopping at the standpipe to run his face under the water pipe on the hard-standing. It's cool and clear down here in the shade of the brick building, and he's momentarily invisible, concealed by the shadows. He shakes the water from his hands and massages wet fingers across his scalp before stepping out into the sunlight. Shielding his eyes, he looks back up the hill towards Martin, who's up on his feet now, keeping watch. The sun illuminates him clearly: his great shadow cast long and thin, his arms limp at his sides, shoulders dipped. Luke can hardly bear the thought of climbing back up the hill in full view of all the other campers, and he's seized by the urge to run. He could just keep on walking around this building and drop down on to the beach via the coastal path. He could lie back against the pebbles and soak in the rays for a few hours, undisturbed by anyone. He could do it; he could do it right now.

But he won't. He'll fill his flask with drinking water and walk back up through the field, avoiding the mocking gaze of the holidaymakers, and he'll let Martin know he's alright. Nothing to worry about, mate. Because he is. He's alright.

Back home on Monday evening, the family sits around the kitchen table for supper, as a light evening breeze blows in through the open back door. Luke sat the first part of his English exam today, and he's still feeling irritable from two hours spent concentrating on his paper in the heat of the school gym. He studies his parents; they chat comfortably, like normal parents in an average family. His father's hand slips around his mother's waist as she stretches over to serve Kitty peas and potatoes. Mum complains about yet another flood from the twin-tub and Dad grumbles that they can't afford a replacement. He jokes about one of his unbearable colleagues at work; she tells him he shouldn't be so unkind, but laughs all the same. Luke observes the simple domesticity of it all, knowing he should be grateful for it, but inexplicably resenting them all the same.

'Good weekend, Luke?' Dad asks.

'Not bad.'

'Cracking weather for it. You've been lucky. How was the tent?'

'Small.'

Mum touches Luke's hand lightly; he pulls it away. 'I still can't believe you're old enough to be riding around on a big motorbike like that on your own, Luke.'

'It's a 50 CC, Mum, and it's a scooter. It's hardly big.'

'Alright, Luke,' Dad says. 'She's a mother. It's natural for her to worry.'

'I'm not *worried*. Just a bit sad that my little boy's all grown up.' She pulls a melancholy face and sprinkles salt over her potatoes. 'You know we're going to miss you when you're gone.'

Luke shakes his head. 'You make it sound like I'm dying.'

'Is Lu-lu going to die?' asks Kitty, her face crumpling up.

'No!' says Mum, stifling a laugh with one hand, reaching out to comfort Kitty with the other. 'Of course not!'

'Bad luck, Kitty. I'll still be coming back to tickle you every now and then.' Kitty smiles broadly, using the diversion to grab a handful of peas and scoot them on to the floor.

'So, what are you up to over the next week or two? Apart from exams, obviously,' Mum asks.

'Dunno. It's Martin's eighteenth this weekend. Expect I'll have to sort out something for him. His dad's a complete arsehole, so I doubt he'll have anything arranged.'

'*Luke.*'

'*Well*. It's true. From what Martin says, he's turning into a bit of a nut job.'

'Poor boy,' says Mum, gazing at her plate. 'You know, I haven't seen his dad for *years*. He always did keep to himself, even when they first moved here. Remember, Richard? We asked him round for a drink, didn't we, when the boys started getting friendly at school? We thought he might be glad of it, as he's on his own. But he didn't come. Said he had too much work on.'

'Nut job,' says Kitty, bashing her spoon on the edge of the table. 'Nut. *Job.*'

Mum scowls at Luke.

'Strange man,' Dad agrees, reaching across the table for the salt. 'Hardly surprising, though, is it? I'd probably be the same if I didn't have a wife to sort all those things out.'

'I think he's shy,' says Mum, 'like Martin. Anyway, we can't let Martin's birthday go by without a celebration. Why don't we have him over for Sunday lunch, Richard? Kitty and I can make him a cake and we'll sort out a little present or something. What do you think, Luke?'

'OK,' Luke says after some thought. 'Why not?'

Dad mops up the last of his sauce with a hunk of bread. 'This casserole's good.'

'It's not bad at all, is it?' Mum replies cheerily. 'Chicken chasseur. I think I've done a rather good job of it. It's one of Marie's recipes.'

Luke shrugs. 'Who's Marie?'

'You know, as in John and Marie? She's a wonderful cook.'

The recollection of the frazzled old dog lady shunts to the front of Luke's mind. 'The McKees? Aren't they the ones who have all the parties?' He looks up, a forkful of food hovering over his plate.

Mum pauses, just a fraction of a second. 'That's right.' Her voice is light and breezy, like when she's talking to the postman or the Avon lady. 'We were there last weekend, remember, when you and Martin were babysitting? What did she cook that night, Richard?' She turns to Dad, who appears deep in thought as he helps himself to more chicken. 'Richard?'

A large dollop of thick sauce falls between the serving dish and Dad's plate. It glistens wetly, and for one collective moment they all stare at it, before the silence is broken by a loud rap on the open door leading out to the back alley.

Kitty waves her spoon in the air as Simon Drake appears in the doorway, a hand loosely hung in his shorts pocket, a lock of golden hair obscuring one eye. 'Uncle Simon!'

'Afternoon, Wolffs,' Simon says, pushing the hair from his face and smiling widely. He indicates for Luke to budge along the bench, and eyes the empty plates with interest.

'Simon – can I get you a drink, sir?' Dad springs up to fetch a couple of beers from the fridge, opening the first and handing it across the table. 'What brings you?'

Mum points to the casserole; Simon nods approvingly, and she fills a plate for him. Kitty clambers out of her seat, padding across the kitchen and out through the back door, the sound of her singing trailing away as she disappears into the garden.

'So, Simon – what did Laura have to say when you rolled in drunk the other night?' Mum gives Simon an annoyed look.

'I was hardly drunk!'

She looks between the two men and scoffs. 'You could barely stand up, the pair of you.'

'Friday night?' Luke smirks. 'You must've been – I heard one of you kick the milk bottles over. You didn't stop laughing until Mum came out and told you off.'

'I did not tell them off!' Mum says, smoothing her hands over her lap. She turns back to the men. 'I was worried about you waking the kids up.'

Simon leans over and kisses her on the cheek. 'Sorry?' he offers, feigning shame.

She doesn't look convinced, still scowling hard as she indicates for Luke to fetch Simon a knife and fork from the drawer. 'Well, I hope Laura gave you an earful when you got home.'

He laughs. 'Believe me, she did.'

Dad raises his bottle in Simon's direction, and Mum smiles despite herself.

'So, how's the new job going?' Mum asks, sitting back in her seat. 'It must be a bit different being in charge, isn't it? Especially when you've got to keep the likes of Richard in line.'

Dad laughs. 'It's about time we got some fresh blood at the helm. Shake things up a bit. Simon's doing a great job.'

'I don't know about that,' says Simon, resting his fork to one side. He nudges Luke and takes a swig from his beer bottle. 'I reckon your old dad's just pleased to have his best mate in the headmaster's seat. He thinks no one will notice how lazy he is, with me there to turn a blind eye.'

'As if!' Dad laughs.

Mum clears the plates and places a defrosted Black Forest gâteau on the table, handing Simon the serving knife as she returns to the sink to wash the forks for dessert. 'Well, I hope you two can learn to pace yourselves a bit better,' she says without turning round, 'especially you, with all this responsibility, Simon.' There's a loud clatter as she drops the clean cutlery on to the draining board.

Simon slices into the gâteau, moving his head closer to Luke's as he passes him a plateful. 'Was she really cross about the other night?' he whispers.

'She'll get over it,' Luke replies, trying and failing to pick up the dessert with his hands.

Dad scoops a deep curl of cream on to his finger and drops it into his mouth, his eyes following Mum's backside as she stretches across the table to pass out the clean forks. He runs his hand up over the smooth contours of her tight slacks and gives her bottom a firm pat. 'Ignore her, Simon,' he says. 'She's just jealous she wasn't out on the town with us, aren't you, love?'

Mum pulls her seat up to join them, her eyes moving from one man to the other before her face cracks into a reluctant smile. 'Yes, of course I am, silly. Now eat your cake!'

The pathway to Martin's front door is accessed via a small wooden gate the colour of driftwood. The house name, which reads 'Shingles', is entirely bleached, leaving only an etched imprint, nailed to the decaying gatepost. Despite their long friendship Luke has only called on Martin a handful of times over the years, as he knows he's not entirely welcome.

'Dad doesn't like visitors,' Martin once told him, years ago, after he'd chased down the road to catch up with Luke, who was close to tears because Martin's dad had just shut the door in his face. He'd only wanted to show off his new roller skates. 'He just gets funny about strangers knocking on the door,' he had added for emphasis.

'But we've known each other for ages!' Luke had replied, angrily swiping at his cheeks with the back of his wrist.

Martin had looked lost, his awkward limbs already too long and gangly for his years. 'Well, he doesn't like people,' he said, and they dropped the subject and headed off towards the seafront to call on Len.

Today is yet another dry, searing day; Luke pushes the gate closed behind him, treading along the narrow path which ruptures with dandelions, limp and broken in the uncommon May heat. Hollyhocks and lupins droop and fall at the path's edge, evidence of a once pretty cottage garden. Stepping around a rusted lawn roller, he knocks on the front door, suddenly conscious of the garden's silence in contrast to the sharp gull cries that carry up from the seafront, haunting and clear. He's nervous that Mr Brazier will answer the door, but he doesn't really have a choice. He's been phoning for days without a reply, and his mum really needs to know if Martin's coming for lunch or not. Yesterday she went out and bought cake ingredients and new candles, saying she'd make it anyway, just in case he does manage to come over. After a minute or so, there's no answer, and he knocks again, before cupping his eyes to peer into the darkness beyond the salty front windows. The bright sunlight from the back of the house cuts through the lounge, casting deep shadows across the disarray of the room. Newspapers pile up against the leg of a wood-framed sofa, while pots and plates cover the sideboard at the rear of the room.

'Bloody hell,' Luke mutters as he scans the mess.

Dropping back from the window, he turns his face to the sky as another cluster of gulls passes over, screeching and cawing until they're far from view. As he turns to leave, he catches the opening whirr of saws in the still air, drifting over from the back of the house where he knows Mr Brazier keeps his workshop.

'Martin?' Luke calls out, pushing back the high grass and nettles that obscure the path along the side of the house. 'Mart?'

The long grasses grow sparser as he reaches the rear of the red brick building, where he comes out on to a large lawn. The workshop sits at the far end of the garden, a huge wooden construction, built across the full width of the plot. It stands with its double doors wide open, the noise of circular saws buzzing and shrieking from within. A wrecked bike lies abandoned at the edge of the path: Martin's old bicycle, the one he'd once used to pedal all over the island with Luke, back in their primary years. Now, it looks tiny, insignificant; a rusting relic from the scrap yard.

Luke reaches the opening to the workshop and leans in. Martin and his dad are at the bench, both of them wearing protective goggles and canvas aprons, bent over their work in concentration. The machine grinds to a halt and the two men look up, alerted by Luke's thin shadow stretching out across the sunlit concrete.

'What the – ' growls Mr Brazier, snapping the goggles up and over his head. A cloud of sawdust lifts and floats around his face, catching like gold in the streaks of light from the glass panels above. His greying hair stands in an angry peak at the crown. 'Who the bloody hell invited you in?' he shouts.

'There was no answer at the front door, so I – '

Martin's dad flings down the goggles and strides towards Luke with such pace that he's sure he's going to hit him. Luke's fists ball up instinctively. Martin catches his father by the arm as he passes; he swings round to face his son, shaking his hand off violently.

'It's *Luke*, Dad,' Martin says, shrinking back, rubbing his dusty hands on the front of his apron. 'It's just Luke.' He must be six inches taller than his father, and yet he looks so small beside him.

Mr Brazier's face is stony grey. He glares at Luke accusingly, before lumbering back to his work, pausing to point his finger at Martin. 'Don't talk to me like I'm a fool, son.'

Martin returns to the bench, his long arms hanging limp. The swirling motes ripple in the light, circling Mr Brazier as he indicates towards a screwdriver, which Martin passes to him.

'What d'you want, Luke?' he barks over his shoulder. 'We're working.'

Martin picks up a pencil, which he nervously twirls between his fingers. There's black paint smudged along the crooked lines of his nose, and something in his expression reminds Luke of the day when he broke it, tripping and smashing his face into the gritty surface of the playground as he fumbled to catch the ball that Len had lobbed over from the field. They were still friends back then, and Len had sprinted over to help, pushing his grubby handkerchief beneath Luke's nostrils to stem the blood flow as they guided him inside to find the school nurse.

Luke takes a single step forward, halting as he notices his shadow shift over the rippled floor. 'Well, it's just, you know it's Martin's eighteenth today?'

Mr Brazier's brow crinkles, and he makes a small grunting sound.

'Well, it's my mum, really. She wanted to know if he could come to ours for lunch.'

Martin taps his Adam's apple once with the pencil, avoiding eye contact with Luke.

'Did she?' Mr Brazier mutters. He reaches across the bench and picks up a tape measure, drawing it out and along the edges of a completed picture frame. 'Thinks he's a bit of a charity case, does she?' He hooks one finger through the corner of the frame and lets it swing, turning to look at Luke for his answer.

'No!' Luke answers. 'No. We just thought, you know – '

'What? That he wouldn't have anything better to do on his birthday?'

'No, but – '

Mr Brazier pulls on his leather gloves and waves Luke away. Martin shakes his head at Luke, a tiny movement, before reaching for his own goggles and fixing them over his face. He turns his back to Luke as the machinery screams into action again.

Luke's skin feels hot and clammy beneath his black T-shirt and he pushes away the hair that sticks to his forehead, as the heat of the sun's rays scorches the skin of his legs through the open doorway.

'She said to ask you too,' he shouts over the noise. It's a lie and he instantly regrets saying it.

Martin's dad utters a harsh cough of a laugh, and he shuts off the machine. 'Really?' He faces Martin, who's gripping a strip of pine between both hands. 'So, what d'you think of that, son?'

Martin doesn't respond. He stares blankly at the strip of wood, as if he's stopped breathing. Outside the wide opening to the workshop, house sparrows chirp and batter about in the dusty patch of earth.

Luke walks away. 'Sorry,' he says, raising his hand half-heartedly as he reaches the fullness of sunshine beyond the entrance. The sparrows scatter and take flight. 'Happy birthday, mate.'

He kicks his way back through the weeds at the side of the house, cursing the nettles as they sting the soft skin behind his knees; cursing Martin's dad. He pushes open the broken gate, jamming it back into place and clicking the latch as he goes. '*Fucker*,' he mutters as he rounds the corner at the top of the road where he left his scooter.

To his surprise, Martin appears, benign and lanky, wheeling his scooter through a concealed hole in the hedge, shaking the wood shavings from his hair.

'How'd you get there?'

'Back gate,' Martin replies. 'We never use the front these days. Too overgrown.' He guides his scooter off the kerb.

Luke stares at him, baffled.

'He said I can come,' Martin says.

'Your dad?'

'Yeah. He said I could have the day off. As it's my birthday.'

Luke wrinkles his nose as he fastens his chinstrap. 'That's big of him.'

Martin shrugs.

'So, what did he get you? For your eighteenth?'

'This!' Martin holds up a ten-pound note. 'Just now. Told me to get myself a few drinks or something. But I'm going to save it towards my camera. Good, huh?'

Luke shakes his head. 'He gave it to you just now?'

Martin looks blank.

'You're joking, mate. He'd forgotten?'

The whirr of saws floats up and over the hedges from Mr Brazier's workshop, and Martin glances in the direction of the noise.

'Not really. Well, kind of, but he remembered in the end, didn't he?'

Luke slaps him on the arm and does his best to smile. 'Yeah. Of course. He remembered in the end.' He watches as his best friend clambers on to his scooter and starts up the engine.

Martin rubs his hands together, and grins through his helmet visor. 'So, what's for lunch?'

It's warm enough to eat outside, so Mum sets out the long bench in the garden, covering it with two mismatched tablecloths, clipped together with pegs. She's wearing an ankle-length dress, in a turquoise and pink floral design, like the flowers that hang from the baskets at the front of the house. Kitty follows her round, placing knives and forks where Mum points, counting loudly as she goes, while Luke and Martin sit with Dad in the deckchairs beside the willow tree, drinking cold beers and watching the birthday table take shape.

''*Appy Birthday to Yoooou*,' Kitty sings, spinning in clumsy circles, making Martin laugh as she stumbles about.

Luke stretches his arms over his head and snaps his fingers. 'Here, Kitty, come and sing Martin his birthday song. Remember, the one we talked about earlier?'

She skips once, then runs across the lawn, darting beneath the branches of the weeping willow and through the teatowel entrance to her clothes-horse den. Martin sits forward in his seat, ducking his head to see where she's gone.

'Wait,' says Luke. 'She's got it all worked out, mate. Special birthday song, just for you – '

The teatowels flap as Kitty pokes her head out. ''Troduce me, Lu-lu!'

Luke pushes himself up from his seat and stands at the edge of the willow branches. He makes a trumpet of his hands. 'Ta-da-da-dahhh! I'm pleased to present, for your ears only… the mar-vel-lous, mechanical Kitty! And today, she'll be singing Martin's all-time favourite song – ' He laughs. '"Fernando"!'

Martin shakes his head as Kitty twirls into the centre of the garden, trailing a fluffy mohair scarf, to the light applause of the gathered family. She raises a dramatically cupped hand against her ear. '*Can you hear the drums, Banando?*'

Luke presses the beer bottle to his mouth to stifle his laughter.

'*They were shiny there for you an' me, flibberdee –* ' She sings and sways across the lawn, filling the lyrical gaps with confident lah-lah-lahs, making up the actions as she goes along, creating balletic arcs with her arms and legs. '*Something in the hair and light – stars and bright, Banando!*'

Mum watches from the table, paused in her duties, clapping in time as Dad hums along, conducting with his forefingers.

'*Lah-lah-lah-lah-lah-lah – same again! Ohhh yes, my friend –* ' She roly-polys three times across the garden and lands in front of the seated men, until finally she reaches her crescendo and jumps to her feet with outstretched arms. '*Banando*!'

Martin puts down his bottle and claps, a slow, happy smile creeping across his face.

'Yee-hah for Kitty!' Luke yells.

'Fank you verry much,' she says, bowing deeply before sprinting over and launching herself at Martin, where she clings to his neck and presses her face against his.

'Well done, Kitty!' Mum calls over on her way back to the kitchen, a bunch of napkins in her hand. Kitty releases Martin, and runs back across the lawn to resume her role as table assistant as Martin settles himself back down into the deckchair.

Dad pats his exposed belly, his eyes firmly closed against the sun. 'She's a star, alright.'

'What d'you think, Mart?' Luke asks.

Martin doesn't answer. He's leaning on to his knees, scrutinising the ground between his feet.

Luke bumps his knee against Martin's, hoping to elicit a laugh. 'I know how much you love *Abba*, mate,' he says.

Martin nods, finally raising his head.

'Mate?' Luke says quietly, noticing the moisture in Martin's eyes.

After a pause, Martin takes a swig of beer and leans back in his deckchair. 'It was nice. Really nice.'

Luke clinks his bottle against his friend's. 'Happy birthday, mate.'

Lunch is a roast, and as usual, it's late. At two-thirty, Mum calls them all into the kitchen to help ferry the various bowls of vegetables and potatoes outside. She ceremoniously places a bottle of white wine on the table and hands a corkscrew to Dad.

'Well, it *is* a special occasion,' she says, casting a sentimental smile in Martin's direction. 'Now, I know we've got pork, but I've made Yorkshire puddings to go with it as I remember they're your favourite, Martin, and there's plenty more gravy if we run out.'

She passes the serving spoon to him, and he helps himself to potatoes. Dad pours the wine, and Martin passes the vegetable bowl back to Mum, fumbling awkwardly as she takes it from him. When she turns away, he stares for a moment at her pretty dress, his gaze lingering on the halter-neck behind her wavy French-pleated hair. Luke smirks, and Martin looks away, drowning his food in gravy with unsteady hands.

'Ahhhhhh,' says Luke, pointing at Martin's plate.

'Bisto!' Kitty yells.

Martin smiles self-consciously and dips his head to concentrate on his food. A light breeze has picked up through the garden, but the sun remains resolute in the sky, and it feels like the height of summer. They eat, and, as Kitty fills her Yorkshire pudding with all the vegetables she plans not to eat, the lads chat about their plans for the coming months, and Dad keeps the wine flowing.

After Mum has cleared the lunch plates, she returns to the table with a Victoria sponge cake, decorated with white icing, Smarties and eighteen candles. Luke watches her, his view softened by wine, as she looks down at Martin with her pretty smile and kind eyes. His mind drifts back to thoughts of the dog woman at the campsite the previous weekend. Last night, still troubled by it, he'd waited until his mother was out of the room before relaying the whole conversation to Dad.

'Oh, yes, I remember Sara Newbury, all right,' Dad told him. 'She only lives round the corner in Grasslands Avenue, but she keeps a caravan down at Caulks' Farm for weekends. I heard that she'd had a bit of a falling out with Marie McKee not so long ago, all over something and nothing. I'm afraid she's just a lonely little lady with an axe to grind.'

'Ah, that's it – Grasslands Avenue. I knew I'd seen her somewhere before – isn't that the house with all the chihuahuas? Anyway, she was making a big deal about those parties you go to at the McKees,' Luke said.

'Well, she would.' Dad laughed. 'She's probably just put out because her invitations stopped coming. Her husband died a couple of years back, and I think she went a bit funny – filling her house up with all those dogs – you know she's got six? Imagine the smell. It's no wonder Marie stopped inviting her.' He picked up his newspaper, folded it down the middle and looked at Luke gravely. 'Here, you might want to get yourself a rabies vaccination if her flea-bitten dog's had a go at you – before you start foaming at the mouth.' He clutched himself at the throat and started gurgling and bulging at the eyes, and Luke laughed too, reassured by his father's typical response.

Here in the sunny cocoon of the spring garden, Luke pushes it from his mind. Kitty stands on her chair to lead the birthday song, crossly gesturing at Luke to join in, stretching across the table to stick her finger into the icing before Martin blows his candles out.

'Wish!' she yelps in Martin's ear, making him jump.

Martin closes his eyes, and rubs his chin thoughtfully. 'OK,' he says, nodding at Kitty when he's done.

'What was it?' she asks, lowering herself back into her seat. She puts her small pink hand on his arm and gazes up at him earnestly. 'A pony?'

'Secret,' he says, and he pats her on the head.

A breeze passes through the branches of the willow, causing the leaves to ripple and sway. One of Kitty's tea-towels snaps free of the clothes-horse and flutters across the lawn.

Gesturing towards Martin, Dad pushes back his chair and stands, easing his free hand into the pocket of his tight polyester shorts. 'May I?'

Martin brings his fingers up to cover his face; Luke pulls them away, laughing.

'Now, Martin, we're all honoured that you agreed to join us on your special day.'

Mum clinks her glass with a spoon. 'Hear, hear!'

'And a little bird tells me you're quite keen to take up photography?'

Martin nods cautiously, looking sideways at Luke.

'Now, I don't know if you're aware, but I was quite the photographer myself, back in my youth.' Dad puffs out his chest, smiling sagely.

Luke helps himself to more wine.

'In fact, in my London days, I was great mates with David Bailey, just before he got his big break.'

'You met him *once*,' Mum says. She hands a stack of side plates to Luke to pass around the table.

Dad looks injured. 'I'll have you know we were very nearly flatmates. If I hadn't pinched his girlfriend, I'm sure we'd still be friends now.'

She shakes her head, addressing the lads. 'And even when they *did* meet, they only exchanged a few words. It was at a party in Battersea, and I was there, so I don't see how he managed to pinch David Bailey's girlfriend with me in tow. *Honestly*, Richard.'

Dad sits down in his seat. 'Jealous,' he says, jerking his head in Mum's direction. 'So!' He reaches under the table, and produces a wrapped shoebox which he passes across the table. 'Happy birthday, Martin! I hope you don't mind that it's second-hand.'

At first Martin doesn't even reach for it; he just sits and stares at the box.

Dad tops up his own wine glass. 'It's just that when Luke told me what you were after, I thought it was the perfect excuse to get myself a new one. So you're very welcome to this old thing. If you'd like it, that is.'

Mum reaches over to stroke Dad's forearm. Martin takes the box, holding it suspended over his slice of cake as Dad bobs his head, encouraging him to open it. He unwraps the paper and opens the lid, slowly lifting the camera out, his mouth drooping in wonder.

'It's a Brownie,' he says, barely audible, gently running his thumb over the buttons and dials. 'But, I can't – '

Dad swiftly brings his finger to his lips, in the way you might do to quieten a class of schoolchildren. 'Shh! It didn't cost us a thing. Apart from the price of a fresh reel of film. And a flash bulb. I'm just glad to see it go to a good home.'

Martin sits in silence, gazing at his gift, as Luke shifts in his seat, eventually breaking the tension by waving at his dad and pointing to the camera.

'Oh, yes – we must capture the moment!' Dad takes the camera from Martin and sets it up at the far end of the table, fiddling and adjusting the timer. 'OK – gather round.'

They all surround Martin at the head of the table, squeezing together to fit into the shot. Mum rests her arm around Martin's shoulder, as Luke makes devil horns behind his head and Kitty clambers up to sit on his lap.

'Ready, everyone?' asks Dad, pulling in his stomach muscles as he sprints back to rejoin the group. '*Cheese!*'

Late in the afternoon, Luke and Martin take the bicycles from the garage and pump up the tyres before cycling down to the rocky beach at Whitecliff Bay. They wheel the bikes down the steep sloping path to the shoreline and prop them against the metal rails in the fading light, clambering up and over the rocks to a secluded spot looking out across the sand. Luke opens his rucksack and pulls out a bottle of Dad's wine, removing the cork clumsily with his old Swiss army knife. They've already had several glasses with lunch, but Luke's in the mood to carry on. Martin stands with his back to the sea, fiddling with his new camera, humming to himself quietly as he slots the flash cube into place. The beaches are still fairly quiet, and, when the last dog walker disappears up the wooden walkway just before nine, the lads are the only people left as the beach nears darkness.

'I can't believe your dad gave me this.' Martin snaps Luke as he pushes the base of the wine bottle into the sand, startling him with the flash so that he slides back off his smooth rock, kicking sand up with the toe of his sandal. He swears as he rights himself, making a grab for the wine bottle before Martin can reach for it.

'Remember when we got stuck out on the rocks, trying to climb round at Culver Down? How old were we – eleven – twelve? It's a wonder we didn't drown.'

'Remember the fat lifeboat man? He went mad at us, didn't he?'

'So did my dad.' Luke laughs. 'Well, it *was* bloody stupid. Of course, it was Len's idea in the first place.'

'Whenever we got into any bother it was Len's idea.' Martin smiles wistfully, fixing the lens cap over his camera. He folds himself on to the rock beside Luke, his large feet burrowing beneath the sand.

'*Len*. I can't even start to imagine what Samantha Dyas sees in him. Stupid little pikey.'

Martin's brow wrinkles. 'He's not a pikey, mate.'

'Well, they live in a caravan, don't they? So, he must be a pikey.'

'They didn't always, though.' Martin looks over towards the rocks at Culver Down. 'They had that nice place along the esplanade, before his dad went off. It's not exactly Len's fault they ended up in a caravan.'

Luke shrugs, taking another drink from the bottle. 'Yeah, yeah. OK, maybe he's not a pikey. But he's still a dickhead. You of all people should agree with that, Mart.'

He hands Martin the wine. It's a clear sky, and the tide is low, gently rippling in the distance. The light of the half-moon catches on the wet pebbles along the shoreline so that they blink and flicker as thin cloud cover steadily crosses the sky. 'Just a couple of weeks until exams are over.' Luke sighs. Martin passes the bottle back to him, and he jams it back into the sand between them.

'You're lucky, Luke, with your folks,' Martin says.

'Yeah, I suppose they're alright.'

'And Kitty. I wish I had a little sister like her.'

Luke doesn't answer for a moment. 'How are things with your old man, mate? When I called for you earlier – well it seemed pretty obvious your dad didn't have a clue it was your birthday. Your *eighteenth* birthday, man.'

Martin reaches forward to scoop up a heap of damp shingle. 'He does his best. It's just he's never been very good at that kind of thing.'

There's a shriek from the coastal footpath overhead; the lads pause, listening intently, until they hear laughter as the young voices trail away.

'I suppose,' Luke replies. 'I guess it's my mum who sorts all that stuff in our house. Birthdays, dentists, school uniforms. All that mum stuff.'

Martin lets the shingle filter between his fingers and on to the sand between his feet.

'You know when you moved here?' Luke asks. 'D'you remember your first day at school, when Mrs Harwood put you next to me in class? I still reckon she did it to take the piss. I mean, I was so small I only looked about five or six. And you were so tall, you looked like a teenager.'

'I wasn't *that* big.'

'You were! Your shoes were massive – and your jumper sleeves were always too short.' He slaps his hands down on his thighs. 'You looked like Herman Munster.'

'No change there, then,' Martin holds up one of his size thirteen feet, waving it in the air, sprinkling sand.

'Nah. It's good to be tall. The girls love it – I wish I was a few inches taller.'

Martin nods his head gently and gazes out over the water, watching the blinking lights passing over the horizon as the faint shush of the lapping waves drifts in and out of reach.

Brushing sand from the back of his calf, Luke shifts on his rock. 'You've never really told me much about before you came here, mate...' He laces his fingers together and stretches awkwardly. He knows Martin isn't comfortable talking about this; he's tried before. Luke watches the side of his face, trying to read his expression.

'Can't really remember all that much about it. I was only eight, and we've never been back since.'

Martin digs his feet further into the sand.

'So, what made your dad choose the island?' Martin's discomfort is pouring off him, but Luke can't seem to stop himself from going on, and he leans forward, trying to make contact, to provoke some kind of an answer.

Martin runs his broad hands across his face, releasing a small groan and dropping his head. 'I think I've had too much to drink,' he mumbles.

They sit in silence for a few minutes longer as the distant lights fade and disappear from the horizon, and Luke decides to drop it. It's Martin's birthday, for fuck's sake.

Martin takes the bottle and drinks until there's nothing left, letting the empty vessel slip from his fingers to the sand with a hollow thud. He turns his head and looks at Luke face-on, the swill of alcohol casting a milky film across his eyes. 'It was an accident,' he says. 'A car accident.'

'Man,' Luke exhales. 'I had no idea.'

'My dad was driving the van when it happened.' Martin turns his hand over and scratches at a callus. 'He was a gardener back then – and we'd just stopped to pick up some new tools on the way back from town. I remember Mum saying to leave it until after the weekend, that she wanted to get home – but he went anyway. He said he had a rockery that wanted breaking up the next week.' He stops mid-flow, staring into his palm like he's reading off it.

For a moment, Luke thinks he's not going to continue. 'And?'

'It was one of those Austin vans, with the covered back – you know? Blue. He stuck the new things in the back of the van, on top of some wooden boxes he'd been meaning to clear out for a while.' He reaches out for the empty bottle, turning it upside down to reassure himself that it's empty. 'It was a country lane, and a bird hit the windscreen. Dad had to brake, hard; the new sledgehammer slid straight over the passenger seat and hit her in the back of the head – right here – ' he traces a line along the base of his skull ' – and that was it.'

'Mate, where were you?' Luke asks.

'I was on her lap. When it happened I slipped straight off, on to the floor of the van, not a scratch on me. He made me get out of the car, but I'd already seen her face and I knew she wasn't in there any more, because her eyes were open, but just staring at me, like a blind person. He shouted at me then, *Get out!* So I got out of the car and fetched up the bird, and sat down at the edge of the field, like Dad told me to, while he ran for help.'

'Man,' Luke whispers again.

'It was a swallow,' Martin says. 'Just a young one. Its tail streamers were short, you see; that's how I knew it was a young one. I wanted to take it home and bury it there, but he wouldn't let me. He took it and hurled it out into the field like a piece of rubbish.'

Martin raises his arm and the moonlight glows white across his hand, before his fingers unfurl and drop to his lap. He stands unsteadily, indicating that he's ready to go. Luke looks up at him, searching for his returning gaze.

'Does he blame himself, mate? Your dad?'

Martin pushes his hands deep into his pockets. 'I know he'd rather it had been me that died that day.'

'That's not true.' Luke gets to his feet with a stagger and they start off towards the wooden walkway. 'How can you even think that?'

They pause at the top path to untangle their bikes, their faces suddenly clear in the white light of the moon. 'Because it's true,' Martin says. 'Because he tells me all the time.'

3

Met Office report for the Isle of Wight, late May 1976:
Maximum temperature 63°F/17.1°C

It's been raining all night, and Luke wakes to the sound of rainwater running through the broken downpipe outside his bedroom window, the trickle and splash of it hitting the concrete path at the front of the house. From beyond his room, he can hear music from the kitchen radio pouring out along the hallway, irritating him as it seeps beneath his bedroom door. Abba's *still* at bloody number one. The front door slams shut as Dad leaves for work, making the metal windows shudder beside Luke's head. He sits up in his bed and pulls back the curtains to watch the white Dolomite reversing down the rain-slicked drive. The car pauses at the rusty gate as Dad checks his reflection in the rear-view mirror before carrying on over the kerb and speeding off along the road. Luke pulls the covers up over his head and drifts in and out of sleep for a little longer, until the grating music from the kitchen radio finally drives him from his bed in search of breakfast. In the hallway, Kitty charges at him with Tiny Tears, hitting him square in the side with a plastic foot.

'*Banando*!' she yells as Luke stumbles backwards.

'Watch it, Kitty! My bloody ribs.'

Mum sticks her head out of the kitchen, frowning. 'Language, Luke. She's only four!'

Kitty hurls the naked doll over her shoulder and roly-polys down the hall. Luke weaves his way through the barrels and siphon tubes which clutter the kitchen floor, stubbing his little toe on a tub of brewing sugar as he reaches across to flick off the radio. Mum has recently discovered wine-making and she's busy setting up her second production.

'Hey, I was listening to that,' she says, shifting the fermentation tank to clear a path.

Luke rummages in the food cupboard, pulling out half-empty cereal boxes and shoving them back in. 'What are you making – red or white?'

'Red. Claret. It'll be ready in six weeks – maybe we can save some for your eighteenth. Thought it would save us a fair bit doing it this way.'

'But the kit must've set you back quite a lot?' He lays a place for himself at the table, setting a bowl and spoon next to the cornflakes packet.

'Yes, but it's an *investment*.' Mum gestures towards the boxes and barrels with a sweep of her arms. 'It will soon pay for itself. And it's not half bad either. Did you try my first batch?'

Luke wrinkles his nose. Dad had bitterly complained of acid indigestion after sampling the first bottles over dinner with Simon and Laura, although Mum refused to admit that the wine was to blame, more the quantity he'd consumed. Luke fills his bowl with cornflakes and pats the pile lightly before negotiating his way over the obstacle course to get to the fridge. 'It wasn't the best wine I've ever tasted,' he says.

Mum refastens her hair in a loose knot at the back of her head. 'It wasn't that bad – just a little tart. And I know how to fix that now, so I'm learning all the time. This lot will be perfect – just you wait and see. Anyway, we've still got eight bottles of that first lot to get through, and I expect it only improves with age. I might open another bottle tonight, see if it's any better.'

Luke watches as Mum fiddles around with two pieces of tubing, trying to fix them together with a joiner.

'I still think we should get some normal drink in on my birthday as well. Lagers. Maybe some Babycham, for the *ladies*.' He grins. 'Just in case some turn up. We don't want to poison anyone.'

She pokes her tongue at him. 'You should have a little more confidence in your old mum, Luke. All your teasing only makes me more determined to prove you wrong – they'll soon be queuing up around the block to sample my marvellous wine.'

Luke opens the fridge and reaches into the door for the milk bottle. 'Oh, God, *Mum*,' he moans, waving the bottle at her. Half an inch of creamy milk swills around in the bottom. 'Who finished the milk?'

'I don't know, Luke,' Mum sighs. 'It's hours since I had my breakfast, and there was plenty left then.'

He drops the bottle back into the fridge door and slams it shut, causing the pickle jars to rattle loudly. 'There's *never* enough left by the time I have my breakfast!'

'Maybe you should try getting up a bit earlier – I thought you were meant to be revising today? Look at the time – it's almost nine o'clock. We've all been up since seven.'

Kitty appears in the doorway, humming and swinging her doll by her side. 'Lazy Lu-lu, lazy Lu-lu.' She smirks as Mum shakes her head and Luke attempts to pour the unused cereal back into the box, scattering rogue flakes on the floor as they miss the packet and bounce off the table.

Mum stands with her hands on her hips, gazing into the garden as the rain continues to trickle down the windows, pooling in shimmering puddles on the outside sill. 'The plants'll be happy,' she says. 'There's been talk of a drought, you know. Though I'll believe it when I see it.'

Luke rolls out his neck irritably. 'So, is there any bread, then?'

'In the bread bin. Where else?' She stoops to continue with her wine production, while Kitty wanders over and starts to fiddle with the barrels, trying to force her doll's leg in through the opening at the top. Luke lets out a frustrated growl.

'Brilliant,' he says, dumping two pasty white crust ends on to the board. 'Just *brilliant*.' Pulling out the grill pan, Luke slaps the bread on to the rack with a clatter. 'I'll be malnourished by the time I reach the mainland,' he says, searching around in the cupboard for jam.

Mum laughs, and she kisses him on the cheek before returning her focus to her wine barrels with a contented little smile.

By mid-afternoon the rain has slowed to a stop and Mum suggests they take a walk to Teddy's Spar. Kitty insists on wearing her full wet-weather gear, including red welly boots and clear domed umbrella. She runs ahead all the way, jumping in the puddles gathered along the pavements and verges, where the rain struggles to drain into the baked earth.

Mum turns her face towards the dappled sky. 'How *refreshing*. I hope we've had enough to bring the garden back to life – the ground's got so hard, it's a wonder anything grows at all.'

At the end of their road they come out into Grasslands Avenue, and Kitty points towards a purple gate on the other side of the pavement, where two chihuahuas yap and snarl through the wooden posts.

'I hate those dogs,' grumbles Luke. 'At least the gate's shut this time. Last time I came this way, they charged out at me, snapping at my heels. Little bastards.'

'*Luke.*'

'Well, they are. I had to chase them back in so they couldn't attack anyone else.'

Mum glances over, before hooking her hand through his arm to speed him along. 'Keep your voice down. That's Sara Newbury's house. You know, Marie's old yoga teacher?'

Luke looks back over his shoulder. 'Oh, yeah. The mad dog lady.'

'Shh! *Yes.*'

'Have you seen inside her front garden? I had a good nosy over the gate when I was putting the rats back in last time. It's massive, and there are gnomes everywhere – hundreds of them. Creepy little things. They're probably guarding the dog shit.'

'*Luke.*'

'*Well,*' he says, as they near the shop. 'She's got six dogs, hasn't she? That garden's got to be one great big dog toilet, if you ask me. I'm surprised the gnomes haven't all gone on strike over working conditions.'

Mum releases his arm. 'Like the rest of the country.'

Outside the shop there's a large puddle, which Luke steps around to hold the door open for his mum. He gestures for Kitty to follow behind her, but instead she takes a running jump at the puddle, soaking him right up to the chest of his fresh white T-shirt. Luke makes a grab for her – 'You little – ' and she squeals, running in ahead of him, straight up the aisle to the sweet section.

He joins Mum, who's chatting to Teddy over the counter.

'Oh, Luke!' she sighs, eyeing his muddy T-shirt.

'But – ' He starts to point in Kitty's direction, then stops himself as he realises how pathetic it would sound.

Mum turns back to Teddy. 'As if I don't have enough washing and ironing to keep me busy.'

'These lads, eh?' His voice is gravelly. 'Always up to some kind of mischief. Ain't that right, Luke?'

Teddy once told Luke he's a real Cockney, but Luke's not convinced he doesn't just put on the accent to impress the holidaymakers.

He pushes his hands into the back pockets of his jeans and nods at Teddy. 'Too true.'

'So, Jo, love, ever give any thought to getting yourself a little job? You know I'm always after a bit of extra help here.' Teddy's on the inside of the lift-up counter, resting his tattooed forearms on the top. 'We could do with a pretty face like yours behind the till.'

Mum reaches back towards the entrance for a shopping basket. 'You know what, Teddy? I'd love to get out to work again, but it's impossible to even think about with Kitty at home. She's at nursery during term time, but that's only half-days. I think I'll have to wait until she's started at school in September.'

'Well, you know where I am if you change your mind.'

The door chime goes and a couple of young lads enter the shop. Teddy gives them a nod and they wander off towards the crisps, jangling their pennies in the palms of their hands.

'Doesn't seem so long since you were that age, does it, son?' Teddy leans further on to the counter, lowering his voice. 'So, tell me – how's your love-life these days, Luke? Up to much?'

'Ah, men's talk,' says Mum, unfolding her shopping list. 'I think I'll leave you to it.' She hooks the basket over the crook of her elbow and makes her way towards the back of the shop, where Kitty's still deliberating over the sweet selection.

Luke rubs the back of his neck. 'Non-existent.'

Teddy pushes himself up to standing and stretches out his back, placing a meaty hand on the top of the till. 'Really? I would've thought you'd have had loads of girlfriends by now.' He reaches beneath the counter for a cigarette, lighting it up between two nicotine-yellow fingers.

'Oh, I've had a few girlfriends. But nothing serious really. I don't know, I'm not all that good with girls.'

Teddy listens earnestly, the side of his mouth rising in a playful leer. 'Still, plenty of time for all that, eh? You'll want to sow your wild oats a bit, before you settle down.'

Luke laughs, flicking his long fringe off his face. 'I'm off to college after the summer – going over to Brighton.'

'So I hear,' Teddy replies. He takes ten pence from a boy who's just dropped a mountain of small chews on the counter.

'Plenty of opportunities there, eh?' he smirks. 'If you know what I mean. That's why they call it *further* education, so I hear.'

For a second they're both distracted by a shrill voice at the back of the shop, greeting Mum. It's Rhona, Teddy's wife. Teddy's face clouds over. 'Tell you what, lad – make the most of it. Being young, I mean. It's gone before you know it. I'll be fifty-nine next week. Who'd've bloody thought it, eh?'

The little boy scoops up his sweets, making way for his friend, and Luke walks down the middle aisle to join his mother. He pauses before turning the corner, to hear the tail end of their conversation.

'So you've never seen anything funny when you've been there?' Rhona's asking. Luke can just see the tips of her fingers resting on Mum's wire basket. 'Sara said they all throw their keys in a bowl!'

Mum laughs. 'Oh, how silly. You know Sara's fallen out with Marie?' she says, in her breeziest voice. 'It'll just be sour grapes. Poor old Sara, she's never been the same since Patrick died. It's a shame, really.'

'Well, yes, she certainly is an odd one – ' Rhona stops short when she spots Luke rounding the corner, and she taps Mum on the wrist, lowering her voice to a conspiratorial tone. 'We'll have to get together for a cuppa, Joanna, and a proper catch-up. I'll give you a ring?'

'What's up with her?' Luke asks after Rhona has disappeared through the door marked 'Private'. It leads to their flat upstairs; Luke knows because he had to go up there one afternoon a few years ago, to fetch his dad who had been out on an all-day bender with Teddy.

'Shhhh!' Mum whispers back. She looks rattled. 'It's nothing. Just a bit of silly gossip – you know what they're like round here. Always after a bit of scandal.'

'What about?'

'Oh, I'm not sure.' She scans the shelves as if she's searching for something important.

'You must know, or else you wouldn't know it's gossip, would you?'

'For God's sake, Luke!' she hisses, grabbing a tin of gammon and slamming it into her basket. 'Will you just drop it?' She tilts her head meaningfully towards Kitty. '*Please.*'

Luke frowns at her hard, and she looks away quickly, busying herself, checking the shopping against her list. He takes the basket from her. 'Sorry, Mum.'

She folds and unfolds the list in her hands. 'I'm just a bit tired, that's all. We've got Simon and Laura coming for supper tomorrow and I'm not really in the mood for it. I don't know why your dad insists on filling our weekends up without asking me. It's not him who has to do all the hard work preparing for it.'

Luke steps back to let a customer pass between them.

Mum scans the list. 'And I was up late last night, waiting for your dad to get back home.'

'Where was he this time?'

'Out with Simon.'

'Again?'

She turns and walks along the next aisle, running her index finger over the plastic product strips. 'They had a staff meeting, and went on to the pub afterwards. You know how Uncle Simon likes to drink.'

Luke hasn't called him *Uncle* Simon since he accidentally said it at school in front of Len, back in the third year. Len took the piss about it for weeks, what with Simon being a teacher at the school, and Luke quickly dropped the 'Uncle' bit at home, hoping no one would notice or mind. 'I know he's Dad's mate,' he says to Mum, 'but isn't the headmaster meant to set a good example? I've never met such a pisshead.'

'What?' Mum replies vacantly, placing a loaf of sliced white bread into the basket.

Luke tuts and turns away, peering around the aisle, towards the sweet shelves. 'Where's Kitty gone?'

At that moment, Kitty yells from the front of the shop.

'Lu-uke!' She's at the till, teetering on tiptoes as she unloads an armful of sweets and chocolate bars on to the counter. Teddy raises his eyebrows as Mum and Luke join her at the till. 'Lu-lu's paying.' Kitty tells him.

'Lu-lu?' Teddy smiles at Luke.

Mum takes the basket from Luke so he can search his pockets for change.

'OK, Kitty. There – I've got 25p. You can have the Toffos and the buttons, and make the rest up in Black Jacks or something. But the other stuff has to go back.'

Kitty snarls and bites his wrist.

'She's a bright spark,' says Teddy.

'Kitty!' Mum gasps, as if she's never seen her do anything so awful before. She shakes her head in embarrassment. 'Sorry, Teddy. She's been pretending to be a dog this week.'

'You *said*!' Kitty whines, narrowing her eyes at Luke.

'I said I'd get you *some* sweets,' Luke replies, rubbing his wrist. He reaches out to ruffle her hair and she ducks away to stand by the entrance with her arms folded crossly over her chest. Luke gives her his stern face. 'I didn't say I'd buy you the whole shop.'

Choking his rough smoker's cough, Teddy tries to conceal his amusement behind a hand. 'And what about this lot, Jo, love?' He bags up Mum's shopping. 'Shall I put it on tick?'

Outside, the cloudy sky is clearing, and they stroll home at a leisurely pace, sharing a bag of peanuts as they walk back along Grasslands Avenue, where the leaves shimmer with fresh moisture. Kitty is content now, her teeth glued together with a toffee. Just as they reach the junction to Blake Avenue, the chihuahuas run out from the purple gate, yipping and snarling at their feet. Kitty shrieks, holding her sweets high above her head.

'Grrrr!' Luke snarls back, stamping his foot towards them. 'Bugger off, you little rats!'

Mum tugs the hem of his T-shirt. 'Luke! *Stop it*. She'll hear you.'

She speeds up to remove herself from the vicinity, as the dogs carry on snapping from a distance, too nervous to continue any further.

'Who cares?' he says, jogging to fall into step with her and glancing back again to glower at the dogs. 'Those dogs are a bloody menace!' He throws a peanut in the air, pausing briefly to let it plop into his mouth before catching up with her again. 'God, Mum. You should chill out a bit, man.'

The chihuahuas give up and trot away, disappearing through the gate as the clouds above their bungalow split and separate, allowing the sunshine to pour through, warm and bright.

'Urgh, those little baldies gives me the willies,' Mum says once they're out of earshot.

'*Rats*,' says Kitty.

'I can understand having one or two dogs,' says Luke. 'But six? Apparently she's obsessed with them, carries photos of them around in her purse, like they're her children. Dad told me she's thinking of setting up a dog portrait studio in her home – taking soft-focus pictures for adoring dog owners.' He laughs, his face freezing mid-smile as he looks up to see Samantha Dyas cycling towards them from the other direction, slowing down as she bumps over the uneven pavement towards Grasslands Avenue.

'Hi, Luke!' she calls over her shoulder as she passes, stopping on the pavement a few feet away, tilting on to one tanned leg. 'I hear you're going to be starting work over at Sunshine Bay tomorrow,' she says. The new sunlight sparkles behind her long fair hair, which drapes prettily around the shoulders of her orange cagoule. When Luke doesn't reply, she twitches her little nose as if amused. 'Philip Beckett told me – one of the managers, you know?'

'Oh, yes,' Luke replies, tugging at his earlobe and hoping Samantha hasn't noticed the flush of his cheeks.

'I'm working there too,' she says brightly, hooking back the pedal with her toe and pushing off. 'So I'll see you up there!' She tinkles her bell and disappears behind the hedge at the corner of their street.

Luke tries to subdue his delight, and avoids eye contact with his mum as they carry on along the path, knowing she's desperate to ask about Samantha. After a moment, she rubs his back. 'Now, *she's* rather nice, isn't she? What's her name?'

'*Mum*. That's just Samantha. She's in the year below me at school.'

'*Just* Samantha?'

'Yes. *Just* Samantha. You know, the vicar's daughter.' He purposely bumps her leg with the shopping bag and she laughs, dodging out of the way. 'Anyway, she's going out with Len, so I doubt very much that she'd be interested in me.'

'Len Dickens?'

'Len *Dickhead*. God know what she sees in him.'

'Pity.' She sighs, scooping up her hair and letting it drop over one shoulder. 'I would've thought you'd make someone a rather nice boyfriend.'

'Oi! Don't write me off just yet. I'm not even out of my teens.'

'No, you're right. I guess you're still my little boy, aren't you?' She puts her arm through his and pulls him close. 'You'll be flying the nest soon, though, won't you?' she says with sadness in her voice.

'It's what we're meant to do, Mum.'

'Oh, I know,' she replies, raising an arm to wave at Dad as he turns the car into their driveway at the far end of the street. 'Just don't be in too much of a hurry to grow up, love, that's all. Being a grown-up... it's not all it's cracked up to be.'

Within twenty-four hours the sun has returned, the moisture from the brief rainfall now sucked from the dry earth as if it never came at all. Luke potters about in the garden with Kitty, killing time before he sets off for his first shift at Sunshine Bay, and avoiding the kitchen, where Mum and Dad are having another argument. This time Dad came home towing a second-hand trailer tent he'd bought from the school caretaker and Mum went mad, telling him she'd rather die than sleep in that mouldy old thing. Why can't they holiday in Italy or France, like other families? she wants to know. A nice little *gîte* in the Dordogne; a hotel in Florence? They've been fighting over it ever since.

Kitty is busy collecting up daisy heads, to decorate the garden of her cardboard insect house. Luke has helped her to separate the box into rooms so that the woodlice and beetles have got two bedrooms, a bathroom and a living room to move about in, and the house now sits in the centre of the garden table, soaking up the afternoon heat. He peers into the box and spots a shrivelling earthworm that Kitty has installed in a sunny corner, whipping it out and throwing it back into the flowerbed before she notices.

'Do you think we should give them some water, Kitty?'

She nods and starts dotting the flower heads around the perimeter of the house. Luke fills an empty margarine tub at the wall tap. 'It can be their bath,' says Kitty, showing him where to put it. She scoops up a couple of woodlice and drops them into the water, poking them under with her finger.

'No, Kitty!' Luke grabs the tub and flicks the water and woodlice out over the cracked concrete patio. They immediately head for the nearest dark crevice, disappearing like miniature tanks, headfirst into the abyss.

Kitty balls up her fists and starts to scream. Luke picks her up under his armpit, and swings her round and round until she stops screaming and starts to chortle instead. When he's sure she's completely over it he puts her on to her feet in the middle of the lawn, where she sways momentarily and topples on to her face. This time her crying is for real, and there's blood where her front tooth has caught the edge of her lip. '*Shit*,' he mutters, rushing to check her over. 'Shh-shh-shh-shh,' he soothes, and he picks her up to whisk her into the kitchen through the open back door.

Mum and Dad are still in there; Mum's angrily pushing a mop around the floor and Dad is propped up against the stove, his arms folded defiantly. He frowns at Luke as he places Kitty on the kitchen table.

On seeing her mummy, Kitty holds her arms out, feebly wiggling her little fingers.

'Oh, Kitty! What happened?'

Kitty's really bawling now, dribbling snot bubbles down Mum's bare arm. 'Lu-lu-u-u-u!' she wails, bouncing a wretched finger towards him.

Mum turns to look at Luke, who's anxiously pinching his chin at the sight of Kitty's bloody lip. 'Luke?'

He drops his hand. 'What? She fell over!'

'Noooooo!' Kitty shakes her head, spreading the snot further. She pulls her head back and glares at him fiercely. 'He *made* me!'

Luke laughs, and looks to his dad for support. 'That's not true. She fell over. She was being silly, doing that twirling round thing she does. God, *Kitty*!'

Kitty throws her head back and howls, and Luke stares at her in disbelief. 'Sod this,' he says, snatching up his crash helmet and stomping from the room. 'I'm off to work.'

'Luke!' Mum calls after him. 'Tell Kitty you're sorry!'

He pauses on the front door step and looks out across the sun-soaked driveway, at the dazzling shimmer of light as it bounces off the chrome of his freshly polished scooter. He thinks about Samantha in her little white shorts, feels the thrill of anticipation bubbling through his veins, and smiles. '*Sorry*, Kitty,' he calls back along the hall, and he jogs across the front drive and sets off.

When he arrives at Sunshine Bay, Luke has to report to the manager's office, which sits at the entrance to the holiday camp. 'Beware Wet Paint' boards lean up against the steps to the front door, highlighting the freshly painted woodwork and jaunty new sign. The door is ajar, and the tinny sounds of the wireless radio float out of the open windows, through which Luke can see Philip Beckett sitting behind the desk, drinking Coca-Cola and concentrating on the large chart in front of him. Luke runs a quick hand across his fringe, before ascending the steps and poking his head through the door.

'Luke Wolff!' Philip grins, standing to offer his hand. 'Welcome, welcome.' He's only a little older than Luke, but already his hair is deeply receding, the peaks of exposed forehead adding years to his appearance. He jangles the keys that hang from his belt loop. 'All set to meet the rest of the gang?'

Luke nods, pushing his hands into his shorts pockets, and he follows Philip as he locks up the office and leads the way to Housekeeping, where he will pick up his kit and meet his new workmates. All along the way they pass various camp workers: gardeners, chefs, maintenance men and cleaners. A group of Suncoats, three girls and a young man with thick black sideburns, sit on the benches outside the ballroom in their bright orange jackets, smoking cigarettes and chatting. The man salutes Philip as they pass and he returns the gesture, winking at one of the young women with a cluck of his tongue. 'Piss off, Beckett,' she laughs, tossing her head back as he returns a showy leer. Her hair falls around her face in luscious dark curls, and her lips are painted pillarbox red. They all look like air hostesses.

'I love it when they're like that,' Philip confides as they round the corner to meet the rest of the temporary staff waiting beneath the Housekeeping sign.

Luke joins the other new starters, slipping in to stand beside Samantha as Philip counts them up and refers to his clipboard to delegate their tasks.

'Hi,' she whispers, flashing a smile and giving him a nudge. 'Do you know anyone else here?'

He shakes his head. Samantha waves at Philip and points to Luke, indicating that she wants to pair up with him. Philip nods and makes a mark on his chart.

'Right! Most of you already know me – if not, I'm Philip. Suzy is the other duty manager, who you'll see tomorrow, so, if you've got any problems or questions while you're here, come and find one of us over in the managers' office. We don't bite – honest! Now, you're in teams of three per chalet: one on beds, one on bathrooms, one on brushing, dusting and windows. Once I've called your teams, head inside and see Brenda and the gang, and they'll take you to your first chalet and show you the ropes. OK? So, Team One – Samantha Dyas, Gordon Lurie and Luke Wolff. Off you go.'

Luke, Samantha and a puny-looking lad called Gordon head inside, and, as soon as Brenda has escorted them to their first room and explained the job, Samantha takes charge. She drops back on to one of the single beds and bounces gleefully, kicking her legs about like a schoolgirl. 'Introductions!' she says. 'If we're going to work together, we should know a little bit about each other.'

Luke inwardly cringes, furtively eyeing Gordon, with his pale skin, National Health glasses and baby-soft hair. He looks like a complete pleb.

'Oh, I'll go first,' Samantha says, smoothing her hands over her tanned thighs. 'I'm Samantha Dyas. Sam. I'm seventeen years old, I live on the outskirts of Sandown, and my father's a vicar. Yes, a vicar! I'm into T-Rex and Dr Hook and Janis Joplin.' She bobs her head towards the boys, inviting them to share too.

Gordon rubs his chin, looking like a wizened old professor. 'Eclectic music choices, young Samantha. I approve.'

Samantha laughs, her eyes wide.

'Well, I'm Gordon Lurie, I'm nineteen and I've just finished my first year at Brighton Polytechnic. I'm staying with my dear old mum in Newport, who incidentally cooks the best moussaka in the northern hemisphere, and what I don't know about music – pop in particular – isn't worth knowing.' He smiles complacently and turns to Luke.

Luke rakes his fingers through his hair, wondering where to start. 'Well, you know I'm Luke – I'm nearly eighteen – '

'Ah, *nearly*,' Gordon croons, amiably leaning in to bump shoulders.

Luke frowns. 'Alright, I'm seventeen, I live in Sandown, and I've just done my A-levels – well, I've got my last two still to do. I like Bowie, Velvet Underground, T-Rex – ' He looks at Samantha for her approval. 'Oh, and I'm off to Brighton Poly in September too. That's if I get the grades.'

'Well, fancy that!' Gordon says. 'Perhaps we'll be neighbours.'

'What about girlfriends?' Samantha asks, raising her eyebrows.

'Not at the moment,' Luke replies, feeling his cheeks colour.

Samantha turns her gaze on Gordon.

'Me? Not *ever*,' he says, and then in a whisper, his hand cupped at his mouth, 'Nor ever likely.'

Samantha jumps up to grab Gordon's hand. 'I know I'm going to just love you, Gordy. And for the record, boys, I *do* have a boyfriend.' She picks up a feather duster and daintily steps up on to the bed, stretching into the far corners to brush away the winter cobwebs. She looks over her shoulder at Luke and smiles. 'Just in case you wondered.'

Simon and Laura arrive for supper that night, carrying three bottles of wine and a large kilner jar of sloe gin.

'He's going through a midlife crisis,' Laura announces, putting the bottles down on the dresser and kissing Mum on both cheeks. Laura's had her hair cut into a short pixie crop, with little dark spikes framing her tiny face. 'He's even started talking about digging up half the garden and planting an allotment.'

'Self-sufficient,' Luke says, holding the gin up to the light. It shines a vibrant burgundy red through the evening glow of the kitchen window.

'Exactly!' Simon pats him on the back, and starts removing the foil from the top of one of the wine bottles. He slides along the bench to sit beside Luke. 'I'm pleased to see that Luke's in harmony with the *Zeitgeist*. Unlike Laura – bloody pessimist.'

'*Realist*,' Laura replies, pulling out a chair to sit beside Dad, kissing him on one cheek and reaching across the table to squeeze her husband's hand. She twirls the shiny black plastic studs in her earlobes and smiles derisively. 'Honestly, I swear he's turning into a *bona fide* hippy – I've never seen you let your hair grow longer than a couple of inches before, Simon. It's almost down to your shoulders.'

'Doesn't stop him looking like a double for Leslie Phillips,' Dad laughs, accepting one of Simon's cigarettes and waggling it in front of his mouth. '*Helllll-ooooo*.'

Simon strokes his pale moustache. 'You know me, Richard, old boy.'

'Anything I can do, love?' Dad asks, as Mum carries a large dish of chilli-con-carne to the table, pushing it along to make room for the boiled rice.

She's wearing a long-sleeved lace blouse, with wrist ruffs that flop over her hands and irritate her as they get trapped between her fingers and the dishes. She pushes at her loose hair with the back of her hand.

'Just go and check on Kitty, will you? Make sure she's asleep.'

'I'll come with you,' Simon says as Dad scrapes his chair back.

They disappear into the hall, cigarettes and glasses in hands, and Mum starts to serve up, letting Laura take over when she remembers the salad she's neglected to take out of the fridge. Luke sneaks a top-up of white wine while her back is turned; Laura smirks and taps the side of her nose.

'How is she?' Mum asks when the men return to their seats. She lights a candle at each end of the table and sits beside Simon.

'Gorgeous!' says Simon, flipping out his napkin and placing it on his lap. 'And, you'll be pleased to hear, fast asleep.'

Luke stretches across the table for the salt. 'You should have kids,' he says to Laura. 'You'd make great parents.'

'Yurgh!' she replies with a little shudder. She pinches the ends of her little black necktie and removes it, fanning a hand over her warm face. 'We'd be a disaster, wouldn't we, Simon? We can hardly look after ourselves, let alone a house full of screaming brats.'

'Not that Laura thinks you two are brats, of course,' Simon adds.

Laura refills her glass, making a point of pinching Luke's cheek affectionately. 'Mmm, delicious supper, Jo. Thanks. Now *that's* one of the few things your People party have got right, Simon.'

'It's not *my* People party. I'm just interested in a few of their policies.'

Laura waves him away. 'Stop being so touchy.'

'What policies?' asks Luke, trying to find a way into the conversation.

'Use less energy, produce fewer kids. It makes sense, if you think about it.'

'Produce *fewer kids*? But life isn't as simple as that, is it?' Mum rests her fork on the side of her plate. 'Sometimes you can't plan those things.'

Laura puts her fork down too. 'Isn't that what the birth control pill is for? It's revolutionised women's lives across the world.' She reaches for one of Simon's cigarettes.

'And all for the better. But we're not robots, are we?' Mum blows the cigarette smoke away from her face. 'You can't tell people how many kids to have, any more than you can tell someone who they should marry. It's about choice.'

'Choice is all very nice, Jo, but we can't go on naively ignoring this economic crisis forever. At some point we have to acknowledge it – and do something about it.' Laura wafts her cigarette towards the men to encourage them to join in the debate. 'Don't we?'

'Telling people how many children they can have is ridiculous. What if they told people they couldn't have *any* kids. Or even that they *must* have kids?' Mum flips her hair over her shoulder. 'You're someone who's already exercised her choice not to have kids, Laura – how would you feel about that?'

Laura sighs loudly. 'Now you're being ridiculous. That could never happen. It's a fact, the planet will always need fewer human beings on it, not more.'

'But the size of the population just isn't an important consideration to a woman who desperately wants a child, is it?'

'It should be.' Laura grinds her cigarette stub into the ashtray and pushes it up the table. 'We're not dumb rabbits, for fuck's sake! If nature has been good enough to bless a family with a child, I think it's perfectly reasonable for a nation in crisis to dictate that they stop there. Stop them all procreating thoughtlessly.'

Mum releases a harsh laugh.

Laura raises her eyebrows. 'It takes more conscious thought to decide *against* having multiple children than it does to let nature take its course. So yes – *thoughtlessly.*'

'*Laura*,' Simon says. 'Time to get off your soapbox.'

'More chilli?' Dad asks, offering the spoon to Simon. He nods, letting Dad serve up as he leaves his seat to fetch a second bottle of wine.

'You know what? In the grand scheme of things, the economy is the least of our worries. It's the dark shadow of progress from heavy industry that's killing us. *That's* what's destroying the fragile ecology of the earth.'

'Bloody hell,' Dad says, banging his knife against the side of his wine glass. 'Time out, everyone. It's a bit early in the evening to start getting this heavy!'

Mum tops up Laura's wine glass and forces out a smile.

'Sorry,' Laura sighs, reaching over to rub Simon's wrist as he retakes his seat. 'I told you – he's having a midlife crisis. So! I hear the McKees are busy planning their next party. What's the theme, Simon?'

'Masks at Midnight,' he replies, subtly withdrawing his hand from hers.

'Sounds like fun,' says Dad. 'It's bound to be, if Marie's organising it.'

The men laugh, and Dad inclines his head to kiss Mum on the side of her face. She tuts, shouldering him off with the briefest of movements.

Luke leaves the table to fetch himself a glass of water, leaning against the sink as he waits for the tap to run cold, glancing back at the assembled adults, at the well-worn rhythm of their drinking and conversation. From here, they appear to act as one, pulsating as they do with shared laughter, with boredom, with pent-up opinions and unspoken desires. At the next bottle they move on to staffroom gossip, and when dessert is served Luke takes his crème caramel to his room, leaving them to it. He can tell by the number of empty bottles already, it's going to be a late session.

4

Met Office report for the Isle of Wight, early June 1976:
Maximum temperature 72°F/22.1°C

There's a little sunny patch in the back garden where Mum can sunbathe naked without fear of being seen by the neighbours. Mrs Bevis on the one side is shielded by a high wall, and on the other side the gardens are only separated by a low picket fence but the house has stood empty for the past year or so.

They're nice gardens, with sloping lawns running down to trees and shrubs at the lower edge. Beyond the dilapidated picket fence, next door's garden has turned into a meadow, overrun by nettles and tall grasses where butterflies and moths hover, collecting nectar from the wild clover and sprawling buddleia.

Luke is on a late shift today, and he sits in a deckchair, his closed eyes hidden behind mirrored sunglasses, sunning his chest. He should be studying, but it's too hot to think. He listens to the sounds of his mother preparing her sunbathing spot, as she crosses the garden in her flip-flops, laying out her towel and fluffing up a cushion she's brought from the living room.

'Gosh, it's beautiful! Not a cloud in the sky.' She sighs contentedly. 'Imagine, if it's like this in June, what on earth will the rest of the summer be like?'

Luke hears her flip-flops land as she kicks them off her feet and on to the patio; they fall with a little slap, amidst the soft buzz of insects and the distant hum of weekend lawnmowers. He crinkles one eye to see her, over by Mrs Bevis's wall. She's wearing her blue bikini, performing her daily stretches, bending to bounce her fingertips lower and lower towards her flexed toes. A pair of sparrows bursts through the leaves of the willow tree, landing on the grass a few feet away, where they flap and squabble like a dance, exploding into the air again to bomb through the branches in neat formation.

Luke wipes the sweat from his brow.

'Tell me when it gets to half-twelve, Luke. I have to pick up Kitty from down the road – she's playing at Susan's.' She drops her bikini top on the grass and steps out of her bottoms, before settling herself face-down on the towel, bunching up her hair so the sun can reach her neck.

Luke pushes himself up out of the deckchair. 'Right. I'll go and mow the front lawn, I think.'

'Good idea,' she replies brightly. 'Don't forget – twelve-thirty! I'm bound to doze off.'

He picks up his magazine and walks back up the garden, glancing in his mother's direction before he reaches the house. How old is she – forty-one – forty-two? He recalls once overhearing his dad telling her she looked like a twenty-year-old from behind, and she'd smiled for a moment, before frowning and asking how old she looked from the front. Thirty, he'd replied, and she'd seemed pleased enough with that.

Out on the drive, Dad's clearing the rubbish from his car, and he looks up as Luke comes through the front door, squinting hard against the bright glare of the sun. On one side of the patchy lawn the grass is green and lumpy, while the other side, where the sun is harshest, is starting to take on a straw-like appearance. Luke's been doing the lawn every weekend since he was fourteen, and he's always quite enjoyed it, watching the stripes appear as he works his way up and down the garden. But last week Dad came home with one of those new hover mowers. Mum went mad, recounting a horror story about a man who'd electrocuted himself by mowing over the flex. Dad had laughed. 'Daft bugger – sounds like he asked for it.'

Luke carries the Flymo from the garage and drops the plug in through the bedroom window. He potters about the lawn for a while, picking up Kitty's toys and throwing them into a heap at the edge of the drive. There's a set of bright plastic saucepans, small to large, each of them with wide-eyed faces, which he lines up along the low front wall in order.

'Hiiiii-yah!' Dad leaps at him from behind, karate-style, causing him to yell and stumble backwards. 'Gotcha! So, where's your mum, then?'

'In the nudist colony, out the back.'

Dad raises his eyebrows. 'Is she now?'

Luke pulls a disgusted face.

'Well, no time for all that, anyway – I'm going to wash the car. She needs a good polish. Want to help?'

Luke reaches for the plastic saucepans and adds them to the toy pile. 'Nah. I'm about to mow the lawn.'

'Well, watch how you go,' he says, indicating towards the cable. He strips off his shirt and drapes it over the gate, pulling a muscle-man pose for Luke. 'Look at that,' he says, inspecting his own bicep.

Luke grimaces and turns away, embarrassed to see Mrs Bevis walking past with her shopping.

'Morning!' Dad calls after her.

'Morning,' she replies, shrilly, dipping her aged head so far down that Luke thinks she might tip over.

'See?' Dad says, patting his bare stomach. 'Still got it. Right, I'd better wash that car before they slap a hosepipe ban on us once and for all.'

Both set to work on their separate jobs, and before long the lawn's looking less patchy. Luke has accidentally hovered the heads off Mum's anemones, and he stuffs them underneath the grass cuttings before anyone sees, before starting on a circuit of the borders, pulling up stray dandelions and weeds to add to the heap. Dad's whistling 'Save Your Kisses for Me' while he gives the car a final rinse with his sponge, stepping back every now and then to check he hasn't missed a bit. He drops his sponge into the bucket and clicks his fingers to catch Luke's attention, as a Regency red Jaguar slows in the road and bumps up the kerb into the driveway next door. Luke rakes the last strands of grass into the heap and rests on the wooden handle, watching, suddenly self-conscious about his naked torso.

A large, balding man steps out of the driver's seat, wearing what appear to be golfing clothes.

'Hello, there!' the man calls over.

'Morning!' Dad replies.

Both men approach the low front wall that separates their two driveways.

'Mike Michaels,' the big man says, offering his hand.

'Richard Wolff.'

The passenger door of the car opens and a woman gets out. She's in her late twenties or early thirties, dressed in white slacks and a bright red shift top. Her hair is a halo of tight, dark shoulder-length curls.

'My wife, Diana,' Mike Michaels announces. He puts his hand on the small of her back. 'Di, this is our new neighbour, Richard.'

At first she appears shy, as her gaze shifts between Dad and Luke, who face her in their shorts and sandals, staring back like a couple of stunned Mowglis.

'Neighbours!' she finally says, her face breaking into a wide smile.

'*Neighbours*,' Dad repeats, planting one hand on his hip, unconsciously slapping his bicep with the other. 'Well, how about that? We haven't had anyone this side for quite some time.'

Luke remains where he is, gripping the end of the rake handle as Diana glances over at him and waves.

Dad turns to beckon him over. 'This is my son, Luke. Come and shake hands with Mr Michaels, Luke.'

'It's Mike!' he bellows, shooting out his arm.

'Hi,' Luke says. Mike's hand is huge and wet with sweat, and Luke's about to wipe it away on his shorts when Mrs Michaels suddenly reaches over the wall to shake hands with him too. Embarrassed that she'll think it's his sweat, Luke mumbles something about clearing the lawn and leaves Dad chatting with them. As he fills the wheelbarrow with grass clippings, he allows himself occasional glances at Mrs Michaels, who's now perched on the edge of the little wall so that her white slacks tighten over her thighs. She's laughing, her fingers dancing like butterflies to emphasise her words. Dad's loving it, standing there in his cut-off shorts and bare chest, next to her fat old husband. Luke can see him pointing at their car, as Mike Michaels hitches up his checked trousers and strokes the bonnet.

Dad whistles over. 'What do you think of the motor, Luke?'

'Very nice,' he calls back, and Mike Michaels rubs his paunch, as if he's just enjoyed a good meal.

A removals van pulls up at the roadside. Mike Michaels claps his hands and strides off towards the vehicle, opening the side door and standing back to let the driver step down. 'Good to meet you, Richard!' he calls over. 'And I hear we have friends in common!'

'Really?' Dad replies.

'Yes – the McKees. We'll have to get you all over one night soon!'

Diana gives a little wave and disappears around the far side of the house, while Mike Michaels lights up a cigarette and starts to direct the two removals men ferrying pieces of furniture from the van and into the house. Dad can't get over to Luke quick enough.

'Well, she's a bit of alright,' he says, rubbing his hands together with glee.

Luke gathers up an armful of grass and drops it into the wheelbarrow.

'Don't tell me you didn't notice,' Dad goes on, nudging his arm with his knuckles.

'Not bad, I s'pose,' he replies. 'Nice hair.'

'And the rest! They both seem nice enough.' Dad's eyes follow the removals men as a collection of potted pampas grasses and yukka plants are placed on to next door's driveway. 'Though he's got to be twenty years her senior if he's a day!'

'Sugar daddy?' Luke smirks.

'Probably. Well, let's face it. I wouldn't think she's with him for his athletic physique.' As he says this he hitches up his shorts and pulls in his stomach muscles, continuing to watch the activity next door. The men unload a set of garden chairs and parasols. 'Looks like they've got a few bob, judging by the furniture. Wonder what he does. Did you see the leather armchairs going in?'

'*Dad*,' Luke hisses. 'At least try to look busy while you're spying on the new neighbours. Try to be a bit more subtle.'

'Good plan!' Dad picks up the rake and starts drawing it across the clear lawn as the heat continues to throb down into their front garden. 'Bloody *hell*, it's a scorcher.'

The removals man holds up a deckchair. 'Where d'you want these, Mr M?'

Mike Michaels holds his hand up to block out the sun. Luke wonders if he ever gets burnt on that great big bald patch.

'Take them straight through to the garden, John. Through the side gate. Here – give me a couple and I'll take you down there.' They pick up the chairs and force open the rusty gate which leads to the back of the house.

Dad stops raking and stretches, yawning loudly. 'I haven't seen much of Kitty today. Is she indoors?' he asks.

Luke looks at his watch. 'Shit!'

At that moment, travelling from the back garden, over the low walls and picket fences, Mum's shriek pierces the gentle summer hum of Blake Avenue. It sounds like a *Carry On* scream, rendered saucily comical by the knowledge that Mum is out back in her birthday suit. Luke covers his mouth with his hand; Dad throws his head back and howls, bringing the palms of his hands down, slap, on to his bare knees. 'Oh, dear, *Luke*. Your poor mother.'

Luke lets the last pile of grass drop to the hard lawn, breaking into a run towards the house. 'She's going to kill me!'

Dad's still laughing as he follows Luke up the front step and into the hall, where Mum has now locked herself in the bathroom, refusing to come out. He knocks on the door, resting against the frame with a fixed expression of amusement on his face while Luke watches on.

'Go away!' she yells.

'So – ' Dad clears his throat ' – you've met the new neighbours? Mike's the tall one in the Rupert Bear trousers. I think the other one's called John. He's the removals man.'

Mum goes quiet on the other side of the door, while Dad reaches over and prods Luke, inviting him to join in.

'Mike seems quite nice, doesn't he, Mum?'

'GO AWAY!'

'Don't suppose he was counting on such a warm reception,' Dad says, deadpan, drumming his fingers on the wall. 'Anyway, fancy a nice cup of tea, love?'

Mum kicks the bath panel as Dad heads off to the kitchen, where he resumes his cheery whistling, and all falls silent again beyond the bathroom door.

'Mum?' Luke says cautiously.

There's a pause. 'What?'

'It's nearly one o'clock. D'you want me to go and get Kitty for you?'

He hears her closer behind the door.

'Thanks, Luke. Yes, please, love.'

Luke stops off in his room to pull on a fresh T-shirt. As he reaches the front step on his way out, he hears Dad calling back down the hall towards his mother.

'That's nice of Luke, isn't it, Jo? Saves you getting dressed.'

Her furious shrieks follow Luke all the way out to the front gate, where he raises his hand to Mike and Mrs Michaels, who stand beside the open doors of the removals van, covering their mouths.

'Nice to meet you, Luke,' Mrs Michaels calls after him as he jogs off down the road to fetch Kitty.

He turns, still running on the spot, to see her raise an elegant arm, the sun casting her in dark relief, her fingers fluttering in the still air.

'You too,' he replies, pulling back his shoulders and running like a man.

On Sunday morning Luke is woken by his alarm at eight, set so that he can drive up to the holiday camp at Sunshine Bay for an early shift. The sound of Kitty's off-tune singing rouses him again as he drifts back into sleep, and he gets up and dressed, paying particular attention to his hair, pinching a squirt of Dad's Bacchus aftershave on his way out. Until the school term ends, Samantha is only working weekends and the odd afternoon, like him, so there's a good chance they'll be put together again. He thinks about Len, and what he'd say if he knew he was spending his days with Sam; he'd hate it. God only knows what she sees in Len. He's passingly good-looking, a bit like a grubby David Essex, but that illusion soon disappears, the minute he opens his mouth. All that glue-sniffing beneath the pier must have addled his brain over the years, just as it did his brother's.

As it turns out, the schedules have all been drawn up for the next two weeks, and Samantha, Gordon and Luke are teamed up for the same shifts. Today they're on the older chalets towards the edges of the camp, and, after Luke's initial awkwardness around Sam, they soon start to relax and chat more easily while they work. Gordon meanders about the bedrooms, stripping off the bedlinen and showing off his encyclopaedic knowledge of the music charts. Luke knows he should find him irritating, with his square appearance and over-familiar chitchat, but somehow he doesn't. Gordon entertains Samantha no end, and it's a good feeling to be with them, working, earning money, having a laugh.

'Of course, "Fernando" is the one to beat,' Gordon says, as they get to work on their third chalet. 'Number one for four weeks on the trot. But it's no wonder really. It's classic pop. I love Abba, don't you, Lukey?'

Luke stops sweeping, looks up from his broom and shakes his head slowly, looking at Gordon like he's mad.

Gordon splutters, throwing his arms up theatrically, disturbing the dusty shards of window light. 'What? You have to be joking! Why not?'

'Because they're, hmm, let me think… shit.'

Samantha hoots with laughter, appearing from the bathroom in her rubber gloves. She brought them from home, saying her mother insisted when she heard that they'd be cleaning other people's loos. Her face glows beneath a light sheen of perspiration.

Gordon sits heavily on one of the twin beds, looking astonished. 'I have never – I mean never – met anyone who doesn't love Abba.' He smiles at Sam and pokes a finger in Luke's direction. 'You're going to be a challenge, young Luke.'

'Oi. Don't call me "young" Luke. Just "Luke" will do fine, thanks.'

Gordon sniggers and swings his feet up coyly, putting his hands behind his head while he earnestly studies the other two, Luke with his broom, Samantha in her pink gloves.

'Good golly, Miss Molly,' he sighs, forming a square with his fingers to frame them in his view. 'Wouldn't you two make the most fabulous couple?'

At the end of their shift Luke returns the cleaning trolley to Housekeeping, before heading back to meet the others in an out-of-action chalet they discovered on their walkabout at lunchtime. The lock is rusted and broken, and there's no end of maintenance work needed to bring the rooms back up to use, but it's still furnished, with a good view across the lawn towards the Suncoats' accommodation block. When Luke arrives, Samantha and Gordon are already there, each reclining on one of the twin beds amidst a fog of fragrant smoke. The windows are all nailed shut and the chalet has a humid, damp odour which reminds Luke of the salt-soaked panels of the beach huts on Sandown seafront, when the holidaymakers have all gone home.

'Lukester,' Gordon drawls as Luke eases the door closed behind him. His eye squints as he inhales deeply. 'Care for a toke, young man?' He holds the joint out, and smiles, watching Luke closely as he brings it to his lips. 'What a cupid's bow to die for,' Gordon sighs, and his eyelids slide shut, his fingers waving lightly, like a king dismissing a serf. He resembles a shrunken old man lying on the bed, pale-skinned and thin-haired, laid out for the coffin.

Luke laughs at the thought, coughing out little chokes of smoke, and Sam budges up on the bed, indicating for him to squish on beside her. She's wearing her tiny shorts again, and as he shifts closer to keep from toppling off the bed he feels the soft brush of her skin against his.

'This is cosy,' she says, reaching across to take the joint from his far hand.

Across the lawn, some of the Suncoats are now congregating between shifts, sharing cigarettes and cans of drink in the afternoon heat. They look so much older, the women curvy and tall, some of the men thick-armed and moustached. Gordon props himself on to his elbows for a better look, commenting on the broad shoulders of the Burt Reynolds lookalike at the centre of the group. 'What a dish,' he says, rolling his eyes as if it's all too much.

'What does your mum think?' Sam asks, craning her neck to look directly at Gordon.

He appears to give it some thought. 'Nothing,' he replies, his eyes still on Burt Reynolds, who has now taken off his jacket to sit on the bench with his arm draped around one of the girls. 'She's too busy arranging my next blind date to even notice my, well – *lack of interest* in the opposite sex. Honestly, she's always trying to pair me up with her friends' daughters, talking about me as if I'm some kind of Greek god.'

Luke laughs, then stops short when Gordon scowls at him. 'Well, you don't look very Greek.'

'Really? Some might say I'm a bit of an Adonis.' He strikes a pose, flexing his puny white bicep as Luke and Sam collapse on the bed, shrieking with joint-fuelled laughter. Gordon sucks in his cheeks, feigning offence, sitting up to roll another, and Luke lets his gaze drift with the blue sky beyond the glass of the window, feeling the beads of perspiration prickle his upper lip.

'So, I hear you know my Lenny?' Samantha suddenly says, startling him out of his daze.

He stiffens, at once feeling exposed as he lies beside her on the narrow bed. 'We were friends at primary school.' He sits up, mirroring Gordon on the bed opposite.

She nods. 'That's what he said.'

Luke waits for her continue, but she just lies there smiling mysteriously. 'Yeah, we were good mates back then,' he says, 'but not so much once we were in our teens.'

'You're not at all how he described you,' she says, and Luke instantly feels defensive, a surge of hatred for Len pushing out through his chest. 'He said you're a bit of a wimp.' She puts a hand up in front of her mouth.

'Nice,' Luke replies, and he turns to Gordon, who's sucking deeply on the fresh reefer. 'I remember that was one of his favourite expressions: "wimp". For anyone who didn't go around intimidating the other kids with their fists.'

'Luke!' Sam gasps, before shrieking with laughter again. 'He's my *boyfriend*. You can't say that!'

Gordon passes the smoke to Luke. 'Oh, I think he can, Sam. I mean, Lenny does sound like a bit of a thug, darling. And I haven't even met him.'

'*Tit-Head*, that's what he used to call my mate Martin,' Luke continues, drawing the smoke deep into his lungs, enjoying the straining sensation behind his ribcage, the light-headed fuzz as the marijuana seeps into his bloodstream. He exhales a thick white column of smoke up into the room, following its trail with his eyes. 'What an idiot.'

'Why Tit-Head?' Sam sniggers, pressing the palm of one hand against his thigh while she stretches across for the joint.

'His surname – it's Brazier,' Luke replies. 'You know, like *brassiere*.'

Gordon and Sam frown, before simultaneously getting the joke, laughing so hard that the tears stream down their cheeks until they flop back against the mattress, exhausted and stoned.

On the way home, Luke stops off at Nan's house. He notices how brightly green her front garden is, sheltered by tree cover, not exposed to the continuous glare of the summer's rays like theirs. When there's no answer, he lets himself in, and finds her asleep on the bed at the back of the house. Her hearing's not so good these days, and she's clearly startled when he knocks on the open bedroom door to let her know he's there.

She makes a big drama when she sees him, shuffling her little legs off the patchwork quilt, telling him she wasn't really asleep at all.

'Just resting my leg,' she says, pushing her feet into slippers and hobbling down the hall to the kitchen to put the kettle on. 'Want to stay for your tea? It's lamb stew.'

'Love to – I'm starving. I thought I could chop up that dead wood out the back for you while I'm here. I know you won't need it till the winter, but I won't be around so much when I'm at poly, will I?'

'What's a Pollie?'

'College, Nan. It's what we call it these days. What about that wood?'

'Well, if you're sure, son. That'd be grand. So? What's new?'

Still feeling slightly wasted, Luke flops into a kitchen chair, dragging another over with the toe of his shoe so he can put his feet up. 'I've just finished work.'

Nan sits on the other side of the table as she waits for the kettle to boil. 'Up at Sunshine Bay?'

'Yup. Though I'm not that keen on the job title. Chalet maid! I'll have to make sure Dad doesn't find out; I'd never hear the end of it.'

Nan coughs, mopping at her pink old eyes with the corner of a hanky. 'Good for you. Might even get yourself a girlfriend, if you're lucky.'

'Maybe. Actually, there's a girl I like working there for the summer, so you never know.'

'Oh, yes? Who's that, then – someone nice?'

'She's really nice, but she's going out with this idiot Len Dickens. Remember, he used to be in my year at school? He's the one who was always giving Martin a hard time.'

'Sounds like a twat,' says Nan, pushing herself up to make the tea.

Luke tugs his earlobe. 'Ha, you're not wrong there, Nanna. Anyway, I get to work with Samantha while he's off being a twat somewhere else, so I guess I'm the winner. And some of the others there are quite a laugh too. It's nice to meet some new people for a change.'

Nan brings the teapot to the table and indicates to the biscuit tin on the shelf so that Luke can fetch it down. He notices she's wheezing slightly and clutching her hankie tight.

'You feeling OK, Nan?'

She waves him off. 'I'm bleedin' old, you daft bugger! I'm fine.' She pours his tea and pushes the mug across the table. The sunlight crosses her hands, illuminating the translucent silver skin and the undulating contours of her veins. 'Your mum and dad alright?'

He blows into his mug before taking a sip. 'They're fine. We've just had a new couple move in next door, so they're trying really hard not to shout at each other in case the Michaelses overhear them. Mum says we'll have to get a proper fence put up in the back garden now we've got neighbours.'

'So, what are they like, these neighbours?'

'She's alright, but I'm not so sure about him.' He lets out a small chuckle.

Nanna's wrinkles deepen around her eyes. 'Go on, spill it,' she says.

He laughs, shaking his head. 'The removals man arrived yesterday and walked straight down to the back of the house with their furniture. Mum was out in the back garden sunbathing.'

Nan links her fingers and cracks her knuckles. 'Well, that's not the end of the world,' she says with a little wince.

'It is if you like to sunbathe naked.'

Nan covers her mouth. 'Oh, dear. Poor cow,' she says.

Luke leans back in his seat, grinning. 'She went mental.'

'Bet it gave the removals fella a bit of a treat.'

'That's what Dad said. But the fat old husband saw too, so she's been trying to keep a low profile ever since.'

Nan gets up and opens the back door to let in some fresh air. 'So, do they argue a lot, then, your mum and dad?'

Luke stretches his arms high above his head in a yawn. 'Oh, small stuff, mostly. But they're always bickering lately.

I think she's just bored, stuck at home looking after Kitty. And you know what Dad's like – he's not exactly the most helpful husband in the world.'

'I feel sorry for her. I mean, I know he's my son, but he can't be the easiest man to live with. Trouble with him is, he thinks he's God's gift.'

Luke screws up his face. 'But they do love each other.'

'Of course they do. And he's got a good heart,' Nan replies. She reaches over the table and pats Luke's arm. 'You've just got to take him with a pinch of salt, that's all.'

Back home, Luke finds Mum in the kitchen with Diana Michaels from next door. They're sitting at the table with the back door open, drinking gin and tonics and cooing over one of the family photo albums. It's just gone seven, and yet the heat of the day makes it feel like early afternoon still, with the scent of honeysuckle drifting in from the back garden. Kitty is sitting on the doorstep, digging around in a flowerpot filled with earth.

'Oh, look!' says Mum as Luke enters the kitchen, still fumbling with his chinstrap. Her cheeks are flushed. 'Here's the other man of the house.'

Luke drops his keys on the dresser and carefully lays his helmet on the wicker chair in the corner.

'Hello, Luke,' says Diana.

He takes a tumbler from the draining board and fills it at the tap, keeping his back to them. 'Hello, Mrs Michaels.'

'It's Diana, *please*! Been anywhere nice?'

When Luke sets his glass down and turns back, he sees she's wearing tiny white towelling shorts and a navy striped polo shirt that clings tightly to her rounded bosom. His cheeks burn and he makes a big show of running his hand across his brow, as if the redness is down to the heat. 'I'm just back from Sunshine Bay. It's the holiday camp. I've got a job there.'

'Oh, how lovely! Are you a Redcoat! Or is it Blue?'

'It's Butlins with the red coats. Pontins with the blue. They call them Suncoats here.'

'How super. We'll have to come down and watch you one night,' Diana says, prodding Mum's wrist for agreement.

'Oh, well – ' Luke tries to interject.

'Oh, yes, *let's*,' says Mum, clearly having forgotten that he's just going to be cleaning toilets and watching the pool. 'We can make a girls' night of it!'

Luke smiles politely at Diana, tearing his eyes from hers when she holds his gaze for a moment too long. 'Where's Dad?' he asks Mum.

'He's gone down to the Crab and Lobster with Mike. And guess what?'

'What?' he says, opening the fridge and scanning the contents.

'Well – it turns out that Mike's got a son about the same age as you.'

Luke pulls out a large tub of raspberry yoghurt and peels back the lid. There's just a thin watery scraping left at the bottom, with a Kitty-sized finger mark running through it. He wrinkles his nose and chucks the tub in the bin. 'Yeah? That's nice.'

'Isn't it?'

Diana takes a delicate little sip of her drink and looks up at Luke. 'He finishes at boarding school in a couple of weeks, so he'll be coming over to stay with us for the summer.' Her hand hovers at her enticing chest. 'We were wondering if you'd mind showing him around a bit? Introduce him to the island?'

Luke's heart sinks; that's all he needs. He closes the fridge door, having found nothing worth eating, and looks at Mum, who smiles at him encouragingly. 'Maybe,' he says, then instantly realises how rude it sounds. 'Of course, I'm working most days, but, you know…'

'Wonderful!' Diana says, bouncing out of her seat to kiss his cheek.

His pulse races as her fingers brush his back, and he smiles again, awkwardly, desperate to leave the room. 'Has anyone phoned?' he asks on his way out.

'Not that I know of,' Mum replies, turning her attention back to Diana. She picks up her empty glass and shakes it playfully, already reaching into the fridge to fetch more ice. He leaves them to it, closing the door behind him, and heads down to the hall phone, where he picks up the receiver and dials. After a few rings, Martin answers the phone.

'Alright, Mart,' Luke says. 'How's it going? Haven't seen you for a while.'

There's a pause at the other end. 'Oh, Luke. Hi. Sorry, I've been working.'

'Me too. Wondered if you fancied a pint tonight? I can tell you all about Sunshine Bay – did you know I'm working with Sexy Samantha?'

He laughs, expecting Martin to do the same, but instead he hears Mr Brazier's voice in the background, as Martin puts his hand over the mouthpiece. His voice becomes muffled while he talks to his dad, before his hand moves away and his voice returns clearly again. 'Sorry, Luke. I don't think I can make it tonight.'

Luke frowns. 'Why not? Go on, mate! I'm gasping for a pint. And I haven't seen you since your birthday, you lightweight!'

'Um,' Martin mumbles, as Mr Brazier's indistinct voice carries on in the background, along with the faint sound of the television, 'we've got a big order on.' He hesitates, waiting for Luke to answer. 'I'd better stay and get it finished.'

'Am I interrupting your supper or something, Mart?' Luke asks, feeling irritated.

Again, he hears the rustle of Martin's fingers over the mouthpiece. '*Martin*,' his dad says, like a growl, before a few more vague words are exchanged and the room falls silent at the slam of a door – no more television noises, no more voices.

Luke waits for Martin's answer. 'Are you alright, mate? Mart?'

Eventually, Martin clears his throat. 'Sorry, Luke. Another time?' And he hangs up, leaving Luke staring at the receiver, wondering if Martin will ever leave his dad and his dust-filled workshop; if he'll ever leave this tiny little island for the world beyond.

5

Met Office report for the Isle of Wight, mid-June 1976:
Maximum temperature 72°F/22.2°C

By mid-June, an oppressive blanket of humidity lies over the island's wilting towns and villages, causing restlessness and torpor. At last exams are over, and Luke and Martin stand outside Ryde cinema, cradling their crash helmets, waiting for the doors to open. It's nearing dark, yet the heat of the day is still upon them, as the crowd throbs impatiently, uncomfortably warm even at this late hour in the evening.

'Do you reckon it will be as good as *The Wicker Man*?' Luke asks, jangling the loose change in his pocket.

'Better.' Martin cranes his long neck to see in through the glass of the closed cinema doors. He's wearing a white T-shirt with a picture of the Michelin Man on the front, one that his dad got free at the garage when they changed a couple of tyres on the van.

'What, better made, or more scary?'

'Both. When they first showed it in London there were people running out of the cinemas, screaming.'

'They always exaggerate that stuff, just to get us all to go along and watch the film. It can't be that bad.' Luke gazes back down the line, which continues to grow as they wait to go in. 'Haven't seen anyone else we know yet. I saw

Samantha at work last night and she said she might come along to see it too.'

'With you?' Martin asks.

'No, you idiot. With Len Dickhead.'

Martin takes a look back along the queue, his sleek new haircut swinging with the turn of his head. He had his first salon cut today, and the stylist has smoothed it under so that he looks like one of the Beach Boys.

Luke smirks and points at the side of Martin's face. 'What's that?'

'Sideburns,' Martin replies, stroking the downy fluff at the side of his face. 'I've been growing them.'

'I think they need a bit more work, mate. They look like pussy willows.'

Martin slaps Luke's hand away and smoothes the hair back over his underdeveloped sideys. 'Cherie said they make me look mature. She said I looked really cool.'

'*Cherie*? Woo-hoo! So, what was she like?'

'About fifty.'

'Bad luck, man.'

Before they can exchange any further insults, the doors open and the queue starts to move inside. Within ten minutes they're sitting in the mid-row seats with two bags of sweets.

A group of lads from their old high school passes up the middle aisle. 'Len,' Luke whispers to Martin, when they've gone by.

Martin stares straight ahead.

'I don't think he saw us.'

A couple of girls run up the steps, dropping chocolate beans on to the carpet, letting them roll down the stairs to be crushed underfoot. 'Len! Lenny!' one of them calls out as she nears the upper row. It's not Samantha. 'Can we sit with you?'

Luke can't help but take a sneaky glance up towards them. The extended group now almost fills the back row, where they shout and chew and flick sweets at each other. He looks away to see Martin staring brazenly up at the group.

'Don't stare,' Luke hisses.

Martin turns back to face the front. 'I'm not.'

More and more people trail in through the open doors, and soon the cinema is completely full. The smoking side already has a halo of fog gathering in the space between the viewers and the ceiling, distorting the pictures on the wall, painting them soft-focus in the dim light. Luke and Martin eat their sweets, occasionally raising a hand to an old schoolmate, watching the girls go by in their short dresses and summer tops. Eventually, the lights go down and the red velvet curtains part to reveal the screen.

Martin's fingers tense into fists and he bangs his knee against Luke's to get his attention. 'Brilliant seats.'

As soon as the first advert comes on, a peanut hits Luke on the back of the neck, swiftly followed by another, which bounces off the top of Martin's head.

'Hey,' Luke yells, turning to look up towards the back row.

The woman in the seat behind him scowls.

'Oy! Tit-Head!' Len shouts from the top.

Luke looks at Martin, sitting head and shoulders above everyone else in the room; he's an obvious target. An easy target.

'Oi! Brazier! *Brassiere!*' Another peanut. 'Tit-Head!'

The steward at the foot of the steps shines her torch up the stairs in warning.

The palms of Luke's hands are sweating and he's suddenly conscious of the airless heat in the cinema, as he and Martin resolutely stare ahead, trying to ignore Len. 'Fuckers,' he mutters under his breath.

'Shhhhh!' says the woman in the seat behind.

'Tit-Head!'

At last the adverts come to an end and the steward sprints up towards the back seats, talking in hushed tones and shining her torch along the row, before jogging back down again and out of view. Silence passes through the theatre and the peanuts stop flying as the screen blacks over, throwing the cinema into complete darkness. Luke hears the rustle of Martin's bag as he shifts the weight of his sweets from one hand to the other. A few last whispers travel around the room, before the screen fills with the silhouette of a small child, casting the ominous shadow of the cross. Luke glances at Martin. His face has that glazed-over appearance, like when he's eating, but there's a small smile at the corner of his mouth.

'Creepy music,' Luke whispers.

'Shush,' says Martin, in time with the woman behind.

Luke hunches down in his seat to watch the film.

It's past eleven when they file out through the foyer into the muggy night beyond the theatre doors. The air has a tense quality, warm and brooding, with not a star visible in the sky.

'What did you think?' Luke asks Martin as they stroll along the shadowed pavement, having to raise his voice over the chatter of the crowd.

Martin's eyes sparkle with enthusiasm. 'I don't know what to say. Radical. *Brilliant.*'

'Yeah, I can see what all the fuss was about now.'

They separate from the mass, taking a shortcut through the alleyway at the side of the building to reach the car park beyond, where their scooters are parked.

'What about that spike – you know, when it came down from the church – right through that guy! Genius.'

'And the nanny. She was brilliant.' Luke eases his helmet over his head and fiddles with the strap beneath his chin. 'Can you imagine if she turned up to babysit? You'd cack yourself.'

A peanut ricochets off the top of his helmet, bouncing up and over to land on the tarmac beside the back wheel of his bike.

Martin pauses with his helmet held half-mast, frozen between his hands and his head.

'Alright, Tit-Sisters?' Across the car park, some way behind them, is Len Dickens, and he's got two of his stupid mates with him, as well as the girls who joined them in the cinema.

Luke shakes his head and turns his back on them, continuing to fasten his chin strap.

'What's the matter?' Len launches another peanut, this one skidding along the path beside Martin's boot. 'Cat got your tongue?'

'Alright, Len.' Luke places a hand on his scooter as if he's about to start it up.

Len laughs, pointing at Martin. *'Hey-hey, we're the Monkees!'* He's moved up close now, flipping Martin's hair with his finger. 'It's that lanky one off the telly!'

The first girl squeals with laughter. 'What's that one called? Not Micky – you know, the one with the bowly haircut!'

'They've *all* got bowly haircuts,' Luke retorts, throwing her a contemptuous look. They look like cheap tarts compared to Samantha, both doughy-skinned and bland in their matching beige tunic dresses and boots.

The taller one blanks him, flicking her hair over her shoulder. 'I know, it's *Peter*, that's the one he looks like. The lanky one. The *dippy* one.'

The smaller one giggles again, and Len seizes the chance to put his arm around her shoulder and join in. His mates stand a couple of feet behind, nodding like a pair of bouncers.

Luke shakes his head again. 'Come on, Mart. Let's get going.'

'Running away?' Len sneers. 'Or maybe you poofs have got other business to get up to? That's it – they're benders!'

Luke feels the heat rising, up through his chest and neck, filling the inside of his crash helmet. 'So, not with Samantha tonight, Len?' he says, watching Len's expression shift.

'What?'

'Just wondered where your girlfriend is.' He jerks his head in the girl's direction. 'Thought you might have brought Sam with you. I was with her last night, and she was telling me how much she wanted to see the film. Just thought you might have brought her.'

'You're talking shit,' says Len, dropping his arm from Amy's shoulder. 'Sam was working last night, you dick.'

'I know,' Luke replies smugly, recalling the coy smile she gave him as they passed on the path at break time. 'She was on a late shift. With me.' He gestures to Martin to get a move on, but he's still standing in the same spot, looking gormless.

Len takes a step towards Luke, along with his mates. 'Come here and say that, Wolff.'

'Bloody hell, Len, give us a break, will you?' Luke says, dropping his shoulders in an exaggerated display of boredom. 'We're not at school now.'

Len launches forward, but instead of going for Luke he reaches up and grabs a fistful of Martin's shirt.

Luke puts his hand out. 'For fuck's sake, Len, what are you starting on Martin for?'

'Because he's not right in the head,' Len replies, maintaining his grip on Martin's shirt as he stands rigid, unresisting. 'Well, aren't you going to fight back, spastic?'

Luke smacks Len's fist away with the flat of his hand. 'What d'you mean, *spastic*? He passed more O-levels than you even took, Len. So if he's such a spastic, what's that make you?' He gives a little scoff. 'An amoeba?'

Len turns to his mates. 'A what?'

'Pond-life,' Luke replies. 'Plankton.' It slips out in a snigger. 'You know, those small slimy things that are so insignificant that you hardly even know they're there. A single-celled organism. You'd have learned about it at school if you'd stayed on long enough.'

Len's face contorts, and he grabs again at Martin's shirt and shoves him backwards into his scooter, so that he and the bike crash heavily against the tarmac.

'You stupid – ' All at once Luke's on Len, thrashing out at him clumsily. His field of vision is distorted by the crash helmet, so his aim is off, and he only manages a glancing blow off Len's shoulder. Len grapples Luke by the back of his neck and pulls him in, landing a powerful, square-on punch in his sternum.

Luke wheezes for breath as he drops to his knees, retching, the helmet weighing heavy on his shoulders. 'Len? What the fuck happened to you, man?'

Len hooks his fingers in through the face of the helmet and pulls Luke up to standing. He can see Martin from the corner of his eye, still awkwardly draped over the collapsed scooter, while the girls stand back now, looking frightened; one has her hand clasped over her mouth and the other won't even look in their direction.

Len jerks his head at his mates. 'He can't call me names like that, can he? I want you to say sorry, Wolff. And your mate. *Tit-Head*.'

He's still got his fingers hooked into the top of the helmet, and Luke can feel the flats of his two filthy fingernails pressed up against his forehead. He jerks backwards to shake him off.

'Stand up, Tit-Head,' Len barks at Martin.

Slowly, Martin eases himself up off the ground and attempts to pick up his bike.

'Leave that!'

Martin eases the scooter back to the floor and stands quite still.

'Right, Wolff. Tell him he's a spastic. *Tell him he's a spastic*. Go on. It's what everyone else calls him but he should hear it from you.'

Still winded from the punch to his stomach, Luke turns to look at Martin, who gives him a little nod. He bends forward, resting his hands on his knees, before pushing himself back up to full height, feeling ridiculous as he stands there in his crash helmet, arguing with Len Dickens. He's had enough.

'OK,' he says, breathing out through pursed lips. 'Tell you what, Len. Why don't I tell you what everyone calls *you*, and then we'll call it quits?'

Len doesn't answer, just clenches his fingers in and out of fists at his sides.

'I'd want to know if I was you,' says Luke, steadfastly staring into Len's eyes.

'What the fuck are you on about?'

'OK, here goes, then. Pikey. Fleabag. Rag and Bone. *Inbred*.'

Len looks momentarily confused.

Luke laughs loudly, the harsh sound of it bouncing off the garage doors and walls which back on to the car park. 'Inbred? It means your mum screwed her own brother.'

Len flies at Luke, knocking him to the ground as he pounds fists into his ribs again and again. He grabs at Luke's helmet with both hands, bringing it repeatedly down on the tarmac, until Luke slips briefly from consciousness. He's tugged back by the panic-stricken screams of the two girls and the tap-tap of their heels disappearing into the distance as they run out across the car park and into the night. 'Len!' one of the mates is shouting, but Len ploughs on, punching and thrashing as if he might pulverise Luke altogether.

Luke isn't fighting back now; he's just lying there, taking it, and he fleetingly wonders where Martin is, because he can't hear his voice.

'*Len!*' someone shouts again, abruptly, and then Len's weight is gone, spirited away. Heavy footsteps retreat, breaking into a run, leaving just the sound of Luke's heavy breath in the silence of the car park, and the distant hum of music from the town's nightclubs along the promenade.

Lying on his back, limp, Luke gazes up at the night sky through the open visor of his crash helmet. The sliver of a new moon is obscured behind a lamppost, so that it doesn't look like the moon at all. He knows he hurts all over, but he can't feel a thing. There's a small movement to his left, and he feels the light tips of Martin's fingers on his forearm.

'Mart?'

The fingers press against his skin. 'I thought you were dead,' Martin says, his voice quiet, shaking.

'I'm so hot,' says Luke, waggling his head weakly, feeling the sweat inside his helmet spreading at the base of his neck. 'Can you get this thing off me?'

Martin bends over him and releases the chin strap, cradling his head as he eases it off. He lowers himself to the ground and lies beside Luke, gazing up at the same patch of night sky.

'I really thought you were dead,' he says, his words turning into a swallowed sob.

And then it rains; heavy, wonderful drops of rain that soak into their T-shirts and slick back their hair.

When Luke and Martin finally arrive home in Blake Avenue, the rain-glossed street is in near darkness and they cut the engines at the top of the road, quietly wheeling their scooters along the path and into Luke's driveway.

'Want to crash here?' Luke whispers, shaking the rainwater from his helmet as he stands on the front doorstep, wincing at the dull corset of pain now encircling his torso.

'Yeah. I don't fancy bumping into my dad this late. I said I'd be back about half-eleven.'

'What will he say when you don't come home at all?' Luke asks, carefully slotting the key into the lock. He turns it slowly and eases open the door.

'Dunno. But I'd rather face him tomorrow than tonight.' Martin rubs the tops of his arms vigorously, smoothing over the goosepimples.

Inside, the smell of sweet and sour sauce hangs in the hallway. The house lights are all out except for the one in the bathroom, which is always left on in case Kitty wakes in the night. Luke grabs a towel from the rail and rubs it over his damp arms and legs before handing it to Martin, who does the same, draping it over the radiator when he's done and glancing at his bedraggled hair in the half-light of the hall mirror.

Luke leads them through to the kitchen, where he flicks on the lights and closes the door with a soft click. 'Dad's been out with Simon,' he says, keeping his voice low. 'Wonder if there's any leftovers.'

An array of Chinese takeaway boxes covers the worktop, and Luke flips the lids off each in turn, unearthing four prawn balls, half a tub of special fried rice and an almost full bag of cold chips.

'Bingo,' he says. As he reaches up into the plate cupboard, a spasm of pain cuts through his ribs, causing him to drop against the sink. '*Man*,' he growls into his fist.

Martin puts down his helmet and helps Luke to the kitchen table where he can ease himself on to the wooden bench. 'Maybe we should've got you to the hospital?' he says, frowning hard.

Luke shakes his head, lifting his T-shirt to look at his injuries properly. His torso is red and blotchy, turning darker around his sides as the bruising starts to come through. 'I'll be alright,' he says, grimacing. 'Just get me some of that food and I'll feel a lot better.'

Martin pinches his bottom lip between his forefinger and thumb. 'But if it gets worse, you'll get it looked at?'

'Yes! And grab one of those bottles while you're at it. I need a drink.' He waves his hand towards Mum's DIY wine rack, still filled with leftover white Château Wolff.

Martin divides the cold leftovers between two plates and places them on the table, along with a couple of glass tumblers, the dusty bottle of wine and a corkscrew. He picks up the corkscrew and bottle, holding the two in place.

'Give it here,' Luke says when Martin hesitates. He screws down into the cork and places the bottle on the tiles between his feet. 'Look, mate. Hold it like this,' he says, showing Martin how to grip the bottle with his shoes, where to place his hands. 'And then pull. I think I'll pass out if I try to do it.'

Martin follows Luke's instructions and swiftly pops the cork from the neck of the bottle. He beams with pride, filling the tumblers to the top.

'Cheers,' says Luke, clinking glasses. 'Now brace yourself – ' They both take a swig of wine and Luke slumps forward, silently thumping his fist against the tabletop.

Martin's bony Adam's apple visibly rises and falls as he swallows. He flexes his fingers in and out with a wince. 'That's strong.'

Luke's laughing, clumsily wiping away his tears. He reaches for the bottle and tops up their glasses. 'It's a bit like vinegar. But I bet it's good for pain relief.'

Martin stretches out his long legs and chews away at the cold chips, gazing into space like a grazing cow. 'Why d'you think Len went so mental tonight?'

Luke shakes his head. 'He's been building up to it for years.'

He thinks of the day when they were thirteen, when the police were called down to the rocks at Whitecliff Bay, where Len's brother had just washed up on the shoreline, a week since he'd last been seen stumbling out of the Jolly Roger at closing time. Len had been one of the last to hear about it; Luke had talked him into cycling down to Blackgang Chine that afternoon, to see if they could sneak in to look at the new season's attractions, and by the time they'd got back, after dark, Len's mother was hysterical, ranting in the doorway when they arrived. Len had dropped his bike against the metal steps of the caravan and pushed his mother inside. 'What's up?' Luke called after him, but Len didn't even look back; he just slammed the door and that was that. Luke didn't see him again for the rest of that summer, and when they returned to school in September the gulf between them had just been too great.

Martin takes a pensive sip of wine. 'I think it was what you said about his mum sleeping with her brother.'

Luke chokes, coughing hard, spraying wine sideways as he tries to catch it behind his hand. 'Oh, yeah,' he says, recovering, wiping the mess from his lap. 'Yeah. That did seem to trigger his psycho attack.' He reaches across the table for the wine. 'I think I touched a nerve there.'

'So, do you think it's true?'

'No, you plank! I just said it to – well, I don't know why I said it. To wind him up, I suppose. I'm just fed up with him hassling you all the time, man. Like I say, he's a fucking idiot.'

Martin looks embarrassed and he looks down at his hands. 'I just kind of froze. You know?'

Luke finishes off the last of the wine and stacks the empty plates by the sink. 'Man, forget it. I know fighting freaks you out. And anyway, he wouldn't have flipped if I hadn't said what I said, so it's my fault. Don't worry about it.'

They creep out of the kitchen and into the living room, in search of cushions to make up Martin's bed. Luke flips on the main light.

'Piss off!' Dad mutters from his sleeping position on the sofa, waving a fist in the air. His eyes are still closed, and he freezes momentarily before his body goes slack again and he flops back against the cushion with a small snore.

Luke pushes Martin backwards out of the room, grabbing a couple of cushions before pulling the door closed. Handing them to Martin, he squeezes his eyes shut, punching out into the hallway in an imitation of his dad, taking a feeble swipe at Martin. He laughs hard, thinking better of it as he clutches his sides again.

'What's up with him?' asks Martin, looking bemused as he follows Luke down to his bedroom.

'He's had a skinful,' Luke replies, indicating for Martin to pull out the sleeping bag from beneath his bed. 'Teachers' night out – it's always the same. He goes out telling Mum he

104

won't be too late, then rolls in shit-faced with a bag of curry, making loads of noise. Trouble is, he's a rubbish drinker. He'll be like a dead man for the rest of the weekend.'

'Why does he do it, then?'

'Peer pressure. It's always a big session when Simon's involved. It drives Mum mad. She kicked Simon out the other night when they turned up late after the pub. I couldn't believe it – I heard her tell him to get back to his own wife and leave us in peace. Dad tried to step in and calm her down, but she wasn't having any of it – I've never heard her talk to *anyone* like that before. She called him a cuckoo.' He picks up one of his own pillows and passes it to Martin to add to the makeshift bed, before helping to roll the sleeping bag out over the cushions. 'Honestly, man. *Teachers.* You'd think they'd know better, what with all that responsibility. Mum always says the trouble with Dad is that he can't bear to miss out on anything. So he's always the last one at the end of a party, always wanting to be at the centre of everything. And even if he's not, he'll try to convince you that he was right there when it all happened. Like the festival they had up at Wootton in '69. He tried telling me he got to go backstage with Bob Dylan, that he was one of the lucky few, 'cos he only played for an hour. Turns out he was round at Nan's house all evening, keeping an eye on things because she was a bit worried about a couple of tents that had turned up in her back garden overnight.' They both laugh. 'Nan says he's one of nature's show-offs.'

'Like a peacock,' says Martin, kicking off his shoes.

Luke steps out of his jeans and pulls on his pyjama bottoms. '*Just* like a peacock.' He eases himself into bed, holding on to his breath to stop from crying out, exhaling slowly. 'Him and Mum will have had a fight when he got back – that's why he's on the sofa.'

Martin balls up his T-shirt and throws it across the room, wriggling down inside the sleeping bag, which only just reaches below his armpits. He lies flat out, his long arms resting alongside his body. 'What do they fight about? Your mum's so nice; I can't imagine her arguing about anything.'

Luke thinks about it for a few moments, replaying the argument he overheard before he went out to meet Martin. Dad had come in from chatting to Mike Michaels over the garden wall, saying that Mike had suggested they pair up for John and Marie's party at the end of the month. Mum lost her temper, and when Dad said Mike was only offering them a lift Mum called him ridiculous and naive and kicked him out of the kitchen altogether.

Luke glances across at Martin lying prone on the floor, his damp hair looking as if he'd never had his posh haircut at all. He pulls the light cord above his bed and shifts himself on his pillow, flinching at the deep ache of his ribs. 'I'm not sure really. Something's going on but I'm not sure what. There's something about these parties they've been going to that's got them all worked up.'

'The McKees' parties?' Martin asks softly.

In the darkness, tiny bursts of white light play behind Luke's eyelids. After a moment's silence, he asks, 'Did *I* tell you about the McKees' parties, mate?'

'No,' Martin replies, haltingly. 'But I've heard about them.'

'Who from?'

'The delivery driver who comes for the picture frames. He was talking about it last week when I was helping him to load up the order.'

It feels as though the air has been sucked out of the room.

'What did he say about them?'

Martin shifts in his sleeping bag, the rustle of it clear and sharp in the darkness.

'Mart?'

After a moment's pause he speaks. 'He said they're all *at it*. That it gets quite wild.'

Luke stares at the slice of light that cuts over the top of the

106

closed bedroom door. The oily swill of takeaway and wine weighs heavy in his stomach and he tries to push away his growing urge to throw up.

'Mate?' Martin sounds worried.

'Yeah?'

'It's probably all rubbish, you know. I mean, your mum wouldn't get involved in something like that, would she? It's bound to be just gossip.'

'Yeah. I know,' Luke replies and he turns over to face the other wall, wincing in pain. 'Night, mate.'

Luke and Martin both wake with pounding heads, as the sun pours in through the front window, illuminating the tiny bubbles clinging to the sides of the half-drunk pint of water that sits on the desk. Luke summons up the strength to push himself out of bed and hobbles across the room, picking up the glass and draining it thirstily.

'Jesus,' he says, running his hands up over his face and sticking his tongue out in a grimace. 'That wine of my mum's is *filthy*.' He eases off his stinky T-shirt and examines his bare torso; the bruises have darkened in the night, coiling around his ribs, up across his chest.

Martin props himself up on to his elbows. 'Does it really hurt?' he asks.

'I think this must be what it feels like when you've been run over. Or kicked by a camel.'

'What will your folks say?'

Luke scowls. 'I'm not going to tell *them*, am I? And nor are you. Anyway, my face is fine, so they'll be none the wiser.'

Martin stands, nudging the sleeping bag away with a bony foot and reaching under the bed for his crumpled trousers. 'What are you gonna do about Len?'

'I won't have to do anything. Except show Samantha *this* when I next see her at work. I'll probably leave it a good few days – make sure all the bruising has a chance to come out. Let's see if she still wants to go out with him when she's seen his handiwork.' He takes a good look at himself in the wardrobe mirror before pulling on a long-sleeved shirt and adjusting the collar.

In the kitchen, they find Dad making tea and toast, whistling along to the radio, a towel slung over one shoulder. Luke goes straight to the sink, filling two glasses with water and dropping a couple of soluble aspirins into each.

'Didn't expect to see you up so early, Dad,' he says. 'Thought you'd still be out for the count. You were in a right state when we got back.'

'People in glass houses,' Dad replies, pointedly eyeing the fizzing aspirins.

Martin takes his glass and sits at the table, swilling the little white pills around in circles until they soften and break up altogether. He's got deep, dark rings beneath his eyes.

'You told us to piss off,' Luke says brightly. He scrunches up his face and punches out blindly in a mimic of his dad. 'Uh? Uh?' He laughs, clutching at his sides.

'Judging by the state of you two, I can only assume *you* had more than your fair share of lemonade shandies. What did you get up to last night?'

Luke slides on to the bench opposite Martin. 'Went to see *The Omen.*'

'Any good?'

'Brilliant. Where's Mum?'

'In bed.' Dad starts to lay out the tray, searching around in the cupboards for the jam.

'Oh, man, that looks good.' Luke reaches out to grab a slice of toast, but Dad repels him with a flick of the teatowel.

'Make your own, you layabout. This is for your mum. Breakfast in bed.'

'So what have you done wrong, then?' The conversation with Martin about the party rumours still lurks at the edge of Luke's thoughts; he tries to push it away.

Dad wipes up a slop of tea from the table. 'None of your business. But I can tell you this, lads – sometimes the easiest thing to do is just say sorry.'

Luke straightens up in his seat, stretching his arms out in an exaggerated yawn. 'I suppose it depends what you've done. Maybe sorry isn't enough, if the crime is too big.'

Dad frowns, picking up the tray. 'What's that supposed to mean?'

Luke fixes an innocent expression on his face. 'Nothing. I'm just saying.' He points at the second plate of toast on the table. 'Is that going spare?'

'That's for Kitty. Which reminds me: you're to keep an eye on her while I go back to bed and have breakfast with your mum.'

'What?' Luke complains.

'Well, it's not as if you've got anything else planned, is it? Just make sure Kitty has her toast – we'll only be an hour or so.' He gives Luke a conclusive nod and leaves the room, calling for Kitty to come in for breakfast.

As Dad disappears along the hallway, Luke pulls Kitty's special chair over and pats Martin on the shoulder. 'Sorry, man.'

'I don't mind,' Martin says as Kitty runs in through the kitchen door, waving a naked Tiny Tears over her head. He picks her up and sits her in her seat, placing the plate on the table in front of her, and rubbing the back of her head as if she were his own sister. 'This'll make you big and strong,' he says, sitting down beside her with a gentle smile.

When Luke's parents finally get up, it's late morning, and Luke is out on the front driveway with Kitty, waving Martin off as he scooters up the road and out of sight. Next door, Mike Michaels strides across his front garden just as Mum steps out on to the path, squinting against the bright sunlight.

'Morning, Mike!' she calls out, wandering over as Dad joins them too, slipping his hand around her shoulders and pulling her close. She has a pink-faced happiness about her. Luke just knows the rumours can't be true.

Mike claps his meaty hands together. 'So, all set to come over to us today? You're in for a treat – Diana makes a *splendid* Sunday lunch.'

'Goodness, yes, Mike! Can't wait!' says Mum in her lightest, brightest voice. Luke can tell she'd completely forgotten about it.

'Wouldn't miss it for the world,' Dad agrees.

'Come over about half-twelve. You all eat beef, don't you?'

They both nod enthusiastically. 'Anything we can bring?'

'No, just yourselves.' Mike rubs his hands together and powers back across his patchy lawn, as Mum and Dad rush into the house to hurriedly get ready. Kitty runs inside behind them, and Luke stops to perch on the front wall, glancing along the balding grass verges and dried hedges of Blake Avenue, as the heat of another scorching day takes hold. His memories of last night have grown surreal in the hung-over clarity of late morning; he closes his eyes to recall the lamplit glow of the darkened car park, and the cool, gentle relief of the rain as it soaked through to his skin. He squats to touch the earth that protrudes beneath the gnarly blades of yellowing verge, feeling the hard contours beneath his fingertips. The moisture is gone, sucked up as soon as it reached the ground, like drops of water on blotting paper, leaving nothing to prove it was ever there at all.

The front door to the Michaelses' bungalow is wide open when they arrive, and Dad knocks on the glass panel, calling out a cheery, 'Hello!'

Mike appears in the hallway, one hand cradling a large gin and tonic, the other outstretched. He's wearing huge beige shorts and a matching short-sleeved shirt, and his downy legs look as if they've never before seen the light of day. At

Mum's insistence Dad has put his legs away for a change, and Luke can tell from his expression that he wishes he'd worn his shorts too, so that he could show off his tan.

'Nice day for it,' says Dad.

'Glorious!' shouts Mike, kissing Mum as if she's an old friend. 'Just like you, my dear!'

'Stop it,' she replies, clearly enjoying it.

They follow Mike through to the kitchen at the back of the bungalow, where Diana is putting the finishing touches to a blackcurrant cheesecake. Her hair is pulled up into a high pleat, and as she turns to greet them Luke notices the tiny dark curls that lick loosely around her slender neck.

'You're here!'

Hurriedly, she dries her hands on the teatowel and embraces Mum, before kissing both Dad and Luke on one cheek. He feels the heat of her hand as she runs it down the length of his back; it's brief, but the imprint remains, mingling pleasantly with the tender bruising concealed beneath his cotton shirt. Dad and Mike head off to the living room to fix up some more drinks.

Diana hunkers down to Kitty's height. 'Hello, Kitty! I've got someone I want you meet. But she's very tiny, so you have to be nice and quiet and gentle with her.'

Kitty looks to Mum for approval, her eyes large dark blue discs in her face.

Diana takes Kitty's hand and opens the adjoining door into a small washroom, to reveal a whirring twin-tub, next to which is a small basket containing a black and white kitten. It blinks and gives a faint mewl. Kitty gasps.

'Isn't she lovely?' asks Diana, picking up the kitten and placing her in Kitty's outstretched arms. The cat wriggles once, and settles sleepily against her chest. 'Now, she's very young, so be gentle. I'll pull the door to, so that she doesn't escape. OK, Kitty?'

Kitty strokes the animal, mesmerised, not appearing to notice as the door closes.

'Well, that's Kitty taken care of for the afternoon,' says Mum, smoothing her wavy hair down with both hands. 'What an adorable little thing!'

Diana screws up her face, lifting the cheesecake from the worktop and sliding it into the fridge.

'I didn't really want it,' she says, 'but one of the girls at Mike's office was so desperate to find homes for these cats that we couldn't really say no. It's all a bit of a bother really, and Mike's not the one who has to clear up after it. I don't know how I'll cope if she starts bringing mice in.' She notices Mum's blank expression and releases a pretty little laugh. 'Sorry, I'm going on, aren't I?'

Luke shifts from one foot to the other, unsure whether he should join the men in the living room or stay here with Mum. He smiles at Diana. She's wearing a smocked white blouse which criss-crosses tightly over her chest, puffing up into sheer white cotton where a half-inch dip between her breasts is clearly visible. 'I like your top,' he says, blushing instantly.

Diana's jaw drops in pleasure. She reaches out to brush the skin beside his ear. 'What a lovely boy you are, Luke! Gosh, if all lads your age were the same – well, the world would be a better place.'

Mum smiles at him proudly. 'He's not so bad, are you?'

Just when Luke thinks it can't get any worse, the men return with the drinks and Mum says, 'And can you believe it, Di, he hasn't even got a girlfriend?'

Dad sniffs back a chuckle and hands Luke a scotch and ice. He takes a sip and tries to look as if he drinks it all the time.

'Is that right?' booms Mike. 'Unbelievable. Good-looking chap like you.'

Luke takes another swig of his drink, willing his redness to fade quickly.

'Not like our Thomas, eh, Di?' says Mike proudly. 'He's always got some young thing on the go.'

'Hmm,' replies Diana, undoing the ties of her waist apron and hanging it up on the back of the door. 'I'm not so sure I'd want my daughter going out with Tom, though. If I had one. I don't think he's always very nice to his girlfriends.'

'Nonsense! He's young – no point getting yourself tied down at eighteen, is there? Plenty of fish in the sea, and all that.'

In the dining room, Diana has laid the table out as if it's a formal dinner, with strands of real ivy draped around the silver candelabra centrepiece. Mike strides over to the seat at the head of the table, indicating where everyone should sit, so that he ends up with Mum and Diana to either side of him.

'Diana, it looks beautiful!' says Mum, running the flat of her hand down her simple lemon dress.

Mike stretches round to pull out a chair for her. 'Di always goes a bit over the top. Habit. These corporate wives, you know?'

'Wish I did!' says Dad, taking a seat on the other side of Diana, opposite Luke. 'Teachers' wives don't measure up in quite the same way, I'm afraid to say.'

'Hey!' Mum laughs, draining her gin and tonic. 'I wasn't always a teacher's wife. Remember, I was once a teacher too, which made *you* a teacher's *husband*.'

'Were you?' asks Diana. 'Were you really? Gosh, aren't you clever?'

'What, to be a teacher? Not really!'

'Subject?' Mike asks, grunting as he pulls the cork from a bottle of white wine.

'English.'

'Girls or boys?'

'Mixed.'

'Hmm. Very good. But of course you had to give it up when you had children?' He passes her a large glass of white wine.

Mum goes to answer, but he cuts her off before she can speak.

'And what about you, young man? What are your ambitions?'

Luke is startled; he'd thought he was safe from conversation for a while. His eyes follow Diana as she leaves the room to check on the lunch. 'Me? I'm off to poly in September.'

Mike hands him an even larger glass of wine. 'Of course. But what are you reading? What's your subject?'

Luke glances at Mum, across the table from him, as she fiddles with the edge of her rattan place mat, tugging at a loose thread. One of her eyebrows is slightly arched.

'English,' Luke replies. 'Like Mum.'

'Right. And is that a very employable subject? What do you plan to do with it, once you're done with further education?'

Whenever he's speaking, Luke notices, Mike never maintains continuous eye contact. At all times he's pouring wine, tucking his shirt under his big belly, checking that everyone's got what they need around the room. He takes a clean handkerchief from his pocket and mops his shiny head where the sun is pouring in through the sparkling windows.

Mike glances at Luke, who's staring at his sunlit bald patch. 'Hmm?'

'Oh. I'm not sure really,' Luke replies vaguely, running his hand through his hair.

Mum's social voice rears up, light and bright. 'He's only seventeen! Let him have a bit of fun first. He doesn't need to think about all that dull grown-up stuff just yet.'

Luke nods his head in agreement. 'Yeah, I haven't really thought that far ahead.'

'Well, you must!' Mike turns to Dad. 'Isn't that right, Richard? It's tough out there – unemployment's rife, the political climate is a bloody disaster, and by the time you graduate it'll be survival of the fittest. Mark my words, Luke. You need to get your ducks in a row if you're to be a success in this world.'

Luke hasn't a clue what he's talking about. He glances at Dad, who nods gravely in Mike's direction.

'I know what you're thinking, Luke,' Mike says, stretching across to top up his still half-full wine glass. 'You're thinking, what's this old man telling me all this for? What do I care? I'm young – I've got my whole life ahead of me. Am I right?'

Luke listens politely, trying to resist the temptation to fiddle with his cutlery.

'I'm right!' Mike roars. 'Ha!'

He slaps his palm down hard on the tabletop. Mum jumps in her seat and lets out a little shriek. She lowers her eyes and brings her hand up to cover her smile.

'I'm right! Listen, we can all remember the three-day week, can't we? A disaster! We've had the unions rising up around us, unsettling the workers. Strikes – power cuts! I mean, the candle industry never had it so good!' He roars at his own joke. 'Inflation – at an all-time high! Immigration – out of control! That's why we need young men like you, and my boy Thomas, to be planning your futures now. We're all relying on it!'

He peers around the table for agreement, his eyes bulging, his face now a deep red colour. When no one answers he lunges across the table to refill Dad's glass, huffing and puffing as his backside returns to his seat. Mum and Luke connect briefly; he quickly averts his gaze and bites down on his bottom lip.

'And don't even get me started on the madness of the Equal Pay Act! Who do these lefties think has to pay for it? Industry pays, that's who. You and I pay; that's who. Equal pay means fewer jobs available all round. Fewer jobs means greater unemployment. Greater unemployment means less spending. Less spending means businesses go under. And on and on and on it goes. Whatever next? A woman at Number Ten if the Conservatives get in! We're stuck between the devil and the deep blue sea.' He exhales, and pours himself another glass of wine, slumping against his chair back, exhausted.

Mum pushes out her chair, wincing as its legs scrape loudly across the parquet floor. 'I'll just see if Diana needs a hand,' she says, and she slips from the room, leaving the three men sitting around the table in silence.

'So,' says Dad after an uncomfortable minute has passed.

Mike holds up his hand and stands, to stop Dad in his flow. 'Back in a mo,' he says, bringing his handkerchief out again, clutching it tightly. He leaves the room through the other door.

Luke lifts his glass to his lips and takes a long drink, arching back in his seat to check there's no one beyond the doorway, before pulling a baffled face at Dad. 'What the hell was that all about? I think he might be a bit – you know?' He taps the side of his head, and lets his tongue loll from the corner of his mouth.

'Shh!' Dad replies, grimacing.

'Where d'you think he's gone?'

'Toilet?'

'Maybe. Do you think we should tell Diana?'

'Don't be daft, Luke. We're *guests*.'

'Yeah, but he might be having a heart attack or something?'

'Of course he's not! He just got a bit worked up.' Dad lowers his voice further. 'Just check he's not on the other side of the door.'

Luke tiptoes over to the doorway and peers round it. 'Nope.' As he returns to his seat, he spots Mike through the glass in the back garden. 'Look!' he hisses, indicating to Dad to turn and look outside.

Beyond the glass, Mike is strolling around the edge of the long garden, taking deep drags on a cigarette, blowing the smoke into the branches of the Wolffs' overhanging tree. His skin has returned to a normal colour now, but he appears to be muttering to himself.

'See?' says Luke. He taps the side of his head again.

Diana pushes the dining room door open with her shoulder, holding out a large roast beef joint. She halts in the doorway with Mum at her shoulder, following Luke and Dad's gaze through the window and into the garden.

'Oh,' she says softly. She places the roast at Mike's setting and points to the centre of the table for Mum to put down the bowl of potatoes she's carrying. 'Back in a sec.'

They watch her slip out into the garden and fall into step with Mike.

'Stop staring!' Mum says. Luke sniggers, and she smacks him crossly on the top of his arm. 'You two bring in the rest of the veg while I go and get Kitty.'

By the time they've ferried all the food in and washed Kitty's hands, Diana's back at the table, looking cool and unflustered.

'Mike's just visiting the bathroom.' She lowers her voice. 'He's been terribly stressed at work recently, and to top it all he's been trying to give up smoking. *Not* very successfully, as you can see.' She gives Luke an apologetic smile, before looking up towards the doorway as Mike reappears. 'Oh, look! Here he is.'

Mike enters the room and claps his hands together in a jolly gesture, pushing his large belly out as he makes a show of deeply inhaling the aroma of food. 'So! Shall I be father?' He carves the beef with enthusiasm, and within minutes an easy comfort has returned to the room.

After lunch, Mum and Diana clear the table and make tea, while Mike pours brandies. They move out into the garden, to sit on softly padded garden chairs beneath the shade of a parasol, while the afternoon sun pulsates across the dry, untended garden. Sluggish with wine, Luke reclines in a deckchair, resting his eyes, enjoying the heat. It's all politics and hairdressers and golf courses and schools, and Luke silently vows he'll never be so square, no matter how old he gets. And Diana has no excuse – she's only young, for

God's sake. He wonders what she'd be like if she got really pissed. He wonders what she looks like without her make-up. Without her clothes…

'Bloody mess out here,' says Mike, gesturing towards the lawn with his glass.

'The lack of rain doesn't help,' agrees Dad. 'Last night's downpour seems to have made no difference at all.'

'Got a man coming in next week to tear it all up. Isn't that right, Di?'

Diana lowers a tray on to the wrought iron table, and proceeds to pour tea for her and Mum. 'What's that, darling?'

'The garden.'

'Oh, I can't wait. We're having a new lawn, flower borders. One of those lovely crazy-paving patios? I'm desperate for a patio!'

Mike snorts. 'She loves to spend my money. Don't you, Di?'

Diana sits down with her cup and saucer, and crosses her legs, hitching her little tangerine skirt higher up her thighs. Luke notices the subtle gradation in skin colour from her ankles to her thighs, starting off a warm honey colour at her feet and growing gradually lighter above her knees, lighter still where her thighs finally disappear beneath the crinkly seersucker hem of her skirt. She kicks off her wooden sandals and re-crosses her legs.

'You won't be complaining when this place looks like a little oasis.'

Luke's eyelids droop behind his dark shades, kept open only by the pleasure of watching Diana, unnoticed. Her foot bounces lightly at the end of her crossed leg and Luke is entranced by the startling white gaps between her toes. He imagines sliding the pad of his finger between them, to feel the cool soft skin concealed within. The sun soaks into his face and his mind loosens and he thinks of Diana's toes, his mind jumbling them up with images of the empty whelk

118

shells on Yaverland seafront, with their chalky exteriors and silky pink apertures.

'You always wanted a pond, didn't you, Luke?' Mum pats his knee, forcing him to rouse himself and rejoin the conversation.

'Uh-huh,' he says, shifting up in his seat. 'Where's Kitty?'

'With the kitten, of course!' Mum says. 'She couldn't be happier, Diana.'

'Oh, please, Jo – call me Di.' She inclines her head towards Mike, amused as he drops into a doze in his chair, his head occasionally dipping and bobbing as he fights sleep. Luke wipes his forehead with the back of his hand, and pushes his long sleeves up his arms as he stretches into a yawn. Mum gasps, briefly waking Mike, who opens one eye and quickly closes it again.

'Luke – your arms! What on earth – ' She puts her cup and saucer down with a little clatter, and rushes over to push his sleeve back, staring at the dark bruising that encircles his right arm.

Luke wrestles his arm back and sits up straight, pulling down his sleeve, shooing her away with a flap of his hands. 'Get off, Mum! It's nothing. I fell off the sea wall when I was with Martin the other day. We were mucking about and I slipped.'

'*Luke*! You could have *broken* it.' She returns to her seat, shaking her head.

'Well, I didn't, did I?'

'Boys will be boys, Jo,' Dad says. 'I was the same at his age. Always up to some mischief or other. I once broke three ribs when Henry Peters dared me to jump off the pier at Ryde.'

'*Really*?' asks Luke sarcastically.

Mike gives a little snore, and wakes himself.

'Yep,' replies Dad, lifting up his shirt for everyone to see. He starts to inspect his brown stomach, sucking it in

119

and clenching his muscles. 'I'm sure there's still a scar here somewhere.'

Mum rolls her eyes and smiles at Diana.

'Anyway,' Mum says, 'I wish you'd be more careful, Luke. You don't want to start your first term at polytechnic with your arm in plaster, do you?'

'I keep telling you, everyone calls it poly these days, Mum, not polytechnic. Anyway, Martin helped me back up, and it was fine. So, no harm done.'

Mike taps the teapot and Diana pours him a cup. 'That was Martin in your front drive earlier, Luke?'

'Uh-huh.'

Mike takes the cup from Diana, and stirs in a large spoonful of sugar. 'Funny-looking lad, don't you think, Richard?'

'Martin? I suppose he is,' Dad says pensively, accepting a cup of tea from Diana. 'We've known him such a long time now, I don't really notice how he looks any more.'

'Freakishly tall, I'd say,' Mike adds. 'And those rather dozy-looking eyelids.'

'Mike!' Diana chides. 'Looks aren't everything, you know.'

'*An-y-way*,' Luke says, trying to shift the topic, resting his head back against the fabric of the deckchair. Light and shade play behind the cover of his eyelids, mottled illuminations cast by the sky's bright glare. For a moment the world stops still, before the brief silence is broken by the buzz of a lawnmower several gardens along, mobilising the group back into conversation.

'So, what are you wearing to the party, Jo?' Diana asks.

'Gosh, I think I'll have to make something new,' Mum replies.

'Something summery,' Diana ponders.

'Oh, dear, frock talk,' Dad jokes. 'I'm sure you'd look good in anything, Di.'

Diana waves him away with a pretty flick of her wrist.

'Flatterer.'

'He's right,' Mum agrees. 'You *always* look amazing, Di.'

A smile of satisfaction spreads over Mike's face. 'Not a bad-looking pair of girls we've got ourselves, eh, Richard?'

Luke resists the temptation to make a retching noise.

Diana smiles. 'Of course, John and Marie's parties are *such* good fun, aren't they? I hear you've been to a few already?'

Luke peers up from behind his sunglasses, alert.

'Yes – ' Mum starts, but Dad speaks at the same time, and they pause awkwardly before he takes over.

'Great fun,' he says, and then, as if more emphasis was necessary, he adds, '*Great* fun.'

'Marie's such a wonderful cook!' Mum says, in a bright voice. 'They're a lovely couple.'

Diana takes another sip of her tea.

'So...' says Dad, clearing his throat, but his sentence doesn't go anywhere.

The comforting drill of the lawnmower ebbs and flows in the distance, and Luke tries to calculate how many gardens away it is. He moves his head slightly, opening one eye beneath his shades. He sees Mike, in his ridiculous big-game-hunter's outfit, sitting upright in his seat, his head angled towards Dad. From this perspective, Mum and Diana now just appear as silhouettes on the far side of the group, beneath the orange parasol. Dad sits directly opposite Mike, his ankle on his knee, bottom lip pinched in concentration between thumb and forefinger. Luke closes his eyes and breathes in the heat of the afternoon, feeling his limbs becoming weightless as he drifts, perfectly afloat.

In a heartbeat he's awake again, as Kitty's high-pitched scream rings out from the house and she appears in the kitchen doorway. Mum and Diana rush to her aide.

'Hurt me!' she manages, in between heaving snivels. She holds out her arm and flops against Mum's legs, her head bowed with the emotion of it all. Mum soothes her, as Diana retrieves the kitten from the kitchen floor and steps out into the garden beside her.

'Right!' Mike stands and claps his hands together, marking the end of the afternoon. 'So, we'll see you at the McKees' party?'

'Oh, yes!' says Diana. 'Party of the year!'

Luke continues to watch them, as if through glass. Dad now stands beside Mum, affectionately running his hand across her back and up over her shoulder, turning up the charm. He pats his chest decisively, and with a flick of his head indicates for Luke to get out of his deckchair and join them. Out on the front doorstep, they go through the formality of kisses and handshakes as Luke waits at a distance, tearing foliage from the overgrown hydrangea bush beneath the front window. He rolls a rubbery petal between his fingers, flicking it into the baked flowerbed, before hopping over the low wall on to his front drive, where he stands in the doorway, watching his parents as they walk around the adjoining gate post and up the path towards him.

'Thanks again,' Dad calls over to Mike and Diana, who have wandered out on to their lawn to see them off.

'Until the party,' Mike shouts back, raising his pasty arm in farewell. 'Richard – we'll definitely pair up, then? I'll drive.'

'Good plan!' Dad replies. 'See you then.'

Mum returns Mike's wave with a startled smile, before setting Kitty down and walking steadily along the path ahead of Dad, avoiding Luke's gaze as she brushes past him in the hall.

'Jo?' Dad says, following her into the kitchen, where she's busying herself at the sink. 'What's the matter?'

Mum shrugs Dad's hand from her shoulder, unaware that Luke is standing in the doorway.

'What's the matter?' she hisses. 'You heard him – *let's pair up*, he said. And what did you reply? *Good plan*!'

'Oh, for heaven's sake, Jo, he didn't mean that!'

'Of course he did. He's been staring like he wants to eat me all afternoon! You'll have to tell him we'll make our own way to the party. Make it clear.'

'I can't do that – that's just plain rude.' Dad laughs.

Mum throws down her rubber gloves and turns, startled to see Luke in the room. 'I've got a headache,' she says, and she kisses Luke on the forehead and disappears into the hall.

6

Met Office report for the Isle of Wight, late June 1976:
Maximum temperature 91°F/32.7°C

Since the downpour ten days ago, the temperature has risen dramatically with no end in sight. Each day, Luke's father returns from school, stripping off his shirt the moment he's through the door, complaining that the children are unmanageable, that the heatwave is driving them all demented. The government should let them close early for the summer holidays, he says. In the afternoons he tunes in to catch what he can of Wimbledon, drawing the living room curtains to block out the glare, occasionally yelling from his seat to share the latest scores or announce that another tennis ball has burst in the extreme heat. Mum busies herself to avoid him, drifting about with Kitty through endless muggy days, retreating to her room to lie down when it all gets too much. Ever since that Sunday lunch next door Luke has kept to himself, working long hours when he can, to avoid the arid tension that crackles through the household whenever they're together.

Today, he has an early shift and he slips from the house quietly, as his parents wordlessly take breakfast in the kitchen. Wheeling his scooter down the driveway, he pauses to check it over, giving the lamp a little polish with the hem of his T-shirt, only looking up as he hears his name called from the next door garden. Mike Michaels strides across his lawn with a young man at his side, and comes to a stop at the low wall that separates them. The lad is wearing torn straight jeans with a black and white striped T-shirt, and his eyes are hidden behind dark sunglasses, making it hard to judge his age.

'Mr Michaels.' Luke nods.

'*Mike*. I insist. Luke, remember we told you about my son, Tom?'

Luke smiles, feeling like an idiot in his happy camper gear. 'Hi.'

Tom half-raises a hand, before hooking his thumbs in his belt loops. 'Alright.'

'You promised to show Tom the sights, didn't you? Well, here he is!' Mike slaps his son on the shoulder; Tom pulls a face at Luke, the corner of his mouth lifting up in a pained grimace.

'Oh, yes. I will – but I'm on my way to work right now.' Luke eases his rucksack on to his back and starts to fiddle with his crash helmet.

'No problem! Tom's got a car, he'll drive you, and he can look into getting a job himself when he gets there. He'll give you a lift back, won't you, Tom?'

Tom doesn't answer.

'Oh, but I don't finish until four. You won't want to hang around that long, will you?'

Tom shrugs. 'I haven't got anything better to do, I s'pose.' His accent is a weird mix; he sounds like a posh boy trying to rough it.

'Good man!' says Mike, giving Tom another slap. 'Go and change into something smarter before you go. No one will give you a job looking like that!'

'Dad, if they don't like what I'm wearing, then I don't want their poxy job. I'm not compromising myself for no one. This is me; take it or leave it.'

Mike glares at Tom and reaches into his shirt pocket for a cigarette. He lights it, maintaining eye contact with Tom while Luke looks on, embarrassed. 'As you wish,' he says before marching back across his bald front lawn with a wave of his cigarette. 'See you later!'

'Pillock,' Tom says, indicating for Luke to follow him to the yellow Cortina parked on the road beyond the drive.

Luke throws his rucksack over the passenger headrest and gets in. For the first five minutes or so, they drive along in uncomfortable silence, only broken by Luke's occasional instructions on direction. 'Nice car,' he says, eventually thinking of something to talk about.

'Cheers,' Tom replies. 'It's a Mark Three. Only six years old.'

'Nice.'

'So, is that your scooter back there?'

'Yeah. At some point I'll get on with some proper driving lessons. I'd like a car some day.'

'The scooter's pretty cool,' Tom says, flipping down his sun visor. 'Though you can't get a girl in the back of a scooter, can ya?'

Luke laughs, turning to see that Tom's not even smiling. He's got a matchstick poking out of the side of his mouth, which he moves lazily between his teeth.

'You're after a job, then?'

Tom curls his lip. 'Apparently so. My old man seems to think I'm turning into a layabout or something. That's why I'm here. He's scared shitless that I'm going to let down the family name, by not being a capitalist bastard like him.'

Luke can't begin to imagine his own dad taking such a close interest in anything he gets up to.

'He thinks he'll have wasted all that lovely money on my crappy education, I suppose. You heard about the punk movement?'

'A bit.'

'It's gonna be massive. But the squares seem to think it signals the arrival of bloody Armageddon. My dad's one of the squares.'

'You live in London, right? There's got to be more going on there than there is here. How come you're on the island for the summer?'

Tom sniffs out a small laugh. 'Now, there's a story. I went to this gig a few weeks back, up in Manchester. Mind-blowing. The Sex Pistols.' He turns to look at Luke as if it's a question.

Luke shakes his head, feeling like a hillbilly.

'Don't suppose it's crossed the water yet. Anyway, they were storming. What a gig!' Tom shakes his head earnestly and rolls his matchstick to the other side of his mouth.

'Turn left here,' Luke says as they approach Kite Hill.

'Anyway. After the gig, we went on to this party, and things got a bit out of hand. I was done for drunk and disorderly, and my stepdad had to come all the way up from London and get me out of jail, 'cos I was only seventeen.'

'You look older.'

'That's the funny bit. I turned eighteen the next day, but the offence happened when I was seventeen so they had to treat me like a minor. *Fucking pigs.*'

The 'fucking pigs' part of the sentence slips out in what's clearly his original posh-boy accent and Luke grins to himself. 'Yah,' he says.

Tom darts him a scowl. 'What's that meant to mean?'

'Nothing. I meant "yeah".'

He points out where Tom should park and walks with him to the managers' office. The ground outside the hut has all but turned to dust in the heat, and even the ornamental grasses around the building are starting to look dreary under the scorching sunlight. Luke sprints up the wooden steps and knocks on the door, where he's greeted by Suzy, the manager on duty today. Last week Gordon told him he'd heard Suzy had a reputation as the camp bike, she'd been through so many staff and visitors since she started here a year ago, and Luke felt mildly insulted that as yet she'd never shown any interest in him at all.

She's sitting behind the desk, drinking a bottle of Coke through a straw, not appearing particularly busy. 'Hello, Luke,' she says, looking straight past him to get a better look at Tom, who has slipped his shades up into his tousled strawberry-blond hair. 'Who's your friend?'

'This is Tom. He's over for the summer. He was wondering if there were any more jobs going.'

'Well, let's see.' She makes a show of moving her books and journals around the desktop, flipping pages and clucking her tongue.

'I told him I wasn't sure – ' Luke starts to explain.

'Hasn't your shift started, Luke?' Suzy interrupts, pointing her pen at the clock above her desk, smirking at Tom as she does so.

Luke feels his cheeks flush. 'Yeah, I'd better get going. The only thing is, Suzy, Tom wants to meet me after I finish. But that's not till four, so he might need to wait around a bit?'

Suzy stands and perches on the corner of the desk, tapping her pen on the palm of her other hand. 'I think that'll be fine, Luke. Tom and I can have a little chat about jobs, and then we'll see if we can't organise a pool pass for the afternoon – how's that sound?'

Tom gives Luke his one-sided smile. 'Cool,' he says.

'Tom can meet you back here later, Luke. Thanks for showing him the way.' Suzy flicks her head towards the door.

Luke glances back at Tom as he leaves, feeling invisible as he pulls the door shut and trudges along the dried-up paths towards the cleaning block and his bucket and mop. He checks the Housekeeping rota and heads up to his first chalet, keeping a lookout for Samantha, who's due in despite the fact that it's meant to be a study day. When he woke this morning, he was satisfied to see that, ten days on from Len's beating, his bruises have just about reached their peak, the colour around his chest and ribs having turned the dark brownyblack hue of an over-ripe banana. Today's his big chance to show Samantha what Len's really like.

'Lukey-baby,' Gordon sings as Luke arrives at Chalet 34. He pauses, a pillow hugged to his chest. 'Bad news. The entertainments team have pinched Sexy Sam for the day – so it's still just you and me.'

Luke carries his trug into the bathroom. 'Why Sam?'

'She's got an art O-level. They're designing the new season's posters this week.'

'Bugger,' Luke mutters, as he squirts cleaning fluid around the rim of the bath.

'I *knew* you were keen on her,' Gordon calls over his shoulder, as he shakes out a fresh bed sheet. 'We can always go and find her when we've finished our shift. I think she's working in the ballroom.'

'Thanks, mate,' Luke replies, and for the rest of the day they work through their list, skipping lunch in order to finish early and meet up with Sam. At half-past three they return their gear to Housekeeping, and Gordon agrees to give Luke a bit of space, taking himself off to the canteen for a Chelsea bun and a cup of tea. Luke rushes across the holiday park, checking his watch as he nears the ballroom, just as Samantha appears through the large double doors, clutching a clipboard to her chest. She looks flawless.

'Hi!' she calls over. 'Haven't seen you for ages!'

'I've been here all along – it's just they like to keep me locked up in the furthest reaches of the place. Don't want me scaring the holidaymakers.'

She laughs.

'What have you been working on today?' he asks. His dad once told him that girls love it when you ask lots of questions. It lets them know you're interested.

'Competition posters for high season. We've done "Elegant Grandmother" and "Miss Model Girl" today. I've got to do "Eligible Escort" tomorrow.' She gives him a little tilt of her head. 'Maybe you could go in for that one.'

He raises his eyebrows. 'I don't think so. Although I'm starting to wish I'd taken art more seriously now – *your* job sounds a lot better than cleaning the bogs.'

Samantha looks quite pleased with herself. 'I suppose it must be. Anyway, these'll be finished soon, so I'll be back on cleaning duties with you two before you know it.'

'So, what're you doing now?' Luke asks. 'Tell you what, I'm melting in this heat. Fancy coming to the pool?'

She bites down on her plump bottom lip, a quiver of a frown dimpling her forehead. 'Oh, I wish I could. Lenny's picking me up at half-four – I don't think I'll have time.'

Luke gives her his puppydog eyes. He's been trying them out lately, ever since one of the women in the laundry room commented when he asked to borrow ten pence to buy a Mars bar. 'Look,' she'd said to her elderly workmate as they folded a large starched sheet between them. 'How could you say no to those eyes?'

Samantha covers her mouth with her hand. '*Stop it* – he's picking me up, so I can't change my plans now.'

'Go on. It's early – you can have a quick swim now and still be out and dressed for when Len gets here. *Go on.*'

He does the puppy look again and is pleasantly surprised when it works.

'I suppose I could fit it in, couldn't I? But don't let me stay in too long. I'll need plenty of time to get dressed and dry my hair.'

'Great!' Luke shifts his swimming bag on his shoulder. 'So, see you in the pool, then?'

In the changing rooms, he strips down to his swimming trunks and drapes his towel around his shoulders so no one can see his bruises until he's ready. He waits in the shaded entrance, watching the other bathers milling about or reclining on the loungers, and he's just starting to wonder if Samantha has changed her mind when she appears from the Ladies' changing rooms opposite. She's wearing a two-piece, sky-blue with a white trim. Her breasts are small and lovely, but it's her legs that drive him crazy. They're so long and lean and tanned, like a tennis player's; he can't stop staring at them. She gracefully walks along the edge and enters via the step rail, turning her back to him as she descends, bending slightly at the hips so that her bottom is clearly framed against the blue and white tiles. Her bikini perfectly matches the blue tiles of the pool.

Gordon appears in the entrance, blocking his view. 'So this is where you were off to, is it? We must be psychic. Give us a sec and I'll be in.' He squeezes past Luke, sucking his weedy stomach in and making a big show of not touching him.

'Just give me five minutes,' Luke whispers. 'I need to talk to Sam without you butting in.'

'Oo-ooh,' says Gordon, pouting his lips. 'Go on, then. I'll hang back a bit.'

Luke knows he's just got to get on and do this, so, taking a deep breath, he strides purposefully to the poolside, where he releases his towel, dropping it on to a lounger. 'Hi, Sam!' he calls over with a wave.

She's in the water, holding on to the far rail, and as she turns her eyes grow wide, and she gasps.

Luke panics and jumps in, but it ends up being more of a bomb-drop, sending a wave of water up and over the edge and soaking most of the sunbathers around the pool. A little girl starts crying, and, as Luke resurfaces, her father approaches the edge, waving an angry hand in the air. 'What the hell do you think you're doing?' He points at the large enamelled Swimming Rules notice, nailed to the wood-panelled wall of the changing room.

Will Patrons Kindly Refrain from: Running. Pushing. Acrobatics. Shouting. Ducking. Petting. Bombing...

'Sorry,' Luke replies feebly, running his palms across his face to clear beads of water from his lashes. He glances around the pool area, where other patrons are tutting and shaking their heads in support of the furious father.

'Sorry? *Pathetic*. We've been giving her swimming lessons all week, and she's just getting her confidence. All it takes is a berk like you in the pool and we're back to square one!'

The man looks as if he's been lying in the sun too long; his round belly is almost purple.

'I'm *really* sorry,' Luke repeats. 'I promise it won't happen again.' He cocks his head to one side to address the little girl directly. 'I promise.'

The man backs away, feeling down for his child's hand. 'Well. Well, you just make sure it doesn't.' He retreats to his sun lounger, his face swiftly disappearing behind the sports pages.

The little girl sits down on the floor with a comic, safely protected from the sun by her father's rotund shadow, and Luke pushes off to glide over towards Samantha. He pulls a terrified face, rolling his eyes in the direction of the fat man.

'*Berk*,' Samantha whispers, giggling as he reaches her.

'*True*,' he whispers back.

Side by side, they swim to the far corner of the pool, where Luke hooks his arm up on the edge so that his upper bruises are clearly visible.

'Luke, I hope you don't mind me asking – ?' Samantha flutters a delicate hand towards his chest.

He looks surprised, pulls his chin in and surveys his torso. 'Oh, this. Oh, it's nothing.'

There's a light splash at the other end of the pool, and to Luke's dismay Gordon starts to swim in their direction. '*Great*,' he mutters.

'Sorry,' Samantha says, looking embarrassed. 'I shouldn't have said anything.'

'No, no – not you! Don't worry about me. It's nothing.'

'Is it a condition?'

'What, this?'

'Like birthmarks or something?'

'No!'

Gordon's now about four feet away and he's swimming back and forth, within hearing distance, glancing up and giving Luke an encouraging nod every now and then.

'Is it contagious?' She recoils slightly as she says it, and her nose wrinkles.

'God, no!'

'Sorry,' she says again. 'I'm being too nosy. It just looks really painful.'

'What's that on your chest, Lukey?' Gordon shouts over. He's on his back now, doing a faultless back crawl across the width of the pool.

'Nothing!' Luke shouts back.

Samantha tilts her head sweetly. 'Anyway, I won't mention it again.'

'No, I'm just being stupid,' he says, suddenly afraid he won't get a chance to expose Len. 'I should tell you really. I got in a fight. I just thought it might put you off me if you knew.'

Samantha looks appalled.

'Well, I didn't exactly get in a fight. Actually, if you want the truth, I just got a right kicking.' He looks down, trying out a wounded expression.

'Oh, my God, Luke! You poor thing.' She throws her arms around his neck and hugs him, and he feels her chest against his, the slightest brush of her bare thigh as she leans in. Gordon swims past again, giving Luke the double thumbs-up while Samantha's back is turned.

'*Piss off,*' Luke mouths silently, and Gordon flips himself under the water to glide away towards the far end of the pool.

'Did you call the police? I hope you went to the doctor's – I mean, it looks terrible!'

Luke shakes his head and gives her his doleful face again. 'I didn't want any more trouble, so I kept it to myself. Martin helped me get home, and I've been trying to hide the bruises ever since, but you can't stay covered up forever, can you? To be honest, I'd forgotten all about it until you noticed.'

She rests her hand on his bicep and he clenches his fist to make it tighten, pleased to see it looks quite manly from this angle. He places his other hand on hers, pats it twice and lets it fall back into the water.

'When did it happen?'

'Just over a week ago.'

She shakes her head and squeezes his upper arm. 'And have you got any idea who it was?'

Luke pinches his chin, in the way he's seen Martin do when he's nervous. 'I'm not sure I want to say.'

Her hand slides up on to his shoulder and she gives him a firm little shake. 'Luke? If you know who it was, you can't let them get away with it!'

He looks up and nods slowly, maintaining eye contact all the while, loving the feel of her warm hand on his skin. 'It was Len,' he says. 'Len beat me up.'

By Saturday morning, harmony appears restored in the Wolff household.

Mum was working at her sewing machine late last night, sitting at her workbench in her mismatched bra and knickers, rushing to finish off her new dress, cursing every time the thread snapped or the bobbin jammed in her old Singer. From time to time she'd call on Luke to hold a seam or adjust a pin for her, interrupting his TV shows, kissing him on the cheek every time he helped out, and he couldn't decide if he was more pleased or annoyed at her change in mood. Right up until that point she'd protested that she wasn't going to the McKees' party; that she'd rather die than go. But on Thursday, when Dad arranged for flowers to be delivered while he was out at work, something in her shifted. *Just you and me*, the card said, and Mum threw herself into pre-party preparations, laying out her dress patterns and rushing into town to pick up threads and sequins from Sew and Wear.

Now, as he steps into the hall from his bedroom, Luke sees the finished dress hanging on the back of the living room door. The fabric is a deep yellow and black print she bought some months earlier, and when you look closely you can make out the intricate Grecian design which weaves around the curves of the dress, up over the low-plunging neckline, coming to an end at the wide plastic loops of its halter-neck clasp.

He finds Mum in the kitchen, frying bacon and eggs with one hand, pulling toast from under the grill with the other. 'You're just in time,' she says cheerily, pointing towards the cupboard for Luke to fetch down an extra plate.

He pulls out a seat and nudges at Kitty to budge up, making her squawk. 'What's the occasion?'

'No occasion.' Mum lifts a fried egg out of the pan and on to a slice of buttered white toast. 'I just thought your dad could do with a bit of help this morning.' She calls out into the hallway. 'Richard! Breakfast!'

Luke fetches the ketchup and impatiently thuds away at the base of the glass bottle. 'What's up with Dad, then?'

'Hangover,' she mouths silently, setting out Dad's plate and stretching across to cut up Kitty's bacon.

'Again?'

'He was out with Simon last night. Blind drunk, the pair of them – I'm surprised you didn't hear them. I had to virtually wrestle Simon out into the street, to stop him waking everyone up. It was gone midnight!'

'He's such an idiot when he's had a few.'

'I'm afraid I wasn't very patient with him – but he can't come round here every time him and Laura have a marital spat. I just hope it's not awkward when I see him at the party tonight.'

Luke sneers. 'Pissheads. You'd think they'd be old enough to know better. And they're *teachers*.'

Mum takes a mouthful of bacon and chews thoughtfully. 'It's just as well I'm not teaching any more. I'd never be able to keep up with the social life. Mind you, Simon hasn't got kids to worry about, has he? I'm sure he'd be a bit more restrained if he had a four-year-old bouncing into his bedroom every morning.'

Luke spears a piece of bacon and folds it into his mouth. Resting his knife and fork on the side of his plate, he makes a big display of stretching out, reaching back to tap his fingers on the wall behind. 'So, what kind of party is it, then?'

'What do you mean?' Mum replies without looking up.

'Well, is it a birthday party? A fancy dress party? Simon said something about masks...'

'It's just a party.' She carries on eating.

'A cocktail party?'

'I don't think so.'

'Or one of those Tarts and Vicars parties?'

'Luke!'

'I bet Dad would like that.'

Mum refills her cup with tea from the pot, and retrieves a piece of toast that Kitty has pushed off her plate.

'I hope Mike's up to it,' Luke says, as he watches Mum stir milk into her tea. 'He looked like he was having heart failure that Sunday – what d'you think's wrong with him?'

Mum lifts her head and stares into the space just beyond Luke's ear. She blinks, and meets his gaze again. 'Diana seemed to think it was stress. And he did calm down a bit after a cigarette, so she's probably right.'

'I reckon she's wearing him out,' Luke grins. 'I mean, he's got to be sixty. At least.'

'Actually, he's fifty-eight. Di said she's twenty-nine – exactly half his age.'

Luke waggles his knife. 'Just as I thought: dirty old man!'

Dad skulks into the kitchen, shirtless, and joins them at the table, wincing as his chair catches on the floor. 'Who's a dirty old man?' His face looks crinkled and puffy.

'Apart from you?' Luke replies, putting down his cutlery and folding his arms.

Kitty waves her toast above her head. 'Berty ole man!'

'*Oh, dear*, Dad. Overdo it a bit last night, did you? You're not looking like such a ladykiller this morning.'

Dad ignores him. 'Is there any coffee, love?'

Mum strokes a hand across his shoulders as she gets up to pour him a mug. 'One or two sugars?'

He rests his face in his hands and puts up two fingers. Luke picks up his knife and fork and continues to eat his breakfast, growing increasingly chirpy as he enjoys the spectacle of his father's hangover. Dad lifts his head as Mum places his coffee mug on the table, revealing a clear film of sweat beading up over his top lip. He returns a withering look as Luke smiles at him from across the table.

'Open the back door, Jo,' he asks feebly, running his hand across his brow. 'It's roasting in here.'

'Silly boy,' she says, planting a kiss on the top of his head and leaving the table to push open the back door, propping a loose paving slab against it to hold it in place. She sits again and resumes her breakfast.

'*Silly*,' Luke agrees earnestly.

Dad continues to ignore him, and attempts a mouthful of bacon.

'Silly Billy,' mimics Kitty. When Dad doesn't acknowledge her, she starts up. 'Silly Billy Gilly Willy Hilly Jilly Pilly Shilly – ' She bounces in her seat, bashing her little hands on the tabletop with each syllable, causing Dad's coffee to slop and spill. 'Quilly!'

'KITTY!' he shouts, so loudly that she shudders, her eyes startled wide.

For a moment her bottom lip quivers, but when she realises Dad isn't taking any notice she slides down from the table and marches across the kitchen towards the open back door. She sets her jaw firmly and slaps her hands on her hips. 'SILLY!' she yells. 'BILLY!' And she stomps into the garden.

A few seconds later, she returns, to push over the paving slab and slam the door shut.

'Little git,' says Luke.

Mum slaps his hand, and starts to clear the table, carrying dirty plates and cups over to the sink. 'No, she is *not*.'

'Dad agrees,' Luke says, noticing the colour starting to return to his father's cheeks.

Dad saws into his bacon and smirks back at Luke. 'I don't know where she gets it from. It's certainly not me.'

'Richard! That's an awful thing to say!'

'Well, maybe she's not a git. But she's certainly her mother's daughter,' he says with a playful smirk.

Mum pulls on her rubber gloves and fills the sink, humming along to the radio as she washes the dishes. After a companionable silence while he eats, Dad mops up the last of his egg yolk and pushes away his empty plate, stretching his arms taut above his head and letting out a long, loud growl as he rises from the table. He picks up his dirty plate and slides it into the washing-up bowl, wrapping his arms around Mum and nuzzling her neck. '*You to me are everything –*' he sings, swaying her gently, and she nestles her face against his.

Luke retches loudly. 'Urgh, you look like a couple of those disgusting French exchange students that hang around the pier.'

Mum squeals softly, as Dad bites her shoulder.

'Who wants to see that?'

Dad laughs and releases her, and starts to rummage around in the hanging basket beneath Nanna's cuckoo clock, pulling out a box of soluble aspirin. 'I've got to sort my head out before tonight.' He pauses to read the thermometer built into the side of the clock. 'Bloody hell,' he says, tapping the glass panel. 'It's already seventy-eight degrees, and it's only just gone eleven! That's got to be a record for June.'

Luke hands his plate to Mum and reaches for the teatowel. 'They say we're in for a heatwave. And they're still talking about a drought.'

'Don't be daft, son,' says Dad, stirring his cloudy aspirin and knocking it back in one wincing motion. 'This is England. We'll be up to our necks in puddles by the time the school holidays come round. That'll be just my bloody bad luck – I'll probably limp over the finishing line in July, just as the skies open up for a washout summer.' He reaches round Mum and drops his glass in the washing-up bowl, before slapping her on the bum.

'So, who else will be at the party tonight?' Luke asks, picking up another plate.

Dad pauses in the doorway, pulling in his stomach muscles and patting his ribs as Mum empties the bowl and gives the sink a wipe-over with the cloth.

'I'm not really sure, love,' she replies. 'It's the first time they've thrown a big summer party like this.'

Luke swizzles the teatowel into a thick rope, and spins it out again. 'But you've been to loads of parties at their place.'

'I wouldn't say *loads*,' says Dad.

Luke watches Mum closely as she wipes down the clean sink a second and third time. 'You were there around Christmas, and I know you've been to quite a few since then. Easter. That weekend in May.'

Mum drops the dishcloth in the sink and snatches the towel off him.

'Alright, Luke! Honestly! You make it sound like we're never here.'

'I'm just saying. You've been to quite a few parties over at the McKees'. That's all.'

She frowns and turns to Dad, who shakes his head despairingly and disappears down the hallway and into the bathroom.

'Yes,' she says firmly. 'But this is the first *summer* party of theirs we've been to. That's all I meant.'

Luke hooks his finger into the belt loop of his flares, hitching them up casually as he leaves the room. 'OK, OK.

Keep yer hair on. It's just a party, isn't it? I don't know why you're getting so worked up.'

By early afternoon, the temperature reaches its pinnacle that summer, peaking at ninety-eight degrees Fahrenheit. Martin cycles round with their fish and chip supper soon after seven, just as Dad is getting Kitty in the car to take her to her friend's house for the night.

'Marteee!' Kitty yells, running to grab his leg, almost knocking him over.

Luke is sitting in the shade on the doorstep, cooling off with a home-made orange lolly, and he calls over, laughing at the state of Martin's old bike, which looks as if the rear mudguard might fall off any minute. 'Where's your scooter?'

'Spark plugs need changing.'

Luke walks across the drive to take the chip parcel from Martin as he wheels his bike beneath the car port, flinching as the knackered mudguard scrapes noisily over the back wheel. 'I thought you were getting a lift with Mike?' Luke calls over to Dad, who's busy wrestling the car keys from Kitty's hand.

'We were,' Dad replies, checking to make sure the neighbours aren't around. 'Your mum said she'd rather go separately.' He lowers his voice. 'In case we want to make an early escape.'

Mum appears in the front doorway, wearing her pretty new dress, with her clutch bag and shawl over one arm. Her hair is curled and piled high, showing off her long neck and the deeply plunging lines of her dress back. There's a scent of musk about her and she smiles brightly, giving the boys a twirl before heading towards the car. 'How do I look?' she asks.

Martin blinks awkwardly, eventually opting for a thumbs-up as Kitty sidles over to hug on to his leg.

'Not bad,' Luke says. 'Nice dress.'

She kisses him, and smiles, brushing her thumb across his cheek to rub away the smudge of pink shimmer lipstick that's left behind. 'Right, Kitty! We don't want to be late for Jessie, do we?'

Kitty sticks her lip out and gives Martin her best sad face.

'Oh, I nearly forgot,' he says, and he squats beside her and rummages inside his rucksack, before bringing out a small troll-faced elephant with blue fur running down its back.

Kitty takes the elephant and gasps, hugging it beneath her chin, looking to Mum and Dad to share her pleasure.

'A present?' Dad asks, ruffling Kitty's hair affectionately. 'That's very good of you, Martin. What's Kitty done to deserve such kindness?'

'My dad gave me a bonus yesterday, and I saw it in the window of Toyman's and just thought – '

Luke nudges her with his knee. 'What do you say, Kitty?'

'Fank you, Marty,' she says, kissing the elephant on the end of the trunk.

Martin looks pleased. 'What are you going to call it?'

Kitty beckons for him to stoop down, then cups her hand around his ear and whispers into it.

'Say it again,' he says, screwing up his face in concentration.

She repeats it, careful to keep it a secret.

'That's what I thought you said.' A smile curls at the side of his mouth and he turns to give Luke a small, happy nod.

Dad checks his watch and slaps the top of the car. 'OK, lads, we'll see you later.' Once Mum and Dad have managed to wind down all the windows, Luke and Martin watch them drive away, with Kitty yelping, 'Hot-hot-hot,' from the back seat until they're out of sight.

'So what did Kitty call the elephant?' Luke asks as they pass through the gloom of the bungalow hallway and into the kitchen.

'Marty. She said it's got a long trunk, like me.' He laughs, rubbing the broken bridge of his nose.

Luke shakes his head, pulling open the fridge door and fetching out two cold beers. 'Tell you what, mate, it's a good job you're not easily offended.'

'She's sweet.'

Luke hands a bottle to Martin. 'She's a little nutter.'

After they've plated up their fish and chips, they eat in the bedroom, with the Velvet Underground playing at full volume, the windows thrown open on all sides. The net curtains ripple as the evening light filters through, falling across Martin's large jaw as he chews mechanically, slowly bobbing his head in time with the music.

'I tried phoning you a few times during the week,' Luke says, 'but no one was answering.'

'We don't hear the phone if we're in the workshop.'

Luke puts his empty plate aside on the desk. 'Thought you might want to know how I got on with Samantha? After I showed her my war wounds.'

Martin raises his eyebrows. 'So you told her about Len? What did she say?'

'She burst into tears,' Luke replies proudly. 'She burst into tears, and threw her arms round my neck, saying, "You poor thing, oh, my God, you poor thing!" over and over again.' He pauses for effect. 'Guess where we were when this happened?'

Martin shakes his head.

'In the pool. Virtually naked.'

Martin continues to stare at Luke, a slow smile forming. 'Really?'

'*Really*. Honestly, mate, it was worth getting beaten up for.' He runs his hands over his ribs. 'I'd do it again, any time.'

'So what happens now?' Martin asks, pushing the crispy bits of chip around his plate.

'Dunno. With any luck she'll dump him, then suddenly find me irresistible. That's the plan, although she's still mainly just doing weekends till the end of term, so I haven't seen her for a few days. I really like her.'

'Lucky you,' Martin mutters, turning over to lie on his front.

'I haven't even asked her out yet, so we'll see if I'm so lucky when she knocks me back.'

Martin gazes out of the window beyond Luke, his expression unreadable.

'Listen, mate. If I do get to go out with Samantha, you can bet she's got a few nice friends she could introduce you to. We could set up a double date, go to the cinema or something?'

Martin focuses back in.

'Yeah, OK,' he says. 'Deal.'

'So, you've finished that last big frame job, then?' Luke asks as they take their plates back down to the kitchen.

'Yep. It's just as well. Dad's back has been playing him up quite a bit lately.'

'I didn't know he had a bad back.'

'I think it's something to do with the way he bends over the bench. It's all one-sided. I'll have to watch out for it when I'm older, I suppose. Anyway, it's got really bad lately – he has to keep sitting down and taking aspirins. He's finally agreed to go see a doctor about it on Monday, so maybe they'll give him something stronger for it. I think that's probably why he's been getting so bad-tempered.'

Luke thinks about his own grandmother, with her weak ankles and crumbling hips and fading vision, and her ever-cheery outlook. Mr Brazier should take a leaf out of her book.

He takes out two more bottles, prising open the caps and passing one to Martin. 'These are the last of Dad's beers, but there's loads of wine in the rack. If you dare.'

Martin raises his bottle.

Luke flips his bottle top into the bin opposite. '*Goal*. On the news, they said it's the hottest day of the year. Actually the hottest day in June since records began. *Ever*.' He looks at

Martin, who's perched on the edge of the kitchen table gently rubbing his nose. A shard of warm sunlight cuts through the kitchen, and Luke feels the pleasant flow of his blood as the effects of the alcohol start to kick in.

'So did you find out any more about this party your folks have gone to?' Martin asks, sliding on to the kitchen bench and picking up a deck of cards. He starts to shuffle them, and Luke notices for the first time how nimble Martin's hands are, so unlike the rest of his lumbering body.

'Not really. One minute they weren't going, then all of a sudden it was action stations and they were going after all.'

'Did they go with your neighbours?'

'Delicious Diana and Fatty Mike. *Beauty and the Beast.* Man, she's another one – she really *is* a bit of alright. I can't stop staring at her. It's embarrassing.' Luke takes a seat across from Martin and swigs from his bottle. 'Anyway, no – I mean, they're all going – but in separate cars.'

'Are you worried?' Martin asks. 'I'd be worried.'

'About what?'

'About the neighbour – about this Mike?'

'Why would I be?' Luke asks, taking the cards from Martin's hands and dealing them out for a game of pontoon.

Martin hesitates, until Luke looks up and meets his eye. 'Because of the way he looks at your mum,' he finally says.

Luke shakes his head and turns away, reaching out towards Mum's wine rack. 'Sod it,' he says. 'In for a penny, in for a pound?' He slams the bottle on the table and fetches a large glass for each of them, filling them to the top and pushing Martin's across the table towards him, like a challenge.

Martin takes the glass and glances at Luke apologetically.

'I tried to talk her out of it, mate,' Luke says, raising his glass to his lips. 'Last night, when she said they were going after all. I said I didn't think they should. And she said, "Don't be so silly, Luke." And I said, "It won't make you happy, if you go. It won't make you and Dad happy."'

'What did she say?'

'She said, "Don't be daft, Luke, we *are* happy." I thought, you could've fooled me. I told her I wouldn't babysit, but that didn't make any difference, they just found somewhere else for Kitty to go – and I can't exactly just come out and ask them about these parties, can I?'

'Well,' says Martin, gingerly tasting the wine.

'Let's forget about all of that,' Luke says with resolve, and they bash their glasses across the pine table, grimacing at the tartness of the nasty wine, but persevering nonetheless. 'So, what d'you fancy doing tonight?' He tops them up, sniggering at Martin's martyred expression. He can already feel his own speech becoming slurred, his blood running slower through his veins.

Martin looks around the room with a bemused expression on his face. 'Nothing much.'

'We should do something. Man, it's the *hottest* day of the year, and we've both got the day off tomorrow. We're young, free and single – we should be out there painting the town red! It is red, isn't it? Well, what d'you reckon? What should we do?'

'What does everyone else do on a Saturday night?' asks Martin.

'Down the pub, I suppose. Or hanging around the arcades getting pissed. I don't fancy that. Some of the girls you see down there are rough as they come.' He pours more wine into Martin's glass. He thinks about Tom next door, who's gone back over to the mainland for the weekend, for some fancy party in Chelsea. '*Yah*,' Luke mutters to himself. It seems everyone but Luke and Martin has somewhere better to be.

'What about Samantha?' Martin asks. 'What do you think she'll be doing tonight?'

'Dunno. Avoiding Len Dickhead with any luck. Can't imagine her ever wanting to see him again now she knows what he's capable of.'

'You should phone her,' Martin says.

'Yeah.'

'You should. What if she met someone else, and you never got a chance to ask her out?'

Luke clumsily swills the wine in his glass. A big slop spills over the edge on to the table. 'Maybe.'

'Why don't you do it now?'

'I will.' Luke doesn't move.

'When?'

'After I've had a slash.' He rises from the table and heads towards the open back door, stumbling slightly as he steps out into the dimming light of the garden.

The balmy air surprises him and he pauses momentarily to gaze up at the pinkly receding skyline, at the outlines of the last swallows of the day, which glide and dip beyond the back wall, where the dry scrubland grasses grow tall. All around the garden are symbols of family life: his mother's sunhat, forgotten beside a deckchair; Kitty's deflated Space Hopper; the clothes horse den, now dismantled and propped against the peeling white brickwork at the back of the house. He pees beneath the willow tree, aiming for the displaced iris bulbs that poke up alongside the new fence separating them from Mike and Diana's garden. Earlier this afternoon, he'd stood on the front doorstep, watching his parents with Mike and Diana as they congregated at the front wall, chatting about tonight's party. Luke had felt a pang of disgust as Mike Michaels ran his meaty hand down the length of Mum's back, letting it rest on the low curve at the base of her spine. She must have known Luke was looking, because she turned to look over her shoulder in his direction, and, when their eyes met, he saw something there that made him look away.

Now, in the quiet of the garden, he stoops to retrieve her hat, drawing back his foot to kick a plastic plant pot up and over the shadowy fence into Mike's garden, where it lands with a feeble crump. 'Fat *fugger*!' he calls out into the night, staggering towards the side of the house and in through the back door.

Martin is still at the table, droopy-eyed with drink. 'Who?'

'Bloke next door. Fat fucker.' He slides on to the seat, his words running together like sludge as he drains the last of the wine into their glasses and waggles the empty bottle overhead. 'You know what, mate? You're right. I *will* phone her. I'll phone Samantha.'

Martin looks confused. 'Now?'

Luke waves at the wine rack. 'Soon as – soon as. Soon as we've had a bit more to drink.' He laughs manically. 'Dutch courage!'

Martin laughs too; it's a soft, rasping sound, like a gently panting dog. 'Tha's good,' he says, tapping the side of his head for no apparent reason. 'She'll like that. She'll like that.'

'But first...' Luke brushes the abandoned playing cards to the floor with a sweep of his forearm. 'But first! You and me are gonna have a game of Truth or Dare.'

Martin pulls his chin in. 'Oh, I dunno – '

'Yup! Truth or Dare. For us old pals. We've known each other ten years. Ten years!'

'We have.'

'Ten years! You're my oldest mate. No doubt.' He reaches across to pat Martin on the arm, but ends up patting the bare wood of the table instead. 'So, can't have no secrets, can we?' Luke slumps forward on to his arms, letting out a sickly burp. He lifts his head, screwing his face up at the taste.

Martin drinks his wine down in one mouthful, reaching for the new bottle and attempting to uncork it in the way Luke has shown him before. The cork snaps off halfway, and he has to go in again with the corkscrew, eventually pulling it out in little crumbly lumps.

'You go first,' Luke says, sitting back, holding his palms out towards the ceiling. 'Arse me anythin'. *Anythin'*!'

Martin stares at a space on the ceiling, appearing to think hard.

'Anythin',' Luke repeats.

'OK, I've got one. Who's your favourite songwriter of all time?'

'No!' Luke shouts, bringing his hands down on the table with a slap. 'Not that kind of thing. I'll start. Truth or dare?'

'Truth,' says Martin hesitantly.

'Have you *ever* done anything with a girl?'

Martin's face goes blank.

'*Truth* or dare,' Luke reminds him.

'Dare, then,' says Martin, inspecting his fingernails.

Luke flops against the table. 'Oh, my God, man. You might as well have said no.' He shakes his head so that his hair swings over his face like a curtain. It's nice and dark behind his hair. 'Tell you what, I'm too wasted to do dares. Let's just play truth. Your go,' he mumbles, flicking his fringe off his face.

'You OK?' Martin says. It sounds muffled to Luke. 'You look a bit weird. You've gone all creamy.'

'Creeea-mmy.' Luke murmurs, before attempting to straighten himself up. '*Truth*.'

'OK,' Martin says. 'Did you really sleep with Tina Jarman in the fifth year?'

'Nope. I made that up. Didn't even get a kiss.' He splutters into his fist.

Martin snorts. 'Knew it. Go on, then.'

'Do you fancy Diana from next door?'

Martin avoids eye contact until Luke gives him a nudge across the table. 'OK,' he concedes. 'A bit.'

'Who doesn't?' says Luke. 'She's a cracker.'

Martin scans the room while he searches for his next question. Cautiously, he asks, 'D'you believe the rumours about these parties?'

Luke scowls, shaking his head slowly. '*No.* That's a stupid question.'

Martin pushes a long strand of hair from his face. 'Sorry.'

'S'alright, mate. My go. Does your dad hit you?' It doesn't come out as he means it to; it sounds as if he's taking the piss.

Martin pauses, then shrugs.

Luke covers his face with his hands. '*Oh, man*. Tha's not cool.'

Martin shakes his head, a brief jerking movement, and pours them both more wine.

'*Man*,' Luke repeats under his breath.

'My go. Are you embarrassed when we go out together?'

Luke drops his hands and gazes across the table at Martin. 'Sometimes.'

Martin looks down at the table and fiddles with the stem of his glass before taking another swig of his drink.

'But hardly ever,' Luke quickly adds. 'You're cool, man. It's all cool. My turn. When are you gonna leave your dad and do what you wanna do, like the photogravvy?'

Martin pushes himself out of his chair and lumbers over to the sink, where he runs himself a large glass of water.

'Mart? Truth! Tha's the deal!'

'No deal. It's a shit game, man. And you're only trying to put off phoning Samantha Dyas. 'Cos you're scared.'

'I'm not scared,' Luke replies, getting to his feet and falling back on to his seat. He tries again, this time managing to move away from the table and walk towards Martin with his finger outstretched. 'I'm not scared, and I'll prove it. If – if – '

He staggers back against the dresser, knocking the McKees' party invitation from the shelves. It drifts to the floor and lands beside the open back door.

'If what?' Martin asks, stooping unsteadily to retrieve the card.

'If I had her number.'

Martin leaves the room, bouncing off the doorframe as he goes. The room sways and recedes as Luke steadies himself against the dresser, listening to the sound of the toilet flushing down the hallway.

'Luke?' Martin calls out. 'Come 'ere a sec.' In the hallway, he's standing at the telephone table beside the front door, flicking through the pages of the phone book. 'It's Dyas, isn't it? Samantha's surname?' he says without looking up. He brings his index finger down on the page with a thump. 'Only one of 'em round here.'

Luke looks at the page miserably.

'So, are you gonna phone her?' Martin lifts the receiver and holds it towards Luke, starting to dial the numbers.

In a sudden burst of courage, Luke grasps the receiver and holds it to his ear, listening to the tinny ringing at the other end. It rings and rings, then, just as relief starts to wash over him, there's a voice at the other end of the line.

'Hello?' It's a man.

Luke grimaces at Martin. 'Hello?'

'Who is it?' the voice says, gruffly. He sounds familiar, and too young to be Samantha's dad. 'Hello?'

Just as he realises it's Len, Luke hears Samantha grab the phone at the other end. 'Lenny,' she says. 'Give it here!' She lets out a little yelp as if she's being tickled. 'Hello?'

Luke drops the phone receiver back into its cradle with a hard crack, and leans out of the front door to puke in the lavender. Martin looks on, his long arms dangling uselessly by his side, until finally Luke seems to have brought everything up. He slams the front door shut and staggers into the bathroom opposite, where he splashes his face with water and gazes critically at his grim reflection in the mirror.

'She's still with Len. He answered the bloody phone,' Luke says, glaring angrily at Martin. He makes a grab for the hand towel and rubs his face vigorously. 'Mart, is it just us? It is just us that's not getting anywhere? All the other buggers are doing alright, aren't they? Len and Samantha! Tom next door – the bloody French exchange students! Even, *urgh*, my mum and dad! They're all at it like rabbits! What's wrong with *us*?' He chucks the towel in the bath and lurches past Martin with a groan.

Martin rubs his nose thoughtfully, and follows Luke back down the hall and into the kitchen.

'So what're you gonna do, then?'

Luke looks up at Nanna's cuckoo clock, and staggers purposefully across the room to pick up the McKees' invitation card and wave it in Martin's face. 'What d'you reckon?' he asks with a drunken gurn. 'Wanna go to a party?'

The lads cycle along the esplanade from Sandown to Yaverland, skirting off up the inland roads, where they stop briefly alongside the small airfield so that Luke can throw up again. He does so astride his bike, bending into the gorse bushes to avoid soiling his fresh shirt.

There are no lights on Martin's bike, so he cycles at the front with a camping torch gripped in his fist, while Luke follows, his feeble dynamo lamp flickering at the rear. It's a breezeless night, and despite the advancing hour the heat of the day is still in the air as they divert through the holiday parks to Whitecliff Bay, picking up pace on the approach to the high coastal edge that slopes down to the pebbles and beaches below. The tide is on its way out, and a wide expanse of sand stretches between the rocks and the water where little clusters of youngsters congregate around small flickering fires, or whoop in and out of the water, half-naked and carefree. Martin and Luke prop their bikes against the wooden railing and stumble along the footpath, until they stop at a spot where they can watch unseen. Among the youngsters Luke recognises kids from the year below him at school; he wonders how they came to be here, so at ease, so uninhibited, as he stands hidden in the shadows, merely a spectator.

Directly below them, two young women sit on the rocks in bikinis and floppy sunhats, with towels draped around their shoulders. A bearded man in cut-off jeans tends to a driftwood fire on the sand beside them, and the muted rhythm of their conversation rises and falls against the gentle lapping of the sea in the distance. One girl starts to sing; it's 'Saturday Sun', one of Mum's favourites, and Luke pictures her standing at the sink with her back to him, her head tilted in thought as she listens to the radio, unaware that he's watching. He looks away from the people below and gazes out across the calm water, his thoughts dividing as his wine-soaked mind trespasses on last night's dream, in which they lost Kitty on this very stretch of beach. It was night-time in the dream too, and as he and Dad ran down the pebbles towards the water's edge they spotted her in the distance, teetering at the end of the furthest breakwater. Luke ran to catch her, and as she fell, he looked into her face and saw it wasn't Kitty at all; it was Mum.

His stomach tenses at the memory.

On the beach below, the second girl joins in the song, and another man comes into view, stooping to pick up a guitar from the shadows. He sits on the rock beside them, the notes of his guitar falling in harmony with their voices, and, although they're only a few years older, to Luke they couldn't be more different. Luke feels stunted in contrast, pathetic.

Martin's eyes flicker in the glimmer of firelight, watching as the first girl drops her head against the shoulder of the man, their voices lifting above the sound of the waves. She turns her face to meet that of the guitar player's, and their lips connect.

Luke and Martin leave the beach and cycle out on to the main road. When they reach Bembridge, they slip along the quiet residential paths, heavy with the night scent of honeysuckle. At the Crab and Lobster they cut around the rear entrance, where the landlord is ejecting a few late drinkers and locking up for the night. They wait in the shadows until they're sure the last customers have moved on, before wheeling their bikes across the small car park and up the grass bank to where the horizon comes into view.

'Leave your bike here,' Luke says, carelessly shoving his bike into a hedge before jogging down the deep concrete steps to the rocky beach below, picking his way over the uneven surface of pebbles and driftwood until his feet finally settle on firm sand. Martin does the same, readjusting his rucksack as he follows with the aid of his torch.

Luke walks out across the empty beach, stopping to scrutinise the seafront properties that overlook the water. 'Mum said it's a modern place – sort of upside-down, with the living room on top.' He points towards the sea wall. 'We'll get a better view of the gardens from up there.' Sprinting towards the crumbling steps, his limbs now move effortlessly, up on to the wooden ledge at the top of the beach, which edges on to the large gardens and gated perimeters of the various seafront houses and bungalows.

Martin follows close behind, his torch light juddering as he jogs to keep up. 'Aren't we a bit scruffy to be going to a party?'

'We're not going in, you donkey! We're just gonna have a look. See what's going on.'

The night seems to grow darker as they tread further along the sea wall, the light from the moon frequently disappearing behind wisps of light cloud cover. As they reach the border to each of the grand houses, they peer over high gates to see if they can spot the party house. Many of the gardens are huge, stretching up towards large properties, most of them too old-fashioned to be the McKees'.

'Bloody hell, there's a bit of money round here.' Luke points to a private tennis court beyond a high screen of wire fencing. It's bathed in floodlight, although there doesn't appear to be anyone on the court, and he uses the light to check his watch. 'Quarter to twelve. It's got to be along here somewhere.'

'Do you think they'll still be there?' asks Martin, as he clambers over a tangle of old buoys and rope.

'They never get back from these things before about two. The party'll still be in full swing.'

As they turn the corner, they hear it: the faint hum of music and laughter in the distance. Luke grabs Martin's elbow, stopping to listen for the direction. He snatches the torch from Martin's hand and breaks into a run, stumbling on the pebbles and dried grass underfoot. The sounds grow sharper in the still night air, drawing Luke on, ever faster, until finally, breathless and alert, he arrives at the boundary to the McKees' property. He knows it's their house; the brightly lit top floor is just about visible through the gaps in the tall wooden gate, showing it to be a fairly new build, unlike any of the other houses along the row.

'This is it!' he whispers when Martin eventually catches up. He shines the torch into his face and sees he's got a smudge of dirt across his cheekbone. 'What happened to you?'

Martin checks the palms of his hands and wipes them down the back of his shorts. 'I slipped back there. It's pitch black without the torch. I'm lucky I didn't smash my camera.'

'You brought your camera?'

'It's in my rucksack. First rule of good photography: always be prepared.'

Luke presses his face to the crack in the fence, trying to get a better look. 'Here, give us a leg up.'

He hooks his arms over the top of the gate while Martin supports him from beneath, a surge of drunkenness passing through him as he's lifted. Beyond the gate is a long, sun-scorched lawn, sloping up towards a manicured box hedge that runs the width of the house. Luke can hear voices coming from the space beyond, but his view is completely obscured by the hedge.

He drops back down, crushing Martin's foot before he regains his balance.

'Gotta be another way in.' He waves his arm loosely towards the dark pathway that runs along the side of the house. 'This way?'

Leaving the beach behind them, they follow the hedge-lined path all the way up to the side of the house, passing upturned wooden dinghies and tangles of rope, until the voices on the other side can be heard distinctly. The lads pause silently in the shadows; strange to be standing so close to the partygoers, unsuspected, invisible.

'Darling!'

Luke almost cries out in surprise, the woman's voice is so close.

'Are you going in? Put the Donovan on, will you? It's five to midnight!' Her voice is shrill, as distinct as if she was standing right beside them. 'Everyone! *Five minutes!*' It must be Marie McKee; she sounds as if she's in charge. There's a clamour of voices, and it's impossible to establish how many or few people there are.

'We need to get a better look,' Luke whispers to Martin. 'This hedge is like Fort Knox.'

Martin takes the torch and wanders back and forth a few times, dimly illuminating the hedge to look for gaps. 'There!' he says, holding the beam on a small opening where the foliage meets the ground.

Luke drops to his belly and carefully wriggles through, stopping far enough back that he's still concealed by the hedge on the garden side. The house and garden are brightly lit with lanterns and candles, and around ten or fifteen guests stand about in their evening wear, their faces hidden behind masks. There's much laughter as one woman prances through the group like a gazelle, lifting her skirt high to show her knickers to all who happen to be looking. Her thighs are toned and athletic.

'Why, Laura Drake, you temptress!'

Luke follows Mike Michaels' voice to where he's standing against the box hedge, a glass in his hand. He's wearing an evening suit, his bow tie open at the neck, and a Batman mask, which looks mental on his puffy bald head. The woman curtsies, lifting her gown even higher. Hard to believe a headmaster's wife would behave like that.

Martin has his camera in his hand. 'What's the light like?' he asks.

155

'Well, you can see them all quite clearly,' Luke replies, 'though they've all got masks on. I can't see Mum and Dad. You take a look.'

He retreats, and Martin crawls through the narrow hole and lies there a while, fiddling with his camera and shifting position.

Luke hunches down beside the hedge, speaking softly into the hole.

'Won't they hear you taking the pictures?'

'No. The music's too loud. And it's bright enough that I won't need to use a flash.'

'What can you see?'

'Just a load of people in masks.'

Luke wanders along the dark path to pee in the shadows; the music volume rises suddenly, startling him and making him stumble. As he zips up his flies, his house keys drop from his pocket, falling at his feet in the darkness. '*Shit*,' he mutters, stooping to retrieve them.

Over the hedge, it sounds as though the number of people out in the garden has increased, judging by the growing voices and chatter. Marie McKee starts counting down: 'Five – four – ' and others join in, while Luke blindly scrabbles about in the dirt, trying to find his keys.

' – three – two – ONE!' The party crowd cheer and hoot, their merry voices drowning out the music and the roar of the distant tide.

A discarded mask lands with a crump on the path ahead, just as Luke's fingers fall upon his key fob. He snatches them up, and sprints back along the path to join Martin. 'What did I miss?' he whispers urgently, dropping to his hands and knees. 'Did I miss anything?'

Martin reaches his hand back through, to pass Luke a spent roll of film. 'Take that, will you? I'm just putting a new film in.'

'What did you see?' Luke asks again, nudging Martin's leg in the darkness.

There's a shriek from the garden, silencing Luke instantly. 'Simon! Stop it, you cheeky dog!' It's a woman's voice, but not one Luke recognises.

More sounds of merriment follow, and from inside the house the music level increases further, so that it becomes hard to make out much more than the closest voices. 'Joanna!' a man's voice bellows, and again it sounds like Mike Michaels. Luke listens intently, his head cocked.

'Who was that?' he asks Martin impatiently.

Martin doesn't answer. Luke hears the back of the camera snap shut, and the click and wind of Martin taking another photo.

'Can you see my mum and dad?' Luke asks, as he tugs on Martin's trouser leg, his voice growing more insistent.

'I got some pictures of them a minute ago, but I can't see them now.' Martin slowly eases his long body back out of the hole. He stands over Luke, fiddling with the shutter. 'I only took a few more on that second film. Didn't want to get caught.'

'What happened?' Luke asks, his voice betraying his growing sense of panic as he pushes up to standing.

Martin starts to pack his camera into his rucksack, taking the used film from Luke and sliding it into the front pocket of his corduroys. 'I took some photos.'

'Jesus, mate! I know what happened with *you*. But what happened in *there*? What happened when they counted down to one?'

'Oh. They threw their masks off.'

'Is that it?'

'No.'

Luke can tell Martin's doing it on purpose; he doesn't want him to know. 'Oh, my God, Martin! So they threw off their masks, and then what?'

Martin tugs at the straps of his rucksack, pretending to check them. Dropping to the ground again, Luke pushes himself back through the hole in the fence. He feels the remains of the acid wine sloshing inside his stomach, pulsating against the cool gritty earth, and a sharp intake of breath catches in his throat as he takes in the scene in the McKees' garden.

There must be eight or ten people in the garden now, the others all having moved inside. Of those remaining, five are in various degrees of undress. Three of them are dancing, while the other two lie on the lawn, concealed beyond the rockery, only their tangled legs visible from his vantage point. The light from the lanterns is strong enough that Luke can clearly see the dark hairs of the man's tanned legs, and the smooth coral toenails of the woman's feet. Two fully dressed men stand on the patio, holding glasses of scotch and ice, chatting naturally, as if they were at a business dinner party. Luke scans the garden again; Laura Drake is one of the undressed ones, dancing with two other women he doesn't know. She turns towards the house and beckons someone over, and Simon – *Uncle* Simon, walks across the lawn, stark naked, and starts to dance too, his hairy gonads swinging in time with the music.

'Hey!' Laura calls over to the couple behind the rockery. 'Come on! There's plenty of time for all that. Come and dance!'

The woman stays in the shadows, but the man sits up so that his head and shoulders are visible in the lamplight. It's Dad.

'In a minute,' he replies, dismissing her with a good-humoured wave. He reclines into the shadows, his feet nuzzling lazily around the ankles of his companion.

Luke's horror rises, like a rush of adrenaline, as his mind flips and whirrs at the nightmare scene before him. He takes a deep breath, and before he knows what he's doing he screams through the hedge at the top of his lungs. '*FUCKERS!*'

The two pairs of legs disappear behind the rockery as if magicked away; one of the men shouts, pointing at the hedge, and the naked dancers shriek and run across the garden towards the cover of the house. Clumsily Luke scrabbles back out of the hedge, stumbling to his feet, grabbing on to Martin in the darkness. Panting and wide-eyed, they run at speed, along the unlit stony coastal path, towards the rising tide and the safety of the dark shore below.

7

Met Office report for the Isle of Wight, early July 1976:
Maximum temperature 87°F/30.7°C

In the week following the party, a strange, airless mood saturates Luke's world. Barely able to sleep in the incessant heat, he finds his nights disturbed by jumbled thoughts and images, his days a tangle of anxiety from which he distracts himself with longer work shifts and afternoons drinking with his new friends. He can't bring himself to contact Martin, ashamed as he is about what they witnessed together that night in Bembridge, and yet he knows Martin is the only friend he has in this, the only other person who might understand. At home, he watches at a distance as Mum busies herself with overdue domestic jobs; clearing out Kitty's old clothes, bleaching the mildewed grout in the bathroom, cooking up excessive batches of sultana-filled rock buns. Luke finds it hard to even look at his dad as he comes and goes from work in loaded silence, and for a full seven days barely a word passes between Joanna and Richard Wolff.

At work on Sunday, after he finishes his final job of mopping down the poolside showers, Luke stops by at the managers' office to meet up with Tom, who's just completed a trial day in the kitchens. Gordon and Samantha finished an hour earlier, heading over to the beach at Woodside on foot, telling Luke to follow with his new friend when he's done.

As he arrives outside the office he's met by Tom, bouncing down the steps, tugging at his belt buckle. He gives Luke a smarmy wink and drops his shades over his eyes.

'Just firming up details with Suzy,' he smirks, jangling his keys from one finger as they walk to the car together. He's only an inch or so taller than Luke, but he walks with such a confident swagger, leading with his hips as if he couldn't give a toss about anything.

'So, did she give you a job, then?'

Tom unlocks the driver's door and slides in, reaching over to open the passenger side for Luke. 'She gave me a nice little job, as it goes.'

Luke stares at Tom as he checks his reflection in the rear-view mirror. 'She gave you the kitchen job?'

'Yep,' Tom replies. 'And the rest.' He sticks a new matchstick between his teeth, hitches up his jeans and starts the engine.

Luke blinks. 'Are you saying what I think you're saying?'

'It seemed to be the deal-breaker. A man's gotta do what a man's gotta do.' Tom shoves Luke's arm with the back of his hand, laughing at Luke's stunned expression.

The shaded greenery of Woodside is still relatively lush, protected from the sun by its canopy of trees and cool shade. Luke watches the houses and gardens pass by as Tom chews on his matchstick, the warm breeze blowing through their hair and ruffling their shirts. He notices Tom's shoes: American Converse. He should get some of those when he goes to college. He should get a new look.

'You got a girlfriend?' Tom asks, breaking into his thoughts.

Luke thinks about Samantha in the pool the week before last, how she clung to him when she heard about Len, how hopeful he'd felt back then. 'Not at the moment,' he replies, turning to look out of his passenger window.

Tom pauses at the junction, waiting for a small procession of horse-riders to pass by, before parking alongside a high hedge, just a road back from the beach. 'My dad reckons your mate probably cramps your style a bit. Martin, isn't it?'

'Bloody *hell*. I don't know what he's got against Martin. He doesn't even know him.' He frowns, waiting for Tom to say something.

'I dunno. He just said he's a bit of an oddball. A bit slow.' He taps his temple.

Luke tries to wind up the window, giving the handle an irritable thump when it sticks. 'That's crap, man.'

'Hey!' Tom complains, leaning into his glove box to bring out a small pouch of tobacco. 'Don't take it out on the love machine! I don't know, do I? I've never even met the bloke – I'm just telling you what my old man said.'

'Well, your old man is out of order.'

They take their towels from the back seat along with the two bottles of Mum's home-made wine that Luke stashed there this morning. They follow the path to the shore in heavy silence, Luke squinting against the sunlight as he suppresses his anger.

'Look, I'm sorry, man,' Tom finally says, turning to face Luke. He holds out a hand. 'I know my dad can be a bit of a dick. *Sorry.*'

Luke pauses, bites down on his lip and considers it, fleetingly wondering what would happen if he just told him to sod off. But Tom pushes his sunglasses up over his head, and he looks sincere. Luke accepts his hand and shakes it once.

Tom drapes his towel over one shoulder, replaces the shades and runs his fingers through his tufty fair hair. 'Look, some of our shifts are bound to be the same – we could drive over together some days? Hang out round the pool a bit, check out the birds after work?' He curls his lip suggestively, and when Luke spots Samantha in the distance, bikini-clad and dipping her toe at the water's edge, he can't help but return his smile.

By nine o'clock it's getting dark and the group are the last people on the beach. They lie in a loose formation on their towels, skin still warm from the afternoon sun and the wine that now flows through their veins. Luke's eyes follow the patterns of stars as they start to appear, blinking hard as they flicker in and out of view. Samantha lies on the towel beside him, while Gordon sits at his feet, cross-legged and bowed in concentration as he rolls yet another joint.

'Man, this island has got more going for it than I realised,' says Tom, sweeping his arms wide as he surveys the moonlit water, the last few inches of wine swilling brightly in the bottle. He's the only one standing – the only one fully dressed, Gordon and Luke having changed into swimming trunks as soon as they arrived. Tom throws back his head and drains the last of the wine, dropping the bottle to the sand with a soft thud.

Luke gazes at Tom, cast as he is in silhouette, at his lean frame and shimmering hair, and he envies him. He envies his certainty, his devil-may-care attitude; his ease. 'You should try living here,' he says, sitting up and taking the joint from Gordon.

Gordon nods agreement. 'Everyone leaves in the end.' It's the most he's said in an hour; Luke can tell from his heavy eyelids that he's already completely stoned.

'But it's beautiful, man. The sea – the sky – the wide open sky. Man, you should try London for a week in this heatwave, and then try telling me this isn't better.'

Sam sits up and curls her feet beneath her, so that her bare back forms a perfect curve. In the moonlight, she looks like a silver statue. 'So, what's it like, Tom? What's it like to live in London?'

She passes him the second bottle of wine and he drinks, wiping his mouth with the back of his hand and passing it on. 'It's cool. Of course.' He grins knowingly.

Sam sighs. 'I'll live there one day.'

She rolls over on to her front, reaching over Luke to stroke Gordon, who has now slipped quietly on to his own towel, curled up beside Luke in a foetal position. Luke reclines between them, his head pleasantly muggy and soft against the sand.

'We should be flatmates, Sam,' Gordon says sleepily. 'And you, Lukey-baby. We can all live together, in perfect harmony. You, me and Sexy Sam.' He pats Luke's shoulder with floppy fingers.

Tom hands the wine bottle to Gordon and stoops to pick up stones, which he throws out across the placid water.

'What about Len?' Luke asks, turning to face Sam, his words harsher than he'd intended. 'Won't you be busy playing happy families with *Lenny*?'

Gordon sniggers, and Sam's eyebrows knit crossly as she glares at Luke. Their faces are so close as they lie side by side on their towels that for a moment he thinks she might just slap him. But instead her mouth forms a smile, and in an instant she's upon him, astride him, tickling him hard, her bare thighs squeezing firm against his ribcage, the fleeting brush of her warm breasts exquisite against his chest. He yells and laughs, gasping for breath between tickling grabs, reaching up to encircle her small waist and inflict the same in return. But she pauses, radiant in the water-reflected light, and looks down at him from her position of power. In this sharp moment of clarity, Luke has no doubt that she's the most beautiful thing he's ever seen; that never again will he feel anything quite like this.

Sam rises up, and stands over him, her hand held out to help him to his feet, her sparkling blue eyes never leaving his. 'Who's for a skinny-dip?' she asks, breaking contact to beckon Tom and Gordon with mischief. In moments, they're stripped to the skin in the pale moonlight, all four of them running like children, hurdling the waves, laughing and, for a short while, carefree.

8

Met Office report for the Isle of Wight, mid-July 1976:
Maximum temperature 76°F/24.2°C

For the first half of July, Luke takes every measure he can to avoid his parents, continuing to put himself forward for as many extra shifts as work will give him, and stopping off to take a meal with Nanna every now and then. Daily weather updates continue to report on the interminable drought, and the beaches and resorts around the island swell with worn-out locals and wilting holidaymakers. Dad has found himself a new project, converting the garage into a gym, and every afternoon, on his return from school, he fetches himself a cold beer and strips down to his shorts before setting to work. To Luke's embarrassment he's managed to pick up a stripy headband, just like Björn Borg's, which he now wears whenever he's doing any fitness-related activity, including planning his gym. Wherever Dad is, Mum is sure to be elsewhere, and Kitty runs from one parent to the other, fretfully chirping at them in a bid to restore normality.

One Saturday morning Luke fills an hour before work playing with Kitty in the garden, helping her to make a log house for the little elephant Martin gave her. They're decorating the floor with willow leaves and yellow rose petals, which attract a swarm of ladybirds that gradually threatens to take over the garden.

'Out! Out!' Kitty tells them, flicking them away one by one.

Luke stretches out on the scrubby grass while Kitty runs across the path to fetch a container from the kitchen. Even this early, it's too hot. He should be happy, but the novelty's worn off now, after weeks of this endless heat. Maybe he'd feel differently if he had a girlfriend to share it with, someone like Samantha. But he knows he's got no chance with Sam; even after all that's happened, she's still with Len. Bloody Len Dickhead.

'There,' says Kitty, poking his face to make him look inside the wooden cigar box she's pinched from the kitchen. Already the box is half full of writhing ladybirds. 'Can't go in the house now.'

'Clever girl,' Luke says lazily, listening to the sounds of her pottering about, humming and chattering to herself as she stoops to work on the log house beside him.

'Love you,' she whispers, and Luke opens one eye to see her kissing the little elephant and laying it down inside the new house.

'Ahh,' says Luke. 'Ellie looks comfy, doesn't he?'

'*Marty*,' Kitty replies with a scornful look. 'He's called Marty.'

Luke laughs. 'Oh, yes, that's right. *Marty*.'

She covers the elephant with a few more leaves before lying down beside Luke, nestling her small head beneath his armpit. 'Isn't Marty your friend now? *Big* Marty?' she asks.

'Martin? Yes. Of course he is.'

She reaches up to slide her finger inside his nostril. 'He don't come no more. Maybe he's got Dutch elm disease?'

Luke bats her finger away. '*No*, he hasn't got Dutch elm disease, Kitty. I've told you, it's just trees that get that, not people.'

'Beth at nursery school got Dutch elm disease.'

'Really?'

'Yes. It was going round.'

He smiles. 'I think that was German measles, wasn't it? Anyway, Martin's fine. It's only because I'm working a lot at the moment, Kitty.'

'Did you break friends?'

'*No*. He's still my friend.'

'Then he should come round and play.'

'I know. Maybe I'll phone him later on, see what he's up to?'

'He can come today!' She jumps up on to her knees and claps her hands together.

'Not today. I'm going to work.'

'But he can come and play with *me*?'

Luke sits up and brushes his hair from his face. 'No, Kitty, he's a big boy, isn't he? He comes to play with me. But he really likes you too.'

'He gave me Marty-ellie,' she says a little sadly, stroking the elephant's soft fur head. 'I want Marty to come here.'

Luke gives her shoulder a squeeze and leaves her in the garden while he goes to get ready for work. In the kitchen, Mum and Dad are in the middle of a serious-looking conversation, so Luke decides to hang around for a minute to find out what it's about. He's not hungry, but he lays out the bread board and starts to make a sandwich, nice and slowly.

Dad huffs irritably. 'Do you have to do that now, son?'

'I've got to go to work in a minute,' Luke replies, without looking up. 'So yes, I do. Pretend I'm not here.'

Mum snatches up the house keys. 'I told you about this weeks ago, Richard. How often do I get a bit of time to myself? And anyway Diana's calling for me in a minute, so I can't let her down.'

'But it's the Olympics!' Dad complains. 'It's the first day of the bloody Olympics!'

'You don't have to watch all of it, do you?'

'No, but I don't know the order of events yet. I'm an athlete, Jo – it's in my blood – you know that.'

'You're a PE teacher, Richard,' says Mum.

Luke lets out a small scoff.

'You might laugh, Luke. But I could've taken my pick of sports – they had me tipped as a competition-level swimmer at one point. It might have been me out in Montreal instead of David Wilkie, if my coach hadn't told me to concentrate on field sports instead.'

Mum sighs heavily. 'Yes, well, it seems there are lots of things you "nearly did" in the past. Surely you can look after Kitty *and* watch the television at the same time?'

Luke chances a quick look at them. They're standing either side of the cooker; Mum's dressed up in one of her favourite frocks, and Dad's shirtless as usual, still wearing those grubby denim shorts. His skin is now so dark he looks like an extra from *Swiss Family Robinson*. Mum is rubbing her temple, looking worn out.

'It's not much to ask, is it?' Dad says. 'I've already agreed to spend less time with my friends, just to keep *you* happy.'

'Simon Drake, you mean?'

'Of course I mean Simon.'

'You've got a family, Richard! Simon's never out of that damned garage of yours, drinking our beer and carping on about his marital problems. As if we don't have enough of our own to deal with! He might as well move in, the amount of time he's been spending here lately. I only asked you to cut it back a bit! It's not good for us – it's not good for Kitty. Believe it or not, *we'd* like to spend some time with you too.'

Dad shakes his head. 'I work hard all week long, and all I ask of you is that I can have a bit of peace and quiet every four years, to watch the Olympics.'

'All you ask of me? If only!'

'What's that supposed to mean?'

'Nothing.' She looks at Luke, glaring at him when she sees him chewing on his sandwich, listening in. She turns back to Dad. 'Every four years, you say? Aren't you forgetting the weekly football? The cricket coverage? The snooker?'

'The wrestling,' Luke chimes in.

Dad shoots him a petulant glance.

'Yes, Richard, you go out to work, but don't you think I'd rather go out to work than stay at home washing your dirty socks, cooking your meals, cleaning your house – '

'Ha! Cleaning the house? Can't see that you do a very good job of it.' He runs his finger along the hood of the cooker and holds it up as if he's just won the battle.

Mum's jaw drops and she's about to launch into her defence when they hear Diana calling in through the open front door.

'Coo-eee! Anyone home?'

Mum throws Dad one last scornful glance, and picks up her handbag. 'So, I'll be home about four or five. Just make sure Kitty has something to eat at lunchtime and she'll be fine. I'll see you later.' She leaves, slamming the front door behind her.

Dad shakes his head as he pushes past Luke and stomps into the living room to turn on the television. 'Thanks, son. *Thanks very much.*'

'What?' Luke mutters, shaking his own head in response. He fetches his uniform from his bedroom and goes straight next door to call on Tom for his lift. He doesn't need to get going for another half-hour, but he can't stand to hang around here a minute longer than he has to.

As Tom starts the engine, Luke gazes back at the house, where he sees Kitty standing on the front doorstep clutching her blue elephant, her little hand raised forlornly. He waves from the car window, and Kitty turns and disappears through the open front door.

The day at work passes in a flurry of hot activity, as everyone in the camp gears up in preparation for the school holidays. Luke meets Gordon and Sam at Housekeeping, where they check their schedule and collect their kit, and Tom leaves them for his day's work in the kitchens.

'Don't forget to give Cheffy a big kiss from me,' Gordon calls after him, as Tom swaggers along the path, his thumbs hooked in his pockets. 'A *dirty* big one,' he adds with a laugh.

Tom looks back over his shoulder, raising an eyebrow over his dark shades. Just yesterday, Chef kicked Gordon out of the kitchen when he called for Tom at the end of their shift, calling him a dirty little faggot. '*Your lot disgust me*,' Chef said, according to Gordon, and Tom had pushed back his sleeves, ready to take him on. But Gordon wouldn't hear of it, told him it wasn't worth losing his job over, and managed to drag Tom away to cool off at the pool. Tom says Chef's a Nazi, the way he orders them about and makes them all wait on him when it's time for his break.

Now, Tom reaches the end of the path and turns the corner, disappearing into the shadows of the kitchen block.

Today they've got more rooms than usual to get through and so they work at double speed, with minimum chat, Luke and Sam on the cleaning, Gordon on the beds. It's hard going in the blistering heat, even in the shade of the chalets, and by the end of their shift Luke's exhausted, sweaty, and ready to go home. After they've dropped off their kit, the trio creep alongside the kitchen windows, trying to spy Tom inside without getting caught by Chef Cockgobbler, as Gordon has rechristened him.

'*Tom*,' Luke hisses through the open window, when they spot him serving up at the hob.

Tom checks his watch and jogs over, talking in a whisper. 'I'll only be a sec,' he says, nodding at the plate in his hand. 'Just getting *Mein Führer*'s supper.' He reaches over for a bread roll.

'Is that for him?' Gordon asks. Tom nods, and Gordon lunges through the window to grab the roll, sticking it up his T-shirt and rubbing it liberally beneath his armpit.

'That's disgusting, man,' says Luke, grabbing it off him and doing the same. He passes it to Sam to repeat the process, who then returns the bread roll to Tom.

He shakes his head, looking unimpressed. 'Man, that's just *wrong*.' He looks over his shoulder before shoving it down his trouser front for a good jiggle, finally placing it ceremoniously on the edge of Chef's plate. '*Bon appétit*.' He spins on his heel and pushes through the double doors to the dining hall, to hand over Chef's supper.

Shrill with laughter, Gordon and Sam sprint off to the pool together, waving back at Luke as they go. The afternoon sun is still scorching, and, instead of hanging around at the car while Tom finishes up, Luke decides to call in at the managers' office to collect his wages. He knocks once and eases the half-open door into the office, where Philip is sitting behind the desk in his swivel chair, rosy-cheeked with the heat, drumming his fingers to a track on the radio. He sways his upper body in time, while Suzy sits slumped on the bench beside the window, glugging back a can of Coke.

'Luke Wolff!' Philip says, making it sound like they're long-lost friends. Suzy looks Luke up and down and jerks her chin briefly as Philip riffles through the pay packets, his head never missing a beat. Luke stands awkwardly beside the desk, his fingers resting on the edge, while Philip continues to search. 'How's your friend Tom getting on in the kitchens?' he asks, smirking at Suzy.

'Fine,' Luke replies. 'I think he gets on quite well with Chef.'

'Good, good. I hear he got on quite well with you too, *Suzy*. Isn't that right?' He snorts to himself, as Suzy throws a ball of paper across the room.

Luke is about to tell Philip he'll come back for his wages tomorrow when finally he locates the envelope, holds it aloft and waves it in the air like a drumstick, to mark the final notes of the song. He hands it to Luke.

'Suppose I should get going in a moment,' Suzy says, sounding bored, not making any effort to move. The sunlight streams in behind her, accenting her shiny, uneven complexion, and Luke wonders if this is what they do all day in the duty office: just push bits of paper around and air-drum to the latest top twenty hits. Suzy gives him a puzzled look, a kind of what-are-you-waiting-for expression, and he backs out of the hut and leaves them to it.

The afternoon's rays are beating down hard now, and beads of sweat quickly rise to his brow as he pauses to lean against the wooden handrail and check his wages. Beneath his plimsolls he can feel the bottom tread of the wooden step, smoothly curved, worn down at the midpoint through years of use. He absently runs his hand across it as he stoops to pick up a dropped coin.

'His lot were part of it,' Suzy says, the words carrying clearly through the crack in the door.

Luke reaches for the stair rail, his eyes focusing on the heat haze that shimmers over the distant lawns.

'You know. That orgy over at Bembridge. I heard his lot were there. His mum and dad.'

As his pulse quickens and his heart thuds against his breastbone, Luke holds on to his breath, too stunned to exhale.

'No way!' Philip replies. 'Aren't they teachers?'

'His dad is – taught me PE in the fourth year. He was alright, as they go. Wouldn't have put him down as a swinger, though. Apparently these parties have been going on for *years*.'

'How'd you hear about it?'

'I know John, one of the taxi drivers at Sandown Cabs. He picked them up after that last party – apparently their car wouldn't start when they went to go home. Anyway, he recognised Mr Wolff from the school. John said the wife was in a bit of a state, couldn't get out of there quick enough. Maybe he was more into it than she was.'

'Flippin' 'eck. You just never can tell, can you? I wonder if Luke knows about it, poor bastard. Here – turn the volume up, Suze. I love this one.'

Luke can feel the burn of the sun across his forearm, where his hand now grips the glistening blue paintwork of the handrail. Beyond the half-closed door Philip whistles tunelessly; Luke stuffs his wage packet into his back pocket and runs across the dusty forecourt towards the car park, where he finds Tom leaning against the car, smoking a cigarette, his face turned towards the sun.

'He ate it,' Tom guffaws as he pulls out on to the main road. 'Chef – he ate the bread roll. The *whole* thing.' He turns up the volume of the radio, his lop-sided smile curling up at the opening bars of Bowie's 'Golden Years'.

'Nice one,' Luke replies, dropping his head back against the headrest and closing his eyes. He breathes slow and deep, letting the music wash over him, knowing he has to confront Mum and Dad tonight. There's no more avoiding it, and the thought of it makes him want to puke. 'Listen, mate, I've got a bit of a headache. Do you mind if we don't talk?'

Tom reaches for a fresh matchstick to slot between his teeth. 'Suit yourself, man,' he replies, and they wind their way back down towards Sandown, Luke dozing lightly in the warm breeze of the open windows, as the sweat and anxiety of the afternoon pools in the small of his back.

Back home, he leaves Tom and heads for his front door, just as next door's car pulls into their driveway. Mum and Diana get out, Mum with one small carrier bag, Diana laden down with several.

'Cooee!' Diana calls over to Luke. 'Did you boys have a good day together?'

He nods, waiting for Mum as she says goodbye to Diana and walks back round the gate and into their front drive. Luke holds the door open for her and they go through the hallway together to find Dad still watching the Olympics in the living room. The curtains are drawn to keep the sunlight off the television screen, and an empty beer bottle sits on the floor beside his armchair. It looks as though he hasn't moved for hours.

'Oh, you're back,' he says idly, rubbing his eyes as if he's just woken up. 'Get anything nice?'

Mum holds up her carrier bag. 'Not much. Just a new pair of shorts and some underwear.'

'Cor! Let's have a look, then!' Dad says with a lecherous chortle as she snatches the bag away.

Luke's stomach contracts as he wonders how to tackle the subject of the parties. He stares at them a moment, before sighing deeply and throwing open the curtains to let the afternoon light in.

'God, Dad, it's like a morgue in here. I swear you haven't moved since I left for work this morning.'

'He's right,' says Mum. 'Have you been sitting indoors *all* day?'

'It's the Olympics!' Dad replies. 'Once every four years!'

Luke pushes open the French doors that lead out into the garden, frowning hard. 'Poor Kitty. She must have been bored out of her mind.' He turns back to Dad, who at once looks startled.

Mum's face alters. 'Richard? Where's Kitty?'

Abruptly, he leaves his seat, striding out into the garden. 'I expect she's just playing nicely out here – ' He returns. 'What about the bedroom?' he says, his voice giving away his nerves.

'Kitty!' Mum yells, her panic immediate. 'Kitty!'

Individually they hurry about the house, calling her name, pulling open cupboards and searching under beds.

'Kitty! It's not funny any more!' Dad shouts at the top of his voice. He stands in the hallway, his jaw slack, a film of sweat forming across his brow. 'Kitty? Come out NOW!'

Mum clasps her hands beneath her chin, her eyes wide with disbelief. 'She's not here, Richard,' she gasps. 'Where *is* she?'

They all rush to the front garden, and stand at the open gate, frantically looking up and down the road.

'Get the Michaelses,' Mum whispers, and Dad sprints over the wall and across their lawn, returning seconds later with Mike, Diana and Tom. The men stand in next door's garden, on the other side of the low wall, as Diana dashes down the path to comfort Mum.

'You've lost Kitty?' Mike asks in his booming voice, a deep crease of concern slicing his forehead.

Mum's crying now, her fingers shakily hovering over her mouth. '*Richard* has lost Kitty.'

Mike reaches over the low wall and rubs her shoulder. He turns to Dad. 'When did you last see her, Richard?'

Dad pinches his lip, staring intently at a patch of scrubby grass growing up through the concrete.

'Richard!' Mum screams. 'When did you last see her?'

He shakes his head, his face ashen. 'Maybe an hour ago? I can't remember! *Christ*!'

'Keep a hold of yourself, man,' Mike says firmly. 'Has she ever wandered off on her own before?'

'Never!' Mum is almost panting with fear, and Luke reaches out and nudges her wrist, but she won't look at him. 'It's *so* hot out here,' she says, barely a whisper, pushing the heel of her hand up over her sweat-beaded forehead. 'It's too hot for her to be out all this time on her own. What if she needs a drink? She's only four!'

'We'll find her, Mum,' Luke says softly.

Mike massages the back of his ruddy neck, and surveys the gardens and the street beyond. 'Richard, have you had any visitors at all today?'

'Only the postman,' he replies. He bends forward, placing his hands on his knees, studying the pavement as if the answer is to be found there.

Mike slaps his back, causing him to straighten up. 'OK,' he says. 'Well, we saw the postman after he'd been to yours, and there was no sign of Kitty then. What about Simon? I saw him coming out of here this afternoon – he might have seen something?'

Mum looks up, her expression suddenly severe. 'Simon Drake was here?'

Dad darts a guilty glance at her.

'*Richard?*'

'I didn't mention it because I knew you'd react like this. He just popped in for an hour or two.'

Luke looks from one to the other, his mind racing. 'Dad? What's wrong with Simon coming round?'

'Nothing,' he snaps, bringing his flat hand down hard on the wall post. His face is coated in perspiration.

Mum throws her hands out, her tears now flowing with ease. 'Nothing? Simon Drake's been round here – again – drinking beer with you all afternoon, and then Kitty goes missing?'

'Mum, what's wrong? Simon wouldn't take her.'

'Oh, for heaven's sake – she just means me spending too much time with him, Luke, not that he's taken her.'

'Who's to say he hasn't?' She turns fierce eyes on Dad. '*Mum?*'

'Stop it, Jo!' Dad shouts angrily, his hands working madly through his hair. 'You're being ridiculous. Utterly ridiculous!'

Diana stands by, looking confused and helpless, as Mike puffs on a cigarette under the oppressive heat of the sun. He takes a step towards Mum, laying a condescending hand on her shoulder. 'Come along, Jo. You know Simon wouldn't do anything like that. Now, let's try to think straight.'

'All I know is my daughter's missing, and if she's not with Simon – ' Mum shrieks, shrugging Mike's hand from her shoulder ' – then who – ?' She breaks off, unable to complete the sentence, sinking on to the low wall and covering her face with her hands.

Dad's face is suddenly animated. 'Oh! And Martin called round looking for Luke – about threeish – yes it was half-three, because I told him you were at work, and he said he might call back later on. He might have seen her?'

'Now that's a different kettle of fish altogether!' Mike bellows, searching his pockets for his car keys. 'Why didn't you say something before, man?'

'What?' Luke says, raising his voice and looking from face to face. 'She's not with Martin. Bloody *hell*. Just wait a minute, will you? I'll go and call him.' Luke runs back inside and picks up the receiver, dialling the number and listening as it rings and rings at the other end. He can see the others from here, gathered at the gate, a vision of paralysed panic.

'Hello?' It's Martin's dad.

'Oh, Mr Brazier – it's Luke here. I wondered if Martin was around.'

There's an uncomfortable pause at the other end, a heavy sigh. 'No, he's not. Haven't seen him since he went off after lunch. I thought he was going to meet you.' He sounds less angry than usual; he sounds exhausted.

'OK – thanks. I was out at work. I expect he's on his way back now.'

Mr Brazier hangs up. Luke's pulse is throbbing, and he races back down the path towards expectant faces, shaking his head. 'He's not there.'

Mike Michaels opens his car door and slaps the roof. 'Right – we need to split into groups to look for them.'

Mum looks from Mike to Dad. '*Them?*'

'Hang on a second,' Luke yells, fury rising up in him. 'You are not seriously suggesting that Martin's got her?'

Mike plants his hands on his hips. 'Look, son. I know he's your friend, but there's something very odd about that boy. Seems to me you're the only one who can't see it.'

'You are *so* wrong about this!' Luke punctuates his words with a pointed finger, as Mum tries to pull him away from the wall.

'Stop!' she screams, her chest heaving as she fails to suppress her sobs. 'Why are we all standing here, fighting, when Kitty's out there on her own…?' Her voice trails away and she covers her mouth with her hand, hastily turning her back to the rest of the group.

'Or *not* on her own, as the case may be,' Mike says gravely, indicating to Tom to climb into the back seat. 'Richard, you come with us – I'll drop you and Tom at different points to search along the seafront.'

Mum catches her breath at the suggestion. 'She can't have got as far as the seafront.'

'Di, you run in and phone Art Brewer down at the station – tell him to get over here, and don't forget to mention Martin.' He clicks his fingers at Luke. 'What's his surname, son?'

'Brazier,' Dad answers, shaking his head as he opens the passenger door.

'Brazier – Martin Brazier. OK, Di? You got that? When you've called him, you and Joanna need to knock on every door along the street and ask if they've seen her. We'll meet you back here in an hour, if not before.'

Luke can feel the blood rushing through his veins as the insufferable sun beats down on the cracked lawns of Blake Avenue. 'What about me? What am I meant to do?'

'Wait here!' Mike shouts from his window as he reverses from his drive. 'Wait here for Art Brewer.' He bumps down the pavement and speeds off along the road, taking Tom and Dad with him.

Still standing on the path outside their house, Mum and Luke wait for Diana to return from her phone call. Mum reaches for Luke's fingers and squeezes them. 'Someone needs to be here when Kitty comes back on her own.'

'You know it's not true, don't you? About Martin?'

Her face crumples again, and she drops against his shoulder, her tears silently soaking into his sweat-damp T-shirt. 'They should check with Simon – he might have seen her on his way out.'

'OK, Mum. I'm sure they will. But *Martin*,' Luke says, his body stiff against hers, unyielding. 'You know he'd never do a thing to hurt her.'

An hour later and everyone has returned home, with still no sign of Kitty. Chief Constable Brewer has arrived with PC Paley, whom Luke recognises as someone two or three years older than him from school. Dad is showing Art Brewer around the house, answering his questions as the PC takes down notes.

'Write that down,' Art tells the PC with a tap on the page. 'No previous instance of wandering off. And Richard, you've phoned Simon Drake?'

Dad nods. 'He says she was still here when he left at half-two. She waved him off from the front door.' He trails off, deep in thought.

PC Paley makes a note, nervously double-dotting the 'i's. He moves aside for Luke, who's been following them around to hear what's going on.

'Show me her bedroom,' Chief Constable Brewer demands, striding down the hall. 'This one?'

Dad holds open the door.

'They normally turn up within a few hours,' Paley tells Luke as they stand outside the door. 'She's probably just wandered off and found a friend. Lost track of time.'

'I hope so,' Luke replies.

Art Brewer appears in the doorway. 'Go and ask Mrs Wolff what the child was wearing, Paley. And find out what the neighbours were doing at the time.'

Luke returns with him to the kitchen, where Mum is at the table with Diana, staring into a cold cup of tea. Mike and Tom are by the back door, unconsciously mirroring each other's pose, their arms folded, feet planted wide.

'Mrs Wolff, could you tell me what Kitty was wearing when she went missing.'

For a few seconds Mum looks wide-eyed, as if desperately trying to retrieve a lost image. 'I was in a rush. I can't remember.' She draws a shuddering breath. 'I didn't even kiss her goodbye.'

'I remember,' says Luke. 'I was with her in the garden before I went to work. She had that flowery dress on, Mum. The one she was wearing on Martin's birthday.'

Mike Michaels shakes his head and sighs heavily.

'What's your problem?' Luke snaps, turning to face Mike, raising a searching hand.

PC Paley turns to Mike. 'And you, sir, you're the neighbour?'

'Yes. Mike Michaels. This is my wife, Diana; my son, Tom. Diana was out shopping with Jo when this ghastly thing happened.'

'Do you have to say stuff like that?' Luke demands. 'This "ghastly thing"? For Christ's sake.'

Mum pushes her cup away and lowers her head on to her folded arms.

'May I ask where you were, sir, while your wife was out?'

Mike's head recoils slightly, a tiny movement, but enough for Luke to notice. 'Next door. At home.'

'Anyone with you?'

Mike looks deeply offended. 'No.'

'And you – Tom? Where were you?'

'With Luke.'

'Up at Sunshine Bay. The holiday camp,' Luke says. 'We work there.'

PC Paley turns back to Mike, jotting a few notes in his pad. 'I'll just have to report back to the Chief. It's possible he'll want to make an inspection of your house too, sir.'

Mike rears up, his face livid. 'I can't say that I like the line of your questioning, young man!' He marches across the kitchen, passing through them, into the hall. 'It's that Brazier boy you should be more concerned with.'

Tom shakes his head. 'Why does he have to make everything about him? Sorry, man,' he says to Luke. 'I don't know what to say. What an *idiot*.'

'*Tom*,' Diana chides, but Tom just glowers at her in response and follows Luke into the hall.

They meet the others heading out on to the front doorstep, Mike now nearly puce with rage, and Dad looking as though he's aged twenty years in an afternoon.

'Relax, Mike,' Art Brewer says. 'Everyone's just a bit fraught, understandably. I'll put PC Paley straight; no one's suggesting you had any part in it. God knows where they find these new recruits.' He rests his hand on Mike's elbow. Sweating and huffing in the afternoon heat, they look like a pair of fattened-up old pigs. 'It won't happen again.'

Mike takes his handkerchief from his pocket and mops his brow. He reaches for his cigarettes, stepping out on to the front doorstep to light one, inhaling deeply as he wanders across the concrete driveway where he perches on the dividing wall.

'I think we're done here, Richard,' the Chief says. 'We've got all our men out, scouring the streets, and we've already sent someone round to the Brazier house to see if they can track down Martin. There's not much more we can do for now.'

'We can keep looking,' Luke interrupts, angrily. 'Can't we, Dad? We'll just keep looking until we find her. Tom'll help.'

Tom and Luke step aside as the PC joins them at the front door. 'So you'll call us?' Dad says, following the officers as they make their way towards the police car parked out on the road. 'As soon as you hear anything?'

'Of course.'

Luke watches, feeling helpless as Art Brewer gets in and slams the door, clicking his seat belt into place and starting up the engine. Dad pats the roof of the car once – and then he freezes, his arm held strangely aloft, as his gaze rests on something further down the street. Luke observes him from the shade of the house, momentarily disconnected as his gut turns beneath his ribcage.

'Jo!' Dad calls out, his voice emerging strangulated. '*JO!*'

His urgency shatters Luke's trance and he jumps to attention, craning in through the front door to shout back into the house. 'Mum! Dad wants you!' He sprints to the gate, as Mike throws down his cigarette to join Dad, and Chief Constable Brewer eases himself back out of the car.

Luke follows their gaze. There, strolling along the road in the bright evening sunlight, is Martin, his face dappled in the shade of the overhanging leaves and branches. He lumbers towards them in his usual loose-limbed gait, his flared jeans flapping about his thin ankles, his mousy hair swaying lankly across one eye. Bony-elbowed arms protrude at right angles as he holds them high above his head, where his large hands steady the small floral bundle of laughter that sits astride his shoulders. It's Kitty.

The next minute passes in a surreal blur of activity, like a film on slow-play: Mum running from the house screaming Kitty's name as Dad reaches above Martin's shoulders to fetch her down; Chief Constable Brewer taking Martin by the elbow and leading him to the car; Mike Michaels waving his arm in the air, barking instructions to the officers. Tom and Diana recede into nothing as sparkling motes of dust rise and fall between the shards of tree-split light, and the heat of the evening sun continues to beat down on the usually quiet street.

'Thank God,' Mum repeats over and over, smothering Kitty with kisses.

Dad stands, limp, his face in his hands, as Kitty reaches towards him from Mum's shoulder, her tiny face crumpling when he doesn't look up. She dangles her little blue-haired elephant from her fingers and starts to cry.

'Aren't you going to handcuff him, Art?' Mike demands.

Art Brewer ignores him, removing Martin's rucksack from his back and passing it to PC Paley.

'Luke?' Martin says feebly. His visible fear makes Luke feel nauseous. 'Luke?'

'What do you mean, handcuff him?' Dad interjects, suddenly regaining his composure. 'You haven't even asked him where he found her.'

'Found her?' Mike splutters. 'He *took* her, man!'

'No!' Luke roars, stepping forward to stand between Mike and Dad.

'Martin didn't take her,' says Mum, hugging the quietly weeping Kitty closer. 'Martin, tell the officer!'

Martin says nothing, his pale mouth hanging open in a dreadful mask of surprise.

'Martin!' Luke says crossly, stepping up close, shaking his shoulder. 'Martin, tell them where you found Kitty. Martin!'

Mike Michaels crosses his arms and puffs out his chest, and Luke sees in that moment just how much he's enjoying the drama. 'God knows what he's done to her.'

There's a collective intake of breath as everyone turns to look at him.

'*Mike*,' Chief Constable Brewer says firmly, releasing Martin's arm. 'Mike, this isn't helping. I'll take it from here. You and your family can go back inside now – I need to talk to Martin and the Wolff family alone. OK?'

Mike shakes his head and backs off like a disgruntled bear, indicating for Diana and Tom to join him. 'You just give me a shout, Richard. If you need me.'

Art Brewer turns to the group with a small nod. 'Now, Martin, why don't you tell us what you were doing with Kitty?'

'I found her,' he mumbles, at last.

'You found her? Where?'

'With the dogs. You know?'

'Are you getting this down, PC Paley?' Art asks impatiently, wrinkling his brow. The young PC tugs at his earlobe as Brewer turns to Kitty. 'Kitty?'

She looks terrified, and her face screws up again as she whimpers into Mum's hair.

'Kitty?' Art repeats curtly, wiggling the trunk of the little elephant to gain her full attention.

Mum scowls at him. 'Kitty, darling? Can you tell Mummy where you've been today? Who were you with?'

Kitty casts a suspicious glance in Art Brewer's direction and throws her head back in an exhausted howl. The little elephant drops from her hands, bouncing to the side of the kerb. 'Marteee!' she screams as she watches the elephant land. 'Marty, Marty!'

Dad's expression is a picture of confusion. 'Martin?'

Luke looks around the group in panic. Mum now seems to be in complete meltdown as she lowers herself to perch on the wall, drawing Kitty up as if she might squeeze the breath out of her.

'Kitty doesn't mean that Martin took her!' Luke shouts, but no one seems to be hearing him.

Martin has taken on that glazed over look, like he does when he's eating, and Luke knows there's no reaching him now. PC Paley is going through his rucksack, and he pulls out the Brownie camera and holds it aloft. 'Chief,' he says, 'it looks like he's used a full reel.'

'We'll drop that in at the chemist's for processing on our way back to the station, Paley,' Art Brewer says, looking at his watch. 'Could be evidence.'

Luke runs his hands up through his sweat-soaked scalp, watching as Art moves closer to Mum and Dad and talks to them in a low tone.

'I think we'd better take him down to the station, Richard. I take it he's over eighteen?'

'*Christ*,' Luke murmurs, as he watches PC Paley cuff Martin and ease him into the back seat of the police car.

'We'll question him fully there. In the meantime, it's important that you give Kitty a thorough checking over – do you understand, Joanna? And if anything seems out of the ordinary, call me and we'll send someone over to take a look. See if you can get any more sense out of her about where she's been. She's clearly too traumatised at the moment, but you may get more from her later.'

'But she's only four,' Mum says, her voice barely a whisper. She looks at Dad. 'Martin wouldn't do anything to Kitty, would he, Richard?'

Luke pushes between them to be heard. '*Mum*. This is Martin we're talking about!'

Dad shakes his head, unable to meet Mum's eye. 'I gave him that camera,' he says, barely audible.

'I'll let you know how we get on,' says Chief Constable Brewer, and he gets into the police car and drives away, leaving Luke with nothing more than the appalling image of Martin's haunted face as it passes by.

The phone rings early the next morning, and despite a restless night's sleep Luke leaps from his bed and into the hall, where he waits expectantly beside Mum in his pyjama bottoms, trying to catch a thread of the conversation.

'Yes, I checked her over. Yes, thoroughly. She's completely fine. No – nothing at all.' She glances sideways at Luke and mouths 'the police' at him. 'Yes. Yes, thank you, Art. Thanks for calling so early. Oh, and Art,' she says, turning her back to Luke. 'How is he? Martin. Did he get home alright?' A pause. 'We're very fond of Martin – I'd hate to think this could have repercussions for him.' She tilts her head, listening to the Chief. 'Good. Well, thanks again,' she says, and she returns the phone receiver to its cradle.

'Well?' asks Luke, running his finger along the ridged glass of the front door panel.

Mum pushes her hand through her hair, scraping it up into a thick bunch and letting it fall. She releases a deep, relieved sigh. 'That was Chief Brewer. They let Martin go late last night. Apparently he'd only bumped into Kitty minutes before we saw him – he'd spotted her playing with the dogs in Sara Newbury's front garden, and he was just bringing her home. Art says they're confident that it was all just a big mix-up.'

Luke pulls at his bottom lip, remembering the grey spectre of Martin's face as he passed by in the police car. 'Not helped by Fatty next door. So, what now?'

'So, nothing. That's it.'

'You say that, but you know what this place is like once people get hold of a bit of gossip. I'll bet Mike Michaels has already dispatched an emergency telegraph to warn the rest of the island. People are bound to ask questions.'

Mum rubs his shoulder. 'Well, if they do, we'll all just have to put them right.' She inspects her face in the hall mirror, brushing a finger under her lashes to wipe away the traces of yesterday's mascara. 'Maybe you should give Martin a call, Luke?' She leans in to stroke his cheek, and smiles gently before running a distracted hand through her hair and disappearing into the bathroom.

For a minute or two Luke stands in the hallway alone, staring at the telephone, building up the courage to make the call. When he does, Martin answers on the second ring, with a weak urgency to his voice that unsettles Luke to his core.

'Mart, it's me,' he says, in his cheeriest voice. 'The police just phoned to say you'd gone home. Are you OK?'

A little puff of breath at the end of the line lets Luke know he's still there. He waits for Martin to speak.

'I'm fine, thanks,' he eventually says, talking with a pronounced lisp, and what sounds like a blocked-up nose.

'What's up with your voice? Are you sure you're OK?'

'Yesss. I'm fine.' Martin has lowered his voice to a whisper.

'Is your dad there?'

'Uh-huh.'

'What did he say, mate? Did the police explain it to him?'

There's a long silence, and in that instant, Luke knows why Martin's lisping; it wouldn't be the first time his dad has knocked him about. 'Mate, it's all going to be alright, you know? You're not in any trouble. Chief Brewer told my mum on the phone; he said they know it was all just a mix-up.'

'Uh-huh.'

'So what are you sounding so worried about, then?'

Martin clears his throat, the pause seeming to go on for an age. 'It's the film from the camera, Luke. They've put it in for processing.'

'So what?' As soon as the words are out, he understands. Martin's talking about the photos he took on the night of the party. 'Jesus,' Luke murmurs. 'The film was still in your camera?'

'I'd forgotten about it. There were two films, Luke – the police only took that one, the one in the camera, and I don't know what I've done with the first one, but I'm sure I'll find it if I have a good look in my room – '

'Alright, alright,' Luke interrupts, his impatience breaking through. He checks along the hallway to ensure he's not being overheard. 'Just slow down, mate. So, can you remember what's on that film the police have got? It's important – are there any pictures of my folks on it?'

'That's the thing, Luke. I can't remember. I just can't remember. My mind's a complete blank.' There's a rattle in the background as Martin's dad enters the room and tells him to get off the phone. 'I've got to go now,' he says, the tremble in his voice close to tears. 'I've got to go.'

The receiver goes down and Luke stares at his own dishevelled reflection in the hall mirror, as the blood drains from his face, and a slow, deep panic sets in. Is this how it feels when someone has died? he wonders. Because right now, nothing, nothing in the world, could make him feel any worse than this.

9

Met Office report for the Isle of Wight, late July 1976:
Maximum temperature 74°F/23.6°C

Since the last smattering of rain in the middle of July, the heatwave is predicted to soar again to Mediterranean levels. Temperatures continue up in the seventies and news reporters continue to talk of almost nothing else. Yesterday, when Luke took Kitty to the marshes in search of newts, the area was desert-dry, the rushes wilting like hay against the sun-bleached wasteland of the ponds. 'Where did they go?' Kitty had asked sadly, slotting a small finger into one of the broad cracks that fractured the heat-baked basin. 'They must have found a new home,' he'd answered, certain that the ill-fated newts were long-dead.

Since that last phone call a couple of weeks back, Luke hasn't seen or heard from Martin at all. He couldn't bring himself to broach the subject of the parties with his parents, not so soon after the trauma of Kitty's disappearance, and so for now he pushes it away, glad to go on acting as if none of it ever happened.

Sweat-soaked work days come and go in a blur of mops and buckets and crisp white sheets, with many an afternoon spent with Tom and Gordon, sunbathing beneath the tamarisk trees of Woodside beach. Samantha seems to join them less and less, as her relationship with Len Dickens

188

blossoms elsewhere, away from the intense glare of Luke's jealousy.

On Saturday Luke has a rare day free, and he passes much of the morning sleeping off his hangover, waking groggy to the sound of Mum cranking up the carpet cleaner in the hall beyond his door. She's still on this obsessive cleaning kick, and yesterday she hired an industrial-strength machine, which she's been flogging to death before it has to be returned to Hopkinson's at the end of the day.

Parched, Luke heads for the kitchen, waving a sleepy hand at Mum, who's now moved into the living room, where all the furniture is pushed back against the walls and windows.

'Can you take your shoes off when you come in and out, Luke?' she shouts over the noise of the cleaner as he pauses in the living room doorway. 'And I'll want to get in your room at some point later today.'

In the kitchen he runs the cold tap, downing a pint of water before filling his glass again and slumping back against the sink, listening to the sounds of the household. Kitty is out in the back yard, poking around the weeds and seeded buddleia, collecting up green caterpillars in a crumpled old Ski yogurt pot. He can hear the clack-clack-clack of her wooden stick as she taps it along the wall and fence panels. '*I'm on the top of the world*,' she sings, repeating the same line over and over again. This is his first day off in weeks, and yet he has nothing to do, nowhere to go. Gordon and Tom are both working today, and Martin's disappeared off the face of the earth. He thinks about bloody Len Dickhead kissing Samantha Dyas, and the strip of brown thigh he glimpsed when she stepped into Len's car after work yesterday; how she turned and blew him a secret kiss when she knew Len wasn't looking.

Luke wanders back out into the hall, where he props himself against the doorframe to the living room, watching Mum. A trickle of sweat runs down the side of her face as she manhandles the heavy machine across the carpet. It grinds and whirrs, sucking grubby water back up its hose and into the clear plastic tank. Beyond Mum, through the open patio doors, Dad sits in his deckchair, bare legs crossed in the sunshine, the rest of him hidden behind his Saturday newspapers. So far, he's kept to his promise of seeing less of Simon, and, while things are hardly perfect between them, there have certainly been fewer arguments than before. Dad flips his newspaper over and lets it drop to the lawn as he folds his arms idly and closes his eyes for a nap.

'Lazy git,' Luke mutters, returning to the kitchen to search for food.

Shortly after lunch, Mum drops a hastily wrapped present into Luke's hands, and asks him to walk Kitty to a party at the village hall while she carries on with the living room carpet. Kitty's wearing a new frock that Mum made up from some fabric offcuts she's been saving, and she dawdles on the path with her little chin jutting out, annoying Luke every time she stops to twirl and shout, 'New dress! Ta-daaa!'

All along the way, Luke notices the scorched lawns and dying plants, mentally noting those gardens he suspects are being covertly watered under cover of darkness. Like most of their neighbours the Wolffs have been emptying their dirty dishwater into the flowerbeds, but recently Mum's been complaining that the tea roses are starting to smell. Last night she dragged him out into the garden and made him sniff the plants, pressing him for his opinion. He'd stood there for ages, inhaling away, until he finally came up with the answer: macaroni cheese – they'd had it last Wednesday. Mum was delighted that they'd cracked the code, and decided that in future they'd only water the garden with bathwater.

Luke and Kitty turn the corner into the village hall car park, where pink and yellow balloons bob against the fire escape bars of the open double doors. Parents and children come and go in the bright sunlight, and Luke chaperones Kitty inside to look for Mrs Forest, the mother of the party girl. It's cool inside the hall, and a dozen or more children noisily clamber and run across the central wooden stage, while a group of parents cluster around the noticeboard amidst much animated chatter. Kitty spots Mrs Forest at the edge of the group, and she drags Luke over to let her know she's arrived.

'It's not a particularly flattering shot,' one of the fathers laughs, peering in to get a closer look at the noticeboard.

Kitty holds the present high up above her head, waving it under Mrs Forest's nose until she gets her attention. The mother takes the gift and points Kitty in the direction of her little friends. 'The girls are in the Wendy house,' she calls after her, and she glances back towards the noticeboard and lowers her voice to a confidential tone. 'God only knows who saw fit to post it up in the village hall, of all places. Where just about *anyone* can see it.'

'Surely that's the whole point!' the man guffaws. Whatever's up on the board has clearly tickled him. 'Someone's certainly got it in for the poor fella.'

Luke rises up on to his toes in an attempt to see what they're all looking at, and the group shifts, giving him a clear view of the photograph pinned to the centre of the board. Full-frontal and entirely naked, the figure on the dried-out grass lawn appears to be posed mid-dance, his arms thrown wide in the bright lamplight. His wavy hair and sandy moustache look lighter in the shot than in real life, and his eyes are concealed behind a black Zorro mask. But still, despite the small disguise, it's clear to all standing around the noticeboard that the man in the mask is local headmaster Simon Drake.

The two-minute jog back home is frantic, as Luke tries to find the words to tell Mum and Dad what he's just seen. His mind is a jumble; he can't let on that he knows about the source of the photos – but neither can he let this just happen to them. He stops in the front doorway, bending down over his knees while he gathers his thoughts, feeling his lunch swilling in his stomach as he wipes the perspiration from the back of his neck and tries to regulate his breathing. Inside, Mum has moved into Kitty's bedroom with the carpet cleaner, and she looks up and smiles at him as he passes. He strides through the house, intending to tell Dad, to force the issue, but in the event he finds he's lost for words. Out in the leaf-dappled warmth of the garden Dad's sleeping peacefully in his deckchair, his arms draped across his lap, hands hanging loosely against the denim fabric of his shorts, a rare, contented ease lingering at the edges of his mouth. Luke stands in the shade of the willow tree, looking down at his father, and he doesn't know what to do. What is there to do? It's already out there. What use is there in him saying *anything*?

Defeated, he returns to the hallway and picks up the phone receiver, irritably bobbing his head at Mum, who pushes the bedroom door shut to muffle the noise. He dials Martin's number and waits. Hollowly, it rings at the other end of the line, competing with the sounds of Mum's machine bumping up against the bedroom door.

'*Answer,*' Luke urges, chewing on a loose corner of thumbnail as the phone at Martin's end rings on and on. Finally he hangs up. 'Mum?' he yells through the closed door, pushing it open and peering round.

She's working at a small ink stain in the corner of Kitty's carpet, feverishly pushing the brush head back and forth over the same spot, her brow furrowed in concentration. She looks up and switches the machine off, running a wrist across her shiny temple. 'Did you say something, Luke?'

He can't tell her. 'Couldn't Dad give you a hand with that?' he asks. 'It looks like heavy work.'

She looks around the room distractedly. 'He only just broke up for the holidays a week ago – the last thing he wants to do is clean the house!'

Luke chews on his lower lip.

'Is there something else, Luke? You look a bit worried, sweetheart.'

He blinks hard. 'Me? No, I'm fine.'

'You sure?'

'Yep! What time does Kitty's party finish? I'll collect her if you want.'

Mum picks up a small wicker stool and places it on the bed alongside a mountain of cuddly toys. 'Actually, I've got to get the machine back to Hopkinson's around the same time, so I'll pick up Kitty on my way back.' She gathers up her unruly hair, twirling it round in one easy movement, repinning it in a loose knot. Dropping to her knees, she reaches under the bed and feels around, eventually pulling out a pair of slippers and Marty the elephant. She stops to gaze at the little toy for a moment, before throwing it on to the pile and turning away to restart the machine.

Next door in his own bedroom, Luke opens all the windows, and closes the curtains so that they flutter and billow in the warm salt breeze, shutting out the endless glare of sunlight and heat. He places Martin's *Young Americans* album on the record player and turns the volume high, flopping back against his pillow, to sink deep inside himself. He clutches at his hair, trying to shift his thoughts away from Martin's reel of film, and thinks about Samantha and Len, about Mark Bolan and David Bowie, about poly and Brighton and London and America; about any place but here. He thinks about Martin and his father and his long-dead mother; he thinks about the swallow that killed her, about the high grass of their garden path and the grief that hides in the shadows beyond their cloudy front windows. And eventually, he sleeps.

Tom beeps his horn for Luke the following day, to drive them up to the holiday camp for work. It's mid-morning, and Luke drains his mug, pausing to kiss Mum goodbye as she sits at the kitchen table nursing her cup of tea.

Last night the phone rang non-stop, the first call coming from Simon Drake, quickly followed by John McKee and a couple of callers Luke didn't recognise. Dad took all the calls, waving Mum away as she stood beside him in the hallway, making knots of her fingers and avoiding Luke's questioning gaze. When Mike Michaels came striding in unannounced as darkness started to fall, it took everything in Luke's power to keep from punching his smarmy face.

'Richard!' Mike boomed, dropping heavily on to the sofa and waving a cupped hand at mum, by way of requesting a drink. 'Time for crisis talks, methinks!'

Mum broke down again and shut herself in her bedroom for the rest of the evening, until she rose this morning, pale and puffy-eyed.

Now, Luke throws his bag in the back of Tom's car and slides into the passenger seat.

'Alright, man,' says Tom. His sun-bleached hair looks as though he's been hacking at it with a pair of nail scissors, and it stands out in crusty little peaks up and over his head.

'I like your hair,' says Luke as they pull away. 'How'd you get it to stick up like that?'

'Hair gel.' He pats the front carefully with the palm of his hand. 'So,' he says, tapping the steering wheel with his thumbs. 'My lot are in a right two an' eight. Seems to me there's a whole load of shit going down in our neighbourhood.' He winks at Luke with a cluck of his tongue.

'Can we just leave it, Tom?' Luke replies with a worn out sigh. 'It's boring.' He puffs a short breath between his lips, and turns to look through his passenger window at the streets and houses that whizz by, wondering why no one's answering the phone at Martin's house. Last night, in between all the incoming phone calls, he'd tried reaching him again and again, without success. He kept trying, right up until midnight, then once more this morning, but still there was no reply.

'Tom, mate – do us a favour and swing a right here, will you?'

Tom pulls up at the kerb where Luke indicates.

'I've just got to sort something out. Wait here – I'll only be a couple of minutes.' He leaves Tom propped up against the bonnet of his car, rolling a cigarette in the sunshine. Luke pushes open the dilapidated gate and navigates his way through the nettles and weeds that wilt and clutter the path to Martin's house. He stops at the faded paintwork of the front door, where a livid red splash radiates from the central panel. Above the letterbox in dripping red capitals is the word 'NONCE'.

The sun hits the dirty front windows directly, making it impossible to see inside, and Luke knocks once with his knuckles, loudly, dropping back from the doorstep to wait. He's about to knock again when the door opens, and Martin's long, sallow face peers around the frame.

Luke frowns hard, holding his palms up.

'I had to call round, Mart. I couldn't get through on the phone.'

'We've had a few nuisance calls,' Martin replies, keeping his voice low, moving out to stand on the step. 'We unplugged it in the end.'

The awkwardness between them is excruciating. 'Mart, what did your dad say about all that police business the other day?'

Martin gives an involuntary jerk of his head, a tiny movement that betrays his fear of being overheard by his father. There's a fading bruise across one side of his face, along his cheekbone and up over his temple.

'Have you reported this?' Luke points towards the graffiti.

Martin shrugs. 'There's no point. We gave up trying to wash it off after the third time.'

Luke looks back down the path to check that Tom's still out of earshot. 'Listen, man, we need to talk about those photos. One of them has turned up – stuck up in the village hall of all places. It's Simon Drake – stark bollock naked.'

Martin stares at him, unblinking.

'Mart? Don't you get it? If someone's got pictures of him, they could have some of my folks. It must have come from that reel of film the police took off you.'

There's a loud clatter from an overhead branch as a wood pigeon takes flight through the trees. Martin nods his head briefly.

'So? Have you remembered if there are any of Mum and Dad on that film?' Luke shoves his hands into his shorts pockets, kicking his foot impatiently against the doorstep.

Martin runs his finger down the length of his nose, his irises moving like clock hands as he retraces his thoughts. 'Well, the first film, the one I put in my pocket – that was a whole reel of the party. I remember that. Then I loaded a new film and only took a few more on that one before we left. That was the one the police took out of my camera when I got arrested.'

Luke rolls his eyes. 'Mate, they didn't arrest you. They took you in for questioning, that's all.'

'It felt like I was arrested,' Martin replies, kicking at the angry patch of red paint that clings to the edge of the doorframe.

'Sorry,' says Luke. He rubs his hands over his face, pushing his hair back off his eyes. 'So, mate, have they returned the photographs yet? I mean, they're still your property, aren't they?'

'Well, that's what was funny. PC Paley came round, yesterday.'

'Funny? Why?'

'Because he wanted to apologise, about the photos.' He nods at Luke, like he should know what he's on about.

'Apologise for what?'

'For losing the photos.'

'What?' Luke's heart pounds in his chest. 'They've lost them? Fuck. *Fuck*.'

'Well, they don't actually develop them themselves at the chemist's – they send them away. And on that day, he said,

196

some of the photographs seem to have got mixed up, and they couldn't find mine at all. Someone else must have been given them by mistake, he said.'

There's a creak as Tom rattles the broken gate at the end of the path. 'Luke! Come on, man. We don't wanna be late!'

Martin looks alarmed; he takes a quick pace back from the doorstep, into the shadows. Luke gives Tom a sharp shake of his head and turns back to Martin, dropping his voice to a whisper. 'Listen, Mart. It's really important that you remember – were there any pictures of my folks on that film?'

'I'm sorry. I just can't remember.' He shakes his head, confused.

'Well, you'd better just let me have that other one, then – ' Luke glares ' – and I'll destroy it.'

Martin turns again to listen back into the house.

'*Mart!*'

'*I can't,*' Martin whispers. 'I've lost it. Well, I haven't lost it, but I can't think where I put it. I know I put it somewhere safe when I got home – but I just can't remember where.'

Blood rushes into Luke's face. '*Christ*, Martin! You'd bloody well better find it.'

'But I don't know where it is.' His Adam's apple shifts like a blockage.

Tom beeps his horn. Luke leans in, pressing up close to the doorframe, keeping his voice low and controlled. 'Do you understand the damage this could do, Martin? Stop being such an idiot! I'm fed up of sticking up for you, you know? It's *embarrassing*.'

Martin blinks, and starts to back away. Luke stomps down the path, pausing to look back though the branch-dappled light of the overgrown hedges to where Martin watches, almost hidden behind the remaining crack in the door. He points a finger at him, alarmed by the menace in his own voice. 'Martin, I'll keep coming back here until you find it.'

As he closes the gate and starts to walk away, Martin's subdued voice trails after him.

'I want my Bowie album back, Luke. *Young Americans*? I want it back.'

'Not until I get that roll of film,' Luke replies, and he clicks the gate shut and returns to Tom's car.

After work, Luke waits for Tom at the front entrance, so that they can go for a swim before they head back home. He's felt nauseous all day, lurching between anger and shame as he tried to stop thinking about the way he spoke to Martin earlier.

As Tom approaches, Luke makes a mental note of how he looks and what he's wearing, thinking of the things he needs to get when he starts at Brighton in a few weeks' time. He'll have to ditch the flares for starters: Tom's straight jeans are definitely much more with it, and the Converse boots are cool. He fingers his own hair, lazily running his hand up through the front of his overgrown fringe; perhaps it's time to get it cut.

Tom stops in front of him, lifts off his sunglasses, and polishes them with the edge of his faded Jaws T-shirt. 'Luke?' he says, slowly easing his sunglasses back on to his nose. 'Mate, you're not one of Gordon's lot, are you?'

Luke doesn't know what to say.

Tom puts a hand on his shoulder. 'I've got nothing against 'em, you know. I mean, Gordon, he's one cool dude. But, just so you know, it's girls all the way with me.'

'What the hell – ?' Luke finally splurts out, laughing.

Tom shrugs, and they start to walk towards the pool. 'Dunno. Just the way you keep staring at me. I mean, I know I'm a thing of beauty, but…'

'Piss off,' Luke says, flipping his foot round to hit Tom in the back of the shin.

Tom's leg buckles, and he skip-jumps out of Luke's way. 'But you do, man. You stare a lot.'

Luke shoves his hands into his pockets and shakes his head, bemused. 'Sorry, mate. Didn't realise. I was just thinking how cool your boots are. Daydreaming.'

'Fair enough,' Tom replies as they walk up the steps and into the pool area. He stands at the poolside, hands on hips, surveying the vicinity with confidence. 'Fair enough.'

Now that the schools have broken up, the place is overrun with families, and Luke is about to suggest giving it a miss when he spots Samantha sitting on the other side of the pool, dangling her legs in the water beside Gordon. Luke and Tom make their way round the tiled poolside, dodging squirming toddlers and stray armbands.

'Aloha,' says Gordon.

'Hey,' Luke says, his heart racing at the sight of Samantha in her bikini. 'Long time no see, Sam.'

She stretches her legs out above the water, flexing her toes. 'Too long!' she replies.

She flutters her fingers at him and Tom, and Luke feels suddenly incongruous in his shorts and T-shirt, overdressed amongst all the swimsuited bathers.

Tom stoops to run his hand through the water, testing the temperature. 'Nice,' he says, flicking the water from his fingers, purposely splashing Sam's face.

'Hey!' she yelps, smacking his calf, laughing.

Luke laces his fingers and cracks his knuckles. 'So, Sam, I wasn't sure if you were still working here.'

She pats the water's surface with her feet. 'I think we've been on different shifts this week. And I had a bit of time off.'

'Holiday?'

'No,' she replies, smoothing her hands down her shins, whipping the water off in little sprinkles. 'I just had to sort a few things out.'

'*Len,*' Gordon mouths to Luke while she's looking away. He lays a hand on Samantha's back. 'But it's all good now, isn't it, Sexy Sam? No more Len.'

'Really? You finished with him?' Luke asks, crouching down beside her.

Samantha's eyes dart up to meet his. 'He stole twenty pounds from my mum's housekeeping tin – I caught him. Dad's been trying to get me to dump him for ages now. I swear he was almost pleased when I told him it was Len who took the money.'

'Thieving gypsy,' Luke says, shaking his head. 'You're well rid of him.'

She looks at him crossly. 'You don't have to sound quite so pleased, Luke. Anyway, he's gone now. My mum wanted to get the police involved, but my dad sorted it out himself.'

'How?'

Samantha shakes her hair back off her shoulders. 'Dad knows one of the managers up at the ferry port – he got him a summer job, directing the cars on and off. To keep him out of my hair, he said. Although Dad said he'd be happier if he knew Len was off the island altogether.' She giggles at this.

Gordon nudges her knee with his. 'It's good news for us, though, isn't it? You're free!'

'Good old Gordy,' she says, slapping his thigh and giving it a squeeze.

'So what's happening, man?' Tom asks Luke, removing his sunglasses and using the arm to scratch the hair behind his ear. 'Are we staying or going?'

Samantha twists her upper body, looking from one lad to the next as she grips an elastic band between her white teeth and gathers her hair into a high ponytail. 'Go and get into your trunks – the water's lovely! Gordon and I were just debating whether to have another swim or not, weren't we, Gord?'

'Yes sirreee,' he replies in a crappy cowboy accent. He swings his legs and starts to hum.

'What d'you reckon, Tom?' Luke asks. 'Wanna go in? Although, of course it'll mean getting your hair wet.'

Tom's hand automatically pats the front of his hair. 'Yeah, yeah,' he replies, feigning a yawn.

'Oh, go on!' Samantha pleads, and she reaches out and tickles Luke on the back of the knee, sending a thrill of electricity up his thigh. He jumps back with a surprised yell, his eyes drawn to the rise and fall of her breasts as she swings her legs round and drops into the pool. She treads water beneath them, beckoning them in, the swell of her chest shimmering in the bright rippling water. Gordon plunges into the pool to join her, and Luke and Tom head off to the changing rooms.

'What about that, then?' Luke says as he steps out of his shorts and hangs them on a hook, feeling happier than he has in weeks. 'Sam's single again. Finally got rid of that dickhead Len. She's nice, isn't she?'

Tom puckers up his chin as if giving the question serious thought, then stretches his arms high above his head in a taut, muscular movement. 'Sam?' he says with a lopsided smile. 'She's not bad at all.'

When he arrives home that afternoon, Luke finds the house quite still. He pauses in the corridor, listening, and follows the sound of the television to the dim curtain-drawn living room, where Kitty lies on the sofa with her elephant, staring vacantly at the TV.

'Where's Mum?' he asks her, pulling back the curtains to let the evening sun stream in.

Kitty squawks, pointing at the television. 'Can't see!'

'It's *Songs of Praise*, Kitty! You don't even like it.'

'Do!' she snaps angrily, and she turns her face into the cushion.

Luke pinches her big toe, making her snigger. 'I said, where's Mum?'

'Bed,' she replies, snatching her toe back and scrunching up like a hedgehog.

'And Dad?'

'Doing the stretchy thing,' she replies, flexing her arms wide. 'With Uncle Simon.'

Luke ruffles her hair and leaves the room, walking back through the hallway and out on to the front path. He finds Dad in the garage, just as Kitty had described, standing at the centre of the concrete space, using his chest expander, while Simon sits on a motheaten armchair in the corner, drinking beer. Dad's teeth are clenched in an agony of exertion as he draws the wooden handles up and out, stretching the rusty-looking coils across his chest.

'Bloody hell, Dad, I wouldn't do that without your top on,' Luke says, making Dad jump back in surprise. 'You'll get your chest hairs trapped in the springs.'

Simon raises his beer bottle in Luke's direction, a slick of foam clinging to his moustache. Dad puts the expander down and shakes his arms out, rolling his shoulders back as if he's limbering up for an important race. 'Good day at work?'

'It was OK. What's with all the keep-fit?'

Dad reaches round and pulls his heel up against his thigh in a stretch. 'I'm thinking of doing the Island Marathon next year.'

'Really?' Luke gives Dad a disbelieving frown.

'Yes, really. I've done it before, you know.'

'No, you haven't.' He turns to Simon and pulls a face.

Dad stares at him, looking insulted. 'Yes, I have. I did have a life before you came along, Luke. Quite an exciting life, at that.'

'So if I go inside now and ask Mum about the time you ran the Isle of Wight Marathon, she'll be able to tell me all about it?'

Dad reaches down and picks up the chest expander, turning his back on Luke and resuming his exercise. 'If she can remember it.'

Simon grins broadly.

'*Dad*. It's hardly the kind of thing you'd forget, your husband running the Marathon. So what was your time, then?'

'Two hours, fifty-four seconds.'

Luke shakes his head and walks away. 'Now I know you're lying,' he says, and he returns to the house to look for Mum.

He finds her in the bedroom, curled up on top of the patchwork bedspread, her back curved away from him. The curtains are open, but the room is gloomy, where the sun has moved round to the other side of the house. Luke stands in the doorway for a few seconds, watching her shoulders rise and fall, trying to establish whether she's sleeping or awake.

'Mum?' he says softly, taking a step closer, wondering if she and Dad have had another argument.

She inclines her head a fraction, letting him know she's heard, and he quietly treads across the carpet to sit on her side of the bed, looking down at her drawn face.

'Mum, are you OK?'

'I'm fine,' she whispers, not meeting his eye. When she does look up, she attempts a smile, only managing a downturned grimace.

'You're not,' he says, putting a hand on her upper arm.

'Is Kitty alright?' she asks, running a loose hand across her face.

He pulls his hand back into his lap, and fiddles with an oil mark at the hem of his shorts. 'She's watching the telly. Dad's in the garage. *Training*,' he says, hoping it will provoke some amusement. It doesn't.

She releases a slow breath and closes her eyes again.

'So I see Simon's here,' he says. 'Does that mean you've sorted things out with him?'

She lies still. The curtains sway lightly beside the open window and Luke surveys the familiar items of his parent's room: Mum's dusty stack of unread books, pushed to one corner of the windowsill; the chair on Dad's side, piled up with crumpled clothes; Mum's dressing table, scattered with perfumes and hair rollers and bottles of gold-capped nail varnish. He glances along the length of her fragile body, his eyes coming to rest on her pretty painted toenails, feeling like he's teetering on the edge of an unfinished dream, about to drop back in.

'Mum?'

She opens her eyes and swipes away her tears, releasing a slow breath before she speaks. 'Simon's going to be moving in for a while.'

10

Met Office report for the Isle of Wight, early August 1976:
Maximum temperature 77°F/25.2°C

On August 5th, Big Ben stops running. Luke stands in the early morning kitchen while everyone else sleeps, eating Marmite on toast, listening to the news on the radio.

Dad appears in the doorway, turning up the volume to hear the end of the report.

'Metal fatigue,' Luke says. 'Apparently it's knackered.'

'Bloody hell,' Dad replies, filling the kettle and fetching down two mugs. 'You know the world's going to pot when you can't even rely on Big Ben any more. And you heard they've appointed a drought minister now? It's a bit late in the day, if you ask me. Should have done something about it months ago. What's he going to do, wave his magic wand and miraculously fill the reservoirs? I don't think so.'

Luke watches his father as he makes the tea and slides four slices of bread beneath the grill.

'Is she OK, Dad?' he asks, placing his dirty plate beside the sink.

'Your mum? She's fine. She'll be even better once she's had breakfast in bed.'

'You know what I mean. You can't have missed the fact that she's been miserable since Simon moved in. She's been in a right state all week.'

'She's just tired. She'll soon snap out of it.' He rubs Luke's back and places a jar of jam on the tray. 'Are you popping in to see Nan on your way back tonight? You haven't been round there for a while.'

'That's what she says about you every time I call round. You should make more of an effort, you know, Dad. She's *your* mum.'

'Well, I've been busy. Stop off and buy her a nice tin of biscuits for me? She'd like that.' He finishes making the tea and loads up the breakfast tray. 'And stay out of the living room, will you, son? Simon might need a bit of a lie-in today.'

Tom's on a different shift, so Luke takes his scooter and sets off alone in the early sunshine, enjoying the peace of the calm roads and avenues. As he turns out of Blake Avenue, he sees Sara Newbury with three of her dogs on the verge outside her gate. Even though it's still early, she's only wearing shorts and a bikini top, and she clutches one of the chihuahuas snugly under her crêpey brown arm. She stiffens as he approaches, obviously suspicious of a helmeted stranger passing by at this time in the morning. Luke is relieved when the Rottweiler takes no notice of him but instead lowers his backside and pigeon-steps around for a moment, feverishly sniffing to locate the optimum patch for his bowel evacuation. Luke slows to a stop a few feet away, conspicuously watching Sara Newbury, confident that she has no idea who he is behind the cover of his crash helmet.

'I hope you're going to clear that up,' he calls through his open visor, keeping his voice friendly and nodding towards the mountain of dog turd that now adorns the scrubby grass verge.

She gasps, furious, and pushes open her purple gate to wave the dogs inside. Luke carries on up the road, feeling the warmth of the morning breaking through, as the hum of lawnmowers and birdsong starts to fill the air. The distant whisper of the sea is always there, a transparent layer that lies beneath all other sounds, as it rolls over the beaches that surround the island, ever constant. Fleetingly, he wonders if he'll miss the island when he's gone; he wonders if it will miss him.

Turning into Lark Road, he stops outside Martin's house and pauses to watch the swallows as they swoop above the rooftop and disappear into the back garden. He props up his scooter and carefully unstraps Martin's *Young Americans* album, removing it from its carrier bag and checking it over to make sure it's not been damaged on the way. He walks up the front path and props it against the doorstep, taking a step back to look up towards the first-floor windows, where the curtains are drawn. The red graffiti has been scrubbed back again, but a shadow of it remains, the flecks over the front step like a blood trail from the house. He hasn't had any contact with Martin since he stopped by with Tom last week; he's got to get that film off him, but he's not sure how to broach it after the way their last conversation played out. Luke knows he was an arsehole, but he doesn't seem to have it in him to apologise, and he's not sure that Martin would want to know anyway. He cranes his neck to look at the upstairs window, blinking at the reflected sun and willing his friend to appear behind the glass and make it all alright again. But the curtains remain closed as the house sleeps on, and Luke walks away, back along the path, and out through the wrecked wooden gate.

Samantha and Gordon are on the same shift as Luke, and after work they decide to avoid the crowded pool and take a swim in the sea instead. Luke's irritated that Gordon wants to come along, that he can't take a hint and let them have a bit of time to themselves, but he does his best to hide it lest Samantha notices and thinks he's an idiot.

They find a quiet spot a little way along the beach, beyond the jetty, and stretch out on their towels, side by side, with Samantha in the middle. The water laps gently against the shingle shore, and the sun beats down in a seemingly endless blanket of heat.

'This is the life, eh?' says Gordon, flexing his scrawny pink toes. 'I thought I'd miss out on the summer holidays, working all the time. But we get the best of both worlds, don't we? Like they say, every cloud has a silver lining.'

'You're like a walking encyclopaedia of clichés,' Luke says. He's propped up on his elbows, admiring the increasingly dark tan of his own belly.

Samantha flicks his ankle with her foot. 'Don't be mean!'

'Well, he is!' Luke replies, resisting the urge to flick her back.

'It's true,' says Gordon, his voice serious. 'I am. My mum's always saying so. There's no smoke without fire.' He sits up, cross-legged, reaching for a pebble to roll between his palms. 'So, what do we think of the current number one?'

'Oh, I love it!' Samantha replies, brushing sand from her towel with a delicate little movement of her foot.

Behind his sunglasses, Luke pretends to stare into space, allowing his eyes to linger on her honeyed legs. 'What is it?'

'Elton John and Kiki Dee. You know – *Don't go breakin' my heart* – ' Gordon breaks into song, shimmying his shoulders like a girl.

'Yeah, yeah – I know it!' Luke interrupts, embarrassed to be sitting with him. 'Thanks for that, Gordon.'

'I know you love me really, Lukester.' Gordon sighs and flops back against his towel as Samantha gives Luke a knowing little smile.

'You do, though, don't you, Luke? Who couldn't love our Gordy?'

Luke grunts, watching a trio of rowing boats pass by, filled with holidaymakers and camp staff. A little girl, about Kitty's age, waves at them, and Luke waves back.

'That's sweet,' says Samantha, lying back and stretching her arms high above her head so that her stomach caves in to reveal two achingly dark hollows where her hips meet the top of her bikini briefs. 'Not many young men would bother waving back, would they?'

'Wouldn't they?' he replies, flipping over on to his front. 'I've got a little sister, so I suppose I'm used to it.'

'Have you?' She rolls on to her side so she's facing him, with her back to Gordon, who's now breathing deeply with his T-shirt draped across his face. 'What's her name?'

'Kitty. She's four.'

Samantha rests her head on her arm and gazes at him, her face looking all dreamy.

'Are you alright now?' he asks, deciding to act on the moment. 'After your break-up with Len?'

She looks down, and then her eyes slowly travel up the length of his body, until they meet his. 'It was a lucky escape,' she replies. 'How about you? Those bruises he gave you were pretty bad.'

'I think it looked worse than it felt.'

'Really?'

He laughs. '*No*. It hurt like hell. But, it's fine now.' He turns on to his side in a mirror of her, pulling his chin in as he checks out his chest and torso. 'See, all gone.'

Samantha reaches over and runs a finger along the groove between two ribs, making him flinch as her fingertip brushes the rim of his bellybutton. She looks over her shoulder to where Gordon lies beneath his T-shirt, and leans in to kiss Luke, her tongue slipping between his lips in a single, shocking movement. She pulls back and smiles boldly, her eyes lingering on the obvious swelling inside his nylon swimming trunks. She presses the flat of her hand against his groin, fitting her pretty fingers around the outline of his cock.

'You're very brown,' she says, increasing the pressure.

'Mediterranean blood,' he replies, holding her gaze.

'You're kidding?' Her hand releases him and drifts to his wrist, and he wonders if she's able to feel his racing pulse through his skin.

'Yeah, I'm kidding.'

Luke is suddenly aware of just how close they are; how her small breasts are pressed together as she lies on her side; how her long fingers now move and caress the sand between their towels. He smiles at her, trying to incorporate his puppydog look at the same time.

'Are you OK?' she asks, lifting her head, looking concerned.

He clears his throat self-consciously. 'I'm fine.'

'Oh, sorry. Your eyes went a bit funny. For a minute there I thought you were going to *faint*.' She pats him on the hand again and rolls over on to her back, draping an arm across her forehead.

A glider sails across the skyline, momentarily casting them in shadow.

'You know, you're right, Gordy,' she sighs. 'This *is* the life. Look at the three of us, lying here under the sun. We're all young, free and single, aren't we? It doesn't get much better than this.'

Luke arrives home by late afternoon, having called in on Nanna on the way back. He helped her out with a few jobs in the back garden and stopped for a cup of tea while she counted out five one-pound notes and slipped them into a brown envelope for him to put by for his birthday.

'How's your pal Martin?' she asked. When Luke tried to avoid the subject, she clucked her tongue disapprovingly. 'Just because you've got all these fancy new friends up at the holiday camp, don't you go dropping Martin. There's no friends like old friends.'

It preoccupied him all the way home, as he grew increasingly anxious about Martin, and about the missing reels of film, and he even stopped briefly at the end of Lark Road, staring up the street towards Martin's house, wrestling with the idea of calling for him. But in the end he decided against it; he wouldn't know what to say.

When he first gets home he thinks the house is empty, as he unlocks the front door and makes his way through the cool, quiet hallway. He rests his helmet on the kitchen bench and goes straight to the sink to splash water over his face and neck, running himself a glassful which he drinks thirstily. It's only as he sets the tumbler down on the side that he hears voices on the back lawn. He pushes open the kitchen door and wanders out into the garden. Mum and Dad and a woman Luke doesn't recognise are standing at the boundary to the Michaelses' garden, talking to Mike and Diana across the fence. Simon Drake sits apart from the group, reclining in one of the deckchairs in his shorts and sandals, drinking beer beside the willow tree. He smoothes his forefinger and thumb across his sandy moustache, as if deep in contemplation.

The woman turns her head and starts visibly when she sees Luke walking towards them.

'Oh, Luke,' says Mum, looking pale and flustered. 'You're home!'

Luke claws at his damp hair. 'Hi.'

'Hello! Marie McKee,' the woman says, an efficient little hand shooting out to shake his.

'Oh – how rude of me!' Mum flaps. 'Luke, darling, this is Marie. You know, as in John and Marie?'

Diana waves from the other side of the fence. From here, he can only see her upper half, and she's wearing an orange bikini top, her shoulders shiny with oil. She smiles at him like a sleepy cat. 'How's work? Luke's working with Mike's Tom, you know, Marie. At the holiday camp.'

Dad and Mike don't say anything, and Luke wonders what they were talking about before he turned up.

'Tom says it's a lovely job,' Diana continues, bringing her hands up to adjust her straw hat. 'They get full use of the pool and all the facilities.'

Dad clears his throat. 'Luke, can you give us a few minutes? Marie only arrived a short while ago, and we just need to have a quick chat with her.'

Luke raises a quizzical eyebrow at Simon, who languidly raises his hand to return a salute. Dad flicks his head towards the back door, to hurry him along, and Luke holds his hands up in defeat, returning to the house and wandering into the cool living room, where the far window opens straight out opposite Mike's fence. He finds Kitty on the other side of the room, flopped out on the sofa with her thumb hanging from her sleeping mouth, and settles into the seat beside her, exhaling a jaded sigh as he eases his shoes off. He can't wait to get off this island; he's sick of being constantly pushed away, sick of being forever on the outside, listening in.

'So, who else saw the photo, Marie?' Mum asks, her voice travelling in through the window, crisp and clear.

Luke sits forward in his seat.

'A better question might be, who didn't?' Marie answers shrilly. 'I mean, could it have been in a more public place? The post office! Good God, it's just about the busiest place in the whole town!'

'Slow down, now,' says Mike, trying to take control. He'd have been good in the army. 'How did you come to hear about it, Marie?'

There's a moment's silence, and Luke resists the temptation to sneak over and spy from the edges of the curtains.

'Joyce Harrison phoned me just after lunch; I was out in the rose garden, spraying the greenfly. I could have died on the spot, and Joyce was so embarrassed. She could hardly say the words – a *pornographic image*, she called it. She said there'd been phone calls all morning long, between the committee members, deciding what to do about it.'

'What a bunch of busybodies!' Mike exclaims. 'I hate to think what kind of fuss the education authorities will make over *your* photograph, Simon.'

'Screw them,' Simon retorts, and Luke realises that he must have had more than one of those beers this afternoon. Simon always swears more when he's pissed.

'Joyce was so apologetic,' Marie continues, 'but in the end she said that, after careful consideration, they were all agreed that I would have to step down from my position as chairman of the Silver Jubilee planning committee.' She lets out a little cry. 'On *moral* grounds!'

Luke hears Mum comforting her, and the lower voices of Dad and Mike discussing the situation to one side.

'Mr Linder from the post office dropped the picture by soon afterwards, in an envelope. He said he'd taken it down as soon as he'd got wind of it, but that he couldn't be sure just how long it had been up on the noticeboard.'

'That was good of him,' Dad says, and the others all mumble in agreement.

'OK. We need to establish who's responsible for these photographs,' Mike says. 'Marie, I'm sorry to have to ask you this, but what exactly were you doing in the picture?'

'I was on the lawn,' she sniffs. 'I'm standing on the lawn, with a glass of bubbly. And there are others in the background, but their backs are turned away. It's quite a close-up, so there's no doubt it's me. *Oh, God –* ' now she almost howls ' – you can see *everything*!'

'But who would do this?' Mum asks. 'First Simon, now Marie. Who's next? I can't bear it!'

There's a sudden atmosphere of alarm about to break out in Blake Avenue, and Luke slides down into his seat, covering his face with his hands as a fresh sense of dread grips him.

'Everyone, just calm yourselves down!' says Mike. 'I'm afraid we're all going to have to steel ourselves for the worst. There's no way of knowing who's behind this, or what, if any, other pictures they have in their possession. Marie! Come on, now! It'll pass. Be forgotten in a matter of days. So, where's John at the moment? Thought he'd be here with you.'

Another pause. 'He locked himself in the study and won't come out.'

'Oh, dear.'

'I think he's having some kind of a breakdown. He started ranting about selling up and moving back to the mainland. He thinks it'll ruin us.'

'Nonsense!' says Mike.

'He's had a shock,' says Dad. 'He'll come round, Marie, you'll see.'

'Maybe he won't,' Simon calls over from his deckchair, his words slurred. 'Maybe the men in white coats will come to take him away.' He laughs heartily as the others clamour to censure him, ticking him off like a naughty schoolboy.

'Take no notice, Marie,' Mum says. 'He's *drunk*.'

Mike claps his hands together – Luke knows it's him, having witnessed the gesture so many times before. 'It must be near cocktail time! Why don't you all come over and join us for a tipple – take our minds off this damnable charade?'

Simultaneously everyone declines, and sounds of the group breaking up drift in through the open window, as they disperse into little islands. Luke gives Kitty a nudge, waking her up. He sits beside her as she rubs her face, peering at him in confusion, her head cocked to one side as she listens to Mum and Dad seeing Marie off at the front door.

'Morning?' Kitty asks Luke, pulling her little legs around and off the sofa.

'No. Nearly night-time.'

'Hmph!' she says, crumpling her chin. 'Stop teasing, Lu-lu!' She slaps his knee and stomps away on wobbly legs, casting a fierce glare back at him as she leaves the room.

Luke flops back against the cushions, and gazes up at the shell-studded lampshade in the centre of the ceiling as the afternoon sunlight slices across his brow, and his mind whirrs. There were only a few party pictures on that reel of film, that was what Martin said, so they might be safe. But what of the other reel, the one Martin can't find? What if that's discovered, and put on display? He's not sure his parents' marriage would survive it.

As if she's read his thoughts, Mum appears in the doorway, with Kitty on her hip.

'Hi, Lukey,' she says in a sad, singsong way. The front of her hair is pushed up, where she's been anxiously running her hand through it.

'Hi, Mum.'

She tilts her head forlornly. 'Are you OK, my boy?'

'I'm OK,' he replies, his eyes never leaving hers. 'Are *you* OK, Mum?'

She purses her pale lips and nods slowly, blinking once. 'I'm fine, my love. I'm fine.'

She kisses the top of Kitty's head and places her down on the carpet, as Simon enters the room, shaking his hair from his face and rolling the tension from his bare shoulders. He's caught the sun, and his skin is scorched a warm tan beneath the fair hairs of his lean torso. Kitty raises her arms and he lifts her up in a bear hug, planting a warm kiss on her forehead. 'Hello, Kit-Kat.'

Kitty squeezes his cheeks between her palms, making him pucker up like a goldfish.

'Blub-blub-blub,' he says, and she squeals with laughter.

Mum gives Luke a final weak smile then leaves the room, and he hears the door to her bedroom softly click shut. Simon carries Kitty out into the back garden to join Dad, who's smoking one of Simon's cigarettes and gazing up at the sky. Luke sits beside the window, watching the two men in their shorts and bare chests, as they stand at the centre of the parched lawn deep in conversation, with Kitty pedalling back and forth on her red tricycle, revived by her afternoon nap. Luke leaves the room and heads straight for the phone stand beside the front door, dialling Martin's number.

To Luke's surprise, he answers the phone on the second ring. 'Hello?'

Luke hesitates, not sure what to say. 'It's me. Luke.'

'Thanks for the album,' Martin replies after a pause.

'No problem. Sorry I kept it so long.'

'That's OK.' Martin clears his throat loudly. 'I'll make you a tape of it. I said I would.'

'It's a brilliant album. The best.' Luke hesitates while he tries to find the right words. He gazes along the hallway at the closed door that conceals his mother, where he imagines her balled up on the bed in the grip of inertia. 'Mart, mate. Can we meet up? I really need to get out of here.'

He can hear Martin's breathing, the low rumble of the TV in the background, even the tiniest sounds of evening birdsong.

'Mart?'

'Alright. Shall I see you by the pier?'

Luke presses his fingers against the back of his neck, trying to ease away the knots that have gathered in little bunches at the top of his spine. 'See you in five minutes.'

When he arrives Martin's already waiting and they walk their bikes along the esplanade, with the pinkly dipping sun at their backs. At first Martin seems to avoid any eye contact, and Luke wonders if this is it – perhaps they're just too different; perhaps this is where it all ends.

'Mart, there's been another photograph. In the post office this time. One of Marie McKee.'

Martin scans the cracks in the pavement as he walks along, taking care to tread between them. 'Really?'

'Yep. She was round at ours just now. They were all out in the back garden, talking over the fence with Diana and Fatty Michaels.'

'That's two, then. Two photos.'

'So, you reckon there's only few on that reel? What – four? Five?'

'More like four.'

'So, there's at least two more photos to come out.'

Martin nods.

Luke reaches out for Martin's handlebars, to make him stop and look up. 'Listen, I know we can't do anything about those photos, the ones the police have lost. So we just have to pray to God that there weren't any of Mum and Dad on there, and that it all just blows over. But the thing is, Mart, you've got this other film somewhere, haven't you? All the time it's not found – well, I won't be able to sleep at night, mate. We need to find it.' He pauses for effect, and Martin nods again, still concentrating hard on the pavement. 'My mum's gone into meltdown, man. You should see her. She cries all the time, and she keeps shutting herself in her room. And Dad's spending all his time in the garage with Simon, pretending nothing's happened.'

Martin rubs his nose, his drooping eyes downcast.

'I don't know how Kitty would cope if they split up,' Luke adds, giving Martin's handlebars a little shake. 'She's only four, you know?'

Martin's jaw clenches, the muscles below his ears standing out like tiny bumps. 'Why did they do it, Luke? Why would they go to a party like that?'

They prop their bikes up against the railings and drop down on to the beach where they can sit against the sea wall in the warm glow of the sunset.

'I dunno, mate. I've asked myself the same thing a million times. I mean, look at us – we're seventeen, eighteen – we've got our whole lives ahead of us. *We're* meant to be out there partying, meeting girls – having sex – not them! *Urghh*. At this rate I'll be drawing my pension before I finally get with a girl.'

Martin sniffs behind his curtain of lank hair. 'Still no luck with Samantha, then?'

Luke laughs briefly, running his fists over his face. 'Not yet, despite my best efforts. But she's finally split up with Len, and she has been giving me a few *very* positive signals.'

'So maybe you've got a chance?'

'I reckon. Listen, Mart, we've got to find that other film, you know. It'd be a disaster if it got into the wrong hands. I think my mum would top herself or something.'

Martin says nothing.

As he gazes out across the sand, Luke spots gnarly old Sara Newbury at the shoreline with her pack of dogs. She's handing out treats, signalling for them to sit, attempting to photograph them before they scatter like mice. Her high voice rises every now and then – *sit!* – *stay!* – before she hands out more treats and tries again, before moving up the beach.

'Keep looking, will you, mate?' he says to Martin, giving him a nudge. 'I won't sleep properly till I know it's been found.'

Neither speaks for a while, as they watch the tide lapping at the shore where the sanderlings run in the shallow waters. The orange-red reflection of the sky stretches across the wet sand and for a moment it feels as if they're the only people on the island, the last remaining inhabitants.

'Have you had any more trouble with the graffiti?' Luke asks.

Martin shakes his head. 'It was just kids. Dad caught them last time and waved his shotgun around to scare them off. It wasn't even loaded.'

Luke laughs. 'So, is everything OK with your dad now?'

Martin gazes out to sea. 'Not bad. He's over at the doctor's at the moment, about his bad back.'

Luke picks up a stone and throws it down the beach, trying to hit a bottle that's washed up on the pebbles. 'You don't have to get home straight away, do you? I thought maybe we could go for a pint?'

'I'd better not. I want to make sure Dad's alright. See how he got on. Hopefully he'll have some better tablets now.'

'Does he take that much trouble over you, mate?'

Martin throws a stone at the bottle, clipping the sand just beyond it. 'He gave me this yesterday.' He reaches into his pocket and pulls out a shiny silver lighter. 'He said it was a present from my mum – said she'd want me to have it. It's a proper Zippo. Look, it's even got his initials engraved on the side.' He flips it open and lights it, *ker-chink*, watching the

218

pale flame dance for a moment before flipping it shut and returning it to his pocket.

'That's nice, mate.' Luke throws again, wondering what use a lighter is to someone who doesn't even smoke.

For a few long minutes they quietly watch the tide rippling gently against the sand as the evening light draws in, until Luke breaks the silence. 'You know, some day you should think about moving out. You can't stay living at home forever.' He turns to look at Martin, who's concentrating on his target. 'Like they say, mate, spread your wings.'

Martin turns away, pretending to search for the right stone.

Luke throws another, this time hitting the bottle and spinning it in the opposite direction. 'Maybe you'd even meet a nice girl if you had a bit more freedom to come and go as you please.'

Martin remains silent, and Luke knows he can't push it any further.

'So, what do you think?' says Luke, handing over a large pebble, and indicating at another bottle a few feet away down the beach. 'We could just go for a quick pint before you go home. What d'you say?'

'Maybe some other time,' Martin says after some time, and he launches his missile.

It hits the glass bottle, spraying shards of green glass far and wide.

Late that night, Luke hears the rattle and thump of Dad and Simon, stumbling in from the pub.

'*Shhhh!*' Dad hisses loudly, as Simon tries to stifle his laughter, and the wooden umbrella stand tumbles over with a crash.

Within moments Mum is in the hallway too, right outside Luke's bedroom door, whispering angrily at the pair of them, telling Simon she's had enough, that he should be back home with his own wife.

'She doesn't want me,' he mutters.

'Can you blame her, in this state? Honestly, Simon, we've had you here for long enough now. Sooner or later you've got to go home and sort things out with Laura.'

'She doesn't want me – and she doesn't want kids.' He sounds like a petulant child. 'You know, Rich?'

'I know, pal, I know,' says Dad, his words coming out slushy. 'Come on, sir. Another drink?'

'Can I go and see Kitty? Say goodnight? Little Kit-Kat?'

'*Richard*!' Mum shrieks. 'This *has* to stop!'

'C'mon, *Jo*, love. He's my bess friend. We can't just throw him out into the street. You go back to bed, love. Go on. *Go on.*'

Their voices move away, and Mum's bedroom door closes, as the low voices of the two drunken men disappear behind the glass door of the living room, and the house is quiet again.

11

Met Office report for the Isle of Wight, mid-August 1976:
Maximum temperature 78°F/25.6°C

There hasn't been a drop of rain for almost six weeks, and the entire island now has a bleached-out appearance, where the grass has scorched dry and the earth ruptures with drought. Out on the streets and pavements the asphalt softens and bubbles, clinging to the soles of flip-flops, scalding the feet of those foolish enough to go barefoot along the esplanade at the height of the day.

On Sunday morning, the phone rings just as Luke emerges from his bed, startling him as he rubs his drowsy eyes.

'Hello,' he answers, his voice groggy with sleep. He was out late after work last night, celebrating his exam results, and his head thumps a dull beat.

'Richard – John McKee here,' says the voice at the end of the line. 'There's been another photograph. It's Laura Drake this time.'

'Oh,' Luke replies, glancing along the hall for signs of Dad.

'Cowardly bastards put it up on the board outside St John's during this morning's service. I thought perhaps it's best if you or Joanna let Laura know. I know things between her and Simon are a little strained of late. Richard?'

'I'll just get him,' Luke replies, and he drops the receiver against the phone stand with a clatter.

In the kitchen, Dad goes off to take the call and Luke pours himself a glass of milk, sliding on to the kitchen bench to sit beside Kitty. He watches Mum as she hangs around by the kitchen door, casually trying to listen in on Dad's telephone conversation, waiting for him to finish the call. When Dad finally returns to the kitchen, he and Mum step out on to the garden path, pushing the door shut to talk together in hushed tones. He might not be able to hear them, but from his kitchen seat Luke can still see the rise and fall of Dad's hands beyond the glass panels, moving through the air expansively, betraying his disquiet.

'What's up?' he asks when they return a few minutes later.

'Nothing, nosy parker!' Dad replies, too merrily.

Mum fiddles with the teatowel, folding it and unfolding it, seemingly oblivious to Luke and Kitty sitting at the bench. 'Don't wake Simon yet,' she tells Dad. 'Let him have a lie-in.'

Dad starts preparing breakfast for the family, punctuating his activities with jovial quips, joking with Kitty while Mum lingers at the back door, gazing out into the garden beyond.

'One egg or two?' Dad asks her, patting her bum as he passes, making her flinch.

'*Richard*,' she hisses.

Dad grimaces at Luke, pretending to look scared behind Mum's back. He's got a cushion zip mark pressed into his forehead from his night spent sleeping on the sofa. Luke found him and Simon in the living room this morning, Dad sprawled out on the sofa, Simon flat out on his camp bed, his arms straight along his sides, his parched-looking mouth hanging open. The room stank of stale beer and ashtrays.

'I'll have two,' says Luke, stooping below the table to tie his shoelaces. 'Two eggs. So, what was that all about on the phone?' He looks up to watch his parents' reactions.

Dad returns to the hob, his back resolutely turned to the group. 'Nothing important.' Mum stares at him blankly and shakes her head, as he strides across the room and switches on the radio, tuning it in to some pop channel before cracking a sizzling egg into the frying pan.

'I'll make the tea,' says Luke, getting up and indicating for Mum to sit in his place. Mutely, she slides across the bench to be opposite Kitty.

'Are you sad, Mummy?' Kitty asks, reaching over the table to pat Mum's hand.

Mum reaches out and clasps Kitty's hand between her palms. 'No!' she says brightly, and turns her face to the wall.

'Mummy?' Kitty pleads.

Mum waves her hand in front of her face. 'I'm fine, Kitty! I'm just a bit hot. I never thought I'd say it, but I'm fed up with this weather – it's just too much now!'

Luke stirs a sugar into his mug, and pushes open the other door into the garden.

'That's better,' says Mum, and she gives him a forced smile as he passes her a cup of tea. 'So, no work today, Luke?'

'No – now I've got my place confirmed, I thought I'd sort out some of my packing ready for September, work out what to take, what to leave behind. The bookshop phoned to say my textbooks have arrived, so I can pick them up tomorrow.'

Dad slides the plates on to the table and sits on the bench beside Mum.

'Goodness, it won't be long before you're off, Luke,' she says, her fingers covering her mouth nervously.

He sits at the end of the table and picks up his knife and fork. 'First week in September – that's when I'll be moving into my rooms. I think lessons start the week after, something like that.'

Mum pushes at her egg yolk with the tip of her knife. 'It doesn't seem like five minutes since you were Kitty's age, and now look at you, nearly eighteen and off into the world on your own – ' She suddenly gasps. 'Luke! Your birthday!'

Luke carries on eating. 'It's this Wednesday.'

'Is it?' asks Dad.

'We said we'd do a party, Richard. Remember?' She looks as if she might cry.

'Did we?'

'Don't worry about it, Mum. Honestly, I'd rather do something on my own anyway. Tom said he'd drive us over to the *Ryde Queen* up at Newport. There's a group of us going from work.'

'But it's your *eighteenth*. You're supposed to do something special on your eighteenth birthday, Luke.' She puts down her knife and fork and stares at her full plate of food. 'I can't believe we haven't organised anything.'

He glances up and sees just how ragged she looks. 'Mum, do you think you should go to the doctor's?'

'What on earth for?' Dad says, incredulous. He turns to look at Mum, who now has her face in her hands.

'That's not normal, Dad,' Luke says quietly, with a nod of his head. 'Look how thin she's got, and she's hardly been outside for the past month – it's the hottest summer of the century, and she looks paler now than I've ever seen her. Sorry, Mum, but it's true.'

Dad crams the last of his toast into his mouth and glares at Luke, chewing it fiercely before washing it down with tea. 'Well, you certainly know how to make a woman feel better about herself, don't you? Nice work, Luke.'

'*What*? Bloody hell, Dad. I only said something because I'm worried! I'm not the one who got her in this state, am I?'

'And I suppose you're trying to suggest I am?' He slams out of his seat, ineptly scraping bacon rinds into the bin.

'The birds could have had those,' Luke retorts, feeling like an idiot the moment he says it.

Mum is sitting upright now, at an angle with her back to the men, walking her fingers back and forth across the table to distract Kitty.

'The birds?' Dad yells. A livid vein throbs on the side of his temple. 'What on earth are you talking about, Luke?'

'I'm talking about you! You and your stupid parties!' Luke shouts back.

'Luke, stop it!' Mum spins round to face him, her eyes wild.

'Do you really think you can keep something like this a secret, Mum? You all think you're so bloody sophisticated, that you can all handle it, you and your big swanky friends – but you can't!'

Simon appears in the doorway, squinting his puffy eyes against the bright light of the kitchen.

'Luke, I'm warning you – ' says Dad, grabbing for the rest of the plates, scraping them so hard over the bin they sound as if they might shatter.

'Please!' Mum beseeches.

The noise is deafening: the music from the radio, the plate-scraping, the shouting and gasping. Luke pushes past Simon, thumping the doorframe as he goes. 'Well, guess what? You're not sophisticated, or special, or clever!'

'LUKE!' Dad bellows, dropping the last plate into the sink with such force that it cracks in two.

'Christ,' Simon says, running a hand through his unruly blond hair and stepping back.

Luke lurches back in through the door and picks up his empty mug, lobbing it across the kitchen to land hard against the broken plate. 'You're no different from that idiot next door. You're just a bunch of – of *fuckers*!'

'Language, Lu-lu!' Kitty screams, silencing them all.

No one speaks, and Kitty sits immobile, clearly stunned that she's managed to silence the room. After what seems like an endless impasse, Luke stoops to kiss Kitty on the top of her head, before leaving the room. 'Sorry, Kitty,' he calls back, and he walks calmly along the hall and out of the house, slamming the front door as he leaves.

On the evening of Luke's birthday, Tom calls at eight to drive them over to Newport. Luke is in the kitchen eating a sandwich, watching Mum as she quietly tends to her wine production, when Tom walks in and knocks at the pine table to announce his arrival.

This afternoon, after three days of silence, Luke finally gave in and spoke to his parents, after they got Kitty to call him out to the garden for a surprise tea party. Mum presented him with a triple-decker sponge cake, iced and decorated with eighteen candles and all his favourite childhood sweets, and Dad handed him an envelope containing eighteen pounds, as well as a brand new Swiss Army knife, shiny and unused. In typical Wolff family style, Sunday's argument goes unmentioned, and despite the forced jollity of the day a cautious atmosphere still weighs heavy.

'Alright, hippy?' Tom reaches across the table and flicks Luke's hair, before noticing Mum hunched down among her wine barrels, checking through the tubes and joiners. 'Hey-ho, Mrs W,' he says, giving her one of his charming smiles. 'Hope you don't mind me letting myself in – the front door was open.'

'Not at all, Tom,' she says too brightly, pushing her hair off her face, rolling out her breeziest voice for Luke's birthday. She puts her hands on her hips and gives Tom a soppy smile. 'It's *so* nice of you to take Luke out tonight – he's really looking forward to it.'

Luke nods drily at Tom.

'No problem. I've been meaning to check out the *Ryde Queen* since I got here. Nice to have someone to go with.' He places a carrier bag on the table and pushes its boxy shape across towards Luke. 'Happy birthday, man.'

Mum tightens the top of her wine barrel and dries her hands on a teatowel, folding it neatly and placing it on the dresser. She stares into space for a few seconds, before noticing Tom's gift. 'From you, Tom?'

Luke pats the shape, rotating it slowly as if trying to guess the contents.

'Sorry it's not wrapped. Didn't think you'd mind too much, Lukey-boy.' He sits astride the bench opposite, resting his back against the wall, casually drumming his fingers on the table.

Luke reaches inside the bag and pulls out a shoe box. Inside is a pair of green Converse All Star baseball boots.

'Mate, this is too much,' he says, holding one up, turning it over in his hands. 'They're brilliant, man. Brilliant.' He slides to the edge of the bench and kicks off his shoes, loosening up the new white laces and easing his feet in. 'Ace,' he says, nodding to himself and smiling broadly. '*And* they're the right fit.'

Mum smiles knowingly. 'So *that's* why you asked for his shoe size last week.'

'I was back home at the weekend, meeting some old mates, and I picked them up then. There's this brilliant place on the King's Road. It's got all the latest stuff – printed T-shirts, studded belts. You should see the woman who runs it; she's proper punk.'

'Ooh, punks,' says Mum. 'Aren't they the ones with the chains and piercings? Sounds a bit brutal to me, all that anarchy.'

Luke ignores her as he readjusts his laces, wishing his mum would go off and do something else, with her stupid cheery voice and fake smile.

'That's where people get it all wrong, Mrs W,' says Tom, stretching out his legs and crossing his ankles on the wooden bench. 'Really, it's a lifestyle – an attitude – a whole new way of expression through music.'

Mum looks thoughtful. 'Interesting. There's always something new, isn't there?'

'You know what, Luke, she's cool, your mum.' Tom rubs his jaw appreciatively.

'*Ha*,' Luke snorts, not looking at Mum.

'It's true, man. She's one cool mamma.'

'Stop teasing.' Mum laughs. She turns away to run a sink of hot water, and Luke pushes the bench out, irritably motioning that they should leave.

'So Mr W's out with my old man tonight, isn't he?' Tom asks from the doorway.

'I think so. Richard and Simon went off to call for him about half an hour ago,' Mum smiles over her shoulder as they leave. 'Have a good time, boys. Look after him, Tom!'

Beside the front door, Luke rummages through the coat cupboard, searching for his denim jacket.

'I wouldn't go expecting your dad back in any fit state,' Tom says as he stands in front of the hall mirror, checking his reflection, first one side then the other. 'My old man's on a mission. Diana and him had a massive fight before he went out. Blazing, it was. Something about these mucky photos everyone's talking about.'

Luke doesn't answer, pretending to be preoccupied in his search.

'Man, you're fine as you are. It's been eighty-two degrees today – believe me, you're not gonna need a jacket. So what d'you reckon?' Tom says, lowering his voice. 'D'you think they're all involved in these wife-swapping parties, then?'

Luke kicks the door shut behind him and pushes his hands into his pockets as they walk down the drive towards Tom's car. 'Nah. They're all too straight. Anyway, I'm just glad to get out of this place for the night, man. I don't need the hassle.'

'But there's gotta be something in it,' Tom goes on. 'I wonder how they do it – is it like picking teams at school, where you all line up and hope you're not the last man standing? Imagine the humiliation, being the last of the ugly swingers to get picked. Ha!'

He unlocks the car and they get in, rolling down the windows to release the built-up heat of the day. Despite the advancing hour the vinyl seats are still hot to the touch, filling the car with a cloying scorched smell. Tom pulls out into the road and slaps Luke on the thigh, before reaching across and opening the glove compartment with one hand, pulling out a half-bottle of scotch. He hands it to Luke. 'Woohoo! The big Eighteen, man! Have a slug of that, get you in the party mood.'

Luke breaks the metal seal, raises the bottle and takes a drink, hooking an elbow out of the window to feel the breeze on his skin. 'Cheers, mate.'

'And nice threads, by the way – I see you finally ditched the flares.'

Luke stretches his legs out to admire his newly tapered black trousers, reaching down to snap off a loose thread that's been left hanging. 'Yeah, I got my mum on the sewing machine this afternoon. They look alright, don't they?'

As he looks up, he sees Martin walking along the pavement towards them, an envelope in his hand. Luke turns his head away too late, and their eyes meet briefly before the car sails by.

'Yeah, you look cool, man,' Tom says. 'Specially with the new boots. The ladies are gonna be falling at your feet.'

'In my dreams. But thanks, Tom. For the Converse – I know they aren't cheap.' He takes another drink from the bottle, winces and hands it back to Tom, who seems to drink it down with ease.

Outside Samantha's house they pull up at the kerb, and before Luke has the chance to get out Tom jumps from the driver's seat, slamming the door behind him. He trots up the pavement towards the large detached house, casually jangling his car keys on his middle finger. 'Wait there,' he calls back as Luke fumbles to open his own door. 'It's your birthday, man – relax!'

Luke watches as Samantha's mother opens the front door and invites Tom in. Tom looks back and leers comically, pointing his thumb towards the mother, performing a thrusting action before he closes the door behind him. The evening sun hits the large Georgian windows of Samantha's house, reflecting the trees and telegraph poles that line her prosperous road. To the other side, a single swallow dips and glides over the long dried grasses surrounding the green, displaying its pale underbody and tail streamers as it passes over. Luke closes his eyes and breathes deeply, taking in the salty dry heat of the island, listening to the distant squabble of gulls as they fight for leftover scraps of picnic down at the seafront. When he thinks of Martin's phone call this morning, he feels a pang of guilty regret about lying; he just couldn't bring himself to invite him along tonight, with his half-mast trousers and Monkees haircut, and so he told him he was working.

'Never mind,' Martin had replied. 'Actually, Dad's still a bit under the weather, so I didn't really want to leave him on his own anyway.'

Luke was relieved at the time, but now he just feels like a bastard. He stretches across the driver's seat to retrieve the scotch bottle, taking two large gulps before returning it to Tom's door pocket, glancing up at the house as he does so. The front door of the house opens and Samantha appears on the top step, glowing softly in a tangerine trouser and waistcoat suit. Her bare arms are a smooth honey brown, and as she approaches the car Luke can see that the front of the waistcoat is cut just low enough to show a sliver of her cleavage. It's only when Tom raps on the roof of the car that he snaps out of his reverie.

'Oi, Luke, jump in the back!'

Without argument, he pushes the door open and lurches out of the front seat. He frowns at Tom over the top of the car as Samantha gets in in his place.

'It's your birthday!' Tom says. 'You're getting chauffeur-driven, man. Just enjoy it!'

Luke gets in, and leans on to the chair-backs with his face between the front seats as they set off in the direction of the estuary. He's so close to Samantha that he can see the fine downy skin on the nape of her neck when she gathers up her hair and draws it round to one side; he wonders if this is the night, if he'll have the courage to make his move. Samantha tilts round to face him and for a breathless moment it's almost

230

as if she's able to see inside his head. Their faces are just inches apart, their eyes are locked, but finally he bottles it, can't maintain the connection for a moment longer, and he flops back against the sweaty vinyl of the rear seat.

'You are funny, Luke,' she says, sliding a hand through the gap in the seats to run her fingers along the length of his thigh, where it rests briefly at the crease of his groin.

He pulls a daft face to make her laugh, and when she withdraws he exhales, wondering what it is she sees when she looks at him. Does she see a man or a boy? This evening he caught his reflection in the bathroom before they set off, and he stopped to stare, feeling as if he'd stepped out of his own body. He gazed at his wiry, tanned limbs, his straight dark hair and large eyes, and even in his new gear he still only saw the boy he's always been.

Before long Tom turns towards the river, slowing down as the bumpy road narrows, and parking the car at the top end of the marina path. As they walk the last stretch, there's an eerie quality in the air, with the man-made bulk of yacht breakers and rusting containers on one side, the low waters of the Medina river on the other. The clink of sails is constant, like tiny bells on the coastal breeze, jingling and chiming as they pass. It's approaching nine o'clock, and the sky is now a vibrant orange-red, casting a warm hue across their faces, turned towards the stately silhouette of the *Ryde Queen* paddle steamer as it gradually comes into full view.

'There she is,' says Tom, his face glowing brightly in the vivid evening light. 'What a beauty.'

The old steamer is magnificent, its huge red funnel protruding skywards, its dark profile like a lino-cut on the low shimmering water. As they draw nearer, music and voices lift towards them, growing in volume.

'Man,' Luke exhales. 'I can't believe I've never been over here before.'

Tom gives him a shove. 'Man, *I* can't believe you've never been over here before!'

Samantha clasps her hands beneath her chin, before hooking an arm through each of theirs, tugging them to speed up as they near the entrance to the ship and the nightclub inside. 'Oh, my God – Gordon is going to love it!' she says, clattering up the steps in her cork sandals. She flicks her hair and dances her fingers along the handrail as the lads follow her up the stairs. 'You know what a disco diva he is!'

After they get past the bouncers and pay to enter, they make their way through to the main deck, where they find Gordon sitting on a bar stool alone, eating a burger. He's wearing a floral shirt with a huge collar, and on the bar in front of him is a cocktail glass complete with glacé cherry and paper umbrella. His baby hair is brushed smoothly over to one side, where it curls thinly around his ears.

'Hey, it's the Holiday Camp Posse!' he calls over, raising his glass. 'Happy birthday, Lukester!'

The bar starts to fill up, and they order drinks, Tom refusing to let Luke put his hand in his pocket and insisting on ordering him a scotch and soda. 'Now you're a man,' he says, 'you'll drink a *man's* drink.'

The panelled walls of the deck are thickly coated in treacly red paint, with hints of navy blue showing through at the doorframes where the emulsion has chipped. More and more people arrive in small groups, many of them looking underage but appearing to be regulars, clustering around the dance floor and commandeering the comfy seats along the edges. The woman behind the bar calls many of the drinkers by name as they jostle to get served, the smoke from her cigarette spiralling overhead to combine with the hazy fug that drifts across the disco lights of the room. With their drinks in hand, they leave the crush of the bar to stand against a polished brass pillar at the edge of the dance floor, sipping from their glasses and surveying the room as it gradually disappears behind a wall of hot bodies.

Gordon pulls a flyer from his back pocket and unfolds it with a flick of his wrist. 'We should check out the other bars too,' he says consulting the sheet of paper. 'There's the Admiral's Disco on the lower deck, and the Normandy Lounge upstairs. One of the girls at work reckons the dance music is in the lower deck, and the oldies are on the upper. Fifties and Sixties stuff.'

'What kind of dance music?' asks Luke.

'You know, classic disco, mainly,' says Gordon. 'Gloria Gaynor. Hot Chocolate. Tavares.'

'It'll be shit,' says Tom, patting his spiky fringe with the flat of his hand, 'but I'm prepared to go along with it for the sake of your birthday, Lukey-boy.'

Samantha finishes her drink, knocking her head back to drain the last drop. 'Yummy,' she says, arching back to shake her hair out. 'Shall we go and explore, then?'

She leads the way as they wander around the various decks and narrow staircases of the boat, checking out the Perspex viewing wall that surrounds the engine room, the Swinging Sixties sounds of the Normandy Lounge and the wooden walkways of the main deck, where groups of youngsters drink and smoke against the deepening red of the sky. Finally, they end up in the Admiral's Disco, where the music is thumping and the smoke-filled room is packed out with people dancing and drinking. At the edge of the dance floor, they congregate beside one of the tatty sofas, and Tom offers Luke one of his cigarettes.

'Why not?' he says, lighting up from Tom's shiny chrome lighter.

Samantha has one too, and she raises an eyebrow at Luke as she puckers around the tip and tilts her face to take a light from Tom. 'Birthday boy,' she says in a lilting voice, pursing her soft lips and blowing a long cool stream over their heads. 'So, what will happen to you this year, Luke? Your first year of manhood.'

Luke inhales his cigarette smoke, hoping he appears older than his years. 'God, it's all change this year,' he replies, leaning back against the pillar, crossing his feet and smiling at his new shoes. 'It's my last shift at Sunshine Bay on Sunday. Then I've got a week free before I'm off to Brighton.'

'Lucky you, Lukey – you get to escape. I'll do it too, you know, in a year or two, when I've saved up some money. I'm not sticking round here any longer than I have to. *London*, that's the place to be.' She taps her cigarette ash to the floor. 'Are you nervous?'

He takes another short puff on his cigarette, enjoying the husky sound it gives his voice as he exhales. 'I haven't given it all that much thought really. Don't know what to expect, I suppose.'

The DJ changes the record and Gordon breaks into a slow dance, swaying his body, snake-like, to Donna Summer's 'Love to Love You Baby'. Luke kicks out at him and he dodges, still dancing and weaving his fingers like a mystic.

'You'll love poly,' Gordon says, still swaying. 'Second year for me. I can't wait to get back. Happy days.'

Luke laughs at Gordon's crazy dancing, and when the track comes to an end they perch together on the edge of the sofa, as the other two make their way through the throng for another round of drinks. Luke watches as Tom places his hand on Samantha's back, confidently easing her through the crowd and chatting to strangers as they gradually disappear from his line of vision.

'You ought to get on with it,' Gordon says, following Luke's gaze. 'It's obvious you like her.'

'Is it?'

'Er, yes! But I wouldn't hang around too long if I were you – she's a pretty girl.'

'I think she's more into you than me,' Luke replies with a little laugh.

Gordon pulls a reproachful face. '*Really*, Luke? I don't think so, do you, honey?'

Tom and Samantha are now completely obscured by the wall of people that surrounds the bar. Luke scuffs at the floorboards with his foot. 'I don't even know if she likes me.'

'Of course she likes you!'

'Yeah, I know she likes me – but does she *like* me? Has she said anything to you?'

Gordon sticks out his bottom lip, lifting and rotating his cocktail glass as he considers the question. 'Not as such. But it's got to be worth a punt, Lukester. What've you got to lose?'

Luke wraps his arms across his chest and grunts.

The music switches again, and Gordon stands, placing his glass on the floor beside the sofa as he starts to dance again, twisting his hips loosely, limp hands worked by pumping elbows.

'Piss off!' Luke says, kicking out to shoo him away. 'Everyone will think we're a couple or something!'

Gordon raises one eyebrow and winks. 'Alright by me, birthday boy.' He swings his hips, throwing in a few disco hand moves, happily antagonising Luke, who squirms with embarrassment on the arm of the sofa.

'They're taking ages,' Luke shouts over the music, trying to get a view of the bar across the darkening room. 'Should we go and give them a hand?'

At that moment, Tom and Samantha re-emerge, each carrying two glasses overhead, Samantha shrieking as she tries to keep the drinks from spilling. The disco lights flitter across her unblemished skin and she hands Luke his drink, kissing him on the cheek as he takes it. His stomach flips and he seizes the moment to kiss her back, catching her on the side of the nose when she turns her head in surprise.

'Ooh! *Two* kisses,' she says, more to Gordon and Tom than to Luke. 'Very French.'

'Ooh-la-la!' Gordon raises his glass. 'To Luke – the birthday boy.'

'The birthday boy!' they chime. They clink glasses and at that moment, as the disco music pounds and the lights shimmer onboard the *Ryde Queen*, Luke's glad to be here, away from the trouble and anxiety of Blake Avenue, here among the beautiful people.

As the evening progresses, they take it in turns to get the drinks in, spending much of the night on the dance floor, where Gordon's eccentric moves attract much amusement. Luke knows he's no dancer but he joins in, letting his body bend to the rhythm of the music, enjoying the dreamlike motion of the strobe lights that pass over their faces and sparkle in the moisture of their eyes. Samantha is a goddess, the central attraction; her hands rise and fall like birds, elegantly circling high above their heads, darting dangerously close to Luke's body as she weaves between them. At one point, she slips her fingers along the waistband of his jeans, lightly caressing his skin before turning her back on him to dance with Gordon.

There's a brief lull in the music, where one track ends and another begins, and they separate, as Gordon goes in search of the toilets and Samantha asks Tom for help at the bar. Luke's view of the lower deck starts to tip and slide, and he staggers towards the stairs, in need of some air. Outside, it has grown dark, but the stars are out in abundance, and Luke ascends the wooden staircase, gripping the handrail and pulling himself up, one heavy leg at a time. He steps over rows of legs and handbags, bumping into a large man and apologising, steadying himself on his way towards the back of the ship. At the stern, he slumps his arms over the railing and gazes across the marina at the clusters of young people wandering about by the river's dried edge, taking a break from the noise and crowd of the ship. Many of them are in couples, clutched together in embrace or strolling unsteadily, hand in hand, and Luke sighs deeply, as his mind drifts back to Samantha and the way she looked at him just now, when she left for the bar with Tom. Tonight's the night; he knows it. Tonight you'll be a man, my son! Luke laughs aloud, turning his back to the view, and he shuts his eyes for a moment, allowing himself to slide down to sitting, to rest his head against the lifebelt. It feels good behind his eyelids, fuzzy and muted as the thump of music vibrates through the ship's metal hull. He can see his mum inside the blank space and he stares at her, concentrating hard while he tries to work out what it is that she's thinking. She's smiling brightly, and her voice has that tinkling quality she uses when it's not for real, but her eyes contain such sadness and he can't quite grasp the answer to it. He recalls an earlier image of his parents standing at the centre of the kitchen in an easy embrace, her head resting upon his chest; his face in her hair, arms loosely wrapped around her waist as they sway to the music on the radio. When was that?

'Not so long ago,' he says, rousing himself, the gritty surface beneath his fingers reminding him where he is. Unsteadily, he stands, holding on to the side and scanning the deck for familiar faces. 'You got the time, mate?' he asks a man who stands nearby.

'Just after twelve,' he replies, and he grins at his friends as Luke makes a lurch, listing across the deck of the ship like a man on the high seas.

The club closes at one. He's got no time to lose. Luke goes in search of Samantha, gulping the night air down as he tries to sober up and invoke the spirit of courage to make his move. He has just reached the stairwell that will take him down to the disco when he sees him: Len Dickens, just a few feet away, beyond the red funnel, beyond the crowd, portside. Luke pauses two steps down, his head cocked and his heart pounding as he stares at the back of Len's head, wanting him to turn round, yet desperate not to be seen. His footsteps fall into a trot as he stumbles down the stairs to warn Samantha, to tell Tom it's time to leave. He presses through the mass of moist bodies, which seems to have doubled in size since he went above board, craning his neck for a sighting of Tom or Samantha. Having no luck in the Admiral's Disco, he heads up to the Normandy Lounge, where tightly clinched couples slow-dance or neck in the corners.

Muttering to himself, Luke pushes his way back through the crowd on the stairs, stopping off for a leak in the cramped toilets. He sways over the urinal, leaning his forehead against the cool glass of the mirror.

'Lukester!' Gordon yells in his ear, and Luke, startled, stumbles back from the wall and clumsily tucks himself back in.

'*Jesus*, Gordon! What're you doing here?'

Gordon steps up to the urinal beside him, where he reaches into his fly, pulls out his penis and gives it a little wiggle. 'Same as you,' he laughs.

Luke steps away so that his back is supported by the doorframe, where he squeezes his eyelids shut and fights the scotch-nausea building up inside his gut.

'Sorry, Lukester. You look a bit squiffy. Are you having a good birthday?'

'Have you seen Samantha?' Luke asks, at once recalling why he's in a hurry to find her. He rubs his face with the heels of his hands. 'S'important.'

'Ah.' Gordon turns away as he carefully washes his hands, flicking his fingers with a revolted expression when he finds there's nowhere to dry them. 'God, you couldn't swing a cat in here. Now, here's the thing – ' He leads Luke out of the door and they jostle through to a clear space in the passageway. 'The thing is – ' he puts a finger to his chin ' – I'm afraid, Lukester, that she and Tom – well, they kind of hit it off.'

Luke stares at him blankly.

'They were all over each other down by the engine room. They left together – about half an hour ago.'

'Together?'

Gordon seems embarrassed for him, and Luke hates him for it. 'Together. *Sorry*. I can't say I didn't see it coming – I mean, I did try to warn you.'

Luke sways, holding on to the wall to regain his balance. 'No, you didn't.'

'I did. I told you to get a move on, didn't I? I said a pretty girl like her would get snapped up quick if you didn't make your move.'

'Yeah, but *Tom*? Where'd they go?'

'Back to his place, I think.'

'So they just left me here?' He blinks.

Gordon reaches out a hand to pat Luke's shoulder, just as Len pushes past on his way down the stairs, ploughing through the mass of people, towards the bar, then disappearing from view. Gordon tilts his head and pulls a sad expression.

'Fuck off, Gordon,' Luke stammers, and, feeling the bile rising in his throat, he forges through the crowd in search of the exit.

The path is dark and long, as Luke stumbles away from the lights and music of the *Ryde Queen*, past screaming tangles of nightclubbers who perch on the edges of rusting girders, or stagger in and out of the shadows cast by the dry-docked dinghies and restoration yachts. His mind is fixed firmly on his target: to make it back to Tom's house and confront him. He pauses by the rusted fencing of the yacht-brokers to vomit on the gritty path, glad to be unseen as he grips his knees, bent over the dust, trying to pull himself together. It's gone midnight and yet it's still so warm; Luke imagines stripping off his clothes and dropping into the Medina, letting the water carry his naked body out into the Solent, to take him away, over to the other side where his new life can begin. He wishes he knew how to cry, as he did when he was a kid; as he did when his Grandad died, or when his cat Zsa-zsa was put to sleep at the vet's.

A buried memory surfaces in the stagnant air, of Len curled up under the canvas tarpaulin of their den in America Woods, red-eyed and exhausted. He'd been missing for two days, after his dad had left again, and it was Luke who eventually found Len and brought him back. They'd shared Luke's chocolate bar – it was Fruit and Nut, he remembers clearly – then he'd given him a backy, with Len sitting on the saddle, gripping on to Luke's belt loops as he stood and pedalled him back to his seafront home.

Luke starts to walk again, knowing he's miles from Blake Avenue, his anger growing with each drunken step. On the Fairlee Road he sticks out his thumb, and before long he picks up a lift that can take him as far as the outskirts of Sandown, where he thanks the bemused driver and stands beneath a lamppost as he tries to get his bearings. Realising he's just a street away from Martin's house, he heads in that direction, suddenly inspired to put things right. The roads are empty, but distant music whispers in the air, drifting up from the seafront where sleepless revellers party through the night on the hottest day in August. Luke steadies himself along the high hedge at the side of Martin's garden, patting it with his hand in a rhythmic motion. When he reaches the break in the hedge, he steps carefully through the narrow black passage and comes out into the garden, with the large workshop to his right and the house to the left. The darkness of the garden is broken by the lights from the workshop, and from the little window at the top of the house. The back door is ajar. Luke remains in the shadows, his back pressed against the hedge, his breath coming in small, shallow gasps; it's gone one in the morning, and he hadn't really expected anyone to be up and about.

As he wonders about Martin, the workshop door swings open and Mr Brazier, looking bent and exhausted, walks slowly along the path that joins the workshop to the house, stopping with his wheelbarrow at the large dry bonfire that now dominates the middle of the lawn. He tips a load of sun-crisped foliage on to the pile and stares at it a moment, wincing as he returns to the edge of the lawn to fetch more garden debris to add to the heap. When he's placed a final offering of orange crates and offcuts around the edges of the bonfire, Mr Brazier stoops to pick up a small can, which he sprinkles around the circumference of the unlit mound. Instinctively, Luke steps back into the shadows of the hedge, as Martin's dad lights a match and drops it on to the lighter fuel. The bonfire ignites with a roar, flashing a sudden light across the garden as the flames engulf the dead leaves and branches, firelight snaking rapidly to the heart of the stack. Mr Brazier steps back from the flames, his face shifting in the flickering light. With his long arms hanging limp at his sides, for the first time Luke can see Martin in him. He stays like this for minutes, the old man, staring at the burning waste until the light diminishes so completely that he appears to fade into the garden, to disappear altogether. With his heart beating hard against his breastbone, Luke eases his body back through the passage in the hedge and runs, dashing through the empty streets of Sandown, his mind fizzing in the balmy night air, until finally, gasping and weary, he arrives on the pavement outside his own house.

Flopping his arms over the wall pillar that separates his drive from Tom's, Luke stares at the two properties, searching for signs of activity. His own bungalow appears to be sleeping; the lights are all out, with every window propped open in the hope of drawing in some cool air. The street lamps cast a white blush across the dead and fractured lawn, illuminating the various discarded toys and buckets that Kitty has dragged out over the course of the day. Luke quietly steps across the lawn to pick up the wooden cigar box he spots pushed under the drooping hydrangea bush. He opens the lid and turns it to the light, appalled to find dozens upon dozens of tiny, shrivelled ladybirds, collected up by Kitty over a month earlier.

A stream of light catches his attention, coming from next door's alleyway, and in a rush of adrenaline he drops the wooden box, scattering the ladybirds far and wide, and sprints across his drive to hurdle the low neighbouring wall. Silently he makes his way to the side door, and stands with his back against the brickwork, hoping to hear the murmur of voices; of Tom and Samantha's voices. The glass panel of the door is ribbed, frosted to obscure its inhabitants. He strains to listen in: there's the snap of a cupboard door opening, the chink of a glass being set down on the side – but no voices.

Luke peers round the corner, attempting to see through the screen, not realising in his drunkenness that his face is now fully pressed up against the frosted door panel.

Inside there's a short shriek and the sound of glass hitting the tiles. In a moment of clarity, Luke recognises the voice as Diana's, and he raps on the glass, calling her name softly to reassure her.

'*Diana*. Diana, it's me – *Luke*.' He presses his flat hand against the clear panel in a gesture of friendship.

The light of the room shrinks as Diana comes close, and speaks through the door. 'Luke?'

'Yes – it's me.'

He hears the clunk and slot of the bolt being drawn, and the door edges open. Diana is standing in the utility room doorway in a full-length kimono, her face stripped of make-up, her wavy hair falling softly over her shoulders.

'Luke? What are you doing here? I thought you were out with Tom tonight?'

'He's not here?' he asks, feeling trivial in the bright glare of the bulb light. He turns and looks along the alleyway to the street beyond, then back up at Diana. She appears years younger without her make-up, more like a pretty teenager than a sexy older woman. Her face crumples in concern as an unexpected sob catches in the back of his throat and he brings his hand up to stifle his mouth.

'Oh, darling!' she exclaims, stepping out in her bare feet, drawing him inside. She leads him through the house and into the soft comfort of her fawn-coloured living room. 'Sit down,' she says, sitting close beside him on the *chaise longue* and clasping his hand. 'What can I get you?' She tips his chin up with a long, manicured finger and regards him earnestly. 'How about a drink?'

Luke is astounded by the beauty of her denuded face, smooth and sensuous in the radiance of the dimmed side lamps. For a moment he's outside of himself, looking in, as he sits there in the middle of this night of madness, close beside

Diana, in her flimsy robe, with her naked face. Just him and Diana. Delicious Diana.

'A scotch?' he replies.

He watches as she rises and crosses the room to the drinks cabinet. The silk of her floral kimono clings to her curves as she bends to take a glass from the bottom shelf, and Luke is certain she's wearing nothing beneath the gown. She removes the lid from the plastic ice tub and picks out three dripping cubes with a pair of silver tongs, dropping them into the cut-glass tumbler and pouring out a generous measure of whisky.

'Aren't you having one?' he asks, when she returns to the sofa.

She plumps up the cushions and crosses her legs, carefully tucking her gown beneath her upper thigh to prevent it slipping open.

'I've had plenty.' She smiles. 'So, tell me what's happened? Why aren't you with Tom?'

Luke swirls the melting ice chunks, and takes a cautious sip. 'He went off with Samantha.'

'Samantha?'

'We all work together, up at Sunshine Bay.'

'And you like her?'

Luke blows out slowly through pursed lips. 'Yup. And Tom knew it. He knew I liked her.'

Diana makes a sad face.

He takes a braver gulp of scotch and laughs harshly. 'I can't believe I thought I was in with a chance.'

Diana nudges him and he smiles reluctantly. 'Forget her!' she says, smacking his knee and snatching away his empty glass. She sashays from the room, calling back from the hallway, 'Tell you what, Luke, I *will* join you in a drink after all. Hang on a second!'

Moments later she returns with a chilled bottle of champagne, which she holds aloft in a pose not unlike the Statue of Liberty. He narrows his eyes, smiling, enjoying the way the light shards appear to bounce around the room in the soft radiance of Diana's movements.

'We'll not let your big birthday pass by as a disaster!' she says, returning to the drinks cabinet, where she unwraps the foil and expertly pops the cork. 'Your mum phoned earlier to say the chaps arrived home just after twelve, and now Mike's crashed out on your sofa next door. He'll be out for the count till the middle of tomorrow, if past drinking adventures are anything to go by.'

Luke laughs, shifting in his seat, his body at last relaxing into the cushions.

'So, we can't let *them* have all the fun, can we?'

She pours the champagne and joins him on the sofa, where they drink and talk and refill their glasses as Diana's gown shimmers and sways before Luke's increasingly bold gaze.

'This is a strange night,' he says, noting the soft chime of two o'clock from the hallway. 'Out on the marina – on the beaches – it's as if everyone is awake, but at the same time it's as if everyone is sleeping – dreaming…' He trails off, trying to make sense of his thoughts.

'And it's not even a full moon,' Diana says, sharing the last of the champagne between their glasses.

'Do you know what I mean?' he asks, the throb of his heart steadily pounding inside his chest.

She inclines her head in thought. 'It's the heat; the endless summer. We live on this tiny island, and no one knows what to do about the sun when it just won't stop shining, so we all go a little mad, because it feels like it's just a dream that will be gone when we wake up tomorrow.' She looks at him for a long time, and he doesn't look away, and at once he knows that she does understand, that she's like him, that she knows his every desire. 'Shall we take these into the other room?' she asks, holding her glass in one hand, slipping the other along the sofa to lace her fingers between his. He pushes his hand against hers so that no space remains between the valleys of their fingers; she presses back, hard, her eyes never leaving his. With a slow, cat-like blink of her soft brown lashes she moves closer still, allowing her gown to fall open, pushing the hair away from his neck to gently kiss behind his ear.

The chatter of house sparrows beyond the window wakes Luke early, forcing him to rise up from the heavy blanket of his hangover. His head feels encased within a tightening shroud of pressure, and his dry tongue sticks to the roof of his mouth. With a lurch of exhilaration he remembers where he is, and he slowly turns his head to see Diana's face, sleeping on the pillow beside him. Her bare shoulder is exposed; his pulse accelerates as he recalls the slip of her skin against his, the smooth strength of her thighs as she pulled him towards her in the darkness of the night.

Arduously, he props himself up on his elbows, flopping back down as the pain screams through his temples. *'Jesus,'* he whispers.

'Morning,' she says, sleepily pushing the hair from her face. 'What's the time?'

He wants to reach for her again, and he blushes at the thought, so unimaginable in the cool light of morning. He knows he might never touch her again. Luke checks his watch, and is relieved to see it's still early, too early for Mike to return and find him in his bed. He closes his eyes and releases a long, slow exhalation of breath. 'Five-thirty,' he replies.

Diana slips into her kimono, and disappears along the hallway, while Luke gingerly gathers his discarded clothes, wondering what to do next. When he's dressed, he follows the smell of coffee to the kitchen, where Diana greets him with a slow smile.

'Hungover?' She hands him a mug of sweet black coffee.

'Yup,' he groans. He holds up the cup, giving her a nod of thanks. 'I guess I'd better get going soon, hadn't I?'

245

She pulls out a chair, indicating for him to take a seat at the kitchen table. 'Don't worry about Mike. He'll still be dead to the world. You'll be off well before he gets back.'

Luke nods, sipping his coffee, every nerve in his body jangling. He glances up at Diana, shyly, her body still vivid in his memory. 'Thanks,' he says.

She tips her head, her pretty curls falling loose around her neck. 'For the coffee?'

'Well, yes,' he says. 'But also – well, last night. I shouldn't have just turned up like that. I probably acted like an idiot. Sorry.'

Diana reaches out to touch his wrist, and shakes her head with a warm smile before returning to the sink to refill the kettle. They remain like this a while, in comfortable silence, with Diana pottering about the kitchen as the dry chill of the early morning drifts in through the open window, and the sparrows chatter on. Luke feels the life returning to his limbs.

He breathes deeply, as the jumbled mess of his parents' lives rears up in his thoughts, unwelcome and bewildering. He thinks of his father, shuddering at the possibility of him and Diana together – or, worse still, of his mother paired off with Mike.

Diana returns to the kitchen table, a tiny vertical line crinkling her brow as she spots the change in his expression. She places a fresh cup in front of him and sits, folding her arms, casually leaning on to the table.

'Are you alright, darling? You're not sorry about last night, are you?' She gives him a crooked smile and reaches out to rub his forearm.

He hesitates, running a finger around the rim of the hot cup, before lifting his eyes to meet hers. 'Diana, can I ask you something?'

She brings her cup to her mouth, blowing on it gently before taking a sip. 'Of course.'

'Promise you won't be offended?'

'I'll try not to be.'

'It's the parties, the ones at the McKees'. And all these photos that keep turning up.'

'Oh,' says Diana. Absently she pinches her kimono together at the chest.

'Well, I know you've been to some of the parties, like Mum and Dad. It's not exactly a secret any more. Apparently, everyone's been talking about it – even before the photos came out.'

She nods.

Luke drums his fingers on the table, feeling his chest throb with toxic poisoning. 'It's just, I don't know – it's just lately Mum's changed so much, it's like she's terrified of everything. She used to be out and about all the time, down the beach with Kitty, chatting with friends in the town – but now, she hardly leaves the house.'

Diana's eyebrows pucker. 'I had no idea it was that bad, Luke.'

'She's pretty good at putting on a brave face in public, but the minute she's on her own she sort of balls up inside herself again.'

'What about your dad?'

'He's the same as usual, pretending everything's normal. But they're hardly talking. It's like this has pushed them so far apart, they don't know how to get back. And it doesn't help that Simon's staying with us. He's not the best influence on Dad.' He rubs his hands across his face, wearily groaning at the uselessness of it all. He leaves the table to run his cup under the tap, filling it with cold water which he drinks down before filling it again. 'Sorry. I don't know why I'm even telling you all this.'

'God, it's so ironic,' Diana sighs. 'Not long before that last party, Marie told me that if Richard and Jo didn't get more involved she was going to stop inviting them.'

'What do you mean?' he asks, placing his cup down and turning to face her. 'What do you mean, "more involved"?'

She looks surprised. 'Oh. Well, it seems they've not exactly been "full participants", if that makes sense.'

'None of it makes any sense.' Luke fetches his new boots from the doorway, and perches on the edge of the seat to lace them.

'Marie said your mum and dad have been to lots of her parties over the years, and they've always been great fun to have around. But apart from once or twice in the early days, when it came to picking partners your mum and dad always stuck with each other. I think it had started to grate a little, with Marie. There were plenty there who would have been very happy to hook up with one or other of them – they're a very attractive couple. But every time it was the same: they'd turn down all offers and choose each other.'

With clarity, Luke recalls the soft coral toenails of Dad's mystery woman on that party night, the woman who'd stayed concealed behind the rockery. He looks at Diana across the table as the light from the window casts pretty ripples around her hair. 'I don't understand why they'd keep going – if they only want each other?'

Diana stands, holding her empty cup aloft as she walks away, across the kitchen to open the side door to the alleyway beyond. 'Boredom, I should think, Luke. Good old-fashioned boredom. Sometimes love just isn't enough.'

'But if they've got nothing to hide, what are they so afraid of?'

She pushes the door back against the wall, sliding the wedge beneath it with a push of her bare toe. 'Oh, *everyone*'s got something to hide, darling,' she says. She kisses him on the cheek and tilts back against the doorframe, where the morning air breezes lightly from the garden, rippling her gown like water.

Luke pauses momentarily, carefully storing to memory the beautiful vision of Diana as she stands in the doorway, knowing it will never happen again. 'Thanks,' he says, barely a whisper.

'Don't mention it,' she replies with a small dip of her head, and then he's gone, out through the side door and over the wall, silently slipping into his own bedroom and under the sheets, where he'll sleep off his hangover for the rest of the day.

12

Met Office report for the Isle of Wight, late August 1976:
Maximum temperature 83°F/28.2°C

As late August heads towards September, the humidity across the country is becoming intolerable, as news headlines claim that Britain is in the grip of the worst drought in five hundred years. The island throngs with locals and holidaymakers, all vying for space on the beaches, any sense of everyday order and work routine having evaporated along with the water from the rivers and streams.

For the twenty-four hours following his birthday an eerie calm settles in Luke's home; Mum and Dad quietly occupy themselves in separate corners of the house, while a subdued Kitty trails between them, giving in occasionally to flop about on the dusty lawn, too hot to complain or whimper. Simon is still with them, but he's been spending more time out of the house lately, since he and Mum had another bust-up last week, when he took Kitty down to the beach without asking her. Nobody calls at the front door, not even the postman, and the telephone doesn't ring at all. It's as if the brakes are on, as if the whole world has slowed to a halt, and Luke embraces the silence, crawling back beneath his bedcovers and disappearing behind a welcome curtain of sleep.

When Friday comes round, he should be working, but instead he rises early and phones in sick, telling Philip he'll be back on Sunday, to collect his wages and say his final goodbyes. 'I'm really sorry to let you down,' he lies. 'I just need a couple of days to get over this stomach bug.' He hangs up, relieved that, for the next couple of days at least, he doesn't have to face Tom and Samantha.

After a shallow mid-morning bath, Luke waters the front garden, trailing back and forth along the hall with buckets of soap-clouded bathwater, which he distributes along the borders, throwing the last of it across the dehydrated lawn. It has become second nature now, to reuse the water. Luke watches as it slowly seeps into the earth, taking long minutes to soak through the hard-baked top layer, into the parched soil below. He replays his conversation with Martin on the phone last night, when he asked yet again about that missing reel of film. Martin was evasive, offhand even, and something in his uncharacteristically cold tone told Luke that he was lying, that he knows where that film is after all.

Luke swings the bucket idly at his side, wandering over to the front wall, where he scans the road beyond his gate. The street is empty, bar a few weary house sparrows that chirp and flutter in the branches of the tree opposite. There's no activity from the Michaelses' house, nor from Mrs Bevis's the other side. It's no wonder; it's so hot, everyone's taken to hiding out in their houses, out of the heat, out of the endless glare of the sun.

Back inside, he finds Mum in her bedroom, sitting up on the bed with Kitty asleep at her side. She's reading a book, holding it up in her left hand, gently twirling a lock of Kitty's hair with her right.

'Anything good?' he asks from the doorway.

She turns the book face down across her lap and pats the bed, as Luke crosses the room to perch on the edge of the mattress beside her.

'You're not working?' she asks.

He shakes his head. 'It's too hot,' he replies, flipping the book round to see the cover. 'It's nice to see you reading again, Mum. Remember when I was little, we used to sit and read together for hours? I loved that.'

'I don't know why I stopped,' she says, gazing across the room with a little frown. 'I used to live for books. Before your dad, reading was my grand passion.'

'Maybe you should try to make more time for that type of thing? I mean, you must get a bit bored, just looking after all of us. Don't you?'

She smiles at him gently. 'It's my job.'

'But it *must* be boring. The same thing, day in, day out? Don't you sometimes wish for a bit more excitement?'

Kitty wriggles on the bed, letting out a little whine as her thumb drops from the corner of her mouth.

Mum brings her finger to her lips. '*Shush,*' she whispers.

Luke lowers his voice. 'I thought I'd go over and visit Nan today, see if she needs anything. Her ankle's still playing her up a bit, so she might want me to pop down the shops and fetch a few things.'

'She'll like that,' Mum says. 'You're a good grandson.' She strokes Kitty's hair, smoothing it from her face, exposing her clear soft forehead. 'I still feel bad that we didn't do much for your birthday, Luke. Why don't I cook you a special lunch before you leave – we could get Nanna over, and Martin? Even Tom, if you like?'

'Not Tom,' he replies quickly.

Mum looks surprised. 'Oh. Well, whoever you like. But we should do something, shouldn't we? It's a big deal, turning eighteen – and going off to polytechnic on your own.'

Luke's staring out of the window, trying to tune in to the sound of a distant aeroplane as it passes over. 'OK,' he says when she nudges him. 'That'd be great.'

Mum closes her eyes, inhaling deeply as her head eases back against the pillow. He watches her for a moment, seeing the tension in her facial muscles, the tightening of her jaw. He places his hand over hers and squeezes it gently.

'Mum?'

'Uh-huh?'

'How long is Simon staying for?'

She opens her eyes.

'Well, it doesn't look as if he and Laura are going to patch things up, does it?'

She looks away. 'I hope it won't be much longer, Luke. I want my home back. I want my living room back.'

'You need to be firm with Dad, you know? Assert yourself. Women's rights and all that.' He smiles, wanting her to smile back.

A single tear runs down her cheek, and bounces off the book in her lap. She reaches out for his face, cupping his cheeks in her hands and kissing him softly on the nose. 'I just want to get back to how things used to be.'

'They will be, Mum, before you know it.' He sits back to look at her squarely, trying to convey his understanding. 'I'd better get off to Nanna's. If I get there early enough, I'll be in with the chance of some lunch. More than I'd get around here.' He smirks, patting her leg as he gets up to go.

Mum covers her face and laughs silently, brushing away her tears, and checking her fingers for mascara. 'Luke?' she says, as he reaches the door. 'There's a job advertised at the library, starting in September. I saw it when I picked up my book. What do you think?'

He stands in the doorway, looking at her and Kitty, noticing the way the sunlight streams in through the net curtains, making halos of their loose hair. 'I think it's a great idea, Mum. You'd be brilliant.'

'You think they'd even consider me?'

He rolls his eyes. 'Mum, they'd be mad not to.'

The wooded approach to Nanna's house ripples with birdsong as Luke slows and turns his scooter into her path. He removes his crash helmet, and pauses a moment to sit in the dappled sunlight, listening to the peaceful murmur of trees and the distant sounds of holidaymakers down at the creek beyond her garden. He could live here, quite happily, quite quietly.

Nanna raps on the window and beckons him in.

'You're just in time for a bit of shepherd's pie,' she says, drying her hands on her apron. She taps her cheek with her finger, and he stoops to give her a kiss.

Nan hobbles across the kitchen to fetch an extra plate, her limp as bad as ever. She winces as she steadies herself on the corner of the table and places the plate down, pausing to gather herself before she returns to the sink to continue with the drying-up.

'How are your aches and pains, Nanna?' Luke asks, taking the teatowel from her and pointing to a chair.

She hands it over and takes a seat. 'I'm alright, son. Tell you what: in 'ere, it's all tickety-boo,' she says, tapping her head. 'It's just the bits on the outside that's gone to seed. Old age, son, that's what it is. Wouldn't recommend it.'

'You'll outlive the lot of us, Nanna,' Luke says, putting away the last of the pots and hanging the towel on its hook. 'Have you heard the birds out there today? They're making a hell of a racket – the woods across the road are humming with them.'

'It's the ladybirds,' she says, rubbing her knee through a wrinkly beige stocking. 'Bloody millions of them; I've never seen the like. Mrs Fenton walked past my window the other day, all dressed in her Sunday best – yellow hat, yellow dress – covered in 'em, she was. Every time she brushed 'em off, more landed – her back was crawling! I called out the window to her, "What's that on you?" Well, you know what a bible-basher she is; probably thinks it's a plague sent to test us.' She slaps her thigh and cackles, her eyes glazed over. 'Oh, flip,' she suddenly says, putting her hands in the air. 'Run outside and turn off the hose, would you, son?'

Luke jogs through the house and out through the doors at the back, to find the hose snaking across the parched lawn, feeding water into the old concrete pond at the side of the garden. He turns it off at the tap and reels it back in so that it's out of view of the neighbours. 'Nanna!' he scolds as he returns to the kitchen. 'Nanna, there's a hosepipe ban, you know?'

She pulls a baffled expression.

'You must have heard about it,' he says, wrinkling his brow to let her know he's not fooled. He sits on the seat opposite her, and kicks off his baseball boots, removing his socks and flexing his hot feet under the table. 'It's all they talk about on the news – drought this, drought that. You can't have missed it, Nan. S.O.S? *Save or Suffer.*'

Nanna shrugs. 'It's for the birds. It's not their fault we've got no water. That nice wildlife bloke on the telly said *they're* the ones suffering – the birds – so I thought I'd put a bit of water out for 'em. They like a bath, 'specially those lovely little house sparrows.'

She eases herself out of her chair and struggles over to the oven, opening up the door to release a hot burst of cooking into the room. She lifts the shepherd's pie out and places it on a pot stand in the centre of the table, handing a serving spoon to Luke as she lowers herself into her chair.

'How was your birthday?' she asks, pushing the hot dish back along the table.

Luke takes a mouthful of food, and chews slowly, thoughtfully. 'Crappy,' he finally says, and he takes another forkful.

'I thought you were going out with that new lad, Tom, and the girl you liked?'

'I did. That's why it was crappy. This is delicious, Nanna. Thanks.'

She serves him another scoop of food as he eats ravenously, enjoying his meal more than any he's tasted in weeks. 'So what happened?'

Luke sighs, and rests his fork for a moment. 'In a nutshell, Nanna, we went out to a nightclub, and we were having a fine old time, until my new mate got off with the girl I really liked and they left me there to get home alone. Honestly, I only went off to get a bit of fresh air for a few minutes and they disappeared. Apparently they were all over each other.'

'And he's meant to be your mate?' Nan purses her lips and shakes her head. 'Dirty bastard.'

Luke splutters, covering his mouth with his hand. He picks up his fork. 'That's why I love coming to see you, Nan. You always know the right thing to say.'

After they've cleared the dishes they take a slow walk around the garden, to see how the plants are doing. So many of them have wilted and died. Nanna points out those that want cutting back, and Luke collects them up in the wheelbarrow as she hobbles alongside him, leaning heavily on her knobbly stick.

'Here we go,' she says when they reach the top end of the garden where the hedge backs on to the creek. She holds out her hand and Luke passes her the secateurs, which she uses to cut and collect a dozen or so rosehips. She slips them into the front pocket of her pinny and hands back the secateurs. 'So when will you next see this Tom fella?'

Luke scrutinises her suspiciously, and picks up the handles of the wheelbarrow as they head back towards the house. 'Sunday. It's my last shift, so I'll probably have to face up to him then.'

'Alright, son. Well, make sure you stop by here on your way to work, eh? We'll give that Tom a little something to remember you by,' she says, patting her apron pocket.

Luke laughs, and helps her up the step and into the house.

On Saturday evening, instead of retreating to his bedroom, Luke sits up with his parents and Simon, watching television. Dad takes the armchair, while Mum and Simon sit either end of the sofa with Luke awkwardly wedged in between. Luke glances at Mum from time to time, wondering what she's thinking as she sets her gaze towards the television, trying to avoid his eyes, trying to act normal. At the nine o'clock news, Dad tops up his and Simon's wine glasses, putting the bottle down when Mum covers her glass with a flat hand, her eyes still fixed ahead. The island still lies beneath a blanket of oppressive heat, and as they watch together in silence Luke's thoughts drift over his night with Diana, back to the warmth of her encircling arms, the soft pressure of her moving hips. Even though he knows it will never be repeated, not with Diana at any rate, he savours the memory, returning to it again and again, a reassuring distraction from the chaos of his life. Sitting here in the uneasy humidity of yet another airless night, he feels entirely disconnected from the events playing out across the rest of the world, as if their island exists alone, in its own little bubble. In Belfast there's news of yet another bombing, while Catholics and Protestants march side by side for peace, many of them pushing prams or carrying babies. The east of England is slowing to a standstill as sudden downpours cause flash flooding, the unexpected volume of water powerless to penetrate the sun-baked fields and hardened ditches. Weather experts say we haven't seen a summer like it in over a century, a summer of such severe drought, of forest fires and failing crops and plummeting milk yields. Thunderstorms in Mildenhall have brought down an American Air Force plane, killing eighteen passengers and crew, while across the Atlantic in Greenland another crashed earlier in the day, killing twenty-three. Even the sporting world is affected by this strange shift, with the England–West Indies match at Lords unexpectedly rained off before close of play. Despite the disappointment of interruption, the spectators, weary from endless weeks of sunshine, stand from their seats and cheer.

'The world's gone mad,' Dad says, taking a sip from his wine glass. 'It's like Bedlam out there.'

So it's a surprise when the day's news ends on a light-hearted report from Notting Hill, depicting the preparations for the bank holiday carnival and predictions that it will pass off peacefully this year. Yet something in the joyous scenes of costume-making and steel drum rehearsals unsettles Luke as he leaves the room and heads for bed. All night long, an imperceptible anxiety tugs at his drifting mind, merging with half-seen visions of Diana, disturbing his humid sleep like an unfinished dream, where the ending is just a whisper away.

Luke's final shift starts at nine, and he arrives early to stop off at the managers' office and settle his final wages. There's a thick cloak of pressure in the atmosphere; overhead, the sun shines brightly on the mainland side of the island, but back towards the west the sky darkens, growing pewter-like in colour.

As he approaches the office he's drawn to turn his face towards the swoop and fall of the swallows that dance high above the building, dipping low to feed on the flying ants that swarm in the angry sky. At the foot of the wooden steps, he discovers the source of the ants: a desiccated mound of soil that erupts from the dusty earth, spewing winged insects like a nightmarish volcano.

He knocks on the office door and enters to find Suzy and Philip both on duty, wrestling for space behind the small desk, where they push papers about and count out event tickets.

'Sorry about the last couple of days,' Luke says when they look up. He shifts his duffel bag from one shoulder to the other. 'I had gastroenteritis or something. Horrible.'

Suzy wrinkles her chin critically. 'Couldn't have been worse timing, Luke. You know it's the busiest weekend of the season? We've been run off our feet.'

'Yeah, like I say, sorry.'

She swipes the perspiration from her upper lip, and ignores him. 'God, it's muggy.'

Philip rocks back in his chair and smiles at Luke, screwing his face up at the back of Suzy's head. 'Ignore her, mate. She's in a bit of a huff, that's all.'

'Sod off, Phil,' she says, continuing to count tickets.

'That Tom fella has copped off with Samantha, hasn't he? I think Suzy was a bit keen on him, weren't you, Suze?'

'No,' she replies through gritted teeth. 'Why would I bother with an idiot like him?'

Philip nods vigorously, rubbing his chin in a show of disbelief.

'So, they're going out together?' Luke asks, casually. 'I had heard something, but I wasn't sure.'

'Suzy gave them an official warning yesterday, didn't you, Suze?' Philip pats her on the back.

'Yup.' She looks at Luke, straightening up and tapping her pen in the palm of her hand. 'Caught them snogging outside the ballroom – they were on duty. We can't have that. Not on duty.'

'You wouldn't do anything like that, would you, Suze? *Not on duty*.' Philip laughs raucously, pushing his chair back and walking round to the front of the desk. 'What a bloody hoot,' he says, and he runs his finger down the rota chart and locates Luke's name. 'Here you are – Luke Wolff – you're over on the far chalets for the first couple of hours, then pool duty after lunch.' He returns to the desk drawer, where he picks out the relevant room keys and hands them to Luke. 'You're with Gay Gordon.'

'So, are Tom and Samantha both working today?' Luke asks.

'Tom is,' Philip says, returning to the desk. 'He was in here about ten minutes ago. He doesn't start till nine. I think he said he was going to have a swim first – you'll probably find him over at the pool.'

Luke pushes the keys into his pocket and jogs down the wooden steps, out along the dirt path to the pool, swatting the insects away as he goes. He slowly edges around the side of the changing rooms, until he can see Tom, who's doing lengths, alone. Luke waits until Tom starts another length away from him, before quietly making his way along the side of the pool and in through the entrance to the men's changing room. Swiftly he reaches into his duffel bag to bring out the envelope of dried rosehip powder that Nanna handed him this morning on his way to work. He hurries to coat the inside of Tom's underpants and T-shirt with the fine powder, before edging out of the changing rooms and dropping back down on to the path, unnoticed.

The morning passes quickly, as Luke and Gordon move from chalet to chalet, by now having got their cleaning routine together finely tuned, with Gordon concentrating on the bathrooms while Luke sweeps out the bedrooms and changes the sheets and towels.

'We're a bit of a dream-team, you and me,' Gordon says with a little flick of his duster.

Luke curls his lip. 'Don't go getting any funny ideas.'

'Don't flatter yourself,' Gordon replies, puffing out his chest. 'You're not my type.'

Luke laughs, pausing to lean on his broom handle. 'D'you know, for a while, I was *actually* worried that you and Samantha might get it together?'

Gordon carries the bucket through the chalet and places it on the front step. He rests his hand on the doorframe. 'Is that really so hard to believe? I mean, look at me!' He holds his arms out wide, and makes a sweeping gesture down his body.

'Don't you get any bother? About being queer?'

'Do you really have to use that expression?' Gordon asks, indicating for Luke to follow him outside as he locks up the room.

'Well, what expression should I use? I've never been friends with a poofter before.'

Gordon yelps with laughter, picking up his bucket and trailing along the path beside Luke. 'I'm pretty sure I'm supposed to find *poofter* offensive too. Anyway, in answer to your question, yes, I get all sorts of bother. More bother than I could even begin to tell you.'

'Then why d'you make it so obvious, if it attracts trouble?'

'Why hide it?' Gordon replies, serious for once. 'I could go through my whole life pretending to be "normal" like generations of men before me. And for what? For everyone else's peace of mind, not my own. What's the point in a life half lived, Lukester? I'd rather take what comes to me. And if people give me a hard time, well, I'll just rub their bread rolls in my armpit and be done with it.'

The leaden sky looks set for early evening in autumn, yet the warmth in the air is growing ever more oppressive. Luke turns to look at Gordon, with his underdeveloped body and baby hair and strange little knobbly hands, and is struck by a profound surge of affection.

'It'll be good to stay in touch when we're both in Brighton,' he says. He unlocks the door to the final chalet, stepping aside to let Gordon pass through.

'You'll never shake me off now,' Gordon replies, flicking at the windowsill on his way through to the bathroom. 'I'll be round annoying you every five minutes. *That's* a promise.'

After a few minutes, Gordon leans out of the bathroom to dump the towels in a pile on the floor, clicking his fingers to get Luke's attention.

'I have to say you're in surprisingly good spirits, Lukester. All things considered.'

Luke opens up the bedroom window to let the stale air out. '*Am I?*'

'And you know, *he's* dropped right off my Christmas card list.'

'Who – Tom?' Luke wipes his forearm across his forehead and starts to strip off the bed sheets.

'Who else?' Gordon adds, meaningfully. He returns to the bathroom, whistling cheerfully.

Luke balls up the sheets and throws them on to the pile, before starting on the second bed.

'So, I guess it'll be a bit awkward, won't it?' Gordon continues, sticking his head out of the bathroom again. 'Next time you bump into him and Sam?'

'We'll see,' Luke replies. He thinks about the fact that he's just slept with Tom's stepmum, and for a brief moment considers telling Gordon, just to see his reaction. He straightens up to chuck a dirty pillowcase at Gordon's head, laughing hard as it flops over his face. 'Now stop asking me questions and get on with your job, you big nancy.'

At lunchtime they line up in the dining hall for lamb stroganoff and sticky toffee pudding. The hall is teeming with holidaymakers, all passing through in between swimming and lawn games, some of them looking painfully sunburnt and shiny from too much time spent by the pool. Gordon starts a 'lobster tally' on his fingers, pointing out the reddest of the guests as they pass from the top of the queue to find their seats in the hall. By the time Luke and Gordon sit down with their trays, the tally is up to eighteen.

'He lives next door to you, doesn't he?' Gordon asks, setting down his tray opposite Luke's. 'Tom?'

'God, you do go on, Gordon.'

'It's good to talk,' he replies, as he fiddles with the salt cellar, trying to unblock the holes that have become clogged up in the damp heat. 'It might help you to forgive and forget.' He smirks to show Luke that he's joking. 'So, how will you exact your revenge, Lukey?'

Luke shakes his head, and picks up his cutlery.

Gordon wrings his hands like the Hooded Claw. 'Well, you must have thought about it? What have you got in mind? Are you going to woo her back? Let down his tyres? Shit on his doorstep?'

'Nothing so obvious,' says Luke, smiling secretively as he shovels in a forkful of stroganoff.

'Intriguing,' Gordon replies. His attention is momentarily diverted, and he rests his fork on the edge of his plate, reaching out to nudge Luke's arm across the table. 'Over there,' he says, and Luke turns to see Tom standing at the front of the queue, looking pained, an angry red rash having travelled up the side of his face and beneath his carefully messed hair.

'*Watch*,' Luke whispers to Gordon, as he attempts to suppress the smile that tugs at the edges of his mouth.

Gordon waves at an irritable-looking Tom, who crosses the hall to sit with them, lowering his head and speaking to Luke as if nothing ever happened, as if everything's just as it was before.

'Man,' he says, leaning in and keeping his voice low, his eyes scanning the room. 'Man, you should be thanking me for a lucky escape, Luke. I'm not even kidding.'

'You think?' Luke asks with a sneer. 'Why's that?'

Agitated, Tom looks from Gordon to Luke as his hand dips below the table to scratch at his groin. 'I think she's given me something. *Samantha*. My skin's crawling, man. I think she's given me the clap.'

On his way home, Luke feels the first drops of rain as he passes through Brading, where several small children jump and scream on the church green, turning their faces skyward to catch the rare nectar on their tongues. All the way back, there are similar glad scenes as locals emerge to watch while the rain grows heavier, bouncing off the parched leaves and soaking into the arid earth of their gardens. For the first time in months, the streets glisten with moisture.

Luke can't bring himself to go straight home, knowing that they'll all still be there: Mum, Dad and Simon, all of them smiling hard as they hold their breath, waiting for the next damning photograph to appear. This morning he found Mum in the bathroom, hacking away at the mildewed grout of the bath tiles, her mouth set in a livid line as the hardened filler chipped and flew beneath her chisel. She looked up at him sharply, flashing him the anger that has, for the time being, taken the place of her deep despair.

Luke parks his scooter on the esplanade and wanders down the sand beside the pier, watching the rain as it hits the water beneath the dark sky. The tide is slow, languorous, sucking up hungry great gulps from the shoreline, only to push them gently back in again. The drops are refreshing on Luke's bare arms, and he inclines his head, pushing his long hair back from his face to feel the cooling trickle of the long-absent moisture. The beach has cleared out entirely; the crowds of sunbathers have gathered up their towels and retreated to the parade in search of ice creams and amusements. Luke turns towards the pier. Drizzles of rainwater spew from its murky railings, forming tiny pools at the footings where it anchors to the shore. A few gulls squawk and peck between the concrete piles, fighting over abandoned sandwiches and taking shelter from the rain.

As Luke watches the birds, a pale face appears from behind one of the struts; it holds his gaze, as if confused, then disappears again. It's Len.

Without a thought, Luke jogs across the softening sand, his T-shirt now slicked to his body, large drips of water hanging from the hem of his shorts. 'Len?' he calls out, as he steps into the gloom beneath the walkway.

Len is sitting with his back against one of the struts, his elbow propped on a large rucksack. He holds out his beer can, flicking his head for Luke to sit with him. Luke rests his palm on the wet pillar, trying to assess the situation, taking in Len's drawn expression, his unthreatening pose. He reaches for the can, takes a swig and returns it before sitting cross-legged against the opposite pillar. 'Alright?' he says.

'You can have a whole one if you want.' Len passes him an unopened can, avoiding eye contact, pulling his jacket close around his shoulders.

For a short while they drink in silence, listening to the slap and drip of the rain beyond the pier. Len takes a ready-rolled reefer from inside his denim jacket and lights up, drawing on it a few times, pausing to look at it closely before offering it to Luke. He takes it, inhaling a few tokes, as the effects stream through his limbs, to linger about the backs of his knees like a heat haze.

'Didn't think you smoked,' says Len.

Luke concentrates hard on not smiling. 'That's good stuff.'

'Should be. It cost enough.'

Luke takes a few more drags, drawing the smoke deep into his lungs, feeling the weight of it pressing in at his ribs. His mind lights on the night Len beat him up, how quickly they'd resorted to childish name-calling, just as they would have done back at primary school. Luke shakes his head. He'd called Len an amoeba. An *amoeba*. He laughs aloud, losing control, sighing between splutters as he stretches across to return the joint. Len scowls at him as if he's an idiot; Luke holds his palms up, still laughing.

'Sorry. *Sorry*. I was just thinking about when you called me and Martin benders. It's just a funny word. *Benders*.'

Len smiles briefly – almost laughs, before he turns away again, bringing his expression under control. Luke puts his face in his hands, trying to pull himself together, feeling the grit of the sand grazing across his skin.

When he looks up, Len is looking at him, square on, holding Luke's eyes for an uncomfortable moment too long. There's no aggression in the look, but something else, something so profoundly sad that Luke's heart stutters in his chest. Abruptly, Len's focus shifts, fixing on some invisible point out at sea. 'You know,' he says, 'I always thought you lot seemed like the perfect family. Your mum and dad were always so bloody cheerful – so pleased to see you.'

Luke stares at him. 'They liked you, Len, you know?' he replies, not sure what use this is now. 'And your mum's alright, isn't she? Well, she was always lovely to me.'

Len scratches his rough stubble with dirty fingernails, and looks back at Luke. 'Mate, d'you know how many stepdads I've had since my old man left?'

Luke shakes his head.

'Seven. That's one for every year my dad's been gone. One a fucking year.'

The rain is coming down harder now, hard enough to force little rivers of water through the cracks in the walkway overhead. Luke shifts position to move out of a stream.

Len grinds the end of the joint into the sand. He tears a corner off his thumbnail with his teeth. 'Some of Mum's blokes weren't that nice.'

'I'm sorry, man,' Luke says, willing Len to turn back to him, but Len's focus is far out over the water, unreachable. Luke pulls his knees up beneath his chin, patting the damp goosepimples beneath the pads of his fingers as he tries to think of something else to say. 'So, where are you off to?' he asks. 'You've got your rucksack with you. Looks like you're off somewhere.'

'Mainland. It's gotta be better than here.'

'But I heard Samantha's dad got you a job on the ferries?'

Len glances at him darkly, and a blush rises to Luke's cheeks. He pushes back against the shadowy pillar of the pier. 'I heard you two split up.'

Len laughs hard. 'Samantha's dad can stick his job. But that Sam, you know, she's just a user. You'll have heard a different story – but you know what, *she* took that money. Granted, we spent it together, but it was her idea in the first place. She knew exactly where to find it. But the minute she got busted, she said it was me. Obvious, really.'

It's the most Len has said to him in years, and Luke feels like a fool. Checking his watch, Len gathers his things and pulls his heavy bag up over his shoulders. Together they leave the gloom of the pier and walk up towards the esplanade, where they stand on the deserted parade, as the ceaseless rain streams through their hair, making rivers over their faces.

'Len, you know Martin?'

Len looks at him, shrugs.

'He's alright, man – he's a good bloke. We all used to be friends, remember? You should give him a break.'

Len pushes the wet hair from his face and turns to scan the curling waves one last time. 'We're not all like the Waltons, Luke,' he says, not unkindly, and he walks away, out across the dimming night as the rain lashes down, never once looking back at his oldest friend, who stands at the roadside, watching until he's disappeared from view.

It's getting late by the time Luke arrives back in Blake Avenue, and he parks his scooter beneath the carport, vaulting over a large puddle to let himself in. Heading through the hallway, he strips off his T-shirt and grabs a towel from the bathroom to rough-dry his hair and mop off his arms and legs.

In the kitchen, he's met by the surprisingly formal assembly of Mum, Dad and Simon, the three of them sitting quite calmly around the table, a Kodak wallet of photos and negatives strewn across the centre of its wooden surface. Luke's heart jolts, his mind a racing jumble of sickness and relief. 'What – ?' he stammers, sliding along the bench to sit beside Simon, across the table from his parents.

Mum pushes the kitchen door closed and reaches across to squeeze Luke's hand. 'Kitty's asleep,' she says.

'Are these – ?' Luke starts, but he can't find the words, and he cautiously picks up the pictures and sifts through the images, one by one.

'It's the last of those bloody photographs,' Dad says. 'Thank God. Let's hope that's an end to it.' He fetches a fourth glass and pours wine for Luke. 'And you know, we had nothing to worry about, your mum and I – we're not even in there.'

Luke studies his dad, bemused. This is the first time he's spoken directly about these parties, the first time he's implied he had anything to fear. Gone is his jokey irreverence, replaced by an earnest calm, his steady hand on Mum's shoulder as she fixes her eyes on Luke's. He turns his attention back to the photos, which, but for just one, are quite harmless – gulls on the esplanade, sparrows in the dust, swallows at dusk. Typical Martin shots of wildlife and birds, the images crisp and clear.

'Have you checked the negatives?' he asks.

Dad nods. 'All there. All accounted for.'

Luke frowns, looking around the group in wordless question.

'It was Sara Newbury,' Dad says in reply. 'I caught her, just a couple of hours ago, outside the library, trying to pin this one on the board.' He waves the final picture and drops it on the pile with a flick of his wrist.

Luke retrieves the photo for a closer inspection. It's a wonderful shot: Fatty Michaels in the altogether, an arrogant smile across his smarmy chops, his copious flesh exposed for all to see. Of all the pictures, it's the one Luke would most liked to have seen on display. 'You should have left her to it, Dad. Fat fucker.'

'*Luke*,' Mum tuts, casting him a brief disapproving glance.

Simon laughs and puts an arm around Luke's bare shoulder, squeezing him once and releasing him. 'You've always been a good judge of character, Luke, old boy.' He lifts his glass and clinks it against Luke's.

Luke runs a weary hand across his brow, looking from the face of one parent to the other. 'So, no more secrets?' he says. 'Please?'

Mum reaches for Luke's fingers, lacing them with hers; Dad nods resolutely and reaches for the wine bottle. 'No more secrets,' Dad says.

A rattle of the kitchen door handle startles them all, and Kitty staggers in clutching Marty the elephant, pausing in the doorway to rub her eyes and squint at the gathered adults. The atmosphere in the room shifts at once; Luke catches the fleeting glance between Mum and Simon, the small shake of Dad's head. He feels exposed, sitting bare-chested in his damp shorts, as ever the one on the outside, the one looking in. It's as if the abrupt change in weather has modified everything, shunted it all off-centre so that, once again, the world he sees is a different version to the one he knew before.

Kitty pads around the table and leans her fuzzy head on his arm. 'Lu-lu,' she says, the words mumbled about her thumb. 'Thirsty.'

Luke slides off the bench and lifts her into his seat, where she clambers up next to Simon while Luke fetches a glass from the cupboard and fills it at the tap. As he turns to take Kitty her drink, his breath catches in his chest. Mum and Dad sit on one side, their clasped hands a tangle on the table top. Kitty stands on the bench beside Simon, leaning into him, her arms draped around his neck, her sleepy head resting on his. The shades of their hair are so remarkably alike, it's impossible to tell where Simon's hair stops and Kitty's starts.

A drop of water slops up over the edge of the glass, plopping to the floor at Luke's feet, the silence of the room now roaring in his ears. Slowly, his eyes turn to Mum's. 'You and Simon?' he whispers.

Mum picks up her glass and drains it, placing it down carefully as she refuses to return his gaze.

'*You* and Simon?' Luke asks again.

'*No!*' she whispers angrily, finally turning to face him. She lowers her voice, inclining her head towards Kitty, like a warning. 'No. It wasn't like that.'

In a fog of confusion, Luke walks across the kitchen, and holds out the glass to his sister. She drinks thirstily, and returns the glass to him before climbing down off the bench and wrapping her arms around his waist. Luke stands at the head of the table, cradling Kitty's head and trying to suppress the trembling of his legs as he waits for someone to speak.

'Why don't I put Kitty back to bed?' says Simon. He slides out from behind the table, gently squeezing past Luke to pick up Kitty and leave the room.

Luke stares at the empty doorway.

'Sit down, son,' Dad says, his voice solid. He scans the table.

All the colour has drained from Mum's face, and she can barely look at Luke as he lowers himself into the seat opposite. The cuckoo clock ticks loudly in the quiet pause, as the rain trickles down the window pane, pooling on the outside ledge. Mum studies the table top; Simon returns to the room and tops up the glasses.

'It's hard to know where to begin...' Dad starts, dipping his forefinger in a tiny bright spill of red wine.

Luke rolls his head back in exasperation, feeling the knots crunch along his neck. 'Bloody hell, *Dad*! Just spit it out, will you? You're killing me here!'

He raises his palms in surrender. 'OK, OK. It's these parties – well, I'm sure you've worked out a fair amount for yourself, son. You've heard the gossip – seen the photographs.'

'It's not how it sounds...' Mum says quietly.

'I know, Mum,' Luke replies, and he sighs deeply, wondering if he even has the energy to go on with this. 'I know. But, right now, I couldn't give a toss about your stupid parties. It's him – ' he flicks his head towards Simon ' – and Kitty I want to know about. What the hell is going on here? Is Simon – is he Kitty's *dad*?'

There's a brief exchange between Mum and Dad, one set of eyes flickering up to meet the other. They both nod. Luke lets a long, slow breath slip out between his lips as the enormity of the revelation sinks in. He scans the kitchen, weighing up his next move. Luke the boy would flounce from the room now, slam his bedroom door, wallop up the volume and shut out the world. But he doesn't want to be that boy any more.

'I don't know if I can listen to any more of this. It just goes on and on. I can't take much more of it.' He breathes deeply, and for a few moments no one speaks.

'Luke, old pal,' Simon finally says, shunting round to face him. 'You really need to hear this. Hear them out, will you?'

Mum rests her hands in her lap and opens her mouth to talk. 'It was just the once,' she says, after what seems like an age. 'Five and a half years ago. That was the first party we went to, and that was the only time either of us ever, *ever* went with anyone else.'

Luke eyes her coldly, waiting for her to continue.

'When you were born, we loved you so much, Luke. All we ever wanted was just one more child – a brother or sister for you, to complete our family.'

She looks to Dad.

'After we'd had you, we tried for another baby for years, son. Years and years. And nothing happened.'

Mum runs a thumbnail around a knot in the wood. 'Eventually, we went to the doctor's and found out the problem was with your dad, not me. He said that my chances of getting pregnant again by Dad were virtually nil.'

'Lazy sperm,' Dad says.

'Bloody hell,' Luke says, shaking his head. He can't believe they all look so composed.

'Simon had met Laura by then,' Mum carries on, 'and they'd told us about these parties, always trying to get us to go along and try it out. Of course, we laughed it off – thought it was just a phase they were going through.'

Simon expels an involuntary chuckle, immediately shaking his head remorsefully. 'I'm sorry, I shouldn't laugh. *Totally* inappropriate. It just sounds funny when you say it like that, Jo.'

Mum glares at Simon, smoothing her hands across her lap.

'Mum?'

'Sorry, Jo. *Sorry*,' Simon says, taking over. 'Look, the whole thing was my idea – let's get that straight before we go any further. You need to know that, Luke. I offered – Laura and I weren't planning for children, and I was happy to help out if I could.' He gestures towards Mum and Dad. 'These are my best friends – what else was there to do?'

Luke shakes his head.

'So we agreed, the party was the best place – keep it simple – if we all went with someone else, there could be no jealousy, no cause for upset. And that, as they say, is that.'

A burst of rainfall hammers against the kitchen window. Luke runs his hands over his face, wishing he could hide behind them forever. 'Man, I don't really know what to say about all this. *Simon* is Kitty's dad?'

Mum and Dad reach for each other, their hands linking, a small sadness passing between them.

'*Richard* is Kitty's dad,' Simon corrects, his brows knitting together, his headmaster's voice rearing up. 'I just provided some of the material needed. Better me than some complete stranger, eh?'

Dad folds his arms and taps the wood with the tip of his forefinger. 'We've so much to thank Simon for, Luke. We wouldn't have Kitty if it wasn't for his friendship. It doesn't change a thing, Luke. She's still your sister. We're still your parents. Nothing's changed – you know that?'

Luke rises and walks across the room, stopping beside the dresser to gaze at the small display of birthday cards lined up along the shelf.

Mum joins him, holding her arms wide. 'I'm so sorry we left it so long, love. There's just never been a good time to tell you...'

He allows her embrace, letting his head drop against her shoulder. Exhaustion pools in his chest.

'We should be grateful for everything we've got, Luke,' Dad says.

Luke raises his head to look at him and Simon, sitting either side of the table, swarthy as fishermen. Simon's hair has been bleached lighter over the summer months, and Luke now sees Kitty so very clearly, with her waving blonde hair and dark blue eyes. Simon studies his fingernails, not looking up, and Luke understands it all, his desire to hold tight to this ready-made family, when he has none. He thinks of Len, alone this evening, walking away into the coursing rain, never

272

looking back. Luke steps back and looks at them all, at Mum and Dad and Simon.

'I am grateful,' he says, and all at once he's compelled to call Martin, to reach out for him across the darkness of this rainswept August night, as the raging wind batters against the windows and doors of the little bungalow in Blake Avenue. He makes his way along the hall towards the telephone stand, where he hovers a moment, gathering his thoughts. He places his hand on the receiver – and it rings, sending a judder of fresh adrenaline through his veins. He lets the phone ring twice, then picks it up, his heartbeat pounding in his ears.

'Hello?' he says with some hesitation. There's a short silence on the other end of the line. 'Mart? Is that you?'

'*It's Dad*,' Martin whispers, his voice muffled as if he's cupping his hand around the mouthpiece. 'He can't get out of bed. Can you come over?'

The rain batters against the glass panels either side of Luke's front door, streaking channels of tears down its frosted vertical stripes. Martin has never asked Luke over to his house. 'What is it, Mart? Is it his bad back?'

Martin's voice is hoarse with fear. 'I've never seen him so bad, Luke. He doesn't know what he's saying. He keeps begging me to fetch the gun and finish him off.'

'I'll get my dad, mate. We'll be there in ten minutes.'

Martin hangs up, leaving nothing more but the desolate whirr of an empty line. Luke stares at the receiver a moment, as his brain shifts gear. 'Dad!' he calls along the hall, already reaching into the cupboard for his raincoat. 'Dad!'

Dad and Simon appear in the hallway, a matching frown on both tanned faces.

'We've got to get over to Martin's place. He needs us.'

13

Met Office report for the Isle of Wight, early September 1976:
Maximum temperature 62°F/16.7°C

Despite the recent downpour, meteorologists and weather experts continue to deliberate over the effects of the ceaseless summer, many claiming it will take years for the water table to return to a healthy level. But to the rest of the country – to the everyday folk in their houses and gardens, in their cars and buses, in their school rooms and offices – the summer of '76 is over; the heatwave has finally broken.

After the service, the small congregation meanders in the sunlit gardens of the crematorium, a sea breeze whispering in the clear air. Luke sticks close to Martin's side, the pair of them wavering quietly beneath the adjacent oak tree, not sure what to do with themselves now that the funeral is over. There's a careful hush among those assembled; it seems many here hardly knew Alan Brazier at all, most having been gathered by Richard and Joanna Wolff over the few days since he died, making up numbers for Martin's sake.

Leaving Nanna sitting on the shaded bench between Simon and the vicar, Kitty runs to Martin, taking him by the hand and pulling him towards the wide, dried-out lawn, where she spins in circles and points out birds perching in the overhanging trees. He looks like a proper man in his new suit, picked out with Mum's help from Chiesman's department store in Newport. Luke joins his parents as they stroll to the edge of the lawn with Teddy and Rhona from the Spar, all of them dressed in black – such a stark contrast to the bleached-out shades of this summer.

'Bless him,' says Rhona, her eyes following Martin as he picks Kitty up and wanders around the edges of the shrubbery. 'He only had his dad, didn't he, Jo?'

Teddy purses his lips, resembling a member of the mob in his Fifties suit, his meaty hands clasped together respectfully.

'Yup,' Luke replies. 'I don't think he's even got aunts or uncles. None that he's ever mentioned, anyway.'

'Such a shame,' Rhona replies.

'He'll be alright,' Dad says, slipping his hand around Mum's waist. Kitty waves from across the lawn; they all wave back.

'So what did the doctors say?' Rhona asks in confidential tones. 'You spoke to them at the hospital, didn't you, Richard?'

He nods.

'They said he'd been ill for months. Initially the doctors didn't spot it was cancer, but, when they suspected it, he just refused to go for tests.'

'Poor beggar,' says Teddy, reaching inside his jacket for his cigarettes. He taps one out on to the heel of his hand, before bringing it to his mouth, continuing to talk around the filter as he lights it. 'What a way to go. Did Martin know he was ill?'

'He knew something was wrong,' Luke replies. 'But he had no idea it was serious.'

Simon joins them and, seeing that Teddy is smoking, appears instantly relieved and reaches for his own cigarettes. Teddy offers him a light, and Luke resists the sudden urge to ask if he can have a fag too.

Dad tugs at his tie, loosening it enough to undo his top button. 'Martin said he'd been trying to get him back to the doctor's for weeks, but he wouldn't have any of it. And then, of course, once we did get him into the hospital, he didn't even make it through the night.'

Rhona gasps softly, absently wafting her hand to bat the cigarette smoke away. Cradling her little handbag in the crook of her arm, she opens it up and brings out a packet of mints, peeling back the crumpled wrapper and offering one to Teddy, who's still mid-cigarette. She drops the packet back into her bag and snaps the clasp shut, shaking her head sadly. 'There but for the grace of God.'

The McKees join the group, looking as out of place as everyone else. Marie embraces Mum, stepping aside as John awkwardly stoops in to kiss her.

'Thanks for coming,' Mum whispers.

'Not at all, darling.' Marie caresses the lapels of her dark jacket, and glances in Martin's direction. '*So* sad.'

Dad shakes John's hand. 'Good to see you, John. Been keeping busy?'

'Always busy,' John replies, sweeping restless fingers through his white hair as Marie holds her arms out to embrace Dad. She kisses him twice, holding on to his upper arm as she talks.

'You know John, Richard! We can't keep him out of the office for more than a few days, or he starts getting withdrawal symptoms.'

Looking at them standing there in their sober suits and greying hair, Luke finds it almost impossible to believe they've so recently been the hosts of these parties. He pushes away an unbidden image of John and Marie mingling among their guests, carrying trays of drinks and nibbles, and letting it all hang out.

'Oh, hello, Luke – and Simon!' Marie says, letting her hand drift away from Dad's arm as she kisses Simon. 'I am glad we came, Richard – it doesn't look as if he knew many people around here, judging by the congregation. So what will happen with Martin now?'

Dad ruffles Luke's hair, just as he used to when he was small. 'We'll help him work it out, won't we, Luke?'

'Maybe I should go and see if he's alright,' Luke says, and he leaves his parents with the others to amble across the crunchy dried grass, hands in pockets, wondering what he'll say to Martin when he gets there.

'Go and find Mummy,' he tells Kitty when she sprints over, and she bombs past, heading back to the edge of the path, where Dad swoops her up into his arms.

Martin is standing at the foot of a young poplar tree, his long arms dangling at his sides, head tilted in concentration. Birds chatter in the branches above.

Luke stops a few feet away. 'You OK, Mart?'

'Hi,' Martin says as he looks round, seeming surprised to see Luke standing there. 'I was trying to show Kitty the chaffinch.'

'She's gone off to find Mum,' Luke replies, cocking a thumb over his shoulder. 'Just thought I'd come and see how you're doing. You did really well in there, mate. It can't have been easy.'

Martin reaches up and snaps off a leaf, turning it over in his large hands, studying the veins closely.

'It was good of your dad to stand up and talk like that – I know everyone probably thinks it's pathetic, but I just couldn't do it.'

'No one thinks it's pathetic, Mart. Christ, you've been through enough without having to get up there and do a big speech in front of a bunch of stuffy suits and hats.'

He moves closer and prods Martin's arm, making him look up. He looks ten again, like an overgrown child dressed in a man's suit, and he smiles weakly, crumbling the leaf between his fingers and letting it fall to the ground.

'The poem he read out was really nice.'

Luke flicks his head for Martin to walk with him, and they follow the line of the manicured hedge until the lawn opens out into the woodland path. 'My mum chose it. I know it's about a carpenter, not a framer, but still – I think it was a good choice. She's written out a copy for you to keep.'

They walk on through the woods, silent but for the soothing twitter of birdsong, and the occasional clatter of the wood pigeons as they rise up through the leaf canopy. The first signs of autumn are more visible here, where the moss-cloaked foot of each tree is joined by an explosion of earthy mushrooms and tiny red toadstools, coaxed out by the recent humidity and rainfall. Further up the older trunks, large, brightly coloured fungus fans out in elaborate formation, wrapping around the bark in vibrant swirls of yellow and orange, its delicate flesh as tender as chicken.

Luke glances at Martin, trying to read his expression, the contours of his long face ever-shifting as they pass beneath flickering slices of early afternoon light. As ever, Martin's focus is in the treetops above as he scans for wildlife, occasionally pointing to the red squirrels that skitter from one branch to the next, searching out food for their winter reserves. At a fork in the path the lads slow their pace, coming to a stop in a warm pool of sunlight that breaks through the parting of leaves overhead. Luke casts his gaze along the rough paths, wondering where each leads to.

'Which way, mate?' he asks, turning to see Martin carefully folding his jacket on to the dusty earth before he reaches up for a low branch and starts to climb the tree. 'What about your new shoes?' Luke laughs. He watches as Martin steadily ascends the enormous trunk, moving surprisingly gracefully for a man of six foot five.

Martin pauses to look back, his movements causing a vortex of dust motes to dance and swirl in the warm pillar of light between them.

'I hope I never have to wear them again,' he says. 'They pinch like hell.' With a bob of his head, he beckons Luke to follow behind.

Once Martin has established himself on a sturdy crook of the tree, Luke goes after him, instinctively using all the same footholds and supports that Martin had scaled moments earlier. Seconds later he's sitting beside him, looking out over the treetops, into the gardens of the crematorium, where he can just make out his parents, still in conversation at the edge of the path. Martin lifts a foot and inspects it, checking out the deep scuffs across its polished toe.

'Look at Kitty,' he says, pointing over to the gardens, where they can see her tiny figure performing clumsy cartwheels along the lawn.

Luke smiles. 'Nutter.' His affection for her swells as he watches her from a distance, oblivious as she is to the events and revelations of this restless summer. She runs past the group of adults; Simon jumps out to catch her and her little arms shoot up in delight as she lets him.

'I don't know what I'd have done without you over this last week, Luke,' Martin says, as he continues to gaze over at the family scene. 'And your folks. It's been – ' He stops short, the muscles in his jaw clenching tight, his nostrils flaring.

Martin's hand rests on the branch between them and Luke presses his own upon it, letting it linger long enough to convey his understanding. 'You're not on your own, mate. You do know that?'

Martin breathes deeply, his hand moving swiftly to remove a tear before it has a chance to fall. 'But the thing is, I *am*.' He turns to Luke. 'I mean, you'll be leaving next week, and I can't stay at your place forever. I'll have to go back home sooner or later – and I just don't know if I can face it, rattling around that place on my own, with my dad not there.'

Luke looks away, focusing resolutely on the group beyond, biting down on his teeth to control his own tears. He thinks of his family: his dad with his well-meaning bullshit and jovial warmth; his mother, quietly bending her will to the needs of them all; and lovely Nanna, who's just there, always the same, with her shepherd's pies and bad language. He sees Martin in his mind's eye, a solitary figure sitting at the table in that cold shell of a house, drinking tea from his last chipped mug, with nothing to look forward to but loneliness, as Luke sails away into the bright world beyond. A tree sparrow lands briefly on the adjoining branch, taking to the air again at the turn of Martin's head.

'But you'll have all sorts of choices to make now, mate,' Luke says. 'You'll be able to do that photography course you talked about? I know it's bad now, but your life could really change, if you wanted it to, Mart. In good ways.'

Martin picks the bark dust off his trousers, smoothing the new material flat against his thighs. 'You know, he wasn't all bad, Luke. Dad. He had a good side to him too, when he wanted. When he let it show.'

Luke nods, watching the dispersing group on the lawn as people head back to their cars to make way for the next service. His parents disappear beyond the screen of trees. 'I know that, mate. Everyone loves their parents, no matter what. I mean, look at my lot. They've hardly turned out to be straightforward, have they?'

Martin lets out a small laugh. '*Swingers*,' he whispers.

Luke laughs too, shaking his head. 'Man, there's more to that story than you could ever imagine.'

'Is that good?' Martin asks, looking concerned.

'Kind of. Well, yeah, it is – it's all good. Maybe I'll tell you over a pint later? Dad and Simon said we ought to take you down the Crab and Lobster, to raise a glass to your dad. What d'you reckon?'

'A beer would be really nice.' Martin nods slowly, his face relaxing for the first time all day. 'Oh, that reminds me,' he says. 'I found this.' He reaches into his trouser pocket and pulls out a small photographic reel.

'The missing film?' Luke gasps, laughing aloud. 'This is really it? Man, that's brilliant news. This one's going straight in the bin where it belongs.'

'I reckon we can do better than that,' Martin says as he cracks open the plastic casing and drapes the long thin negative over the branch between them. He takes the silver lighter from his inside pocket and holds it up to show Luke. 'I knew it would come in handy.'

Luke watches as Martin snaps off a small twig and holds out one end of the film, reaching across to light it. It quickly takes light, small licks of fire travelling up its length as Martin feeds the other end of the film up over the branch until nothing remains but an oily patch of tar.

'Now you can forget about it,' he says, and he clicks his lighter once, ker-chink, and returns it to his inside pocket.

There's the crunch of footfall on the path below. Luke brings his finger to his lips, and they both incline their heads to listen out.

'So that's where you've got to,' Dad calls up, stepping back so they can see each other clearly. 'Are you boys smoking? Look at this, Jo,' he calls back along the path.

Luke turns back to Martin, talking softly. 'Mart, promise me one thing. When I'm over at college – you'll come and stay with me some time? Check out the courses, see what you think of the mainland?'

Martin stares at him. 'You'd really want me to?'

'Of course I would, you idiot,' Luke replies. 'Honestly. I'll be mad with you if you don't.'

Mum and Kitty fall into view, and together with Dad they stand in the light clearing, shading their eyes and peering up into the tree.

'*Two little dicky birds sitting on a wall,*' Dad says in a sing-song voice.

Kitty squeals as she spots them. '*One named Peter – one named Paul!*' She points up at their dangling legs, clapping her hands. 'Come down, Marty! Time to go home.'

Martin waves at her, and when Luke turns to face him he sees eyes full of tears.

'Are you boys fit to go?' Mum asks. 'Simon's dropping Nanna back at ours so she can check on the casserole. It's beef, Martin – your favourite.'

'Are you OK?' Luke whispers.

Martin rubs the bridge of his nose, taking a long breath. 'I'm fine,' he says, and he gestures towards the trunk for Luke to begin their descent.

'Hope you can get down from there,' Dad calls up, 'because I'm not sure I'm up to tree-climbing these days.'

At the bottom, Mum links an arm through Martin's and together with Kitty leads the way through the dappled woods, with Luke and Dad at the rear. They arrive at the car, parked alone in a small sunny patch to the side of the crematorium. Kitty and Martin squeeze into the back seat, Kitty yelping as he squishes her face with his gangly elbow.

'Mum?' Luke says, hesitating before he climbs in beside them. 'I was just wondering…'

From the other side of the car Dad folds his arms on to the roof, listening intently.

'I was just wondering if you'd ever thought of taking in a lodger?' He indicates towards the back seat of the car. 'I mean, my room's going to be empty – and I think he needs family around him at the moment.'

Mum and Dad exchange the briefest of glances, before Mum turns to kiss Luke on the cheek with a small nod. He wedges himself into the tight back seat alongside Kitty and Martin, and the five of them head off home along the winding roads to Sandown.

At midday the following Sunday, Dad arrives home with Nanna in the car, having fetched her from Wootton Creek for Luke's leaving lunch. Luke meets them on the driveway, taking Nanna's arm as she hobbles up the front doorstep, where Martin is waiting just inside the door.

'Marty, my love,' she says, dropping Luke's arm and reaching up for Martin.

He stoops awkwardly, and she takes his face in her hands to regard him sternly before kissing his pale forehead. 'Don't you worry about a thing, son. You've got us now.' She releases his head and continues to limp along the hall and out through the open doors to the garden, where Mum is setting out the long table.

Together, they sit in the gentle sunshine, enjoying the warm breeze that ripples through the leaves of the weeping willow, Dad at one end of the table, Nanna at the other, with Mum, Kitty, Luke and Martin on either side. *Young Americans* plays from the record player in the living room, a leaving gift from Martin to Luke, his own copy to take with him to his new digs. 'So you don't have to keep pinching mine,' Martin said this morning, as he handed it to him with a bashful smile. They eat and talk at ease, the natural rhythm of the family guiding the conversation, any silences comfortable; the laughter abundant. Simon has gone now, moved into the box-room of one of the teachers from school, a hard-drinking bachelor from the maths department. Dad reckons he'll be lucky to keep his job, if the authorities get wind of those photographs. 'We'll just have to hope for the best, my friend,' Dad told him, as they stood on the doorstep and waved him off yesterday. 'Business as usual,' Simon replied, and he kissed Mum, and then Kitty, before shaking Luke by the hand and driving off in his car with a cheery toot-toot.

Now, Luke watches Martin across the table, as he chats quietly with Kitty, patiently listening to the trivia of her little world, nodding and contributing in the right places. Luke thinks about the enormity of Martin's trauma, and wonders whether he'd have coped so well himself; whether he'd have been as strong.

'We'll take Kitty to Blackgang Chine, won't we, Luke?' Martin asks, loosely waving a hand to catch his attention. 'Next time you're back over? I've been telling her all about Nurseryland.'

Luke smiles, fighting the lump that threatens to rise in his throat. 'Yeah, of course we will, mate. And they've got dinosaurs, Kitty, and Cowboys and Indians. You'll love it.'

Delighted, Kitty thumps the table with the flats of her hands, knocking a few loose streamers from the table, so that they flutter and trail across the lawn in the breeze. As it's a double celebration, Kitty has insisted on balloons, and they're tied everywhere – on fence posts and branches, window hinges and bucket handles – where they bob brightly in the light wind.

'So, tomorrow's the big day, son?' Dad says as Mum starts to clear away the lunch plates. He opens three beer bottles and hands them down to the lads and Nanna, opening a fourth one for himself and raising it ceremoniously.

'Yep, the big adventure,' Luke replies, the reality of it suddenly upon him.

Mum puckers her chin sadly. 'I can't believe it,' she says, picking up Nanna's plate and resting a hand on her shoulder. 'Are you sure you wouldn't prefer some of my wine, Nan?' she asks.

Nan wrinkles her nose and taps her beer bottle. 'This'll do nicely, love. Not so keen on the fancy stuff; gives me gut rot.'

Mum briefly disappears into the kitchen, returning with a big dish of shop-bought Swiss roll and custard, Luke's favourite childhood pudding. As she serves up, he reaches across the table to take the bowl from her hands, noticing the tears in her eyes.

'*Mum*. I'll be back all the time. It's only Brighton – it's no distance at all.'

'I know,' she says. 'Ignore me. I'm just being a big baby. Thank goodness we'll still have Martin to keep us company. You can keep us up to date on what Luke's up to, Martin. He's bound to tell you more than he will us!'

Martin looks into his bowl bashfully, unable to disguise his gladness. He picks up his spoon, and takes a large mouthful of pudding before looking up again.

'I think we should get a picture,' Dad announces, breaking into the hush that has fallen over the table. 'Capture the moment for posterity. What d'you think, Martin?'

As Martin fetches his camera from the kitchen, Dad pulls up a trestle to set it up on, and directs everyone to move in and huddle around Nanna for a group shot. Kitty clambers up over Martin's shoulders, to cling like a tree frog about his neck, where she squeals and wriggles as they wait for the camera to be ready.

They're interrupted by the bellowing voice from next door's garden. 'Afternoon!'

Dad puts the camera down, and they all turn towards Mike Michaels, who's resting his pasty forearms on the fence that separates the two gardens. After a second, he's joined by Diana, looking radiant in her oversized white sunhat.

'Afternoon, Mike,' Dad replies, friendly but reserved. 'Diana. Lovely day, isn't it?'

'Superb,' Mike agrees, his greedy gaze roaming over the lunch table, taking in the balloons and streamers that adorn the garden. 'Are we missing out on a party?' he says, clapping his hands together loudly.

Luke hasn't seen Diana since their night together, and he can hardly bring himself to look at her as the fleeting recollection of her skin on his slides across his memory. He fiddles with the edge of the tablecloth, before setting himself to the job of clearing away the pudding bowls.

'It's Luke's last day,' Dad replies. 'He's off to college tomorrow.'

'Oh, that's marvellous!' Diana calls over, forcing Luke to stop what he's doing and look up. She holds on to the top of her hat to prevent the wind from snatching it away. 'You must be so excited, Luke?'

'I am,' he says, turning to face her, attempting a natural smile. He knows he should be ashamed of their night together, yet right now, gazing across the garden fence into her cat-like eyes, he feels only pride. Diana blinks at him once, so kindly and with such warmth that he knows all is well, that she wishes him only good things. 'What about Tom?' he asks. 'Has he gone back to London?'

'Bet he was *itching* to get back,' Nanna giggles, nudging Luke's leg.

'Last week,' Mike replies, momentarily distracted by a streamer that flutters on the fence post by his face. He bats it away with the back of his hand. 'Anyway! You know how we love a party, Richard. Aren't you going to ask us over?'

An embarrassing interval passes as Mum and Dad lock eyes, each waiting for the other to answer. 'Well, you know –' Dad stammers.

'No,' Nanna interjects from her seat at the head of the table, reaching up to take Luke's hand. 'Sorry, love. It's strictly family today.'

Dad looks relieved and he shrugs at Mike apologetically. 'Another time?' he says.

Mike balks, his puffy chin pulling back. 'Why's he there, then?' He nods accusingly at Martin. '*He's* not family.'

Martin sits motionless, his gaze fixed on the camera, as if he's still waiting for the button to go off.

Nanna bangs her hand on the table. 'He bloody well is!' she says, loud enough to alarm Kitty, who drops down from Martin's back. Kitty looks furious.

'He's *not*,' Mike replies, as if the subject's up for debate.

'*Mike*,' Diana hisses, now out of sight.

'Yes, he is,' Mum says, and she rests her hands on Martin's shoulders. 'He's moved into Luke's room. He absolutely *is* one of the family, Mike. Aren't you, Martin?'

Martin bobs his head once, his expression still blank.

On the other side of the fence, Mike scowls, his knuckles still gripping the top of the panel. Dad runs his hands through his hair and sighs, exasperated, shaking his head as he meets Luke's eyes, and takes his wallet from his back pocket. Leisurely, he walks towards the fence and stands before Mike, where he opens up his wallet and hands him the photograph.

Mike's brows rise in disgust as he takes in his own naked form, and he looks up at Dad with a confused little shake of his head.

'I didn't want to do this, Mike. But quite honestly, you're a bully. Martin here – you know what he's been through lately, and still you treat him like this. He's ten times the man you'll ever be, Mike, and, while I'm giving you this photo here, to do with as you wish – put it up on your mantelpiece if you like – I just want you to know: we've still got the negatives.'

Mike backs away from the fence, his livid red face disappearing from view, before the sound of his back door slamming puts a final close to the conversation.

As the rest of the family return to position for the photograph, Luke catches Dad's arm and holds him back.

'Are you alright, Luke?' he asks.

'I'm fine.' Luke looks across the lawn towards the party table, where the rest of the family are busy trying to work out the best arrangement for the photograph. 'Only – there's just one more thing I wanted to ask you, Dad, about all that party business.'

Dad rests his hand on the fence top, the breeze rippling through his hair. 'Go ahead, son. I promised you, didn't I? No more secrets.'

Luke clears his throat.

'So – when Mum went off with Simon at that first party – who did you end up with?'

Dad looks shocked at first, before his mouth breaks into a reluctant smile. He shakes his head and starts to laugh. '*Shit.*'

'What?' Luke asks, starting to laugh himself. 'I'm right, aren't I? Was it Marie?'

Dad pinches at his bottom lip, as if weighing up whether to tell him or not. 'No – it wasn't Marie, son,' he finally says, his eyes welling up as his chest rises and falls between embarrassed groans.

'So *who*, then?' Luke demands through a bemused grin. 'You said it yourself. *No more secrets.*'

Dad clamps his hands over his face and hangs his head in shame, speaking through the muffle of his fingers. 'It was – it was Sara Newbury.'

Luke shakes his head in disbelief, as the laughter rolls up through his ribs. 'Oh, man, talk about the short straw,' he gasps, reaching out to prod his dad, who's running a finger beneath his lashes to wipe away the tears. 'Oh, *man*,' he repeats. 'Tell you what, if this doesn't cheer Martin up, I don't know what will.'

'Don't you dare,' Dad growls, putting a hand on the back of Luke's neck and pulling him in for a rough hug. 'Now, what about this photo we're trying to take?'

The two men jog across the dried grass, where Luke takes his assigned place between Martin and Nanna. Kitty clambers back up over Martin's shoulders, while Dad slips an arm about Mum's waist, sucking in his stomach muscles as the camera timer counts down for the family portrait. 'OK, everyone, after three. Three – two – '

A pair of swallows flies over the garden, arcing through the air.

'*One!*'

Luke and Martin turn their faces towards the birds, a shared thought, locked in time as the shutter comes down and the moment is captured.

Acknowledgements

The characters and events in this novel are all inventions. Yet the places – the beaches, hilltops, towns and villages of the inimitable Isle of Wight – all exist as inspirations to *Summer of '76*, as do certain facts of local and national history.

I couldn't have written this book without the help I received from a number of people. My sincere thanks to:

My readers – for your kind words, your generous reviews and for coming back for more – thank you.

The magnificent team at Myriad Editions. Thanks to Candida Lacey, Corinne Pearlman, Emma Dowson, Linda McQueen and Holly Ainley – with a special mention to my editor Vicky Blunden, whose literary skills and sharp insight are second to none. To my agent, Kate Shaw, thank you for your boundless support and encouragement – it's really good to know you're there.

My writer friends, in particular Jane Rusbridge, Gabrielle Kimm, Jane Osis and Juliet West. Heartfelt thanks for your good company, conversation and laughter.

The Met Office Library and Archive – for providing superbly detailed weather information from the 1970s, an element that formed the backbone of this book from the first word.

Wightlink ferry company, for their generous sponsorship granting me regular passage to the Isle of Wight, without which this novel might not exist. And for hosting my Solent book signings – my favourite gigs of the year.

I'm indebted to the many island folk I've met over the years: the staff, captains and crew of Wightlink ferry company – and their passengers – for their endlessly fascinating stories; DJ Dave Cannon for his first-hand knowledge of the *Ryde Queen* nightclub; the fishermen at Medina Quay for their recollections of teen spirit '76; Paul Armfield at Waterstones in Newport for his solid support since the start; the authors of Wootton Bridge Historical, whose website has been a great source of information, inspiration and enjoyment. Thank you all for generously sharing your memories and history of island life in the 1970s. Despite all this first-class input, inaccuracies relating to the island may still exist, and I claim them as mine alone. Perhaps we might put them down to artistic licence.

Much love to Colin, Alice and Samson, and all my family and friends for their encouragement, kindness and patience – you know who you are.

And finally, thank you to David Bowie, for *Young Americans*.

A F T E R W O R D :

Book Group Guide   294

Extract from *Glasshopper*   296

1. How does the novel conjure up the atmosphere of the heatwave of 1976?

2. Does the representation of that period chime with your own memories?

3. The novel is told from Luke's perspective, but did you identify with other characters in the story?

4. Are there any real villains?

5. Does Luke's work at the holiday camp remind you of your own first summer job?

6. Do you think the McKees' parties could happen in the modern day or are they specific to the spirit of the 1970s?

7. Do you think the characters would have behaved as they did if it hadn't been such exceptional weather?

8. Should Joanna and Richard have acted differently, particularly in terms of concealing or revealing the truth about Kitty's paternity?

9. To what extent could the novel be described as a portrait of a marriage?

10. Does the novel make any judgements about good or bad parenting?

11. How might Joanna's experience have been different if the story had had a contemporary setting?

12. Did your feelings about Diana change as the novel progressed?

13. Would you consider any of the characters to be feminist?

14. In what ways does Sam use her power over men?

15. Do you blame Mr Brazier for Martin's lack of confidence and ambition?

16. Could Luke have been a better friend to Martin?

17. What do you make of Luke's friendship with Tom?

18. What might the future hold for Martin?

19. Are the sorts of issues and events the characters are dealing with particular to life in a small community? What aspects are universal?

20. How does Luke change in the course of the book? What do you think the future holds for him?

If you liked *Summer of '76*, you might like Isabel Ashdown's critically acclaimed debut novel *Glasshopper*.

Observer **Best Debut Novels of the Year**
London Evening Standard **Best Books of the Year**
Winner of the *Mail on Sunday* **novel competition**

For an exclusive extract, read on…

Glasshopper

ISABEL ASHDOWN

WINNER OF THE *MAIL ON SUNDAY*
NOVEL COMPETITION

Jake, November 1984

I love November. I love the frosty grass that pokes up between the paving slabs, and the smoke that puffs out of your nostrils like dragon's breath. I love the ready-made ice rink that freezes underneath the broken guttering in the school playground. And I love the salt 'n' vinegar heat inside a noisy pub, when everyone outside is walking about in hats and gloves with dripping red noses.

This one Saturday afternoon, Dad and me are down the Royal Oak, getting ready to watch the match. Dad tells Eric the landlord that I'm fourteen, so I can come into the bar so long as I only have Coke. Not that I'd want what they all drink.

Dad shouts over, 'Fancy a bag of nuts, Jakey?' and I give him the thumbs-up from the corner seat we've bagged. It's great today because it's just me and Dad. Andy's on some boring Scout trip, and he won't be back till teatime. And Matthew – well, he just sort of disappeared a few weeks back. One morning I got out of bed, and went into Matt's room to wake him up with this fart I'd got brewing. It kills him every time. Anyway, this one morning, I go into his room, and he's not there. His bed was empty. So were his drawers. He'd taken all his clothes and records, so I knew he wasn't planning on coming back any time soon. Even his aftershave had gone. When I went in to tell Mum, she said, 'He'll be back when he's hungry,' and she rolled over and went back to sleep. But he didn't come back. Dad says he's old enough to leave home if he wants to, now he's seventeen. But I know that Dad wishes he knew where Matt was. The thing is, Matt couldn't stand being around Mum any more, and Dad's still in his bed-sit, so he couldn't have him there. It's not ideal, Dad says, but what can you do? The worst thing is, Matthew had only just got on to this Youth Training thing that was going to teach him bricklaying. He was gonna make a fortune, he said. I wish he'd phone or something. I could ask him if they've got YTS at his new place.

'There you go, Jake, lad.' Dad puts the drinks down on the round table, and settles into his seat. 'We should get a good view from here, son. Here, 'ave you seen the new TV Eric's got up on the bar? It's the business – Teletext, eighteen-inch screen, remote control – the works. Reckon I should save for one of them, shouldn't I, lad? Trinitron.'

It's a really nice telly.

'So, what's new, Jakey? How's it going at school? You still in the footie team?'

That's one of the things I like about Dad. All his questions are dead easy, and we never run out of things to say.

'Yeah, it's all cool. Because we're in the second year, we're doing Classical Studies, and it's brilliant. We're learning about Odysseus. He has quests, and he has to kill monsters and cross oceans just to get back home. There's a Cyclops and sea monsters and loads of other stuff. It's brilliant – you'd love it, Dad. I think it's my best lesson now. Miss Terry's giving us Greek names as she gets to know us. Simon Tomms is Poseidon, Emma Sullivan is Artemis. She's still thinking about mine.'

'Your mum got me to read *The Odyssey* when we were courting. And *The Iliad*.' He takes a sip of his beer and smacks his lips loudly. 'You'd like *Jason and the Argonauts*, son. Now that's a good film. There's this one bit, when the Argonauts run into seven skeletons and they rise up from the earth, wielding swords and marching like soldiers of the dead. I tell you, that was one of the greatest achievements of twentieth-century film-making, Jake. And it was bloody creepy too. There's a film to stand the test of time.'

He takes another swig from his glass, wiping the froth from his top lip with the back of his hand as he looks around the pub.

'And Mrs Jenkins chose my bonfire night picture for the corridor display this week. She said that it's "highly original".' I do her high-pitched voice to make Dad laugh. 'It'll be stuck up in the corridor, so everyone will get to see it when they come for Parents' Evening.'

'Parents' Evening,' Dad says, dabbing his finger in the dew around his glass. 'Is your mum going?'

'She says yes. I mean, she signed the slip saying she would. And I gave it back to Mr Thomas.'

'When is it, son?'

'Some time at the end of the month,' I answer. I know what he's getting at.

'Well, if there are any problems, you give me a ring. Here's 10p for the phone box, in case you need to phone from school. Stick it in your pocket. You can get me at the workshop. Alright, son?'

I smile at him, sucking up my Coke through two straws. It feels different drinking Coke out of two straws instead of one. If I had to choose, I think I'd go for one straw. It's less gassy. I wonder what Odysseus would choose, one or two. Mind you, Coke wasn't even invented back then.

'Dad, I don't s'pose you know what Mum's done with our library cards, do you? It's just they won't let me take out – '

'Stu!' My dad shouts across the crowded pub.

Stu's this new mate of Dad's, and he's come to watch the match too. Sometimes, when he comes to the pub, he brings his son with him – Malcolm. Malcolm's the same age as me, and he's mostly OK, but sometimes a bit of an idiot. Once I saw him trip up this little kid in the pub garden, on purpose, just for a laugh. Then this other time we saw some woman struggling with a pram in the paper shop, and he helped her lift it over the step. Dad reckons Malcolm's a bit of an oddball. I think Malcolm's OK.

'Alright, Bill mate!' Stu bundles over with their drinks, grinning at Dad, unwrapping his scarf and hat. 'Glad to see you could make it. This should be a good 'un, eh? Room for two more? Budge up, Jakey boy.'

Dad's pleased to see Stu. 'Just in time for kick-off, mate. Good timing.'

Malcolm's cheeks look all shiny and red with the cold. Like apples. We nod at each other, and then Eric whacks up the volume, and shouts, 'Alright lads!' and everyone turns to the TV as the players run on the pitch and take position.

Stu lights up a cigarette and squashes further into the seat so that I have to budge up to get out of his smoke.

'Should be a good match,' he says knowingly, leaning on to his knees like an excited kid.

Dad agrees and helps himself to one of Stu's fags. 'Just the one,' he says to me with a nudge.

As it turns out, the match is a really boring one, and by half-time it's still nil-nil. In between, Dad and Stu give us each 30p and let us go off to get some sweets from the newsagents. We leave them in the pub getting another round in.

On the way back from the shops, Malcolm tells me about the BMX he reckons he's getting for his birthday next week. They're dead expensive, and I ask him how his dad can afford it. He squats down next to a drain in the road and drops his lolly stick through the gaps, before carrying on along the path.

'It's 'cos him and my mum are divorced. 'Cos I live with Mum and Phil. So Dad always tries really hard to get me a better present than them. Then they say stuff like, who does he think he is, flash git, and then they get me something great too. It's brilliant. Win-win.'

Sometimes I don't get Malcolm, but he's got a point. It does sound quite good.

'Is Phil loaded, then?' I ask.

'Nah. But they get the money from somewhere. That's what counts.'

Malcolm looks like a spoilt kid. He's too big, and too chubby, and his black hair is a bit square. But he talks like he thinks he's cool. He shoves his hands in his pockets and pulls out a liquorice shoelace, shovelling it all in at once.

'What about your lot?' he asks, an end of shoelace poking out the corner of his mouth. 'Do you get good stuff off them? I mean, they've split up, haven't they?'

We reach the phone box on the corner of Park Road.

'You ever played "Mrs McSporran", Malc?' I ask him, heaving open the chipped red door, releasing the stench of old piss and cigarette burns. Malcolm's frowning at me like I'm a right prat. 'Come on,' I urge him, as he stands outside the glass, chewing.

Half-heartedly he comes inside, which is a bit of a squeeze with his chubby belly.

'It'll be a laugh,' I say. 'Watch the master at work.'

I dial 100. 'Reverse call, please,' I tell the operator. I give her a made-up number and name – 'Yes, Albert' – and we wait for the connection.

Malcolm keeps looking around, to see if anyone's coming. He looks really nervous.

'Hulllooo!' I shout when the operator puts me through. 'Hulllooo? Is that wee Ethel McSporran?'

Malcolm's eyes are like saucers, and his mouth has dropped open like a cartoon.

'Ach, Ethel! D'ye need any haggis, Ethel?' I hoot, as the woman on the other end tries to explain that I've got the wrong number. 'Och, Ethel, pipe down, will ye, wee lassie! Ye dinne wan' iny haggis? Hoo aboot some bagpipes?'

Malcolm has tears welling up in his eyes.

'Eh? Oor hoo aboot a kilt?' This one is so high-pitched that I crack up too, and just manage a final 'Tatty-bye,' before hanging up.

Malc is thumping his fists on the glass, choking on his Hubba Bubba.

'You're nuts, mate – ' he splutters, still chuckling, his shiny cheeks redder than ever.

I offer him the receiver – 'Wanna go?' – but he shakes his head, laughing, pushing out of the phone box backwards. As we carry on back towards the Royal Oak, we see an old dear sat at the bus stop on the other side of the road. She looks quite sweet, with a big shopping bag on the floor by her little brown shoes, and she seems to be smiling at everything. I notice the bag's made of a kind of plastic tartan material. Malc sees it too, because he snorts and shoves me.

She's a little way off, and I come to a stop facing her over the road, hands on my hips, legs wide. In my deepest Scottish bellow I shout over to her, 'Hulllooo, dearie! D'ye wanna haggis?'

The little old lady tips her head to one side, like she's trying to hear better.

Malc tugs at my sleeve, and screeches in a rubbish accent, 'Oor perhaps a hairy sporran!' and we tear off down the street before she has a chance to get a good look at us.

An old man with a poofy little sausage dog waves his newspaper angrily at us as we run past.

'Bloody hooligans!' he shouts, like a character from *Benny Hill*.

I smirk at him, running backwards so he can see I'm not scared of him. His dog cocks his leg and pisses against the litter bin, and the steam rises like smoke as it trickles down the pavement and off the kerb.

When we get a safe distance away we stop, hands on our knees, catching our breath between sobbing laughter. A gobstopper slips out of my mouth on to the toe of my plimsoll, before rolling along the pavement and coming to a stop by Malcolm's foot. We look up at each other, and now we're almost screaming, holding our bellies and gasping like we've got asthma.

'Was she Scottish, then – ' Malcolm asks as we get a grip of ourselves '– the woman on the phone?'

I shake my head.

'Then what's with all the Scotch stuff?'

'Dunno, it's just kind of funny,' I answer. 'Shit! I forgot the oatcakes! You should always ask if they want any oatcakes!'

As we get closer to the pub, we run out of things to say for a bit.

'Malc, do you do Classical Studies at your school?'

Malcolm wrinkles up his nose, and snorts, 'Yeah. Why?' like he can't believe I just asked it.

'Oh, nothing, really. Wanna jaw-breaker?' I say, offering him the bag, and then we turn the corner, across the road from the pub, and Malcolm nudges me, grinning.

'Fuckin' 'ell mate – look at the state of that!'

And there's this woman, swaying around outside the door of the pub, arguing with Eric the landlord. She looks like she's just crawled off a park bench, wearing a summer dress and slippers. She must be freezing. Eric is shaking his head – sorry, love, no chance – trying to get rid of her. There's a match on, they don't need this kind of bother.

Malcolm's laughing; he doesn't know it's my mum. I try to act normal, pull a face, rummage in my sweet bag.

'Yeah, fuckin' 'ell,' I reply. My head's throbbing. 'Malc, mate – I need a waz. You go on in – tell Dad I'll be there in a minute.' And I pretend to head off towards the pub's outside loo.

Malcolm nods, stuffing in more sweets, looking the drunk woman up and down as he passes her in the doorway. Eric the landlord spots me, shakes his head as if to say, don't worry about it, Jakey. For a moment, I'm stuck to the spot. I just stand and stare at the back of her head. She's like the Gorgon, and I've turned to stone. Quietly, I walk over and slip my hand into hers, and lead her away from the pub.

'I'll make you a nice cuppa, Mum. I think we've got some logs out the back. It's cold enough to make a fire, I reckon.'

Mum shuffles along beside me, shivering silently, till we reach the house. We get inside and she wraps her arms around me and sobs against my shoulder.

'You know I love you, Jakey. Never, ever forget that, darling. I love you.'

MORE FROM MYRIAD EDITIONS

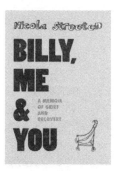

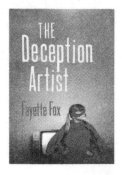

MORE FROM MYRIAD EDITIONS

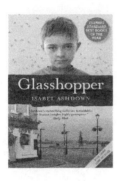

MORE FROM MYRIAD EDITIONS

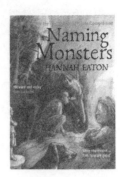

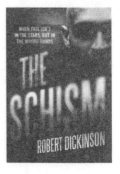

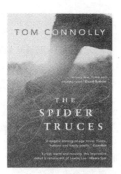

To stay in touch with Isabel Ashdown

Visit her website: www.isabelashdown.com
Facebook: /IsabelAshdownBooks
Twitter: @IsabelAshdown

To find out more about Myriad Editions

Myriad Editions

Visit our website: www.myriadeditions.com
Facebook: /myriad.editions
Twitter: @MyriadEditions